The Dawn Country

BY KATHLEEN O'NEAL GEAR AND W. MICHAEL GEAR
FROM TOM DOHERTY ASSOCIATES

NORTH AMERICA'S FORGOTTEN PAST SERIES

People of the Wolf   *People of the Mist*
People of the Fire   *People of the Masks*
People of the Earth   *People of the Owl*
People of the River   *People of the Raven*
People of the Sea   *People of the Moon*
People of the Lakes   *People of the Nightland*
People of the Lightning   *People of the Weeping Eye*
People of the Silence   *People of the Thunder*
People of the Longhouse
The Dawn Country: A People of the Longhouse Novel
*The Broken Land: A People of the Longhouse Novel**
*The Black Sun: A People of the Longhouse Novel**

THE ANASAZI MYSTERY SERIES

The Visitant
The Summoning God
Bone Walker

BY KATHLEEN O'NEAL GEAR

Thin Moon and Cold Mist   *It Sleeps in Me*
Sand in the Wind   *It Wakes in Me*
This Widowed Land   *It Dreams in Me*

BY W. MICHAEL GEAR

Long Ride Home   *Coyote Summer*
Big Horn Legacy   *The Athena Factor*
Morning River

OTHER TITLES BY KATHLEEN O'NEAL GEAR AND W. MICHAEL GEAR

The Betrayal
Dark Inheritance
Raising Abel
Children of the Dawnland

www.Gear-Gear.com

*Forthcoming

The Dawn Country

A PEOPLE OF
THE LONGHOUSE NOVEL

Kathleen O'Neal Gear and
W. Michael Gear

A TOM DOHERTY ASSOCIATES BOOK · NEW YORK

This is a work of fiction. All of the characters, organizations, and events portrayed in this novel are either products of the authors' imaginations or are used fictitiously.

THE DAWN COUNTRY

Maps and illustrations by Ellisa Mitchell

A Forge Book
Published by Tom Doherty Associates, LLC
175 Fifth Avenue
New York, NY 10010

www.tor-forge.com

Forge® is a registered trademark of Tom Doherty Associates, LLC.

ISBN 978-0-7653-2017-9

First Edition: March 2011

Printed in the United States of America

0 9 8 7 6 5 4 3 2 1

*To Mike D. O'Neal in memory of the lost years
when we didn't get to see each other.
It's great to have you back in this world.*

B.C.

13,000	10,000	6,000	3,000	1,500

PEOPLE *of the* WOLF
Alaska & Canadian
Northwest

PEOPLE *of the* EARTH
Northern Plains & Basins

PEOPLE *of the* NIGHTLAND
Ontario & New York &
Pennsylvania

PEOPLE *of*
the OWL

Lower
Mississippi
Valley

PEOPLE *of the* SEA
Pacific Coast & Arizona

PEOPLE *of the* RAVEN
Pacific Northwest &
British Columbia

PEOPLE *of the* LIGHTNING
Florida

PEOPLE *of the* FIRE
Central Rockies &
Great Plains

A.D.

0	200	1,000	1,100	1,300	1,400

PEOPLE *of the* LAKES
East-Central Woodlands
& Great Lakes

PEOPLE *of the*
WEEPING EYE

Mississippi Valley
& Tennessee

PEOPLE *of the* MASKS
Ontario & Upstate New York

PEOPLE *of the*
THUNDER

Alabama & Mississippi

PEOPLE *of the* RIVER
Mississippi Valley

PEOPLE *of the*
LONGHOUSE

New York
& New England

PEOPLE *of the* SILENCE
Southwest Anasazi

The
DAWN
COUNTRY

PEOPLE *of the* MOON
Northwest New Mexico
& Southwest Colorado

New York
& New England

PEOPLE *of the* MIST
Chesapeake Bay

Skanodario Lake

Canassatego Village

The Lands of the
People of the
Dawnland

Forks River

Rapid River

Quill River

Quill River

IROQUOIA

Singleleaf
Village

Wild River
Village

Hawk Moth
Village

Bog
Willow
Village

Pine
Hill
Village

Nonfiction Introduction

As those of you who read the introduction for *People of the Longhouse* know, during the thirteenth and fourteenth centuries, the size of Iroquois villages began to grow. Archaeologists call this "population aggregation," meaning that more and more people were crowding together within the palisaded walls of villages. We see these expanded longhouses at places like the Furnace Brook and Howlett Hill sites in New York, where archaeologists excavated houses that were 210 and 334 feet long. This Middle Iroquoian period also saw the people becoming increasingly dependent upon maize-bean-squash agriculture. As in historic times, men cleared the fields, built the houses, and hunted, while women were the farmers. They cultivated the soil, planted, tended the fields, harvested and stored the crops. When women began to account for more and more of the food, their lineages also probably became the dominant social avenue for prestige.

At around AD 1400, the first evidence for individual tribes appears. Differences in pottery styles, burial customs, and types of houses demonstrate divisions between Iroquoian groups. As well, small villages began to amalgamate with larger ones, forming cohesive social groups, or, we suspect, nations.

AD 1400 is also the time when the Iroquois were building the most impressive longhouses, and many were elaborately fortified. At the Schoff site outside of Onondaga, New York, the people constructed a longhouse 400 feet long, 22 feet wide, and nearly as tall. The palisaded settlement may have housed 1,500 to 2,000 people, consisting of many different clans.

For archaeologists, this type of aggregation is a telltale sign of interpersonal violence. Simply put, people crowd together for defensive purposes. Cannibalism also first appears in the Iroquoian archaeological record at this point, in the form of cut and cooked human bones.

The Dawn Country takes place at this critical moment in time.

Why did warfare break out? The fact that the climate had grown cooler and drier certainly contributed to the violence. We know that droughts were more frequent, growing seasons shorter, and we can tell from the skeletal remains that food shortages were more common. Larger villages deplete resources at a faster rate. Game populations, nut forests, firewood, and fertile soils would all have played out more quickly, which means the Iroquois must have had to move their villages more often. Moving may have brought them into conflict with neighbors just as desperate for the food resources.

At the Alhart site in the Oak Orchard Creek drainage in western New York, archaeologists found evidence of burned longhouses and food, and the dismembered remains of seventeen people—most of them male. Historically, it was common practice for women and children to either be killed on site, or taken captive and marched away while the male warriors were tortured to death. The fragments of a child's skull were found in one storage pit at the Alhart site, and the skull of a woman in another storage pit. As well, fifteen male skulls were found in a storage pit on top of charred corn, and were probably placed there as severed heads, in the flesh. Some of them were burned. Two had suffered blows to the front of the head. These are just a few examples of warfare. For more detailed information, please read the nonfiction introduction to *People of the Longhouse*.

Let's take a few moments to discuss the Iroquoian perspective on captives. By the 1400s, as it was in historic times, warfare and raiding for captives was probably the most important method of gaining prestige in Northern Iroquoian societies. When a person died, the spiritual power of the clan was diminished, especially if that person had been a community leader. The places of missing family members literally remained vacant until they could be "replaced," and their spiritual power—which was embodied in their name—transferred to another person.

Historical records tell us that during the 1600s, the Iroquois dispatched war parties whose sole intent was to bring home captives to replace family members and restore the spiritual strength of the clans. These were called "mourning wars." Clan matrons usually organized the war parties and ordered their warriors to bring them captives suitable for adoption to assuage their grief and restock the village. When the captives arrived in the village, they were stripped, bound hand and foot, and forced to run a gauntlet where they were struck with clubs, burned with firebrands, cut with knives—but not killed.

After the torture, the tribal council assigned the captives to families that had lost loved ones to the enemy. Sometimes prisoner exchanges occurred, and the captives were returned to their own peoples, but usually one of two things happened: They were either adopted into their new family, or the adoptive family could condemn the captive to death by torture. If he was adopted, he *might* be given the name and title of the dead person he replaced. Such adoptees underwent the Requickening Ceremony. In this ritual, the dead person's soul was "raised up" and transferred to the captive, along with his or her name.

This may seem odd to modern readers, but keep the religious context in mind. The Iroquois believed that each person had two souls. While specific traditions vary slightly, in general, the afterlife soul of those who died violently could not find the Path of Souls in the sky that led to the Land of the Dead. They were excluded from joining their ancestors in the afterlife and doomed to spend eternity wandering the earth. The souls of men and women killed in battles that were not "raised up" were believed, according to some Seneca traditions, to move into trees. It was these trees with indwelling warrior spirits that the People cut to serve as palisade logs, thereby surrounding the village with Standing Warriors.

Iroquoian oral history speaks of this as a particularly brutal time, a time when the Iroquois almost destroyed themselves, and clearly the archaeological record supports their stories.

The Dawn Country

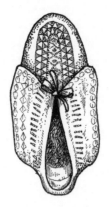

One

Nightfall had silenced the mountains. No owls hooted; no trees snapped in the cold wind that swayed the branches. There was only the faint roar of the fire in the distance.

Sonon pulled his black cape more tightly around him and studied the frozen ground. The warriors' feet had hewn a dark swath through the frost that glittered in the gaudy orange halo. His gaze followed their trail to the burning village. The Dawnland People had called it Bog Willow Village. Yesterday it had contained over one hundred houses.

He hadn't expected the village to be this bad.

As he walked toward it, ash fell around him like fine flakes of obsidian, coating his cape and long hair, turning them gray. The forty-hand-tall palisade that surrounded the village had burned through in too many places. That had been their doom. They must have watched in horror as the enemy streamed through those gaps and raced across the village, killing everything in their path.

He turned back around to stare at the victory camp. Hundreds of celebrating warriors danced to the sound of drums and flutes. Most were from the Flint or Mountain Peoples, but the war party had contained a few Hills People warriors, too. He knew them from their distinctive tattoos, and the designs painted on their bows and capes.

On the far side of the camp, near the river, captive women and children huddled together, shivering, watching their captors with wide stunned eyes. Before dawn came all would be sold and marched away to enemy villages. The lucky ones would be adopted into families and spend the rest of their lives trying to forget this night. The others wouldn't have to worry about it.

Sonon took a breath and let it out slowly.

There were still times when he woke to the sound of screams that existed only inside him. For many summers he'd thought they were the cries of his twin sister, and he'd been ravaged by guilt. When he'd finally realized the voice was his own, the pain had eased a little. The day they were sold into slavery, he'd seen only eight summers. He wasn't a warrior. There was nothing he could have done to save her—or himself.

He clenched his fists so hard his nails bit into his palms. He had to go down there, into the village. No man wished to admit he was afraid, but . . .

He forced his legs to walk. At first, only a few bodies lay alongside the trail, but as he neared the palisade the number increased. Desperate villagers must have fought to get outside and run headlong into a line of waiting archers. Bodies, bristling with arrows, had piled up around each gap in the defensive wall. The last few to make it outside probably had to shove their way through a mound of dead.

Sonon carefully stepped around the carnage and ducked through the charred hole in the palisade. The heat struck him first. He threw up an arm and squinted against the glare to see what remained of Bog Willow Village. In less than twenty heartbeats he was sweating, struggling for air. The smoke was so thick it was almost impossible to breathe.

Five paces away an old woman sat on the ground with her face in her hands, rocking back and forth in dazed silence. A few other survivors stumbled past. They moved methodically, searching for loved ones or bending to collect precious belongings: a dropped pot or basket, children's toys.

I'm over here. See me?

Sonon stopped, and tiny tornadoes of ash spun away from his sandals. They whirled through the firelit shadows. Was it just his fatigue? It sounded like a boy's voice.

Cautiously, he veered around a collapsed wall and began searching the debris. Twenty paces later, he almost stumbled over the child.

Two small arms extended from beneath a buckled wall.

Sonon knelt and pulled the boy from the heap of smoldering bark. Most of his hair had been singed off. He'd seen perhaps six or seven summers. For a time, he just held the boy in his lap and listened to the crackling roar of the fire. Somewhere in the conflagration, muted voices shouted names . . . and went unanswered. Occasionally, orphaned children darted by.

When he could, he staggered to his feet and carried the boy between the burning husks of two houses, then stepped through a gap in the palisade wall and trudged down to the river's edge, where he gently rested the boy on the shore. In the wavering glare, the boy's half-open eyes seemed to be alive and watching him.

Why do I only hear them when the struggle is over? Are the voices of the dead only audible to those trapped in eternal night?

Sonon tenderly adjusted the boy's cape, pulling it up around his throat to keep him warm. "It's all right," he said. "I'll make sure they find you. Your clan will take care of you, and you'll have no trouble crossing the bridge to the afterlife. Your ancestors will be waiting for you."

Though he was a man of the Hills nation, he knew the ways of the Dawnland People. They believed that the unburied dead became Ghost Fires, angry fire-beings that could not cross the bridge to the afterlife and were forever doomed to remain around the deteriorating bones. The Bog Willow Village survivors would not leave their beloved relatives to that terrible fate, not if they could help it. That meant someone would come looking for this child. His body would be ritually cleaned and prepared for the long journey; then his family would sing him to the afterlife. Having the boy out here in the open would make it easier for his relatives to find him.

Sonon wiped his soot-coated face with the back of his hand and looked out across the river to the opposite, willow-choked bank. Beyond it, towering black spruces caught the reflections in the water and seemed made of translucent amber wings. The river itself, coated with ash, had an opaque leaden sheen.

He stood up and turned back to the village. For ten heartbeats, he just breathed and studied the palisade. People from distant places did not understand that each log was a Standing Warrior. Among their peoples, the angry souls of dead warriors were excluded from the Land of the Dead, so they moved into trees. They remained in the wood for centuries, until the tree disintegrated and their souls were forced to seek new homes. It was these trees that the People cut down to make their palisades. That meant that every log was a warrior still keeping guard, still protecting his or her people.

He wondered what the Standing Warriors must be feeling. Not so long ago, they'd watched this little boy racing happily across the plaza, seen him playing ball and dish games with his friends, heard his laughter ringing through the village on quiet summer afternoons. Their grief must be unbearable.

Sonon whispered, "No one could have held off such an assault. It wasn't your fault. You did the best you—"

Voices drifted from the river. He turned.

A birch-bark canoe quietly slipped through the smoke, parting the river like an arrow, heading south. An old woman rode in the bow. She was dressed like a man and wore a long black wig, but a few greasy twists of gray hair stuck out around the edges, framing her deeply wrinkled face. Even if she hadn't been in disguise, he would have known her. A thousand summers from now, as he walked the earth alone, he would hear her footsteps in his nightmares.

Four children lay together in her canoe, crying. Three warriors with paddles swiftly drove them forward. Close on the heels of the first, another canoe pierced the darkness—with three more captive children.

As the canoes passed, waves rippled outward and washed up on the shore near the dead boy, leaving delicate ribbons of firelit foam at his feet.

Everything about tonight felt strange and surreal. As though Sonon was locked in a trance and could not wake, his heart thumped a dull staccato against his chest.

At least a few of the children had escaped. Earlier in the evening, he'd helped them . . . as much as he could.

When the canoes vanished into the darkness, he looked at the western mountains. He couldn't see the pass through the smoke and falling ash. The trail the escaped children had taken was the fastest way back to the lands of the People of the Standing Stone. But there would be many others on that trail: survivors of the village slaughter, orphaned children, and a few wary men who'd left the victory camp early, trying to beat the onslaught of warriors who would crowd the trail just after dawn.

Very softly he called, "Stay strong, Odion, and you'll be all right. You'll—"

I'm here. Right here. Please find me?

Sonon squeezed his eyes closed for several long moments. It was a girl's voice.

He clenched his fists again; then he tramped back up the hill, ducked through the gap in the palisade, and trotted into the roaring inferno to search for her.

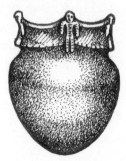

Two

Odion

I'm alive. . . .

I pull my knees up beneath my woven moosehide blanket and gaze out at the night-dark forest, where frozen trees glitter in the starlight. An eerie elation washes through me. I have survived eleven summers and never felt this curious brew of terror and utter joy before—the odd euphoria of a captive suddenly freed from horror.

As I was just a few hands of time ago.

Hope vies with the flashes of hideous memory. I squeeze the terror into a black place hidden deep inside me and blink at the camp.

Our tiny fire glimmers in the depths of a narrow valley that cuts through a rocky mountain ridge. Clumps of trees surround the small meadow. The staghorn sumacs—scrub trees—grow four or five times the height of a man and have dark smooth bark that reflects the dancing shadows cast by the flames. Beyond the sumacs, a thicket of thorny plums spreads fifty paces in every direction. Frost covers the fallen fruit and makes the forest floor seem as though it's paved with round white rocks.

Frigid silence reigns in the night, punctured only by my companions' breathing and the occasional popping of the flames. Though I know Mother and Father guard me—and five other people sleep nearby—I jump every time Wind Mother rattles the trees, or flames leap as they chew through the sweet-smelling plum branches. My ears strain to hear enemy steps in the night.

I look first at Mother, then turn my eyes to Father. They guard opposite sides of the camp, and for a long time I'm not sure they're real. So many times in the past moon, I imagined them standing just like this only to be shaken out of dreams and back to horror.

Is it truly different this time?

When Father turns to smile at me, tears of relief silver my vision. My anxiety drains away, leaving me exhausted. No matter how long I live, my best memory will be the sight of Mother and Father running out of the forest with their war clubs swinging, killing the men who held us captive.

As I live it again, the strange euphoria intensifies, sharpened to a deadly edge by the fear that this freedom can't last. They are coming for me. I know it.

My little sister, Tutelo, sleeps beside me. She rolls over and heaves a sigh. I turn to make sure she's all right. She has a doehide pulled up over her head in the manner of a hood. Only her pretty oval face with its turned-up nose gleams in the firelight. She has seen eight summers pass.

Behind her, Baji is stretched out on her back. I can't be certain, but I think she's staring up at the campfires of the dead that sprinkle the night sky. Every so often, I smell the acrid scent of the burning village that clings to my moosehide blanket. Is Baji thinking about what happened earlier tonight? About the gigantic warriors' camp outside of the flaming village, the screams and cries of orphaned children . . . the laughter of warriors covered in blood?

Baji has seen twelve summers. Long eyelashes fringe her dark eyes. Her small nose and full lips are perfect. Long black hair spreads across the blanket around her. She was captured in a raid and sold into slavery the day after I was.

Images flash behind my eyes: *Girls thrown to the ground by brutal men . . . suffocating sobs . . . Gan—*

A terrified cry climbs my throat. Barely audible. No one else seems to hear. Except Baji.

She rolls to face me and mouths the words, *Are you all right?*

I shake my head, aware that the terror has broken loose inside me. Will I ever be able to completely wall it away down in that black space between my souls? For the moment I can only blink at the hot tears and try to control the fear.

Baji wraps her blanket around her shoulders, rises, and tiptoes over to kneel beside me.

"What's wrong?" she whispers.

I stare up at her. "I dreamed there are warriors coming."

"Warriors? From the victory camp? Or *her* warriors?"

"I don't know. Maybe hers."

She shakes her head violently, and long black hair flies around her shoulders. She's just as afraid as I am. "No, I—I don't think so. Why would they come after us? She bought new children from the destroyed village. She doesn't need us any longer."

The evil old woman who buys and sells captured children is a powerful witch. She can hear conversations from a day's march away. I'm afraid she's listening to us right now.

I whisper, "They're coming, Baji. I swear it. I feel the warriors' footsteps in my heart."

For a long time Baji looks out at the firelit shadows that sway in the trees, as though searching for hidden men. Then she curls up beside me and stares at me. "Even if she is coming after us, we have a good head start. And your mother and father, and the two Hills People warriors they brought, will protect us."

"I know." I want so desperately to believe it's true.

Baji wets her lips and whispers, "I'm more worried about Wrass and Zateri. Do you think they're all right?"

A deep ache fills my chest. Our friends, Wrass and Zateri, are still the old woman's slaves. Somehow, I think it's my fault. We were separated when the rescue happened. I should have called out to them, or gone to find them. Instead, I just ran away with Mother and Father. I ran as hard as I could.

"It's not your fault," Baji says, as though reading the tracks of my soul. Is she feeling the same guilt I am? After the horrors of the past moon, we are closer than friends, closer than family. "It's a miracle that we escaped with our own lives."

"I know, I just—"

"And we're going back for them. Tomorrow morning. Your parents promised. They wouldn't lie to us, would they? We *are* going back to rescue Wrass and Zateri, and the other children, aren't we?"

I have to think about this before I answer. ". . . My parents wouldn't lie to us."

But I'm not sure that's true.

My gaze drifts to where Mother stands. Most people know her as War Chief Koracoo from Yellowtail Village of the Standing Stone People. My

Father, Gonda, is her deputy. Women war chiefs are rare, and being honored with the title requires unusual courage, intelligence, and skill. Mother is a powerful and respected leader. She's a tall woman, muscular and long-legged. Her war club—the legendary weapon known as CorpseEye—is propped on her shoulder.

Just seeing her calms my fears. But I miss her long black hair. After the attack that destroyed our village, she cropped it short with a chert knife. Among our people it is a sign of mourning. The short jagged locks fall around her ears as though sculpted. Her gaze is fixed on the darkness just beyond the circle of firelight, as though she hears something, or someone, on the starlit mountain pass above us. We came over that pass two hands of time ago, and are now on the western slope.

I breathe in the icy air and say, "We should try to sleep, Baji. We're going to need our strength. Tomorrow is going to be a hard day."

"I'll try if you will." She tugs her blanket up around her chin and snuggles against me. The feel of her body against mine sends a warm sense of security through me. In less than sixty heartbeats, she is sound asleep.

But my eyes will not close. I stare up at the dark winter sky. The flickering campfires of the dead look oddly hazy. I realize it's because even here, across the mountain, smoke from the burned village still streaks the sky. I try not to think of the people who lived there, of the dead and dying, of the shrieking children who were taken captive. The destruction of their village allowed us to escape.

Will the war and suffering ever end?

Behind the lies of safety that I tell myself, I feel the presence of Gannajero watching me across the dark distances.

Her warriors *are* coming.

I feel their footsteps pounding in my chest.

Three

War Chief Cord's breath frosted before his face and hung there like a small starlit cloud, ghostlike in the frigid air. He continued struggling up the slope. Above him, through the frost-coated trees, the trail was nothing more than a black gash.

The night had frozen the jagged terrain, turning it into a still and sparkling wasteland so bone-cold that nothing stirred. Even the Forest Spirits and lost souls who usually roamed the trails had fled to their hiding places beneath rocks and in secret holes in the ground. The vast silence was eerie, as though an otherworldly blanket had descended to compensate for the echoed screams, the ululating cries of victory, and the terrified shrieks of the dying that had washed the slopes last night.

Behind him, he heard the rasping moccasins of the handful of his warriors who'd lived through the battle, but he didn't turn to look. Instead, he focused on the trail ahead. Their lives rested upon making it to the pass that was hidden high above them.

Cord pulled his wolf-fur hood closed beneath his chin. He stood twelve hands tall. Snake tattoos covered his cheeks and ropy arms. He wore his hair shaved on the sides, leaving a black roach in the center and a long braid hanging down his back. He had seen twenty-nine summers pass. His wife had once told him he had the burning eyes of a Spirit-possessed shaman. In the summers after her death, however, he knew he radiated only a glacial cold. As if his souls and this frigid night were perfectly matched.

He carefully studied the dark slash of trail.

How far to the summit? He and his men would only find safety on the other side of the pass. Or would they? All night long they had been pursued by a small group of enemy warriors, survivors of the Bog Willow Village fight. Their leader was cunning, instructing his men to show themselves for fleeting instants to tempt Cord's warriors to waste arrows. But long before the arrows struck, their targets had vanished into the darkness.

Cord shook his head. His men were growing careless, desperate. They'd lost friends and loved ones in the battle. Each feared he would be next.

Gravel crunched. He turned.

Strung out behind him, his four men climbed with their heads down. Shoulders and hoods glittered with frost crystals. They did not speak, needing every morsel of strength to sustain the climb.

How long since any of them had slept? Each man was exhausted. Cord could see it in the occasional trembling of a leg, or a head suddenly snapping up from where a man had fallen asleep as he walked. As if the horrors of battle were not enough, the great blind forest—brutally cold and unnaturally still—had rousted every shred of arrogance from their souls. Where once they had preened and paraded in their finest quillwork capes and shell jewelry, now they struggled just to place one foot in front of the other.

When his men drew nearer, he motioned for them to keep going. One by one, they stepped past him with barely a glance.

They wore knee-high moccasins, long war shirts, and wolfhide coats with the hair turned in for warmth. Gray-furred hoods encircled their faces. Each time a man exhaled, his breath settled upon his bristly hood, creating a thick rime of frost. Unstrung bows and quivers rode on top of packs stuffed with loot. Belts clattered with hafted chert knives, sharpened deerbone stilettos, stone-headed war clubs, a food pouch, and water bag.

When the last man walked by, Cord lifted his hand to the sky and measured how far the constellations had moved since his last stop: two hand-widths, the distance across his palm twice. Dawn was another six hands of time away.

He fell into line behind Neyaw and continued up the steep rocky trail. The darkness and cold pressed down, as though to smother that last warm spark in his body.

A cry—half howl, half wail—sounded on the trail below them and echoed through the night. Almost inhuman, it sent a shiver down Cord's spine as he stopped short, staring back down the dark trail.

Dzadi—now in the lead—stopped dead in his tracks and lifted his nose to scent the wind. A tall and muscular warrior, his face was dominated by an enormous jaw that protruded outward and down until it almost seemed to rest upon his bearlike chest. Dzadi had seen thirty-four summers, most of them at war. He wore the puckered burn scars that discolored his face and arms like badges of honor. Last summer, Dzadi had been captured by the People of the Landing. Through indomitable will and cunning he'd managed to escape his captivity; the scars would be with him forever as a reminder.

The howling cry came again, piercing the darkness like a knife. Hollow, wolfish, it sliced upward to a final shrill note that seemed to hang in the night and shook a man to his souls.

Cord tilted his head, determined the direction. Directly beneath them, down the mountain, through the maples. Was it the same group of survivors? Or another? Perhaps several had merged.

"Was that a . . . a wolf?" Young Wado asked, locking his knees to keep his legs from trembling.

Cord's men shifted, glancing uneasily at each other. No wolf could fill its voice with that desperate, hungry rage. Somewhere inside them, they all knew it.

Dzadi worked his way past the other warriors, touching a shoulder or confidently gripping an arm to steady a man; then he came to stand beside Cord and hoarsely whispered, "They're still following us."

"We have to keep moving."

Cord took the lead again, muscles trembling, struggling toward the distant notch that marked the pass. On the other side they would strike the trail that led west: home to the People of the Flint, and safety.

When they came to a thickly forested section, he told his men, "Be careful. Watch your footing. Every time you trip over a root, it drains you that much more."

Below, the cries rose and fell, wild with mockery, as though their pursuers knew there was no escape.

Cord lifted his gaze to the rolling mountains. High above him, hidden behind waves of peaks, was the rocky defile known as Elbow

Pass. Steep switchbacks zigzagged up the mountainside. Their enemies were driving them toward it like deer into a killing pen. Once
they reached the switchbacks—if they reached them—their pursuers
would block the trail below. He and his men would be forced to continue climbing upward. There was no other way.

Two hands of time later, they reached the base of the switchbacks
and squatted on their haunches in a copse of willows. His men were
gasping for breath, and the scent of stale sweat filled the air.

"We haven't heard them in a while," Ogwed panted. He'd seen
eighteen summers. A handsome youth with an oval face and flat nose,
he'd lost three children and his wife in the battle that had destroyed
Wild River Village. He turned sad eyes on Cord. "Do you think they
gave up?"

Cord untied his water bag from his belt and took a long drink. Every
eye was upon him, waiting for his answer. When he'd drunk his fill,
he lowered the bag and tied it to his belt again. "Maybe, but I don't
think so."

A grim smile rearranged Dzadi's scars. "There is only one pass."
He nodded toward the Elbow above. "That's the route home. They
know it as well as we do."

"But they might think we broke off, tried to skirt the mountain
through the rough terrain," Wado suggested hopefully. The youngest
warrior in his party, Wado had only seen sixteen summers. "Maybe
they just decided to go home and take care of their dead relatives?"

Cord closed his eyes, desperate for even a moment's rest. "We hit
them hard, Wado. As hard as they hit us. Would you give up?"

Wado hung his head and seemed to be considering; then he whispered a miserable, "No."

Ogwed glanced around the circle and sheepishly asked, "Can we
sleep for a while? We haven't slept in two days, I—I'm not sure how
much longer I can run."

"Eat something," Cord instructed. "Food will give you strength."

Ogwed pulled a strip of elk jerky from his belt pouch and chewed
it in silence. The other warriors did the same, jaws working deliber-
ately, trying to get food in their bellies before the last brutal climb.

Cord examined their downcast faces. Two men had their eyes
closed, trying to nap while they chewed. Their heads kept bobbing
and jerking up. Though no one grumbled, they looked disheartened
and soul-dead. Warriors pushed to the brink began to think their
Power was broken, that they'd been deserted by the Spirit World.

When that happened they would start to disappear, drifting away one by one.

Dzadi murmured, "Being out of arrows doesn't help our situation. We shouldn't have wasted them on those wild shots at our pursuers."

"How many arrows are left between us?"

Dzadi rubbed his huge jaw as his gaze scanned the quivers. "Neyaw has two. That's it. Maybe if we—"

A long shriek—mournful as a death cry—interrupted him. Dzadi listened to it before he finished. "If we can reach the pass and set up a trap, it might make them pause long enough for us to escape."

"Perhaps." Cord's gaze flitted over the youngest warriors, and Dzadi knew what it meant: *Maybe we can buy enough time for them to escape, but you and I will not.*

Dzadi expelled a breath. "I can't believe this. Over four hundred attacking warriors, from so many different peoples and villages, survived the attack. Why have they fixed on us? There are plenty of other war parties out in the forest trying to make it home."

Around a mouthful of food, Wado stated the obvious: "It's easier to slaughter a war party of five than a party of one hundred."

Cord soberly tightened his fists. He'd already lost too many warriors in the battle—men and women he'd grown up with. People he'd loved and respected. And it looked as though he might lose the ones around him in the next hand of time. He'd been a fool to make this raid. He'd tell that to his elders when he returned—if either was alive. Both matrons had been badly wounded in the attack on Wild River Village, making decisions in haste, probably afraid they were dying.

Cord had argued against joining forces with the other Flint and Mountain People war parties to make this strike, saying they needed to bury their dead and make their way to a new village for protection before they considered any retaliatory action. The matrons had disagreed—and the rest of the village council was dead. He had never disobeyed the matrons, but he wished with all his heart that in this one instance, he had refused.

He got to his feet and looked down the mountain at the dark maples and boulders.

Ogwed said, "War Chief, maybe we should send out a scout? We don't even know for certain that they're enemy warriors. They could be part of the alliance. Maybe even some of our own people."

Wado's eyes brightened inside his frost-rimmed hood. "That must

be it. They're not after us. They're just behind us. They're Flint warriors. We should contact them! Let them know we're brothers."

Neyaw snorted in derision. He had a bulbous nose and slits for eyes
and wore his long black hair coiled and pinned over his left ear. The
style made his hood look lopsided. "You're a young fool," he com-
mented, with the authority of a man who'd seen countless battles.

Wado glared, but did not reply. He knew better than to cross Neyaw.
For the slightest provocation, Neyaw had been known to crush men's
throats with a blow from his war club, then string their teeth for a neck-
lace.

Exhaustion pulling at his senses, Cord swayed on his feet. For several moments, he had the unearthly feeling that they were already
dead—just ghosts wandering through a spectral enemy land, condemned to run forever with no hope of reaching home. The sensation
was so powerful that it stunned him. He lifted a hand and rubbed his
eyes. "Finish eating. Let's go."

He didn't wait for them.

The steep switchbacks were filled with ice-coated rocks and gravel
that rolled beneath his moccasins. Many times he lost his footing and
had to claw at the rocks like a dog to keep going. His men fared no
better. Grunts and curses laced the air, accompanied by the sounds of
scrambling hands and feet.

When they were two-thirds of the way to the top, Cord stopped
and turned. Ogwed and Wado were crawling up the slippery path on
their hands and knees. Neyaw had fallen far behind. Dzadi glanced
up at Cord, saw that he'd stopped, and heaved a sigh of relief as he
clambered up to him.

Cord braced his wobbling legs. "What do you think?" He gestured
to the men with his chin.

"Not all of them are going to make it home."

Cord tilted his head to look up at the pass. In the pewter gleam, the
deep V that resembled a bent elbow was filled with the glistening
campfires of the dead. He gazed at them longingly. After the pass, for
rested men, it wasn't more than a hard two-day run back to the nearest Flint village, and home.

Home? Where was that now? His village had been burned, the familiar longhouses destroyed. Any homecoming was only going to be
filled with grief as he realized how many relatives and old friends were
gone.

At the thought, an almost unbearable sadness filled him. His wife and son were long dead, victims of the endless warfare. Two summers ago his daughter had been claimed by his wife's clan—as was the way of the Flint People, who traced descent through the female. Children were clan property. Little Arum was greatly loved and cared for among the Bear Clan, and, of course, he saw her often. But his life was a husk of what it had been three summers ago.

"Dzadi, listen," Cord said quietly. "I have nothing to go home to. If we have to sacrifice someone, I—"

"One man can't do it, old friend. You know that. You and I will stay together."

"I *can* do it. Not for long, but for long enough that the rest of you can get away."

Dzadi smiled, and the taut, shiny skin of his burn scars reflected the starlight. "Our people need you. I'm the expendable one, Cord. I'll stay."

The walls of black rock that created the switchbacks seemed to be leaning down to listen better, and Cord wondered how many desperate men had stood on this very spot and spoken these very words. How much blood had these rocks absorbed? Cord swore he could hear the land itself laughing at him, laughing with the deep ageless wisdom that comes from watching thousands of puny men toil and die, crushed by the weight of their own fears.

"I've seen you fight, Dzadi. I know you'll kill half of them before it's over, but—"

Dzadi pointed down the mountain. "There they are."

Cord swung around. Dark shapes moved through the shadows at the base of the switchbacks. More appeared. Two, three, four, then too many.

Dzadi lowered his arm. Occasionally, fangs flashed and pricked ears swayed against the frost-lit background. Headdresses?

"Wolf Clan warriors," Dzadi whispered, shaken for the first time. "May the Spirits of the Dead help us."

Shadows spread out among the tree trunks. Shapes appeared, then vanished, then moved again higher up the trail.

"How many do you count?" Dzadi whispered.

"Maybe twenty. Maybe more." Cord exhaled a long tense breath.

"They're persistent. Surely they don't think we have captives with us?"

"They may."

After the battle, the women and children captured at Bog Willow had been rounded up and herded into the victorious warriors' camp. Many were sold to the highest bidder. Cord remembered seeing two Traders who specialized in child slaves—though in the commotion, some of the captive children had escaped. Most were caught and dragged back within a few hundred heartbeats, but it had caused quite a stir for a time, briefly interrupting the feasting, dancing, and general revelry.

Dzadi hissed, "This is not looking good."

Cord filled his lungs and bellowed, "Come on, you lazy dogs! Hurry it up. Move! *I said, move!*"

His three men staggered and stumbled up the steep trail with agonizing slowness. The human wolves below them darted back and forth around the switchbacks. Cry after cry erupted and echoed through the trees.

Cord's men betrayed their fear by scrambling up the slope, panting as they ran for their lives.

Four

*I*s *this what it feels like to die?*

Wrass eased to his side on the packs in a birch-bark canoe. The violent pain in his broken skull blurred his vision, leaving him dizzy and nauseated. Vomit continually tickled the bottom of his throat, and his bowels squirmed like shivering eels.

But the blows had been worth it.

Some of the others got away: Odion, Baji, Tutelo. Even Hehaka.

Too bad Zateri had been recaptured. In that, he'd failed. He would have gratefully given up his life to save Zateri. Like him, she had been Gannajero's captive for too long. Unlike him, she'd been sold to a lot of different men. Perhaps sold was the wrong word. They'd bought her for a hand of time to use in ways that would have earned the men death if their relatives ever learned of it. Gannajero, however, specialized in ensuring that no one ever found out about her children, or what happened to them.

The farther south Wrass' captors paddled, the thinner the clouds became until they drifted through the night sky like translucent veils of charcoal silk. He watched them pass. Sometimes they looked like feathers slowly falling to earth. Two canoes bore Gannajero, her captive children, accomplices, and packs south from Bog Willow Village. Gannajero's canoe, where he lay, was in the lead.

He tried to concentrate on the river's tangy smells. Old leaves had piled along the shores, creating moldering borders that suffused the air with the musty scents of just-past autumn.

The only sounds on this cold night were the soft swishing of oars and the whimpering of the new children who lay beside Zateri in the canoe that followed them.

For a time, he let himself drift on the waves and think of home—which he rarely did, because it hurt too much. Yellowtail Village had been burned to the ground in the attack, but by now the survivors would have found a new place to rebuild and would already have cut hundreds of logs for the palisade. They might even have the palisade finished, and had perhaps begun building longhouses. He remembered Grandmother Sayeno telling the clan elders, two moons before the attack, that if they were smart they would ally themselves with a larger Standing Stone village. That way they could help protect each other. He wondered where the survivors had gone. Bur Oak Village was the closest large Standing Stone village. Perhaps they'd gone there to rebuild Yellowtail. If they . . .

"We have to find Hehaka." Gannajero's sharp voice rose from the bow. "It's the only way."

The old woman had been speaking quietly to her deputy Kotin for two hands of time, but as her voice grew more desperate it got louder.

Kotin replied, "But by now Hehaka could be halfway to Standing Stone country. How can one little boy—"

"Don't tell me what I already know!" she snapped.

Wrass turned in time to see Kotin shrink like a water bladder being wrung dry.

"Yes, all right," Kotin mumbled, taking a stroke with his paddle.

Wrass cautiously lifted his head, wincing at the pain. Two warriors sat behind him, alternatively paddling and steering them through the frozen night. They wore capes against the cold, skin caps on their heads, and did their best to look in any direction but at Gannajero.

Wrass let his gaze trace the canoe's sleek gunwale, following it forward to where Gannajero sat in the bow. The old woman wore a new cape made of finely smoked deerhide and decorated with circlets of seashells and flashing twists of copper. She had seen around forty summers. Greasy twists of graying black hair framed her deeply lined face, framing her toothless mouth and that shriveled plum of a nose.

And her eyes . . . Her eyes were black bottomless pits that seemed to have no pupils. Looking into them was like gazing into a well of hopeless terror that froze a person's souls. Whatever Gannajero was, nothing remotely human ever seemed to look back.

Kotin leaned over her hunched form like a hunting heron about to spear her with his long nose. He reminded Wrass of the *hagondes*—cannibal Spirits who carried off bad children in a basket. Grandmother Sayeno and her sisters had seen one once. It had been walking near an old longhouse and was clearly visible in the moonlight. The Spirit's nose had been so long it almost touched the ground. They'd tried to catch the Spirit, but it had let out a hideous scream and vanished into the forest before they . . .

"That little boy, as you call him," Gannajero snarled, "is valuable in ways you'll never understand."

Hehaka? Valuable? Wrass made a face, only to wince at the pain it caused him.

Three children rode in the canoe just beyond Wrass' feet: two girls and a boy. The boy had seen perhaps seven or eight summers. The girls were a little older, ten or eleven. All had been captured during the Bog Willow Village battle, and sold to Gannajero. They were Dawnland People. At the sound of the old woman's voice, the boy curled into a tighter ball and started crying. The two girls continued to sleep fitfully.

"Are you all right?" Wrass asked the boy in the Dawnland tongue. He was good at languages. He had always listened intently when Traders came through, trying to learn as much as he could.

The boy turned to peep at Wrass from beneath a skinny arm. He was half Wrass' size, with a narrow face and an unkempt mass of chin-length black hair. His blade-thin nose kept quivering and dripping. A ratty cape—made from woven strips of weasel hide—covered his shoulders. "No, I'm c-cold, and my throat hurts."

Wrass inched forward, lifted his cape, and draped it over the boy like a blanket. The boy slid backward, pressing against Wrass as he cried.

Wrass drew him closer. "Shh. Don't cry."

"I can't stop."

"Believe me, it doesn't do any good." Wrass stroked his arm. "You need to get some sleep. You have to be strong."

Above the rocky riverbank a shrubby blanket of winged sumacs seemed to roll on forever beneath the dark maple trees that fringed the winter sky. The campfires of the dead gilded the shrubs with an opalescent sheen that made them appear to shimmer as the canoes passed.

The boy whispered, "What's your name?"

"Wrass. I'm Bear Clan from Yellowtail Village of the Standing Stone People."

"I'm Toksus of the Otter Clan from Bog Willow Village."

"Toksus? That's a good name. How old are you?"

"Eight summers." The boy suddenly twisted his head to look up at Wrass. "My parents are coming, aren't they? They must be right behind us by now? Have you seen them?"

Wrass let out a deep breath. When he'd first been captured, the strangling mixture of fear and hope had been unbearable. "Toksus, I'm not going to lie to you. You have a lot of hard days ahead. But I know this for sure: Someone *is* looking for you."

Toksus stared up with swimming eyes. "And . . . they'll find me soon?"

"I'm sure they will."

"My parents are alive. I saw them! When the Flint warriors rounded up all us children after the battle . . . as they marched us away . . . I saw my parents standing in a line with twenty other people. They were being guarded by six warriors."

Wrass' headache made it difficult to think, let alone speak coherently and gently. The scene Toksus had described was common enough. The captives would be divided up, given to warriors who had shown merit on the war trail or during the fight. The warrior who ended up with Toksus' mother could kill her, or keep her for a slave. Were the latter the case, she was already being marched away to the west, hands bound behind her. The only value his father would have would be as a source of body parts to be carried home as trophies. But he couldn't tell the boy that.

Wrass wet his lips. "Someone is looking for you, Toksus. That means you need to stay alive, or all their efforts to rescue you will be for nothing."

Toksus wiped his eyes on his sleeve and blinked at Wrass. "Are you just saying that?"

The warriors paddling in the rear chuckled, amused.

Wrass turned his back to the men and softly said, "Among my people, if anyone survives an attack, they always form a search party to try and get their families back. Don't your Dawnland people do that?"

"Yes."

"Then if your parents are alive, they're trying as hard as they can to find you."

Some of the tension went out of the boy's shoulders. "But how will they find me, Wrass? If we were traveling on land they might be able to track us. We're in a canoe, headed downriver toward the lands of the People Who Separated."

Wrass nodded. "It will be more difficult, but a good warrior would still be able to find us. Is your father a warrior?"

"He—he's a Trader."

"That's even better. He's protected by the power of Trade." A stab of pain splintered his thoughts. "He—He can s-safely stop at any village along the shores. A-Ask if people have seen us pass by. The important thing to remember is that he's not going to give up, Toksus. He'll keep looking even if he—"

"Enough!" Gannajero shouted, rising in the bow. She extended a skinny arm from beneath her cape, and a talonlike finger pointed. "Land there, on that sand spit."

A din of questions erupted as the warriors steered the canoes to shore.

Kotin leaped into the water and dragged the bow onto the sand. The canoe rocked violently when Gannajero climbed out. Wrass struggled to keep from throwing up, the rolling of the boat adding to his dizziness. He gulped for fresh air and watched Gannajero tramp away into the forest.

Kotin just shook his head and absently scratched his crotch. The two new girls jerked awake and sat up. Wrass glanced at the warriors behind him. They were staring hard at the old woman where she'd stopped just inside the line of trees. She seemed to be staring up at the interlaced branches overhead, as if they held the answer to some great secret.

The older girl, who had a broad nose and long eyelashes, hissed, "We should try to run."

Wrass hissed, "In the name of the Ancestors, no!"

They turned distrustful eyes on him.

He leaned closer to them. "What are your names?"

The older girl gave him a suspicious look, but answered, "I am Auma. This is my cousin, Conkesema. We are Otter Clan."

"I am Wrass of the Standing Stone People. I grew up in Yellowtail Village. *Please* . . . listen. No matter what happens, you mustn't be any trouble for the warriors. *Don't* try to run, or—"

"Why not?" Auma replied sharply. "If I have a chance, I'm going to run as hard as I can! Are you such a coward that you won't try?"

Just the anger in her voice made Wrass' head pound. He squinted against the pain. "Auma, the first day I was a slave, a girl ran. Gannajero told Kotin to shoot her. The arrow took her through the lungs—"

"They killed her? Just like that? They didn't even try to hunt her down and bring her back?"

"They killed her without a second thought." Wrass glanced at the warriors. "We need to stick together, to wait for the right moment; then we'll all make a run for it. But we have to wait, to plan. Do you understand?"

Auma's expression said she wasn't sure she believed him. She cupped a hand to her friend's ear and whispered something. Conkesema blinked, appeared to think about it for several moments, then nodded faintly. She had waist-length black hair and a perfect oval face. A small white scar marked Conkesema's left temple.

Auma gave Wrass a wary, sidelong, look. "For the moment, we will do as you say, but only because we saw no Standing Stone warriors among those that attacked our village."

Wrass said, "None of my people attacked you. I was held captive just outside the big warriors' camp after the battle. I spent half the night searching for any sign of Standing Stone warriors. If I'd seen one, I'd have risked trying to run to him."

Auma's brown eyes glistened in the starlight. "How long have you been a slave?"

"I think it's been most of a moon now. I'm not sure. My m-memory is shaky."

Her eyes tightened. "Can you tell us what's going to happen to us?"

Toksus stopped whimpering to listen.

Wrass considered, then chose the truth. "The worst you can imagine. You will obey, or be beaten with war clubs for the slightest offense. Men will come to Trade for time with you . . . and they'll do things that would get them killed back home."

They glanced at each other with wide eyes, and Wrass knew exactly what they must be thinking, because he'd thought the same things the first night on the trail.

Auma blurted, "What are you *talking* about! The men will take us home and adopt us into their families. That's how it works!"

"Yes. Normally," Wrass replied. "But this is Gannajero. Sometimes the child is killed when the man is through with her. Some are marched away never to be seen again. Some are just purchased for the night."

Toksus choked on a suffering sound.

Auma swallowed hard. In a dread voice, she said, "I don't believe it. We're just children. If any man did that, his own relatives would hunt him down and kill him as something sick . . . soul-diseased!"

"They would," Wrass nodded. "If anyone found out. That's why they march for days to find Gannajero the Crow. They—"

Toksus gasped a breath, and everyone went stone still. He stared at them for a few instants, then leaned forward and in a hushed little-boy voice, sang, *"The Crow comes, the Crow comes, pity the little children, beat the drum, beat the drum, grab the young, and run, run, run."*

"Where did you hear that?" Auma asked.

He looked around the circle. "My grandmother used to sing me that song when I was little, to scare me. Is it about her? About Gannajero?"

All of their gazes shifted to the old woman standing amid the willows and silver maples. She might have been paralyzed, her head cocked as she stared up into the bare branches.

Wrass said, "Probably."

"There has to be something we can do," Auma hissed in panic. "We—"

"There are some things. . . ." Wrass felt suddenly dizzy. He closed his eyes. The emotions affected his headache like stone hammers striking his skull. His nausea was getting worse.

"What?" Toksus asked.

Wrass took several deep breaths to steady himself. "First, d-don't cry. After a while, it irritates the warriors. They'll thump your skull to stop you. Second, just do whatever they tell you to. Don't argue. Don't complain. Just . . . do it. The less trouble you are, the longer you will live."

No one said a word. They just sat in the canoe, breathing hard.

Finally, Auma turned to him and gestured to his swollen, battered face. "You must not have listened to your own advice."

Despite his thundering headache, Wrass smiled. "I helped four friends escape last night. The miracle is that the warriors didn't kill me for it."

"It looks like they tried," Auma noted.

"Did they make it?" Toksus propped himself up on his elbows. "Did your friends escape?"

"Yes." Tears leaked from the corners of his eyes. He might not do anything else right for the rest of his life, but last night . . . he had. Odion, Tutelo, Baji, and Hehaka were free. Safe.

Auma frowned out at Gannajero. The woman gave a crowlike cackle and began to pace. Her hunched figure passed back and forth through the tree-filtered starlight. Over the lapping of waves and the faint sigh of wind through the branches, Wrass could hear her talking to herself, the words indistinct mumbles.

Kotin stood just up from the bow, hands propped on his hips, lips pressed into a hard line. He didn't seem eager to interrupt the conversation the old woman was having with herself.

Auma said, "Who is Hehaka? Do you know?"

"One of the boys I helped escape."

"Why does she want to go back and find him? With all the warfare, she can Trade for plenty of boys."

Two warriors—apparently out of patience—climbed out of the second canoe and stalked over to Kotin. Their low voices were barely audible over the sounds of the river, but they wore worried expressions. They kept gesturing to Gannajero.

Wrass glanced across at the canoe they'd left, seeing his friend Zateri raise her head. She gave the warriors a wary look, then met Wrass' eyes. He could see her concern as she took in his battered and swollen face.

Wrass turned his attention back to the warriors, trying to read their lips. To Auma, he said, "There was something special about Hehaka. He'd been her captive for seven summers. He—"

"Seven *summers!*" Toksus started shivering. "And he never got away?" His voice turned shrill. "She might keep me for seven summers? That's the rest of my life!"

Wrass was still watching the warriors, and thought he saw Dakion say: *She's insane. . . . Leave her. . . .*

Toksus grabbed Wrass' hand. "Tell me! Why didn't she ever sell him?"

"Somehow, and I don't know how, he kept her safe."

Auma asked, "How could a captive boy keep her safe?"

As Wrass watched Kotin make a dismissive gesture to Dakion, he said, "Hehaka once told me that he'd tried to escape, but she'd always ordered Kotin to find him and bring him back. He once heard Gannajero tell Kotin . . ." His voice faded when Gannajero suddenly whirled around and stared at the assembly of warriors. She was breathing hard, her chest rising and falling. The men went utterly still, like mice when an owl's shadow passes overhead.

"Kotin, come!" Gannajero ordered.

Kotin said something to the other warriors, backed away, and hurried to where she waited under the trees. A filigree of dark limbs stained the paler gray behind her. Gannajero's voice was indistinct, almost a singsong. She shook a fist in Kotin's face, and he threw out his arms as though in surrender.

Wrass barely heard Gannajero say, ". . . plotting against me. Don't you . . . he'll find me."

But Kotin clearly replied, "We're far away from his country. We won't be going back for many summers. He'll *never* find you!"

Gannajero went silent. She appeared to be thinking about that.

The group of warriors on the riverbank shifted. Dakion had his eyes narrowed menacingly. He said something to Ojib that made the man nod.

Kotin glanced their way, put a hand on Gannajero's shoulder, and guided her deeper into the trees.

Wrass lifted his left hand from beneath his cape and felt his forehead. His fever raged, but he—

Toksus gasped suddenly and pointed at Wrass' hand. "What happened?"

Wrass looked at it. The pain in his head was so staggering, he'd forgotten about his little finger. He flexed it. "Gannajero sawed off the tip with a chert knife."

"Why? What did you do?" Auma asked.

"Nothing. She needed a flesh offering to consecrate the eaglebone sucking tube she was going to use to suck out a man's soul."

Their horrified expressions gave Wrass the queer sensation that he had just stepped over the edge of a cliff . . . and it was a long way to jagged rocks below.

"She sucked out a man's soul?" Toksus hissed. "Why?"

"She's Gannajero the Crow. A witch. She sucked out the man's afterlife soul and blew it into a small pot that she carries in her pack."

Starlight coated Auma's face with a wash of silver. "She has a pot filled with souls?"

"Yes. She took Hehaka's, too. She got mad at him one night and sucked his soul into that pot. Then she told him that when he died, she would carry his soul far away before she released it."

"So that he could never find his relatives again, and he'd be doomed to wander the earth alone forever?" Toksus asked breathlessly.

"The old woman doesn't like to be crossed."

They all turned to peer intently at Gannajero, who was waving her skinny arms while Kotin slouched, as if under assault.

Barely audible, Toksus whispered to Wrass, "There's something inside me. It feels like a snake, coiling around." He put a hand to his chest and winced. "Do you think she cast a spell—?"

"You're just scared."

Toksus licked his dry lips. "But it feels like more. Are you sure she didn't shoot a witch's pellet into my heart?"

"When she curses you, you'll know it. Hush. Here she comes."

Gannajero strode back to the canoe and climbed into the bow. Standing like some perverted bird, she stared at Wrass first, then, one by one, at other children. They tried to shrink through the bark hull.

"Come here, boy." Gannajero gestured to Toksus.

"W-Why?" He huddled against Wrass.

"We're going to make camp, and I'm going to feed you first," she said in a bizarrely kind voice. "Aren't you hungry?"

"Yes."

"Then come." Gannajero's voice might have been a doting grand-mother's.

Wrass bit his lip, desperate to protest, any words dying in his throat as the old woman fixed him with her soul-eating, empty eyes.

Shaking like a leaf in a hurricane, Toksus walked across the packs toward her. When he got close, she grabbed his arm and jerked him out of the canoe.

Toksus yipped in fear as she dragged him into the small clearing surrounded by silver maples and shoved him to the ground. "Stay there or I'll slit your throat."

"What about the others?" Kotin asked.

"Leave Hawk-Face. He's too sick to run, but bring the girls. Tie them over by that tree."

Hawk-Face. That's what she called him. She had unpleasant nicknames for all of her children. Zateri's was Chipmunk Teeth because her two front teeth stuck out.

Wrass sank back against the packs. All he wanted was to close his eyes and sleep forever.

Five

By the time Cord reached the massive chunks of rock that clustered at the base of the pass, he was stumbling and gasping for breath. He propped himself against a stone slab and waited for his men to catch up.

Dzadi emerged from the darkness first. The old bear slumped down in the middle of the trail and flopped back against the rocks. Panting, he asked, "How . . . many? How many—?"

A long wailing howl pierced the darkness and was answered by shrill yips from lower on the trail: Wolf Clan warriors calling to each other across the lone and silent mountain.

Cord tried to count the dark shapes of his men coming up the trail. "I only see two."

"Are you sure?"

Cord searched for a time longer before he said, "We lost one."

"Which one?"

"I'm not certain yet."

Twenty heartbeats later, Ogwed trudged up along the trail. Five paces behind him, Wado was keeping himself upright by sliding his back along the rock wall, side-stepping up the switchback with his knees quivering. Both looked like they might drop at any instant.

"I don't see Neyaw," Cord said.

Dzadi bowed his head. "I'm not surprised. The fool probably decided to hide somewhere. Sneaked away with his tail between his legs."

Cord didn't answer. His gaze fixed on movement. Two switchbacks down the trail, a stone's toss to the south, stood a cluster of boulders girdled by plum and sumac. A circle of dark forms coalesced around the boulders. Cord watched them close in on the rocks.

A shrill cry, triumphant, almost made Cord jump out of his skin. As it echoed away, bows twanged. A man screamed in pain and fear, the sound buried beneath a din of snarls and yelped war cries. Black forms writhed over the boulders.

If Cord hadn't known better, he'd think it was a pack of wolves downing a struggling deer.

Ogwed cried, "Is that Neyaw? Neyaw!" He started to turn back, but Dzadi brought him down hard in the middle of the trail.

"Leave it be, boy," Dzadi said. "He's gone."

If it had been daylight, their Dawnland pursuers would have sacrificed Neyaw to their Sun God and eaten his flesh, giving the best parts, the brain and tongue, to their most honored citizens. In the darkness, they were, perhaps, dispensing with the ritual.

Dzadi patted Ogwed's shoulder, then released him. "Neyaw was a fool. Don't you make the same mistake. Don't fall behind."

The young warrior sat up and stared down the trail. Suppressing tears, Ogwed said, "He didn't deserve to die that way."

Wado added, "We are Flint warriors. We should all die in great battles, fighting to protect our people. That's what warriors do."

Dzadi exchanged a sad glance with Cord, then raised his eyes to the narrow defile just above them. The black chunks of stone resembled huge stair steps.

"Get up," Cord ordered. "We have to make the pass while they're busy with Neyaw."

"But we need to rest. I can barely walk!" Wado objected.

Dzadi said, "You'd better be able to run, boy."

As they climbed, the war cries grew louder—enough to throw his warriors into short-lived panics where they almost shoved each other off the blocks in their haste to reach the pass.

When they crested the trail and staggered into the gap, Cord could see the forested hills of Flint country in the distance; unwarranted joy warmed his veins. The trail down the other side of the mountain was a silver slash that cut through a thick sumac-and-hickory forest. Even staggering and half-dead, they could run it in their sleep.

Behind him, Dzadi cursed and stamped his feet.

"What's wrong?" Cord called.

"We lost another one."

"What?"

"Wado's gone."

Cord leaped down from the high point and searched their back trail with care. Nothing moved. The desolate frozen-hearted wilderness had swallowed all sound, save the ragged breathing of the men beside him.

Ogwed stared up at Cord. "Do you think they got him?"

"He might have run off," Cord replied gently.

"Or maybe he fainted and they found him. That's why we didn't hear a ruckus," Dzadi said without thinking.

Horror sparkled in Ogwed's eyes. "You mean they found him, gagged him, and they're cutting him to pieces and swallowing his flesh while he watches? That's it, isn't it?" The youth's eyes rolled around in his head, darting this way and that as though he was on the verge of bolting into the blackness.

Cord said, "Stop wasting breath. We're going home."

He climbed back up and perched on the highest block of stone to survey the country to the west. Lines of tumbled and irregular hills, softened by the winter-gray mat of forest, stretched out before him. There, just beyond those ridges, lay the familiar forests, streams, and fields of home.

Or what was left of them.

Feeling hollow and drained, he started down the other side at a shambling trot. He couldn't feel his legs, though he knew when his moccasins hit the ground: Each step jolted his body. Dzadi and Ogwed struggled along behind him.

When they rounded a bend, a tiny light flickered. A campfire. Down the western slope of the mountain, perhaps one-half hand of time away. Friend or foe? He'd worry about it later. Right now, they had only one task: to stay on their feet.

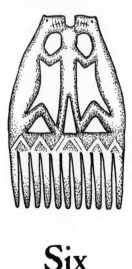

Six

Gonda turned when his eleven-summers-old son, Odion, sat up in his moosehide blanket, as though he'd heard something, and tipped his head to listen to the night. The boy was twenty paces away, sitting beside the Flint girl, Baji. They both looked terrified. Odion's shoulder-length black hair hung around his face in a mass of tangles, and his dark eyes had gone wide. His gaze was riveted on the dense plums and sumacs that created an impenetrable thicket on the northern slope.

Odion tilted his right ear toward the east, then turned to Gonda. Almost breathlessly, he said, "Father? Do you hear that?"

Gonda shook his head. Odion pointed up the mountain toward the pass.

"Are you sure, Son?"

Odion and Baji nodded in unison.

Gonda quietly walked around the fire where the other children and the two Hills People warriors, Sindak and Towa, slept rolled in blankets. His former wife, War Chief Koracoo, stood guard there. She obviously hadn't heard anything either. She stood with her back to him, vigilantly keeping watch on the trail that led up the mountain. Her red leather cape, painted with a blue buffalo, looked black in the faint light. Her legendary war club, CorpseEye, was propped on her shoulder.

As Gonda approached, she didn't turn. She knew the sound of his steps better than her own. They had been married for twelve summers—until she'd returned to find their village burned to the ground. Then she'd set what remained of his belongings outside their smoldering longhouse and, according to the ways of the People of the Standing Stone, divorced him. He walked to stand at her shoulder and whispered, "Odion heard something. Did you?"

The tiny lines around her black eyes deepened. After the devastating attack on their own village, Yellowtail Village, they'd both cut their hair short in mourning. Chopped-off black locks framed her beautiful oval face. At the age of twenty-seven, she stood twelve hands tall—very tall for a woman—and had a straight nose with full lips and a wide mouth. "No. Earlier, I thought I heard wolves, perhaps human wolves, near the pass, but . . ."

They both stood absolutely still and listened. During the attack, several of the Yellowtail Village children had been stolen by the enemy. Last night, they'd rescued their own children—Odion, and their eight-summers-old daughter, Tutelo—plus a Flint girl named Baji and another boy, Hehaka, whose people they did not yet know.

Koracoo's head tilted to the right. Gonda held his breath. Bitter cold gripped the forest; it had driven the sap out of the trees, freezing them solid and leaving their mighty hearts dreaming of spring. They were too cold even to pop and snap with minor temperature variations.

Yet Gonda heard snapping in the distance. And it was rhythmic.

"Men. Running."

"Yes," Koracoo whispered. She spun around to survey the camp. Her gaze lingered on the children. "One of us should remain by the fire while the rest of us hide."

"I'll be the bait. Go. Get the others up and packed."

Koracoo trotted away, rousted everyone from his or her blankets, and ordered them to pack. Hands flew, rolling blankets, stuffing belongings into packs. Then Koracoo sent Sindak and Towa out into the northern sumac thicket with the four children. She lightly trotted to hide in the plum grove to the south of the fire.

A herd of deer thrashed through the plums, startling Gonda into instinctively grabbing for his war club, but they trotted past and disappeared into the forest.

Gonda walked back and crouched before the fire. Reluctantly, he placed his war club to the side, near the tripod where the boiling bag hung, and pretended to be warming his hands before the tiny blaze. Far off, branches cracked as men staggered into brush and trees, then curses erupted, and finally feet stumbled down the mountain trail. Thirty heartbeats later, they arrived.

Gonda subtly gazed at the vague forms that moved at the edges of the firelight. They stood just beyond the weave of leafless plum trees. Gonda calmly added another branch to the flames and mentally noted the location of his war club. He could have it quickly, but not as quickly as they could shoot an arrow through his heart. Sitting clearly visible in the fire's gleam, he made an easy target.

"Since my heart is still beating," he softly called, "I assume you've decided not to kill me. Why don't you come in and get warm." He looked straight out at their dark forms and gestured to the logs pulled up around the little blaze. "You're welcome to the stew that's left in the boiling bag."

A hissed conversation ensued beyond the trees. From the corner of his eye, he saw Koracoo shift, getting ready.

Full into the firelight, his legs shaking, walked a tall man wearing a finely tailored wolfhide coat with the hood pulled up. He had a long pointed nose and cold eyes. Serpents were tattooed on his cheeks, and he had an ugly knife scar across his square jaw. The man moved with a mixture of mistrust and careless desperation. His legs were shaking as though he'd been running flat-out for days. "You're from the Standing Stone People," he noted in a deep voice as he took in Gonda's accent and the distinctive rectangular cut of his buckskin cape. "What are you doing here?"

Again, Gonda gestured to the logs situated at angles around the fire. "Please sit down and call in your friends. I mean you no harm. You look like you can use some rest."

The man swallowed hard and said, "There's no time to rest. They're right behind us. If you value your lives, you'll collect your belongings and join us."

Gonda's head jerked up. He'd said your *lives*, not life. So he knew Gonda was not alone. Had he glimpsed Sindak and Towa? "Who's behind you?"

"Dawnland warriors."

"Survivors from the Bog Willow Village attack?"

"Probably."

Gonda slowly got to his feet. "Who are you?"

"I am Cord, of the Turtle clan of the Flint People, war chief of Wild River Village. Or at least, I was."

Gonda's hackles rose. Cord's men still hadn't come in. Was Cord the decoy for the pack? Was he supposed to keep Gonda busy while the rest of his men surrounded the camp, cutting off escape? How many were out there? Gonda clenched his uplifted hands to fists. "Why are they chasing you? Were you part of the war party that destroyed Bog Willow Village?"

Cord nodded. "Yes."

"Why did you attack them?"

Through gritted teeth, Cord answered, "They destroyed my village, Wild River Village, eight days ago, but I don't have time to explain everything." He used his chin to gesture to the places in the forest where Sindak, Towa, and Koracoo hid and said, "Since your friends have not killed me, I assume you are all bystanders in this, though I can't fathom what you're doing this deep in Dawnland country. Either join us or let us pass. A fight will help neither of us."

Gonda lowered his hands, and called, "Koracoo? Everyone? Come out."

"Koracoo?" Cord said, and clutched his war club more tightly. "War Chief Koracoo of Yellowtail Village?"

Koracoo stepped out, eyed him hostilely, and said, "That's right."

They faced each other like two stiff-legged dogs about to lunge for the other's throat. Cord stared hard at CorpseEye, Koracoo's war club. It was old and made from a dark wood that did not grow in their country. Legend said that CorpseEye had once belonged to Sky Woman herself. Strange images were carved on the shaft: antlered wolves, winged tortoises, and prancing buffalo. A red quartzite cobble was hafted to the top of the club, making it a very deadly weapon—one Koracoo wielded with great expertise. Throughout their territories, CorpseEye was known as a frightening magical weapon, capable of sniffing out enemies even at great distances.

Cord spread his arms in a gesture of surrender and said, "I have never met you in battle, and hope I never have to. I know your reputation for courage."

"And I know yours, War Chief Cord. I also have dreaded the possibility that we would, someday, meet. Are you headed home?"

"Yes, we—"

Sindak and Towa pushed out of the trees, herding the four children before them, and the expression on Cord's face swiftly changed. He looked like a man who'd just been condemned to death.

"Blessed gods," he said. "You have children with you?" His gaze went over the two boys and two girls, as though assessing their ages and how fast they could run. "If you don't want Dawnland filth feeding them to their dogs, you should come with us. *Now.*" He lifted a hand and called, "Dzadi? Ogwed? Come out."

Two warriors stepped from the trees. The first thing Gonda noticed was their empty quivers. Then he saw the men. The big bear of a man had a wide, heavy jaw and pink burn scars mottling his face and hands. He slitted his brown eyes menacingly. The other warrior was young, perhaps seventeen or eighteen summers. He had a catlike face, with a broad nose. Both men had to lock their trembling knees to keep standing.

"How long have they been chasing you?" Gonda dumped out the boiling bag, rolled it, and tucked it into his belt. Then he slung his pack over his shoulder and cautiously picked up his war club.

"For just a few hands of time, but we haven't slept in two and a half days. Now, *hurry,* they're coming." Cord swung around to look up the mountain trail.

"How many are there?"

"Twenty. Maybe more."

A faint far cry split the air, then was joined by a cacophony of yips and snarls that persisted for ten heartbeats before dying away.

Gonda's skin crawled. "Wolf Clan." He looked at Sindak and Towa, who were staring at the newcomers uncertainly. Gonda ordered, "Sindak, Towa, split your arrows. Give half to Cord's men."

Cord looked at him, taken aback.

As did Sindak, whose jaw dropped. "But Gonda, these are Flint People. Our sworn enemies." Sindak had seen nineteen summers. Shoulder-length black hair framed his lean face. He was homely, with a hooked nose and deeply sunken brown eyes.

"Do it," Koracoo ordered.

Sindak hissed something disparaging but unslung his quiver, counted the arrows, and walked forward to hand four of them to Cord, saying, "I'd appreciate it if you didn't shoot me in the back with my own arrows."

Cord replied, "I only shoot cowards in the back."

"That doesn't make me feel better, War Chief." Sindak glared as he walked back to stand beside Towa.

Towa was a handsome youth, with waist-length black hair, a straight nose, and eyes like midnight. "Koracoo, are you sure about this? I don't—"

Annoyed, Koracoo answered, "Don't make me tell you again."

Towa reluctantly pulled three arrows from his quiver and handed them to Cord, who distributed them.

With genuine gratitude, Cord said, "You go first with the children; we'll cover the back trail," and gestured to the path that led down the western slope of the mountain.

"Sindak, you lead," Koracoo ordered. "Towa, follow him. Children, you'll be next in line. Gonda and I will be behind the child—"

Sindak interrupted, "Cord and his men should run in front where we can watch them, War Chief."

"Move, Sindak," Koracoo ordered.

Sindak shook his head, but he and Towa trotted down the trail with their war clubs in tight fists. The children fell into line behind them, followed by Koracoo and Gonda.

Odion led the children at a fast clip, his moccasins leaving dark splotches in the frost. The two girls, Tutelo and Baji, ran practically on his heels. Hehaka, however, lagged behind. He was a strange boy, not quite *right,* though Gonda hadn't had enough time to discover exactly what was wrong with him. Perhaps he'd simply been a slave for so long he didn't know how to deal with his sudden freedom.

Gonda looked back over his shoulder and saw Cord and his men staggering after them. If they made it more than a few hundred paces before their shaking knees gave out, he'd be amazed.

Seven

Odion

I scramble up the steep trail behind Sindak and Towa. I'm exhausted, but I'll never give up. When we reach the crest of a low hill, I look back over my shoulder. Baji is right behind me. Tutelo and Hehaka walk ten paces away. Mother and Father are close on their heels. But the Flint warriors are strung out far apart, staggering more than running. I scan the moonlit forest, where pine needles shimmer and the bare branches of oaks seem made of polished silver. I don't see the people chasing us, but their yips echo at regular intervals. Every time I hear them, my throat constricts as though the huge hands of the gods have closed around it. "Sindak," I say, "give me a weapon. You have three stilettos tucked into your belt." I extend my hand.

The warrior stares at me; then his eyes narrow in respect. He pulls a deerbone stiletto from his belt and hands it to me. "Don't let anyone know you have this until you need it."

"I understand." I tuck it into my belt beneath my cape.

Sindak turns around and frowns at our party. "Towa, let's stop for a few moments and let the Flint warriors catch up." His hooked nose shines with sweat. Despite the cold, the run has made us all hot.

Towa halts and walks back to stand beside Sindak. His brows draw together. He's tall and broad shouldered. His long black hair hangs over the front of his cape. "I thought you didn't want them to catch up."

Sindak heaves a sigh and shrugs. "If it were my choice, they wouldn't be here at all, but I'm too much of a coward to stand up to Koracoo."

"That's wise, friend. She'd crush your skull without a second thought."

Sindak gives him an askance look. "That's not true. There's a war party behind us. I'm at least moderately valuable."

Towa chuckles. "Always the optimist."

Baji walks to my side and says, "Odion? Are you all right?"

"Yes, are you?"

"Just tired." She gazes back, looking beyond the Flint warriors into the dark forest where our pursuers must be. For a time, there is silence; then she whispers, "Odion, do you think these are the warriors you dreamed about? The footsteps you felt in your heart? Maybe it wasn't *her* warriors."

I blink, considering, and say, "No. The steps . . . I recognized them. One was K-Kotin's." When I can't say his name without stuttering, my blood goes cold. Kotin is Gannajero's deputy. The scariest of her warriors. He hurt so many children . . . including Baji. I sneak a glance at her, thinking maybe I shouldn't have said his name out loud; then my fingers go tight around the stiletto beneath my cape.

Baji rubs her nose on her sleeve. Even if I didn't know her, I would recognize the hate twisting her face. "Who else's steps?"

"Waswan's. You know how he shuffled?"

She jerks a nod. When she exhales, her breath shakes as it comes out. "I hope you're wrong, but if not, we need to be ready for them."

"Yes, I—"

Behind me, Sindak says to Towa, "You're brooding. Stop it."

"I'm not brooding," Towa replies.

"Yes, you are. You've been brooding ever since you saw Chief Atotarho in the warriors' camp last night."

"I *thought* I saw him. I'm still not sure."

Baji and I stare at each other and turn to study them. Sindak is scowling, while Towa looks worried.

Sindak whispers, "Aren't you ever going to tell me the secret orders he gave you just before we left the village?"

My gaze jerks to Baji in surprise and find her glaring at Towa as though she's just discovered he's a spy and longs to get her hands around his throat.

Towa goes still. He doesn't blink or even seem to be breathing. After a time, he replies, "I can't. You've never kept a secret in your life."

"I won't tell! And I already know it has to do with the sacred gorget he gave you. What are you supposed to do with it?"

Towa grips his war club in both hands. "That's none of your concern."

"You're just worried about what your mother will say if you betray our chief."

Towa nods. "Yes, I admit it. The fact that she'd order me flayed alive in front of the entire village does have some small influence on my loyalty."

Sindak smiles and looks back down the trail again. "Someday soon you're going to have to decide if that loyalty is worth your life, friend. Or, more importantly, if it's worth mine." He gestures to me and Baji. "Or the children's lives. Think about that."

Towa's voice goes low and serious. "I've been thinking of little else, Sindak."

Sindak stares at him for a long time. "Good. Now, do you think we've let them catch up enough, or should we—?"

A shrill howl erupts and echoes across the icy woods.

I shove between Sindak and Towa and charge up the slope, taking the lead.

Baji's steps are close behind me.

Eight

Grandmother Moon edged over the horizon, and her light ran across the mountains in a silver wave. The silent forest seemed to awaken. Gonda watched as a bare breeze swayed the branches.

The silence had been unbroken except for the sounds of their own moccasins striking the frozen earth, and the hunting yelps of their pursuers. Every now and then, the Dawnland warriors sounded closer, and the panicked children whimpered and threw themselves down the trail in an uncontrollable rush. Except for Odion. He acted as their leader, scolding them for getting too far ahead, keeping them in line. Once, he'd been forced to shout at Hehaka to stop running. And told the enemy their exact whereabouts. Each time the children made a sound, Cord and his men clenched their jaws and stoically stared straight ahead.

Gonda turned around to check on the Flint warriors. They were still there, still on their feet, staggering up the trail through a grove of gigantic sycamores. He almost couldn't believe it. They had the endurance of starving wolves on a blood trail.

Gonda looked ahead again. The children had started to stumble. One of them, he couldn't tell which, was gasping hoarse breaths, as though his lungs were desperate for air. They couldn't keep this up much longer.

He glanced at Koracoo. The lines around her eyes were tight. She knew it, too.

When the trail entered a narrow ravine lined with boulders, Koracoo threw an arm out in front of Gonda, and said, "Stop. We're being foolish."

Gonda halted. Cord and his men staggered to a stop beside them. Sindak and Towa whirled, and Odion held the children in a group, waiting.

"Why are we . . . stopping?" Cord gasped.

"We can't outrun them," Koracoo said. As she turned to face him, the frost crystals on her hood winked. "The children can't continue this pace, and you and your men will die on your feet if we try to. This is as good a place as any to make a stand."

"Make a stand?" Ogwed said in shock. The youth's entire body shook. If he cracked into a thousand pieces in the next heartbeat, it would surprise no one. "They outnumber us three to one! We won't be standing for long. We should—"

"Let her finish," Cord said, and stared at Koracoo with calm, utterly exhausted eyes. "What do you have in mind, War Chief?"

She looked around, studying the terrain. The ravine was fifty paces long and, in places, twenty or thirty hands deep. Granite boulders, smoothed into egg shapes, lined the slopes. In the crevices between the boulders, trees and brush grew. Some of the trees stood two hundred hands tall.

Koracoo said, "We have to try to talk to them. If we can—"

"Talk to them!" Ogwed exclaimed. "Have you lost your wits, woman? They don't want to talk, they want to kill us! We have to run until we—"

Koracoo strode to within a hand's width of him and with soft, implacable precision, said, "Are you prepared to fight me? If you *ever* challenge me again, you'll have to."

Ogwed blinked as though stunned. He backed away. "I . . . I don't want to fight you."

Cord said to Koracoo, "How do you plan to get the enemy to sling their bows long enough to exchange words?"

"I'm still figuring out that part." She scanned the terrain again, apparently devising her strategy. "The first thing we have to do is lure them into the drainage. That way, if they refuse to talk, we can keep them busy long enough for the children to make a run for it."

Cord smiled. "You realize, of course, that while they are pretending to talk with you, their warriors will be moving through the trees, surrounding us? When they're in place, it will be a simple matter for them to push us down into the ravine and slaughter us like spring deer."

Koracoo smiled back, but it wasn't pretty. Gonda had seen it before, and it made the hair on his arms stand up. Wisps of hair fell over her high cheekbones, making her eyes seem huge and impossibly black. She had one of those perfect female faces that made men stare. Koracoo replied, "Then I expect you and your men to fight to the death, War Chief. No one is to lay down his weapons. The longer we're on our feet, the more time the children will have to escape."

Cord bowed his head and nodded. "Of course."

Gonda scanned the terrain, noting the positions of the boulders and trees. "There's a rock shelter near that pile of boulders. I say we hide the children in there."

Koracoo nodded, "Towa, Dzadi, please see to that."

"Yes, War Chief," Towa said, and walked toward the children.

Dzadi hesitated. He turned to Cord and lifted his brows questioningly.

Cord said, "Go."

Dzadi reluctantly stalked over to join Towa.

Koracoo continued, "Sindak, I want you and Ogwed across the ravine, behind that thicket of dogwoods."

Sindak nodded, and he and Ogwed trotted away.

It disturbed Gonda that she'd split up the warriors, separating friends and forcing men from different peoples to work together. He'd never approved of that strategy. Gonda believed men fought harder with a friend at their back. But his way did not create alliances. Hers did. If an "enemy" warrior saved your life, he was no longer the enemy. She might be a war chief, but she was a peacemaker at heart. And that was another thing he'd never approved of. Peacemakers generally ended up dead.

"What about me, War Chief?" Cord asked. "Where do you want me?"

Koracoo studied the ravine with a practiced eye. "I want you with Gonda, up there." She aimed her war club at the south side of the ravine.

Cord studied it, considered, and nodded his approval. "Good thinking. We'll have clear shots."

Gonda and Cord trudged up the slope to take their position.

Nine

Bright, tree-filtered moonlight streamed across the forest. Cord shifted, and his movements repeated in vast amorphous shadows on the surrounding boulders. When Gonda frowned at him, he went still. Fatigue had made him as stupid as a clubbed dog. If he wasn't careful, he'd get himself—and everyone else—killed. The true sign of his fatigue was that he was almost past caring. He sucked in a deep breath. The night breeze carried the damp exhalations from the kicked pine duff underfoot. He concentrated on the scent, using it to focus on staying awake.

"Are you all right?" Gonda whispered, barely audible.

Cord shook his head, and Gonda nodded in understanding. Gonda was a warrior. At some point in his life, he'd probably been in similar circumstances, so exhausted his brain seemed to have gone to sleep with his eyes wide open.

"Do you want to sleep for a few moments?" Gonda asked. "You don't have to be awake until we see them. It might help."

Cord shook his head. "No. I'm not sure I'd wake quickly enough. I have the feeling that when I can finally sleep, I won't awaken for days."

"All right. But we can't afford to have you dozing off in the middle of the fight."

"I won't." *Blessed gods, let it be so.*

Gonda turned to watch the trail again. He was a thin, wiry man with a round face. His short black hair had been chopped off with a knife, and he had a heavy brow that resembled a shelf over his brown eyes. Unlike the Flint People, who sewed finely tailored coats, he wore a plain buckskin cape that blended perfectly with the forest shadows—as was the way of the Standing Stone People. Dark splotches of blood spattered the cape's front. Recently, he'd been in a deadly battle.

With whom?

Cord's thoughts wandered, imagining the fight, and his head started to fall forward. He jerked upright and shook himself. It took an act of will to keep his eyes open. Whether he wanted to or not, very soon, sleep would claim him. His body would simply be unable to stave it off.

"What are you doing in Dawnland country with four children, Gonda?" he asked softly. "Are you uncommonly brave, or dim-witted?"

Gonda answered without taking his gaze from the trail. "Well, it's a long story."

"Tell me, if you can. It will help me keep my eyes open."

Gonda glanced at him and smiled faintly. "Twenty days ago, our village was attacked and destroyed by Mountain warriors. They stole several of our children. Koracoo and I went after them. In the process, we had occasion to stop at a Hills People village, Atotarho Village—"

"Why would you stop there? Atotarho is an evil old sorcerer, and he hates all Standing Stone People. As well as Flint People, for that matter."

"Well, that's another tale. Let's just say that Atotarho's daughter had been captured in a raid, and he believed she was with our children."

"Why did he think they were together? That makes no sense."

Gonda braced his elbows on the boulder, supporting his bow and whispered, "Do you know the name Gannajero?"

Cord's heart seemed to stop. He pinned Gonda with cold eyes. "Gannajero the Crow. She's a Trader. But what she Trades in is so abominable, men have been trying to kill her for more than twenty summers. If she weren't so cunning, none of us would ever mention her name again."

"Soon, I will personally make certain her name is forgotten."

Names were clan property. Immediately after birth, a child was given a name that had belonged to a revered ancestor. After the deaths of evil people, names were retired forever and no one mentioned them again.

Somberly, Gonda said, "Gannajero purchased our children, as well as Atotarho's daughter."

Cord bowed his head for a long moment, trying to blot out the horrors he was seeing on the fabric of his souls. Gannajero bought and sold children to satisfy the unnatural appetites of men who deserved to be dead. He wondered if Gonda and Koracoo had reached their children before anything bad had happened to them. "How long ago did you rescue your children?"

"Last night. Gannajero was in your victory camp, buying and selling children."

Cord licked his dry, cracked lips. "I don't recall seeing a woman Trader."

"Nonetheless, she was there, with our children."

That meant they'd been Gannajero's slaves for more than half a moon. Too long to have gone unharmed. "Sindak and Towa are Hills warriors. Atotarho's?"

"Yes. He sent them with us to help rescue his daughter—or so he said."

"You doubt it?"

In a low, seething voice, Gonda replied, "I doubt every word that came out of Atotarho's mouth."

"You are wise, Gonda. He has a reputation for deceit that is unrivaled—except perhaps by Gannajero's."

As Grandmother Moon rose like a glowing ball over the treetops, she painted the forest with seashell opalescence. Every twig appeared to have been hand-polished to an unearthly shine.

Gonda said, "Gannajero still has one of our village children, a brave boy named Wrass."

"Why do you say he's brave?"

"He sacrificed his own freedom last night to make sure the other children got away. Every moment that we are delayed here, our chances of saving him grow slimmer."

"How old is he?"

"He's seen eleven summers. He's four moons older than my son, Odion."

An ache entered Cord's chest and gradually filtered through his entire body. "My son had seen twelve summers."

"Had?"

"Yes, he—he was killed, along with my wife, when the Mountain People attacked Wild River Village two summers ago." Cord had been standing on the palisade catwalk when he'd heard Lazza, his wife, scream. She'd been clutching both children's hands, dragging them through the thick smoke, trying to outrun five warriors with war clubs. It was a miracle his daughter had survived the blows to her head.

Gonda whispered, "Blessed gods, when will we stop killing each other?"

"When we all have food in our bellies. But not until then. The gods must give us back the rainfall and the warmth, or our great-grandchildren will still be fighting."

Hunger stalked the land, and had for a long time. The elders said that the past one hundred summers had been unusually cold and dry. That's why the corn, beans, squash, and sunflowers rarely matured. The growing seasons were too short. Meager harvests made people hunt harder, but after so many summers, the animals were mostly hunted out. When people couldn't feed their children, they had to take what they needed from nearby villages. Stealing had become a way of life. When it failed, war became necessary. The battles had gotten particularly violent in the past twenty summers. No one was safe.

"As a boy," Gonda said, "I remember the elders telling stories of a time when hundreds of small villages scattered the countryside. Can you believe that? People felt safe enough to live in small villages?"

"It was a different world. I do not believe we will ever see that again, not in our lifetimes."

Gonda exhaled hard. "No, but sometimes at night, I dream of it."

For as long as Cord could recall, smaller villages had been combining for defensive purposes. They built larger longhouses to accommodate the increased population and moved in together, then surrounded the new village with a thirty- or forty-hand-tall palisade of upright logs. Sometimes, they built two or three layers of palisades.

Cord surveyed the locations of the other warriors. On the opposite side of the ravine, Ogwed hid with Sindak behind the dogwoods. Cord could just barely see the outlines of their bodies through the dense tangle of branches. His gaze moved. Twenty paces up the slope, Dzadi and Towa were almost invisible in a pile of tumbled rocks. Just to their right, the four children had slithered into the low rock shelter; it was barely big enough for them to lie flat on their bellies. He could not see or hear them. They were as silent as the dead.

Cord did not know where Koracoo had hidden, but it was a measure of his exhaustion that he'd been content to allow her to lead the party. That and the fact that she had a powerful presence. Dangerous. Competent. And heart-stoppingly beautiful.

Without being consciously aware of it, his nocked bow sank into his lap. He heaved a breath and braced his forehead against the cold gray boulder. He needed to save his strength. Surely he could just close his eyes for an instant without . . .

His breathing instantly fell into deep soothing rhythms. Five heartbeats later, his dead wife knelt before him and smiled. *Lazza, what are you doing here?* He lifted his hand. She took it and kissed his calloused palm, then lovingly rested her cheek upon it. *I know you're tired, my husband, but you mustn't sleep. Soon, but not yet.*

A moccasined foot lightly kicked him. "Cord? They're coming."

Gonda's voice had been very soft, but Cord woke breathless, rigidly still. "How far away?"

"Two hundred paces up the trail."

"How long did I sleep?"

"Maybe sixty heartbeats. Not long."

Cord gripped his bow, shook himself awake, and rose into position. He aimed down at the trail that ran along the base of the boulders.

A short time later, one hundred paces away, just beyond the range of their bows, a circle of dark shapes came into view, melted together, and whines and yips erupted. All around the circle, vague forms slinked through the moonlight.

"I don't believe it," Gonda hissed.

In the brightest patch of moonlight a boy of no more than twelve summers appeared. He moved with commingled distrust and daring, cautiously observing the shadows, then walked into the ravine. His nostrils flared and contracted, then flared again, as though he'd caught their scent but wasn't certain where they were.

Cord studied him. He wore no cape or coat. His ribs stuck out through a threadbare shirt, and his stomach had shrunken up tight against his backbone. His lean face had the desperate alertness of a dog that hasn't eaten in days.

"He's starving," Gonda whispered.

"Don't get sentimental. He and his clan killed two of my men tonight."

Gonda's mouth tightened into a white line. "He looks hungry enough to have swallowed them whole while they were still screaming, moccasins and all."

"In one case, I think he did."

"Why would they send a boy?" Gonda whispered. "Do they think we won't shoot a child?"

"I'm staying my bow, aren't you? Is anyone else letting fly?"

Gonda gave him a knowing glance. "Good point."

The boy stared up at the boulders in a strangely wistful way, patiently waiting for something. What? After perhaps one hundred heartbeats, he loped away to rejoin his comrades, and a whimpering, snarling cacophony arose.

Gonda released the tension on his bowstring. "I wish they wouldn't do that."

"It does fray a man's nerves, doesn't it?"

"What do you think they're up to?"

Cord squinted at the moonlit trail. "The boy's telling them where each of us is hidden—at least those he could spot." He frowned at two warriors who had curled up on the ground, in the manner of sleeping dogs, taking rest when and where they could. Another lazily stretched his arms over his head and yawned. Three, wearing wolf headdresses, were engaged in a ritual he did not understand. They crawled forward on their bellies, ingratiating themselves to a tall warrior. Close by, two more were jealously slinking up and down the trail. The thing that most interested him, however, were the four people sitting together as though in council. Elders?

Cord said, "I see thirteen."

"But you and I both know there are more out there."

"Yes, probably working their way into position around us. Do you think the four people sitting in the circle are elders?"

"I certainly hope so. That could bring some wisdom to this confrontation."

Aggrieved warriors hunting down the people who'd murdered their families lost all reason. Their intent was simply to avenge their loved ones. Elders, however, could generally see through the emotion to the future repercussions of such slaughter. Often, they stayed the hands of their warriors.

After another five hundred heartbeats, one of the children in the rock shelter began talking, then crying.

"Hallowed Ancestors," Gonda said, and called, "Sindak? Do something!"

Before Sindak could speak, Odion ordered, "Stop it, Hehaka!"

It didn't stop. Finally, one of the boys slid out. "I'm not staying in there!" Hehaka cried. His face was lit by the moon, but the rest of him remained in shadow. As he rose to his feet, he might have been a disembodied head bobbing through the forest.

"Hehaka? Get down!" Odion ordered.

Cord observed as Hehaka scrambled through the maze of moonlight and black shadows, heading down the slope to where Koracoo stood amid a cluster of boulders.

Odion lunged from cover and hurled himself after Hehaka, shouting, "Take cover! They're going to kill you!"

Hehaka shouted back, "I don't care!"

Odion dove for Hehaka and knocked him to the ground with a *whump*! Hehaka shrieked as they rolled and fought.

The girls crawled out and ran for the two boys. In less than ten heartbeats, all of the children were out of the rock shelter—and clear targets for their enemies.

Sindak raced down the slope, grabbed Hehaka by the hand, and led all the children behind the boulders near Koracoo. Cord could see them clearly.

The children whispered plaintively and leaned against Koracoo's legs for protection. The youngest girl, perhaps eight, kept tugging at Koracoo's cape and pointing out into the trees, as though to get her to look at something.

This seemed to agitate the Wolf Clan. The whole group sprang to its feet and pressed forward tentatively, each cocking an ear to listen to the children's cries, as though hoping to recognize a voice.

Cord counted the visible warriors. "There are only eight now."

Gonda jerked a nod. "I know. That means the others are behind us."

"We need to spring the ambush soon."

"When a few more have walked into the ravine, Koracoo will—"

Odion said something to Koracoo, and she bent low to whisper with him. After twenty heartbeats, Odion walked down the steep hill and into the bottom of the ravine. He had his spine straight and his hands up, which spread the moosehide blanket knotted around his shoulders and revealed his chest to anyone who wanted to let fly.

"Koracoo is using your own son as the bait?" Cord said in disbelief.

There was only a hint of fear in his voice when Gonda replied, "Odion must have asked to do it. I don't hear any bows singing, do you?"

"Not yet."

Rustling and snapping sounded in the forest as warriors shouldered through the brush, getting into better position. Their faces were silvered by the moonlight, and he could see them smiling, displaying an arrogance Cord knew well—the arrogance that fills a warrior when he knows he's won. It was an arrogance of possession. The prey already belonged to them. The kill was just a matter of time.

Gonda swung around toward the noise. "They're tightening the circle."

Cord used his nocked arrow to point. "I'm most worried about those three. See them?"

In the bottom of the ravine, three youths bellied along the ground, moving toward Odion.

"If they capture your son, what will you do?" Cord asked.

"When it happens, I'll let you know."

Odion clenched his fists and stood tall, though he must be terrified. Admiration warmed Cord's veins. "Someday soon that boy is going to make a fine warrior."

Gonda glanced down at him, and his lips twitched. "You would not have said that one moon ago. I considered my own son to be a coward. He was afraid of everything."

"That flaw isn't apparent tonight. What changed?"

Gonda blinked thoughtfully. "Something. Gannajero."

Cord knew better than to ask any further questions. Such dramatic changes were only born in terror and pain. He returned his gaze to the bodies slinking toward them through the moonlight. Warriors seemed to be everywhere. Their pursuers were growing bolder, venturing well into bow range. On the opposite side of the ravine, two black shapes scrambled to within springing distance of Sindak and Ogwed. What was Koracoo doing? It was well past time to shout the command to fire. Of course, when that happened, they would likely all be killed.

Cord hissed, "Why haven't they loosed their arrows? They could have killed four or five of us by now, and captured the rest."

"That's why Koracoo is waiting. She's trying to figure out what they are up to first. A man should never taunt a bear that has him treed. The bear might, after all, just walk away."

"A wise move." If he'd had his wits about him, he'd be doing exactly what Koracoo was—waiting.

The unknown boy emerged from the shadows and walked up the ravine to meet Odion. Though the Dawnland boy was frighteningly thin, little more than a skin bag stretched over knobby bones and stringy muscles, he was a head taller than Odion. If it came to a fight, Cord suspected the wolf-boy would win.

To his right, Cord saw Koracoo's dark form step from behind the boulder where she'd been hiding. Was she preparing to kill the unknown boy if he attacked her son?

"The boys seem to be talking," Gonda said. "But I can't hear . . ."

Before he knew what was happening, Cord's eyes fluttered closed. When he jerked out of the doze, it startled Gonda, who snapped, "For the sake of the gods, Cord!"

"F-Forgive me." A spasm of fear went through him. He got on his knees, drew his bow again, and fought to keep his eyes open. The boys were gesturing with their hands.

"Stay awake," Gonda warned, "or I'll shoot you myself."

Rage briefly surged through Cord's veins, then vanished. This man had children to protect. He had every right to demand alertness. "I will."

Odion backed away from the unknown boy and called, "Mother? They're looking for a Trader named Tagohsah."

"Tagohsah?" Cord said in surprise. "He's a Flint Trader. A despicable character. What do they want with him?"

Gonda said, "Stay down. Let me do the talking." To the boy, he called, "I have heard of Tagohsah! He's a Flint Trader, but he's not here. Why do you wish to find him?"

"He has my cousin!" the boy shouted back. "A ten-summers-old girl."

Cord leaned against the boulder and whispered to Gonda, "She was probably one of the children stolen during the Bog Willow Village raid. I'm sure she's already been sold."

"Let us pray she was not sold to Gannajero."

Koracoo cupped a hand to her mouth, and shouted, "Tagohsah is not here, and we know nothing of your cousin. Go away and leave us in peace!"

The tall warrior rose from the midst of the "elders" circle and walked toward the unknown boy. He wore a cap made from the shoulder skin of a moose; the long hairs of the moose hump formed a bristly crest down the middle of his head. Two feathers were tied to the crest, and they bounced with his steps. A sheathed knife rested on his breast, hung from a cord around his neck. In addition to his slung bow and quiver, he carried a war club with a ball head, probably made from the root crown of a hardwood tree. "We have you surrounded. You can't escape. Stop lying! We know you were part of the war party that attacked our village. We followed you from their camp."

Cord stared at Gonda. "They don't want you, Gonda. You didn't hurt them. If you're smart, you'll give us up to protect your children."

"Well, frankly, I would, but my former wife stubbornly protects her allies. Even if they are Flint People."

As though she'd heard, Koracoo called, "I am War Chief Koracoo from Yellowtail Village of the Standing Stone People. We did not attack you. Though you are correct, you did see us run away from the warriors' camp last night."

"You *are* Standing Stone," the man replied, and sounded confused. "I can tell from your accent."

The man carried on a brief conversation with the other members of his clan, then turned back. "My elders tell me there were no Standing Stone warriors in the attacking war party. What were you doing in their camp?"

"We weren't in their camp. We went there to rescue our own children from the monster, Gannajero. *She* was in their camp. When our village was attacked and destroyed by Mountain warriors, my son and daughter were stolen and sold to Gannajero." Koracoo walked out into the moonlight, giving them a clear shot at her. "Tell me your name."

"I am Wakdanek, a Healer of the Dawnland People. It is my daughter, Conkesema, who is missing, as well as many other children. I saw Tagohsah buy Conkesema from one of the men who attacked us."

"Then you and I should talk, Wakdanek. We are all being fools here tonight. Let us see if we share a common goal."

"We may, War Chief Koracoo, but I fear—"

"Wait, Wakdanek." A short hunchbacked woman waddled forward. Her feet slapped a clumsy rhythm as she crossed the frozen ground. She wore a conical cap that covered her ears. A frizz of white hair stuck out around the edges.

"She must be fifty summers old," Gonda observed. "Look at that snowy hair."

The old woman stopped beside Wakdanek and studied Koracoo,

who stood on the ravine's lip twenty hands above her. "I am Shara, an elder of the Otter Clan. Come down, War Chief. I want to hear your story of Gannajero. That is a name I have not heard in more than twenty summers, and it terrifies me to hear it now."

Koracoo tied CorpseEye to her belt and started down the steep incline, moving with slow precision, letting them see her hands at all times.

Cord's gaze shifted. During the conversation, the Dawnland warriors had taken the opportunity to crawl closer to their prey. He could see one youth, perhaps fourteen summers, openly lying on his belly in the moonlight. A short distance away, another boy crouched half-hidden behind an elderberry bush. While Cord watched, the boy opened his mouth, and saliva drooled down his chin. He licked his lips in anticipation.

Cord aimed his bow at the boy and struggled against the overpowering need to sleep. Even with death looking him straight in his face, his body wanted to give up. The need was like a calm pool of warm water; it kept seeping up around him and taking hold of his senses with gossamer hands, then silently dragging him down, down. . . .

"Stay awake!" Gonda snapped.

Cord roused with a sudden gasp. "It's getting . . . difficult."

"I understand, believe me, I do. But we need every pair of eyes right now. When this is done, you can sleep for as long as you wish."

Cord chuckled softly. "Forever, maybe. If they have their way."

Ten

Wrass huddled in the canoe with his cheek propped on the cold gunwale, watching the camp almost hidden in silver maples. His fever must be very high. He seemed to be trapped in a hazy sparkling bubble where nothing was quite real. The blurry warriors didn't walk—they seemed to jerk from one place to another, shooting about like diving swallows. Nothing but fog and the great river existed beyond the camp's boundaries. It was still night, but the warriors had risen, and went about building fires, rolling blankets, cooking breakfast. The smell of frying porcupine drifted from the warriors' fire to his left.

Wrass lowered his eyes to the water that lazily flowed by. The warriors had dragged the canoe half out of the river onto the shore, but the stern was still in the water. He could see his reflection. At eleven summers, he was tall and thin. Normally, he had a narrow face with a beaked nose, and sharp dark eyes . . . but the beatings had left his face badly swollen and purpled with bruises. Dried blood matted his long black hair to his forehead and cheeks. For most of the night, he'd alternately slept and vomited.

"Get the children up. We're going to be going soon," Gannajero ordered. "And bring me the sick boy—and the youngest one."

Wrass lifted his gaze. Gannajero crouched beside Kotin near a campfire. The two had been together for a long time.

"Which sick boy? Hawk-Face or—"

"The Dawnland brat."

Kotin's shoulder-length hair flopped around his ears as he stalked across camp. He had a square face with a mouthful of broken yellow teeth, and he wore a soot-stained buckskin cape. He moved like a tall gangly stork.

He kicked one of the new warriors awake. "Akio, get the children up. We'll be leaving soon. And bring the two Dawnland boys to Gannajero."

Gannajero had hired Akio at the big warriors' camp last night. He had seen perhaps sixteen summers and had a florid face and pudgy body.

"Yes, Kotin. Don't worry." He sounded very eager to please.

Akio puffed as he waddled through the camp. Where was he from? Wrass had heard someone name his village. He tried to force his brain to work, to think, but the pain in his head was so overwhelming he could barely move without throwing up.

The pudgy guard stabbed one of the sleeping children with his war club and ordered, "Get up. We'll be leaving soon. You two. Come with me."

Six heads lifted. On the far side of the group, Zateri stood up. Her black hair glistened in the firelight. She was skinny and short for her ten summers, eight hands tall, and had a round "chipmunk" face. Her two front teeth stuck out slightly. She glanced at Wrass.

As the new children woke, the crying started. The two Bog Willow girls had fled their burning village dressed in thin doehide dresses. They stood huddled together, whimpering. The boys refused to stand. Toksus lay curled on his side on the ground, sobbing against his cape. The other boy tried to sit up, but fell weakly back to the ground. He didn't even seem to have the strength to cry. Zateri and the new Flint girl stood a short distance away, talking while they watched the guards. Auma and Conkesema walked over to join them. They were all shivering.

And that's how it would be for many days.

It was part of Gannajero's method of breaking new children. They would freeze and starve. When the evil old woman finally decided to throw them a rock-hard biscuit or ratty blanket, the children would weep their thanks while they groveled at her feet.

Involuntarily, his gaze darted to the left.

The old woman rose. *Gannajero the Crow, black, black as coal.*

She walked over to a fire and sat down with two warriors. In the orange gleam, the greasy twists of graying black hair that fell around her wrinkled, toothless face looked like handfuls of baby snakes. "Where's Hehaka's blanket?" she demanded to know.

The warrior sitting with his back to Wrass shrugged. "I don't know. Why?"

"I want it, Dakion, that's why," Gannajero snapped. "Find it."

The man rose and walked away. A short while later, he returned and handed her a blanket. The old woman clutched it to her lips, as though it were a long-lost child, and started whispering. He thought he heard her singing a song. Was she witching the blanket?

Wrass closed his eyes. If he just concentrated on breathing, maybe the pain would ease.

A few instants later, he heard steps. The canoe rocked. He opened his eyes to see Zateri walking toward him across the packs.

"Z-Zateri," he whispered. "Are you all right?"

"I'm worried about you." She put a hand to his fevered brow, and fear tightened her brown eyes. "Your fever is dangerously high, Wrass. I brought you food. You need to try to eat." She pulled a wooden cup filled with smoked eel from beneath her cape and slid it into his limp fingers.

Wrass closed his shaking hand around the cup and stared at the food. Gingerly, he pulled an eel from the cup and brought it to his lips. The smell made his stomach squeal. He took small bites.

"Wrass, have you been chewing the strips of birch bark I gave you?" She sounded desperately worried.

"Yes . . . but most came right back up."

She reached into the top of her knee-high moccasin, drawing out several willow twigs wrapped in yellow cloth. "I cut these twigs from the river just a little while ago. They'll be bitter, but they'll help with the pain and fever. Then you have to drink, Wrass. Your headache will only get worse if you don't drink. And I need to bandage your head with this cloth."

"Z-Zateri," he stammered around a mouthful of eel. "Since the beatings, I keep stuttering. Will it go a . . . away?"

As Zateri watched him struggle to swallow each bite, her dark eyes glistened with tears. "I think so, Wrass. A long time ago, I saw my mother Heal a warrior who'd been clubbed in the head. His headache was so bad that for many days he couldn't speak at all; then he stammered uncontrollably for many more days. But, finally, he was all right."

She soaked the yellow cloth in the river, then gently tied it around his battered head and knotted it. "This cloth was dyed with musquash root a moon ago. I hope some of the Spirit medicine is left. It will make the swelling go down." She gave him a serious look. "But if you start feeling even sicker, rip this off your head and get in the river fast to wash as much off as you can."

"I will."

Grieving people often used the roots of musquash to kill themselves. It was a powerful poison, though it smelled pleasantly like raw parsnip. "Where did you get the cloth?"

"I . . ." She lowered her gaze. "I Traded for it with Dakion, one of the new warriors. He's from the Mountain People."

Wrass studied her downcast eyes. She didn't want to look at him. Knowing what she must have Traded, sick rage warmed his veins. He searched the camp for the warrior who'd hurt her. But he said, "How are the new ch-children?"

"Scared and hungry. Just like we were. There's one boy, Sassacus, who is very sick. I think he's about your age, eleven. But I'm really worried about the youngest Dawnland girl. Her cousin says she stopped talking after she saw her mother killed during the attack on Bog Willow Village. And she's *too* pretty, Wrass."

He closed his eyes, understanding what that meant. "Conkesema."

"Yes. She's ten summers. The other girls are eleven and twelve. One, Neche, is from the Flint People."

"What's wrong with S-Sassacus?"

"Auma says he's been sick several days. I don't know why Gannajero bought him. It doesn't make any sense."

Wrass pulled out another piece of eel and ate slowly. "If you can . . . tr-try to see that the boys get in this canoe . . . with me? I need to . . . talk to them."

Zateri wet her lips nervously, but nodded. "I'll try. When you've finished the eel, dip the cup in the river and drink. Promise me? Drink and chew the willow twigs."

He nodded and rested his temple against the cold gunwale, continuing to eat. When his cup was empty, he dipped up water and slowly sipped it. His headache was so bad he longed to climb into the water and drown in the icy depths.

Zateri said, "I'd better get back before they—"

A sharp cry rent the darkness.

They both jerked around. Akio was dragging the two boys across camp by their bound hands. Every time Sassacus stumbled, Akio wrenched the ropes so that they cut into his bloody wrists. Toksus sobbed uncontrollably.

When Gannajero saw them coming she knotted Hehaka's blanket around her shoulders and let out a hideous shriek. It sounded like a dying eagle. The warriors around her fire leaped to their feet in surprise.

Gannajero rose and spread her arms as though they were wings and she was preparing to take flight. Her cape wafted in the breeze.

Akio frowned uneasily at her as he hauled the boys over and shoved them to the ground at Gannajero's feet. Toksus sobbed, while Sassacus just quietly stared at the fire.

Akio said, "Would you like me to—?"

"Guard the other children. If anyone escapes, it will cost you your life."

Akio hurried to stand over the girls. A short distance away an uneasy circle of warriors formed. The men muttered darkly to each other.

Gannajero cocked her head, first one way then another, studying the boys like a curious bird. "What's your name, boy?"

"Sassacus," the sick boy bravely said. "What do you want from me?"

Without taking her eyes from his, she said, "Kotin. Bring my pack."

He grabbed it from beneath a tree and carried it over. Gannajero took it from his hand. "Bind their feet."

Kotin knelt, pulled short ropes from his belt—as though he'd been expecting this—and tied the boys' feet. Then he stepped back.

Gannajero drew a chert knife from her pack. Both boys stared at it. Her voice started low, barely audible, just a soft *caw, caw, caw,* as she hopped around in an eerie dance that resembled Crow hunting Mouse in a field. Her steps were light, almost graceful.

As his heartbeat thundered, pain stampeded through Wrass' head. "Oh, no, dear gods." He struggled to get up, to get out of the boat and run to the boys, but Zateri grabbed him around the shoulders and dragged him back down.

"Don't move!" she whispered. "You're in no condition to fight a bunch of warriors."

"But you know what she's about to—"

"You can't stop it!" she said. "None of us can. I don't want to lose you, too!"

Gannajero let out a shrill cry and plunged the knife into the sick boy's back; then she leaped away.

The impact threw Sassacus forward. He shouted, "What?" and tried to twist around to see what she'd done.

Toksus screamed, flopped on the ground, and rolled away. He didn't make it two paces before Kotin grabbed him by the feet and dragged him back. "Stay here you little worm, or I'll cut your—"

"Let him go, Kotin!" Wrass cried. "Leave him alone!" He flailed uselessly against Zateri's arms. When had he gotten so weak?

In his ear, she pleaded, "Stop it, Wrass! Please?"

Kotin glared at Wrass, and his gaze promised death a thousand times over. Where she held him, Zateri's arms started to shake. Kotin looked like he was debating whether or not to walk over and crush Wrass' skull for good.

"Please, please, Wrass!" Zateri hissed.

Gannajero's bizarre birdlike squawk made Kotin shift his gaze to her. With her arms spread, the old woman tiptoed forward to loom over Sassacus.

The boy wept, "Why are you doing this?"

She tucked her dripping knife in her belt and pulled Hehaka's blanket from around her shoulders. As she held it in front of Sassacus' face, she said. "See this? Smell it. I want your soul to go find him for me."

Sassacus blinked at her like a clubbed dog. "What?"

"Smell it!" She put one hand behind Sassacus' trembling head and jammed the blanket over his nose. Blood was streaming down his back. It looked black in the firelight.

Sassacus writhed and tried to squirm away, but as more and more blood filled his lungs, his strength failed him. He sagged in her arms, sobbing so hard he couldn't breathe.

Gannajero tossed the blanket aside and turned toward Toksus.

"No!" he screamed and fought against Kotin's grip. "Let me go! She's going to kill me, too! Let me go!"

Gannajero threw back her head and let out a bloodcurdling shriek that seemed to echo from the trees. Toksus froze.

Gannajero's cape resembled gigantic wings as she leaped upon Toksus like Eagle downing Rabbit, knocked him flat, and clamped her hands around his throat. Toksus kicked and shrieked, "Help me! Someone help me! *Wrass?*"

Wrass fought against Zateri's arms, but she held him tighter and whispered, "Don't! Don't even think about it. It's too late now."

Tears streamed down Wrass' face as he watched Kotin grab the boy's legs and pin Toksus' feet to the ground.

"Stop it! Let me go! Please, please!"

Gannajero leaned over until her shriveled nose almost touched Toksus' and stared into his panicked eyes. "I'm not going to kill you."

Choking and writhing, Toksus could only stare at her with bulging eyes.

Zateri's hold momentarily relaxed, and Wrass saw the disbelief that slackened her face. "Do you think she's telling the truth?"

"No." Wrass shook his thundering head. "She's lying. Just like always."

As Gannajero's gnarled fingers tightened around Toksus' throat, he croaked like a tormented frog. *"Don't hurt me!"*

"There, there," Gannajero soothed. "Don't be afraid. This isn't going to hurt."

Toksus thrashed as her grip tightened, cutting off his air. It took a long time. When Toksus' eyes rolled back in his skull and he went limp, a hideous smile came to Gannajero's face. She crawled off the boy and walked over to Sassacus. Her black eyes flickered in the firelight.

"Is Sassacus still alive?" Zateri whispered to Wrass.

"Probably, but just b-barely. It takes a while to bleed to death from a punctured lung."

Gannajero twined her fists in Sassacus' shirt and dragged him over to Toksus. A faint groan climbed Sassacus' throat.

Wrass felt as though his heart had turned to wood. Every beat sounded hollow, empty.

"Help me," Gannajero told Kotin.

They lifted Sassacus on top of the younger boy; then she straightened Sassacus' arms and legs. Finally, Gannajero knelt and arranged Sassacus' gaping, bloody mouth right over Toksus' mouth.

"What's she doing?" Zateri said. "I don't understand."

Wrass shook his head. He felt numb. "I don't know."

It took another twenty or thirty heartbeats for Toksus to start coming around. His eyelids fluttered; then he suddenly gasped in a huge breath and woke staring straight into Sassacus' dying eyes. His high-pitched scream lanced the night. He writhed like a fish out of water, trying to get away, and managed to shove out from under Sassacus.

Gannajero rose to her feet.

"You caught it," she said. "Good."

"Caught . . . wh-what?" Toksus gasped, and fell into a coughing fit.

Zateri glanced at Wrass with terror glittering in her eyes. "Witchery," she whispered. "She made Toksus catch his last breath."

"You mean . . ." Wrass stared at the boy. "Sassacus' afterlife soul is inside Toksus now?"

"That must be what she was doing. What else could it have been?"

Gannajero pulled her knife from her belt and bent over Sassacus. He was lying on his back, staring blindly up at the glittering campfires of the dead. He looked strangely peaceful.

As though she'd done it a thousand times, Gannajero slipped her knife into Sassacus' right eye socket, severed the tissues that attached the eyeball to the skull, and popped it out into her waiting hand. Then she cut out the left eye.

Toksus looked stunned. He peered at the eyes without blinking or moving. The girls on the other side of camp sobbed until their guards threatened them with war clubs.

"Cut little Toksus loose," Gannajero ordered in an unnaturally kind voice. "Sassacus' afterlife soul knows what it must do. Give Toksus that special bag of dried huckleberries, then let him go."

"The *special* bag?" Kotin asked, as though to clarify which bag.

"You heard me, and give him Hehaka's blanket to take with him. We wouldn't want him freezing to death," she said with a toothless smile.

Toksus' head suddenly jerked up. "You're going to let me go?"

"Of course I am. But don't eat those berries until you see someone. Understand?"

"All right."

Gannajero didn't even glance at him. Her gaze was riveted to the grisly prizes in her hand. She walked away clutching the dripping eyes to her chest.

As she passed, her warriors watched her with bright, alert gazes.

Zateri whispered, "How can Toksus live with a stranger's soul inside him?"

Wrass shivered. "I don't think he can. At least not for long. The souls will be fighting each other for control of the body."

Kotin turned and glared at Wrass; then his evil gaze fell upon Zateri, and a shudder went through her.

Zateri gently touched Wrass' shoulder and got to her feet. "I'd better go."

"Be careful," Wrass said.

"You, too."

She made her way down the length of the canoe, where she jumped ashore. The guards watched her through slitted eyes as she walked back to the terrified girls.

Wrass returned his gaze to the boys.

Kotin had freed Toksus and tossed a bag of huckleberries down in front of him. Toksus just stared at it while he coughed and rubbed his injured throat.

Wrass studied him. Could Toksus sense another soul slipping around inside him? And what about Sassacus? Was he confused? It must be terrifying to suddenly find yourself in an unfamiliar body.

"We're leaving," Gannajero announced. "Get the children in the canoes."

Conkesema and Auma climbed back in the canoe with Wrass. The Flint girl went to the other canoe with Zateri.

After the warriors were all in their places, with paddles in their hands, Gannajero knelt beside Toksus and gave him a hideous toothless grin.

"Find him for me."

"Who?" Toksus wiped his runny nose on his cape. "Who am I supposed to find? That boy? Hehaka?"

Gannajero rose and climbed into the bow of her canoe. "Shove off, Kotin."

Kotin pushed the bow off the bank and leaped inside.

The current caught them and carried them downstream.

Toksus stood alone on the bank, crying and scanning the darkness with terrified eyes.

"Who am I supposed to find?" he shouted.

The canoes rounded a bend in the river. Wrass lost sight of him. His nausea intensified. He eased back onto the packs and fought to keep the eels from slithering back up his throat.

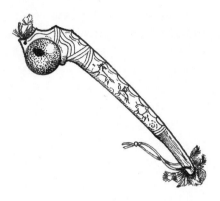

Eleven

Frozen rocks and icy pine needles kept sliding beneath her moccasins as Koracoo carefully maneuvered down the frost-slick ravine. The only sound was her steps crunching frost. It was as though the blood in Great Grandmother Earth's veins has stopped flowing, and Koracoo moved through a vast lifelessness. Instinctively, she glanced around to make certain of the positions of her warriors. They were all watching her, waiting to see what happened next.

When she reached the ravine bottom and started toward the two boys, her gaze shifted to the Dawnland people. Even the way they stood told her a great deal about them. The warriors moved constantly, their weapons aimed, keeping track of her, but they were sluggish, either exhausted or starving. Perhaps both. Desperation made warriors reckless. She needed to proceed with great caution.

Just before she got to Odion's side, the Dawnland boy hissed in his face, "We're going to kill you. We're going to kill all of you."

Odion didn't flinch. He bravely stared into those enormous, hungry eyes, and replied, "My people didn't hurt you. Until just a little while ago, I was a slave. I never even saw your village until after the attack."

"What about the other warriors with you? I know some of them killed my family. I *saw* them."

Koracoo's feet sank into the spongy bed of old autumn leaves as she put a hand on her son's shoulder. "Odion, please come with me."

Odion walked very close to her as she continued toward the elders.

Koracoo knew little about the People of the Dawnland except that where her people traced descent through the female, they traced descent through the male. Because of that, males had more power in their society than females. She doubted there were any female warriors among them. Let alone war chiefs. How would they treat her?

The tall warrior and the boy followed a few paces behind.

Koracoo headed directly for the hunchbacked woman with the white hair. Elder Shara had a strange face, gaunt and sad, with deep wrinkles. Skin hung from her bones as though all the meat had been sucked out. She wore a tattered moosehide cape that hung down to her midthigh, and thin deerhide moccasins. As Koracoo got closer, she saw that the elder's cape was a landscape of mended holes that resembled stitched scars.

The Dawnland People are even worse off than the Standing Stone and Flint Peoples.

No wonder Dawnland war parties had taken to raiding deep into their countries. What they did not understand was that the five nations south of Skanodario Lake had raided each other so often there was little left for anyone else.

She stopped in front of Shara, and the old woman eyed her coldly. "Why did you bring the boy?"

"He has seen Gannajero with his own eyes. I have not."

Shara looked Odion up and down. "Very well. Come and sit with us, War Chief."

Shara waddled back toward the three old men surrounded by six warriors with war clubs. Koracoo and Odion followed.

Koracoo glanced over her shoulder at Wakdanek. He was a big raw-boned man. His skull appeared to have been carved into relief by a blunt knife. He'd seen perhaps thirty summers.

When they reached the elders' circle, Shara lowered herself to a hide-covered litter—probably used by the warriors to carry the elders—and looked up at Wakdanek. "Build a fire, will you, Nephew?"

"Of course." He trotted away.

Shara wore a conical cap, but the three old men had pointed hoods that fell to their shoulders. The lips of the men shrank over toothless gums, and their sharp, jutting chins appeared to have been whittled to resemble hatchet heads. But they had the burning eyes of enraged wolves.

Shara pointed to the ground. "Sit, War Chief."

"Thank you, Elder." Koracoo knelt in the elders' circle, and Odion stood beside her.

She watched Wakdanek go about assigning tasks to the clan boys. Four raced away to crack dead branches from the trees. Two of the four hauled the branches back and respectfully piled them near the elders. A short while later, Wakdanek carefully shouldered between two old men, removed the pack from his back, and began searching inside. He set a small pot and a bag on the ground. From the pot, he poured coals—probably saved from his dinner fire—then tipped the bag up and sprinkled dry shavings of wood upon them. Finally, he bent down to blow on the coals. It took time for them to blaze to life again, but when at last flames crackled, he began adding twigs, then branches, to build up the blaze.

Shara extended her knotted, twiglike fingers to the warmth and shivered. "War Chief," she said, and tilted her head to the old man immediately to her left. "This is Winooski. Next to him sits Kinna, and beside him is Maunbisek. We are all that remain of the Bog Willow Village council of elders. Yesterday morning we numbered twelve." She shifted to bring up her knees and propped her elbows atop them. "Tell us your tale of Gannajero. What makes you think she's alive?"

Odion shivered at the mention of her name, and Koracoo saw tears blur his eyes. He tried to wipe them on his blanket before anyone saw, but the elders were all looking at him.

Shara gently asked, "Your mother says you've seen her with your own eyes, boy. Is it true?"

"Yes, Elder."

"Are you sure it was her? She's been gone from our country for more than twenty summers. It's hard to believe she would return. The last time she was here she barely escaped with her life."

Odion clenched his fists hard. "It was her. Her men called her Gannajero. Except for last night. At the big warriors' camp, she disguised herself as an old man and ordered her warriors to call her Lupan."

The elders all leaned forward to examine Odion, as though trying to decide if he was telling the truth. He stared into each of their eyes in turn.

Koracoo explained, "My son, and the other children with us, were held captive by Ganna—"

"Bah! She's dead." Winooski waved a skeletal hand through the air. Among the People of the Standing Stone, it was an insult to interrupt a war chief, but perhaps here, if she was a woman, she did not deserve respect.

Koracoo proceeded cautiously. "No, Elder, she's very much alive."

"Gannajero died twenty summers ago! I don't know who held them captive, but it couldn't have been Gannajero."

"I agree," Kinna said. "Twenty summers ago every village for a moon's walk had a war party out to kill her. Surely someone must have accomplished it. Even if she lived, why would she return to almost certain death?"

"Perhaps," Koracoo replied calmly, "because she escaped last time, she figured she would this time. All four of the children we rescued last night confirm that their captor was Gannajero. Surely there are not two women Traders with the same name."

"No," Shara said with a shake of her head. "It would be a death sentence. The second would change her name to avoid being mistaken for the first."

Maunbisek peered at Odion through one eye. It was a curious wolflike gesture that made Odion stiffen. "What is your name, boy?"

"Odion."

To the other elders, Maunbisek said, "Have any of you ever seen Gannajero?"

Whispers went around the circle. Heads shook.

Maunbisek tightened his jaw. "No? I didn't think so. Well, I have, and I'm inclined to believe Odion. But since the rest of you don't, let's test him. I saw Gannajero twenty-two summers ago. She was just getting started in her 'business.' My village had been attacked. I was tied up, being held hostage, when she came in to buy children from the victorious warriors. I will never forget her face—though I realize she is older now, some things never change. So, Odion, tell me what she looks like."

Odion lifted his head, and the tendons in his neck stood out. "She has seen maybe forty summers. Graying black hair hangs in greasy twists around her wrinkled face, and her eyes are black pits. Empty. Her toothless mouth is puckered, and her nose looks like a sun-withered plum. She has a hoarse voice; it sounds like sandstone boulders rubbing together."

While he talked, Maunbisek's expression slackened. The old man wet his lips and looked away. "Well, that's enough for me. The eyes and voice are the same. Believe me, once you've looked into those soulless eyes and heard that voice, you never forget. The age is correct, too." He glanced at the other elders. "She's back. And she was Trading for *our* children last night, buying them from the warriors who destroyed our village."

As Grandmother Moon rose higher into the night sky, the deep wrinkles that lined the elders' faces resembled thick black spiderwebs. They muttered softly to each other for a time.

Koracoo said, "She still has one Yellowtail Village boy, a child named Wrass—and many other children from a variety of villages. We mean to find them. We'll be leaving at dawn."

"Maybe you will. Maybe you won't," Shara said. "You said your children were being held in the warriors' camp last night?"

"Just outside. In the forest. I suspect Gannajero is too smart to ply her Trade openly. That's why she wore a disguise. If the warriors had known who she was, they would have killed her instantly."

"Except for her despicable clients, you mean," Maunbisek said.

"Yes."

Kinna and Winooski leaned sideways to speak softly; then Kinna asked, "There were children from other villages with her, more than just Yellowtail children?

"Yes. I know for certain that Chief Atotarho's daughter, Zateri, was there, and—"

"Atotarho?" Kinna half shouted. "He is evil! A *Tsi-noo*. How do you know his daughter was there?"

Koracoo frowned and glanced curiously around at the elders. "What does *Tsi-noo* mean? I don't know that word."

"A *Tsi-noo* has no soul. He lives by eating the souls of others. His heart is made of ice. *Are you helping him?*"

Koracoo replied, "We will rescue his daughter, Zateri, if we can. We will also rescue any other child who happens to be in Gannajero's possession when we attack. Including yours."

Nervous whispers filtered through the elders. While they talked, Wakdanek knelt beside Koracoo and quietly asked, "Did your children see any of the girls she bought last night?"

Koracoo turned to Odion. "Can you answer that, Odion?"

He nodded. "I think she bought five children. Three were girls. But I only saw them from far away. They were roped together."

Wakdanek softly said, "My daughter, Conkesema, has seen ten summers. She has long black hair—it hangs to her waist—and a small scar on her forehead." He lifted a hand and drew it across his left temple. "Did you see her?"

Odion tilted his head uncertainly, and the moonlight reflected from his round face, turning it a pale sickly color. "Maybe. There was a girl about ten summers with waist-length black hair, but I wasn't close enough to see the scar."

"Are you sure she was in Gannajero's group? The group she'd just purchased from our village?" Pain tightened his eyes, and he clearly hoped that Odion would say that she hadn't been in that group, but elsewhere in the warriors' camp.

"She was roped with Gannajero's children."

Wakdanek lightly squeezed Odion's shoulder. "Thank you. You're a brave boy."

Shara waited until Wakdanek rose before asking, "You said you rescued several children last night. Who were they?"

"We freed our two children, plus one girl from the Flint People, named Baji, and a boy named Hehaka, whose people we do not know."

Suspicious, Winooski said, "Why don't you know? Have you asked him?"

"He says he can't remember his people."

"Was he that young when he was captured?"

Koracoo looked at Odion, who said, "Hehaka was captured when he was four. He's been Gannajero's slave for seven summers."

Maunbisek pinned Koracoo with hard glistening eyes. "Do you know our tradition of the Ghost Fire, War Chief?"

"No."

"Among our people the dead are always buried, because the Spirits of the unburied dead remain around the bones as living fire that can destroy anything they touch. Many of our children are now Ghost Fires. Because of Gannajero. I didn't tell you earlier, but my own son was taken by her twenty-two summers ago. I watched her buy him, and I never saw him again."

Sorrow filled his eyes, and she suspected he had mourned that child for most of his life.

"Then you do not wish to delay us for long, Elder. To have any chance of catching her, we must leave before dawn."

Their ancient faces drew tight with indecision.

Wakdanek said, "Elders, if you will allow it, I would like to go with War Chief Koracoo to help her free the children being held by Gannajero."

"Do you think your daughter is there?" Shara asked.

"I fear she may be. But it doesn't matter. There are Bog Willow Village children there. One of us must try to rescue them."

Shara thoughtfully twisted the parchmentlike hands folded in her lap. "I understand, Nephew, but we need you here. Very few of us escaped the slaughter—almost none of our warriors lived."

Wakdanek's face fell, but he tipped his head in obedience. "Yes, Aunt."

Maunbisek lifted a hand. "I cast my voice to allow Wakdanek to go in search of his daughter and the other children. One warrior, more or less, will make no difference to our survival."

Winooski sucked his lips in over his toothless gums. After a time, he blew out a breath and said, "If it were me, I wouldn't care what the council said. I would go find my daughter. Let him go, Shara."

Shara's gaze moved to the last council member. "And you, Kinna? What do you say?"

Kinna's pointed hood was canted at an odd angle, as though he'd accidentally tugged it to the right. "Before I vote, I have a question for Maunbisek."

Maunbisek frowned. "Yes?"

"Did you search for your son?"

Maunbisek's eyes clouded. He bowed his head. "I searched for moons. I traveled from village to village, asking if anyone had seen Gannajero or a boy resembling my son." He shook his head. "I never found a single trace of him."

"Knowing that, would you do it again?"

Maunbisek's head snapped up. "Of course I would. If I hadn't searched, I'd always feel as though if were my fault because I'd given up. I'd be certain I could have saved him if only I'd tried. Now, and for the rest of my life, at least I can say I did my best to find him, even though I failed."

Kinna lifted his gaze to Wakdanek, and the man's shoulder muscles went tight, bulging through his shirt. "We must let him go, Shara. He will hate us if we don't. And I, for one, could not bear it. I have loved Wakdanek since he was a boy."

Wakdanek whispered, "And I you, Uncle."

Koracoo looked around. Were Kinna and Shara husband and wife? The touching way they stared at each other suggested they might be.

Shara sighed and nodded. "War Chief Koracoo, do you have any objections to Wakdanek accompanying you on your journey?"

Koracoo gave him a hard look. "I welcome anyone who is good with a bow, Elder. Is he?"

Shara softly said, "He's the best shot in the village, though he prefers Healing to killing. Go, Nephew. I pray that Tabaldak, the Owner of the world, watches over you."

"Thank you, Elders. I'll gather my things." He trotted into the darkness.

Shara turned to Koracoo. "If you get into trouble, War Chief, look to Wakdanek. For fifteen summers, he has been studying the ways of the Healer. His skills in that regard may save more lives than his skill with a bow. Now, help me up." She extended a hand.

Koracoo stood and supported the old woman as she rose to her feet. "If there are no further questions from the council, I'll walk the war chief back."

The three old men shook their heads.

Shara held Koracoo's elbow as they headed toward the ravine. Odion followed a step behind.

"Your council is wise, Elder. I'm grateful to you."

"Don't be too grateful, Koracoo." Her old eyes scanned the lip of the ravine, moving methodically through the boulders. "Our warriors want revenge, but I'm tired, as are the other elders. We just want to go back and bury our dead; then we must find a new place to rebuild our village. That's why we did not demand to know the identities of the other members of your party. However, I suspect you have Flint warriors with you who were involved in the attack on our village. They are your enemies as much as ours. At some point, they will turn on you. Then, I wager, you'll have more on your hands than you've bargained for."

Koracoo hesitated. Finally, she carefully answered, "I won't forget your words, Elder, and I'll do my best to guard your nephew's back."

Shara clutched Koracoo's elbow tighter, as though afraid of falling. "We will camp here tonight. But you should not, Koracoo. Get as far away as you can. I fear some of our young warriors may not agree with the council's decision."

Koracoo turned. "Odion, quickly, find your father and tell him the elders' words."

"Yes, Mother."

Odion charged away, scrambling up the frosty slope toward the boulders where Gonda hid.

Twelve

Odion

The old leaves are icy. They slip beneath my moccasins as I climb the steep side of the ravine. Just before I reach the top, my feet go out from under me, and I have to claw at exposed tree roots to keep from rolling back down the slope. On all fours, I manage to crawl to the lip of the ravine and pull myself over. The scent of frozen earth is strong.

Breathing hard, I see Father standing with his bow half-drawn, aimed down at Shara where she talks with Mother. War Chief Cord is asleep, lying curled on his side against the boulder.

Father says, "I didn't have the heart to wake him."

I whisper, "Father, Elder Shara says they will camp here tonight, but we must not. She says she's not sure her warriors will agree with the council's decision to let us go."

Father's mouth drops open. "They're letting us go? Are you sure?"

"Yes, Father. And Wakdanek is coming with us, to search for his daughter and the other Bog Willow children."

Father releases the tension on his bowstring and sags against the rocks. "Unbelievable. I thought we were dead."

"Should we wake War Chief Cord now?"

Father looks down at him. The man is sound asleep, his mouth ajar. "Not yet. He needs every moment he can get. We'll wake him after your Mother has finished her talk with Elder Shara, and—"

Shara steps away from Mother, tips her head back, and howls like a wolf baying at Grandmother Moon. It is a lonesome sound that echoes through the cold night air. War Chief Cord does not even move. In the distance, a pack of real wolves yip, and howl back. Instantly, all the warriors hiding in the brush or behind rocks stand up and trot away, down the hill to assemble around the circle of elders.

Father looks amazed. "Those chilling calls sound so real, even the wolves answer them. Odion, find the other children. Bring them here immediately."

"Yes, Father."

I run away toward where Baji, Tutelo, and Hehaka hide in the boulders. As I near them, Tutelo pats her lips with her hand, telling me to be quiet; then she points. Her pretty face is tight with wonder.

I follow her hand to a cluster of downy juneberries. Some of the scrub trees are forty hands tall, but most are young, and more like shrubs. The undergrowth spreads two hundred hands in every direction through the boulders. The shriveled, reddish purple fruits that cling to the branches look pitch black in the moonlight.

"What are you looking at?" I squint hard, searching, and whisper, "The Dawnland People are letting us go. Father wants us to come right now."

Tutelo hisses, "Odion. You're not looking. Don't you see him?"

"Who?"

With fear in her voice, Baji whispers, "It's a Forest Spirit."

Up the hill, beyond the juneberries, I can make out the dark triangular shapes of pines so tall they seem to pierce the belly of Brother Sky. My gaze lingers on the frost-covered ground. Against the white earth there is something utterly black—as though the object absorbs all light. A boulder? No. In the moon's gleam, even the rocks glitter. What . . .

Odion.

I feel the whisper like fire in my lungs. I can't move.

Tutelo smiles. "See, Odion? It's Shago-niyoh. He's back."

For a long while, the only sounds in the night are the soft hissing of Tutelo's breathing and the slamming of my heart against my ribs. The Darkness turns, and there is a sustained glow, as though it is staring at me with one silver eye.

I don't know what it is. There are many supernatural creatures that inhabit the forest. This may be one of the Faces. The Faces are Spirits who control sickness. They can cure or kill. They often appear to Healers in their dreams and instruct them in the usages of sacred plants, or confer upon them the power to cure diseases afflicting people, animals, or crops. Our people carve their images upon trees, or posts erected at gates, but most importantly upon masks—False Face masks.

"I don't see anything," Hehaka says, annoyed. "What are you looking at?"

My gaze slides to Hehaka. He is my age, eleven summers. He has a face like a starved bat's, all ears and flat nose, with black beads for eyes. Shoulder-length black hair hangs over his cheeks. He was Gannajero's favorite slave. I know he has seen many horrors, and I should feel sorry for him, but I don't. I can't. I fear that if he could, he'd run back to her and tell her exactly where we are, maybe even lead her to us.

Tutelo says, "Shago-niyoh came to warn us that Gannajero is looking for us."

Hehaka lifts his head and stares at us. His beady eyes glint. "She *is* coming. She's coming for me. Soon."

"What are you talking about?" Baji asks. Her hands clench to fists.

Hehaka whispers, "Gannajero will never let me go."

"Why not? You're just a boy," Baji says harshly. "Just another boy. She has new boys now."

"It doesn't matter! Every time I ran away, Kotin hunted me down and dragged me back. She's coming for me. You'll see. There's a warrior on the trail right now. Gannajero will recapture all of us again. Then she'll punish the three of you. She'll sell you to bad men."

An enraged sob constricts Baji's throat. She starts shivering and can't stop. Tutelo keeps watching the Face, but I glare at Hehaka. He lifts his chin arrogantly, proud that the old witch wants him.

"Go away, Hehaka," I order.

He lifts his nose and sniffs our scents like a curious predator, then tramps away down the hill toward Father and War Chief Cord.

"Are you all right, Baji?"

She sucks in a halting breath. "Yes. Thanks for making him go away. I was on the verge of strangling him with my bare hands."

"He doesn't know any better," I say. "His souls are wounded."

I return my gaze to the Darkness. The frost beneath it has ceased to twinkle, and as Grandmother Moon rises, the shadows around it do not move. How can that be? It is as though the Spirit exists in a bubble where time has stopped.

Very faintly, the pines rustle, and I'm sure there are dark wings amid the shadows.

None of us breathes. The frosty pines and leafless hickories glitter. This Darkness that calls me by name seems to have the ability to step inside the forest shadows and hide, waiting. But when we need him, he's always there. I don't und—

Father shouts, "Odion? Tutelo? We're almost ready!"

We each take one last look at the dark moonlit forest, and Tutelo hisses, "Shago-niyoh says Wrass and Zateri are alive."

Baji glances at her. "Is he talking to you? Can you hear him? Right now?"

Tutelo nods.

"Ask him—" Baji begins.

Father's shout interrupts her, *"Odion,* bring the children now!"

"We're coming, Father!"

The other children run away.

I take one last look at the moonlit forest. He's still out there. I know he is. I feel his presence moving through the trees. In some strange way that I don't understand, he has become my Spirit Helper.

I call, "Thank you, Shago-niyoh," and turn to run to Father.

Thirteen

As Grandmother Moon wavered through the clouds, the forest went from bright to impenetrably dark in a few heartbeats. The boulders two paces from Sindak resembled hunching beasts. He glanced at them, scanned the swaying pines, then folded his arms and gave the Flint warriors a lock-jawed stare. They were engaged in a discussion that sounded vaguely hostile, at least as hostile as men about to fall on their faces could sound. Koracoo and Gonda stood silently, listening.

War Chief Cord's hood rested on his back and Sindak could get a good look at his face for the first time. His hair was shaved on the sides, in the fashion of Flint war chiefs, leaving a black bristly ridge down the center of his skull, and he had evil-looking serpents tattooed on his cheeks. He was curiously unpretentious. Most war chiefs seemed to be taken with their own wiles. Although his current lack of pretension could result from the fact that he was so tired he could barely stand, it looked genuine. When Cord shook his head at something Ogwed said, his long pointed nose cast a shadow across his cheek. *"What if it was your daughter, Ogwed?"* he asked. *"Or your niece?"*

Sindak leaned sideways toward Towa and whispered, "What are they arguing about? I can only hear part of their whispers."

"I don't know, but if they were smart, they'd wait until later to argue, after we're far enough away that the Dawnland warriors can't use their malevolent expressions as an excuse to kill them."

Sindak replied, "I agree. I saw up close the looks on the boy warriors' faces. I suspect any excuse to toss a piece of our hearts into their mouths would do."

Sindak tightened his folded arms and glared at the Flint warriors. He kept catching a few words of their conversation: *Flint children . . . can't just . . . I'm going home!*

Sindak said, "I don't like them."

"Why? Just because they've been slaughtering our people for generations?"

"That's only one reason. I also don't like their hair. They're not going with us, are they? Surely they will continue on westward to Flint country?"

"I think that's what they're arguing about."

Koracoo lifted a hand and called, "Baji? Come over here, please."

Sindak and Towa watched the slender girl trot over to stand between Gonda and Koracoo.

"Let's move closer so we can hear better," Sindak said.

They both casually drifted up to stand behind Odion, Tutelo, and Hehaka.

"All right, Baji," Gonda said, "repeat what you told us earlier."

The moonlight tipped Baji's lashes in silver as she looked up at Cord. "Last night in the warriors' camp, I saw a Trader selling a Flint girl. She was about my age, twelve summers."

Koracoo said, "Baji would know a Flint child, Cord."

The war chief's exhausted eyes tightened. "As I would. Just by the way she moved. Who sold her to Gannajero? Did you see?"

Baji glanced at the other Flint warriors, probably judging their moods. Ogwed was scowling unhappily at her. "He was a Flint Trader. I've seen him before in our village, but I don't know his name."

Cord said, "Was he an ugly little man with rotted teeth?"

"Yes."

"Probably Tagohsah."

The young warrior, Ogwed, threw up his hands. "War Chief, if we join these people, they will take us deeper into Dawnland country. Our people need us to help defend the new village while it is being built. We have no right to go traipsing off after a missing child, just because she *may* be Flint."

Dzadi's massive protruding jaw moved as he ground his teeth. "I agree, Cord. If we'd seen the girl with our own eyes, maybe, but—"

"I'm not lying!" Baji clenched her fists at her sides, daring any man to call her a liar out loud, so she could rip his throat out.

Sindak smiled. That little girl had fire in her belly. Someday she was going to be a frightening clan matron.

Cord said softly, "I believe you, Baji. And I won't take the chance that Gannajero might have one of our children in her possession. If War Chief Koracoo does not object, I'll send my men home and continue on with her party."

Koracoo stared at him with unblinking eyes, as though evaluating the quality of his soul. She hesitated for a long time, clearly considering the ramifications, before she said, "Do you realize that at some point Wakdanek will ask if you were part of the war party that attacked his village?"

Their gazes locked for such a long time that everyone else started to shift and tighten his hold on his weapons. Finally, Cord replied, "I do."

"I don't want any trouble between you. Is that understood?"

"Perfectly."

"Then gather your things. We'll be leaving as soon as Wakdanek arrives."

"I'll be ready." Cord braced a hand against the boulder where he'd been leaning and stood tall and straight before his men. "Dzadi, tell the elders what happened at Bog Willow Village. Let them know I will be home as soon as I can."

Dzadi glanced suspiciously at the Standing Stone and Hills warriors. "Be careful, Cord. I don't trust your new 'allies.'"

Cord smiled grimly; then he turned to Baji. "Baji, I want you to go with Dzadi and Ogwed. They will make sure that you are cared for until our people can find your family and return you to them. You'll be safe. I give you my oath."

Baji looked longingly at Dzadi and Ogwed, as though she wished with all her heart to go with them. Her voice quavered when she said, "I can't. I promised a friend that I would come back for him with a war party."

"What friend? Another Flint child?" Cord asked.

"No, he's Standing Stone. His name is Wrass. He . . ." Tears constricted her voice. "He saved me. Saved us. Last night, he killed the warrior who was guarding us and told us to run. I saw him. He took the dead warrior's club and walked right into the middle of the camp and poured a bag of poisonous plants into Gannajero's stew pot. Her warriors beat him half to death. I'm not going home until we save him."

Odion and Tutelo walked up to stand shoulder to shoulder with Baji, creating a unified front. Only Hehaka hung back.

Odion said, "None of us are going home until we save Wrass and the other children."

Cord frowned. "Are you sure, Baji? I have to be honest with you. It won't help any of us to have you along on this trip. Children can be deadly on a war walk. They slow warriors down, and when it comes to a fight, they are distractions. Many of the warriors here are more likely to die because of you. Do you understand?"

She lifted her chin. "I am of the Flint People. I understand. But do you understand that I gave my word? I won't go back on it."

Cord exhaled hard. "There's no time to argue about this." He looked up at Koracoo. "War Chief, if it is your decision that she stays, I will take Baji as my personal responsibility. She is of my people. When the fight comes, leave her protection to me."

Koracoo glanced at Baji, and sadness lined her face. She'd obviously been hoping Baji would go with Cord's warriors. It would have been one less thing to worry about. She simply said, "After what she's been through, it is Baji's decision. And if you wish to protect her, it is your right."

Cord turned to Dzadi. "Leave, old friend. Make it home safely."

Dzadi stepped forward and embraced Cord hard enough to drive the air from his lungs. "We will be waiting for your return, War Chief."

"Tell my daughter I love her."

"I will."

Dzadi reluctantly backed away. Turning, he and Ogwed trotted west.

Gonda put a hand on Cord's shoulder, and the man locked his knees, as though the slight weight might cause them to buckle. Gonda noticed and removed his hand. "Can you run for one hand of time?"

"If not, leave me. I'll catch up."

In an utterly serious voice, Koracoo replied, "We will."

She studied Cord in detail, as though absorbing every quaking muscle; then she subtly shook her head and turned to stare over the lip of the ravine at the Dawnland Healer trotting through the moonlight. The long hair of his moose-hump cap glimmered in the light. As he climbed up the steep wall of the ravine, the sheathed knife resting on his breast swayed back and forth. In addition to his slung bow and quiver, he had a ball-headed war club in his fist and a small pack on his back.

"What do you think of him?" Towa whispered to Sindak.

"He looks too hungry for me to ever be quite comfortable around him. I think I'll sleep with my blanket knotted around my vulnerable throat."

"Don't be silly. You're not going to get any sleep."

"Really? Why not?"

"Because the first person Koracoo will allow to sleep is War Chief Cord, so he doesn't slow us down. The second person will be Wakdanek, so she can keep an eye on him. I wager that you and I, my friend, are going to be standing first watch, followed by Gonda and Koracoo."

Sindak had his eyes on Cord and Wakdanek. They both had faint amiable smiles on their faces, which was as good a way as any to hide their fangs. Sindak tried to imagine himself in Wakdanek's moccasins. Surely he suspected that Cord had participated in the attack. If Sindak had been standing in the presence of one of the warriors who'd destroyed his village and slaughtered his family, he'd be filled with murderous rage. He might have to bide his time, but he *would* even the score. He suspected Wakdanek was thinking the same thing.

Wakdanek said, "We can't go back over the pass. There will be too many warriors. I'm going to lead you along a tributary that curves south; then we'll follow another trail to return north to the warriors' camp."

Koracoo said, "That is acceptable."

The night had gone quiet again, and bitterly cold. Sindak longed to be on the trail, running, so he could warm up. Down by the campfire, the Dawnland elders sat, their gaunt faces gleaming orange in the light. Warriors prowled around them like young wolves. Frequently their faces shone as they gazed up at Sindak and Towa.

Sindak leaned closer to Towa to say, "I hope Koracoo knows what she's doing. I think those two are trouble. When it is least convenient, I suspect they're going to kill each other."

Fourteen

Grandmother Moon's face cast an opalescent glitter across the land, silvering the mist that wreathed the dark maples and leafless sycamores. The night was so quiet. It was as though the many voices of the forest had been silenced all at once by some great catastrophe.

Sonon stopped to listen. It wasn't often that a man stood in such deafening silence that he was truly alone with himself and the enormity of his failures. Eternity seemed to open its eyes.

For a few blessed moments, he bowed his head and let the sensation filter through him.

Then he clutched the boy's body against his chest and continued picking his way down the frozen bank toward the river.

Ice filled every hollow. The footing was treacherous. He breathed a sigh of relief when he reached the edge of the water, where willows clotted the shallows. Around the stems, he saw fish feeding. Concentric rings expanded each time they broke the surface.

The pithy fragrances of old autumn leaves drifted on the breeze. He sucked them deep into his lungs. His arms had been trembling off and on for two hands of time. The constant struggle of battling the ice to stay on his feet had taken his strength. He didn't know how much longer he could carry the boy. Soon, he'd be forced to drag him.

But for now, he just held him close.

In a barely audible voice, he sang, *"The crow comes, the crow comes, pity the little children, beat the drum."*

As though the old song called her, a soft rhythmic pushing of air stirred the depths behind his eyes, and he knew she was sharing his vision. Staring out through his eyes. As she had since he'd seen six summers. Sometimes, especially at night, the beating of her wings was so frantic, he would rise from his blankets and run as hard as he could until dawn, when she finally went back to sleep.

He gazed down at the boy's face. His eyelids sunk into his empty eye sockets. His blood-soaked shirt had frozen stiff. In the wash of moonlight, the boy's oval face resembled a ceremonial mask carved from wood and painted a luminous white.

Sonon let out a shaky breath and plodded on down the shore.

He could not say why it began. Not exactly. He knew only that by the age of six, his sister, Jonodak, had seemed to spend all of her time wandering an unfathomable labyrinth that twisted down forever into her own souls.

He remembered with perfect clarity the day Jonodak suddenly looked up at him, squinted, and snapped, "What are you doing sitting there?" As though Sonon should have known it wasn't his place and he ought to move.

He and his sister were twins. They'd been inseparable. For the first time in his life, he'd felt like an outsider looking through a thin veil into her world. A visitor from a hazy place where Jonodak had once lived, but no longer did. And he knew at that moment that she had left him behind and traveled beyond to the realm where no one could reach her.

The horror began when they turned eight.

He'd awakened one night to feel a sharp chert blade slicing through his throat. Then, just before dawn, she had picked up a rock and slammed it into his face. It was impossible to set the shattered bones, so the village Spirit elders had just left it alone. Since that night, his nose had bent to the right like one of the False Faces.

A few days later, his sister had attacked three other children in the longhouse. *Poor Skaneat.* He'd seen barely four summers. Sonon's parents had been hysterical. They'd called in every Healer in the village and demanded to know what was wrong with her. One old man told them that Jonodak's afterlife soul had wandered away and gotten hopelessly lost in the forest. He'd said her body was nothing more than a slowly deteriorating husk.

Human souls were things of mystery. One day a person felt fine. The next day, an overheard conversation, or the loss of a beloved friend, turned the world into an alien wasteland where death seemed less strange than simply going on.

Sonon understood, of course, that he was just as mad as Jonodak.

The difference was, he didn't mind. For him, the madness was a kind of sanctuary, a sacred cocoon spun in the dark emptiness of his heart. Properly guarded, the madness became rock-solid armor. It kept out pain. It protected him from the reflection he saw in people's eyes.

It allowed him to simply go on.

His sandal slipped on a patch of hidden ice, and his feet went out from under him. He fell hard, landing with the boy's stone-cold body still clutched to his chest. The wind had been knocked out of him. For a time, he just lay gasping, staring up at the moonlit Cloud People who blew across the heavens with their bellies gleaming.

When he could, he sat up and gently laid the boy aside so that he could struggle to his feet. His legs shook. He spread them to brace himself.

The fragrances of the river smelled powerful here. The earthiness of waterlogged wood mixed pungently with the tang of frozen plants and moss.

"I'm sorry," he said as he reached down and twined his hand in the boy's bloody shirt. "I can't carry you any longer."

He dragged the boy across a frozen rivulet and up a low rise . . . and stopped. Ahead of him, a dark shape moved through the moonlight.

The other boy. As he walked along the bank, the child wept inconsolably.

Even from this distance, Sonon could smell the child's fear-sweat. He forced his trembling legs to move faster. The dead boy's body thudded over rocks and sticks and finally caught on an upthrust root. Sonon had to jerk hard to dislodge it. By the time he'd freed the corpse, the younger boy had disappeared among the shadows.

Sonon straightened. For a few brief instants, he did not hear the river or the wind sighing through the willows. The sanctuary in his heart had transformed into a vast realm of dust and darkness. For more than twenty summers, he'd been trying to save them, to make sure their families found them so they wouldn't have to face the torments that he . . .

The torments that every lost soul endured.

He looked down at the dead boy. Long black hair covered his face. Sonon knelt and tenderly brushed it away; then he slipped his arms beneath the boy and staggered to his feet.

As he carried him down the shore, he murmured, "When you see me at the bridge, remember that tonight one person cared."

Fifteen

Sindak spread his feet and yawned. He stood half-hidden behind a spruce trunk near where they'd made camp on the western bank of the Quill River. The sound of rushing water filled the darkness.

To the north, above the smoldering ruins of Bog Willow Village, stringers of smoke stretched like the fingers of doom. Every now and then the sky gleamed suddenly orange and Sindak knew flames had burst to life again. Had it only been a few hands of time ago that he'd been sneaking around the huge warriors' camp, trying to find the stolen children? It seemed like days. At dawn, when they could see, he assumed they would trot north along the river to try to pick up Gannajero's trail.

And probably find nothing.

"*Will* find nothing," he hissed, barely audible.

By the time they arrived, the camp would have broken up and the warriors would have trotted off toward home. Hundreds of feet would have trampled the ground, leaving thousands of tracks and trails shooting off in every direction. Many of the departing warriors would have been pushing captive Dawnland children before them, so finding a child's track would be of little help. In fact, picking out Gannajero's trail in the chaos would take a miracle.

Sindak turned to stare at the small clearing thirty paces away where four adults and four children lay rolled in blankets. The fire had burned down to a bed of glowing coals. Gonda and Koracoo lay to the north of the children, Wakdanek and Cord to the south. Everyone appeared to be asleep. Though Sindak found it hard to believe that either Cord or Wakdanek could sleep in close proximity to the other, apparently both were beyond caring about debts of honor.

He swung his war club up and propped it on his shoulder. Across the clearing in the copse of white cedars a faintly blacker splotch marked the place Towa stood.

Sindak wondered what they'd do if they failed to find Gannajero's trail. Atotarho was not known for being gentle and kind. In fact, his enemies accused him of being the most powerful sorcerer in the land. They said he had an army of *hanehwa* that hunted down his enemies. When he'd been a boy, Sindak's mother had seen a skin-being in the forest just outside of Atotarho Village; it had been human-shaped, translucent and shiny, floating through the trees as though sculpted of mist.

Movement caught Sindak's attention. No more than twenty paces away, through the weave of thick bayberry trunks, eyes flashed. A wolf. A real one.

Sindak slowly pulled his war club from his shoulder and gripped it in both hands. The leafless, gray branches of the bayberries resembled skeletal fingers reaching for the sparkling campfires of the dead. The trunks grew closely together, too closely.

"I thought we'd lost you," he whispered.

Right after they'd left the ravine, a pack had dogged their steps, appearing and disappearing loping along their back trail. But as they'd neared Bog Willow Village, the animals had vanished. Sindak had assumed they'd been drawn away by the odor of dead bodies rising from the burning village.

A barely audible "huff" echoed, the sound made by a startled deer. Towa's signal. Sindak turned to look at his friend and saw him pointing to an especially thick bayberry copse, where another pair of eyes glinted.

"Yes, I see them," Sindak whispered.

He and Towa both started walking slowly back toward the camp, and the shining eyes flashed between the trees, paralleling their courses.

When they stood three paces in front of their sleeping comrades, Sindak whispered, "Why aren't they at the village gobbling down freshly roasted meat?"

Towa's brows quirked. "You're a sympathetic soul tonight. Do you think we should try to shoot one? It might scare away the pack."

The two pair of eyes joined, then separated again, and shone like four small silver moons. More eyes appeared, weaving through the brush. A big pack. The bayberry trunks were barely a hand's width in diameter, but there were hundreds of them. "Those saplings are as thick as dog hair. An arrow will collide with a trunk or branch long before it pierces flesh."

Towa gripped his war club in both hands. "They're staring straight at us."

"Impudent, aren't they? Sindak watched the eyes coalesce into a line just inside the trees.

"There must be ten or twelve of them."

"Well, if we can't shoot them, maybe we should charge out there and try to scatter them?"

Towa calmly replied, "I saw a buck do that once. He charged right into the middle of the pack with his antlers swinging. He managed to gore several before they brought him down and chewed out his still-quivering heart."

Sindak irritably shoved a lock of hair behind his ear. "You never like my ideas."

"Maybe we should wake Koracoo? Her ideas are generally better than yours."

"I'm not waking Koracoo until the wolves have my heart in their teeth. But you can . . . if you have a death wish."

Towa shifted his weight to his other foot. "On second thought, the wolves could just be passing through, headed for the village."

"You want to let them surround us, eh?"

Towa scratched his cheek. "Let's just watch them for a while. There's something I want to talk to you about."

Sindak had known Towa his entire life. He could tell from his friend's expression that lives might depend upon this discussion. "Are you finally going to tell me?"

"I'm not telling, I'm discussing. Or rather, asking questions. Why would Chief Atotarho have been in the warriors' camp last night?"

"How would I know? Maybe he went there to Trade. Maybe he went there to visit old friends. Maybe he—"

"Maybe he went there to meet Gannajero?"

Sindak turned to stare at him. Towa was grinding his teeth. Sindak could see Towa's jaw moving in the starlight. "Why would you say that?"

"Well, if Koracoo is right, and Gannajero is Atotarho's long-lost sister, I was thinking that maybe they're working together."

The silence stretched until Sindak thought his nerves might snap. The wolves were slowly twining through the trees, coming toward them.

Sindak said, "That's the kind of thinking that makes men do desperate things."

"Think how I feel. I've been working on this problem for almost a moon."

"How am I supposed to help you if I don't know what your secret orders are?"

Towa seemed to be wrestling with himself. "My friend, each day that passes, I like these orders less and less. If I tell you, then you'll be obliged to keep the confidence, and I don't want to put you in the position of—"

"Having to disobey them? Which is what you're considering doing?" He could tell when Towa was second-guessing orders. He'd seen him second-guess often enough in battle.

One of the wolves yipped, and two others answered with barks. As though grateful for the chance to change the subject, Towa said, "Somebody needs to decide whether or not we ought to move on. You know how wolves are. If they're really starving, the rest of the night will be a cat-and-mouse game. They'll sneak up and surround us; then two will charge snarling and yipping to keep us busy—"

"—while three or four others dart into camp and drag off our packs, or maybe one of the children," Sindak finished.

Despite the care they'd taken to be quiet, Wakdanek sat up in his blanket and expelled a long breath. "Where are they?"

Sindak pointed to the undergrowth of bayberry. "Over there. Why?"

Wakdanek threw aside his blanket and rose to his feet. The rough-hewn angles of his gaunt face looked eerie in the moonlight. Almost . . . not human. More like a carved wooden mask. His size added to the effect. Towa and Sindak both had to look up to him. "Why don't you two build up the fire while I handle this?"

Sindak blinked. "What do you mean 'handle' it?"

"Just wait here."

Wakdanek stalked toward the trees, and Sindak said, "Do you think he's going over there to scold them?"

"Maybe he's the one with the death wish. I say we circle around behind the bayberries, just in case he needs rescuing."

"You're in favor of *rescuing* a Dawnland warrior?"

"It'll give me more time to consider what else I want to say to you," Towa said, and silently trotted south, toward the deer trail they'd followed to get here.

Sindak grumbled and tiptoed into camp to gently lay a few branches on the glowing coals. In less than ten heartbeats, flames licked up and sparks flitted into the night sky. Sindak waited for someone to wake. No one did.

When Towa slipped into the striped forest shadows, guilt overwhelmed Sindak's good sense. He trotted to the north and entered the trees just above where the wolves congregated. Black shapes slipped through the darkness less than ten paces away.

Strangely, the Dawnland Healer never bothered to turn around and see where Sindak and Towa were. He marched straight ahead with his jaw clenched. When he reached the edge of the bayberries, Wakdanek started whimpering. It was a low pathetic sound, like a hungry pup calling for its mother.

The wolves pricked their ears. Sindak saw one, probably the lead female, lift a foot uncertainly and peer directly at Wakdanek.

"My brothers," Wakdanek said softly. "I saw a herd of deer just beyond that rise over there." He pointed. "Please go hunt them. We are your relatives. We don't want to harm you."

Sindak sneaked around until he could see two big males hiding behind a head-high pile of windblown leaves that had frozen against a rock outcrop. Wakdanek stood five paces from them. Had they wanted, the animals could have knocked him down and gutted him before he'd run three steps.

One of the wolves barked at Wakdanek; then the entire pack let loose in a spine-tingling chorus.

The skin at the back of Sindak's neck crawled. He cautiously worked his way over to where Towa stood.

When Sindak got close enough, he could see Towa's wide-eyed expression. He whispered, "You look petrified."

"No. I'm just annoyed that my bladder is weaker than I thought."

The eerie bark-howling conversation continued for another twenty heartbeats; then Wakdanek let out an authoritative series of barks, and the pack went utterly silent. As a final act, Wakdanek started growling. The low deep-throated sound made Sindak long to run. The sensation of threat rode the air.

Sindak watched in disbelief as the female loped away, followed by most of the pack. The two big males remained for a time longer; then they, too, chased after the pack.

Wakdanek propped his hands on his hips and expelled a breath. He made no moves to return to camp. He just stared out at where the wolves trotted away through the darkness.

Sindak softly called, "Do you do cat calls? I've always wanted to shoot a cougar."

Wakdanek jumped when Sindak walked out of the shadows five paces from him.

The Healer squinted. "I didn't even see you out there! Where's your frien—"

"Here." Towa stepped from the trees to Wakdanek's left.

Wakdanek swung around so fast he stumbled and put a hand to his heart. "Blessed Spirits."

"So . . . ," Towa said. "We scared you, but the wolves didn't?"

"I am Wolf Clan. Wolves are my brothers. I find humans a lot more frightening."

"Oh. Me, too. I'm a warrior." Sindak frowned when Wakdanek didn't respond. He made an airy gesture with his war club. "As you are, yes?"

"I'm a Healer," Wakdanek replied. "For me there is no glory in wounding or killing people."

Towa said, "You must find that truly mystifying, eh, Sindak?"

Sindak scratched the back of his neck with his war club. "Yes. The only joy in war is coming home to a woman with wide adoring eyes who wants to know how many people you killed."

Towa stared at him. "Don't tell me that Puksu greeted you that way? I don't believe it."

"Puksu? Hardly. She was always sitting at her mother's fire when I arrived home, bad-mouthing me before she even knew I'd disgraced myself in battle."

Puksu had recently divorced him, thank the Spirits. He was heartily glad to be rid of her constant belittling voice. Even now he could hear her whine in his head: *What did you do this time, my husband? Shoot one of our own men in the back?*

Wakdanek asked, "Who is Puksu?"

"My former wife, the Soul-Eater."

"Ah."

Sindak scowled at the darkness for a while before he said, "Come on; let's get back to camp. If we're attacked by humans out here, I doubt Wakdanek's barks and howls will save us."

Sindak let Wakdanek get several paces ahead; then he grabbed Towa's arm to stop him and whispered, "I trust that you've decided to tell me more about your secret orders?"

Towa looked like a condemned man waiting for the ax to fall. "Give me some time. I need—"

"To figure out what treachery Atotarho has planned?"

"I wish you wouldn't finish my sentences. It's—"

"Unnerving." He released Towa's arm. "Especially when I'm right."

Sixteen

As the howling of wolves penetrated his sleep, Gonda flailed weakly and heard Sindak say, *"Go back to your blankets, Wakdanek."*

Gonda flopped to his opposite side and slowly sank back into the jumbled dream. Memories collided, showing him fragments out of sequence and time. . . .

I crouch in the prisoners' house in Atotarho Village. Wind gusts outside and breathes through the wall behind me, chilling my back. I wrap my cape more tightly around my shoulders, but I'm not going to be warm tonight, or perhaps, for the next moon. The damp, cold house stretches forty hands long and twenty wide. The walls are not of bark construction, but sturdy oak planks reinforced with cross-poles. The odor of mildew pervades the dark house, and insects—or perhaps they are mice—skitter across the floor. Koracoo sits on the floor two paces away with her back against the wall. In the moonlight that penetrates around the door, I can see the outline of her body. No one but me would realize how desperately worried she is. I see it in the tension in her shoulders and the way her jaw is set slightly to the left.

"They can't be that far ahead of us," I say. "The tracks were only one day old, and it looked like the warriors were herding eight or nine children. That many captives slow men down."

Koracoo leans her head back against the wall and looks at the roof.

Tiny points of light sparkle. Holes. If it rains, by morning we will be drenched.

"Koracoo, what will we do if Atotarho does not release us in the morning? Have you considered that? It would be a great boon for him to capture War Chief Koracoo and her deputy." I pause, watching her. "We *must* get back on the children's trail as soon as poss—"

Abruptly, I'm on the trail, staring down at the wolf-chewed corpse of a young girl. Koracoo says, "She is not one of our children."

The birds have pecked out her eyes and devoured most of the flesh of her face. Ropes of half-chewed intestines snake across the shells. The broken shaft of an arrow protrudes from her chest. A short distance away, an elaborately carved conch shell pendant rests. It is gorgeous. A False Face with a long bent nose, slanted mouth, and hollow eyes stare up from the shell.

I walk closer and search the area around the mangled corpse for any clues that might reveal her killer. We've been following sandal tracks, distinctive ones with a herringbone pattern. I bend down, pick up the shell pendant, and subtly tuck it into my belt pouch without Koracoo seeing me. I know she would not like this—I am disturbing the dead and risk ghost sickness—but I have the sense that this pendant—

I'm back in the prisoners' house. Warriors' voices hiss. Feet shuffle, and shadows pass back and forth, blotting out the silver gleam that rims the door.

"Open the door," Chief Atotarho orders.

Atotarho moves painfully, rocking and swaying as he enters the house with his lamp. He has seen fifty-two summers, and has braided rattlesnake skins into his gray-streaked black hair and pinned it into a bun at the back of his head. The style gives his narrow face a starved look. He was once, a long time ago, a great warrior. But now, his black cape covers a crooked and misshapen body. To the warriors, he says, "Close the door behind me."

"But . . . my chief, you can't go in alone. There are two of them. What if they attack you?"

"I will risk it. Close the door."

As the door closes, the lamplight seems to grow brighter, reflecting from the plank walls like gigantic amber wings. Atotarho wears a beautiful black ritual cape covered with circlets of bone cut from human skulls. When the lamplight touches them, they wink. "War Chief Koracoo, Deputy Gonda, I must speak with you in confidence. Is that possible between us?"

Our people have been at war for decades. It is a fair question.

Koracoo rises to her feet. "You have my oath, Chief. Whatever we say here remains between us."

I get up and stand beside her. "You have my oath, as well."

Atotarho comes forward with great difficulty. "Forgive me, I cannot stand for long. I need to sit down." He lowers himself to sit upon the cold dirt floor and places his oil lamp in front of him. "Please, join me." He gestures to the floor, and I notice that his fingertips are tattooed with snake eyes, and he wears bracelets of human finger bones. "This will not be an easy conversation for any of us."

We sit.

Koracoo asks, "What is it you wish to discuss?"

The old man doesn't seem to hear. His gaze is locked on the lamp. The fragrance of walnut oil perfumes the air. Finally, he whispers, "Stories have been traveling the trails for several moons, but only I believed them. She has been gone for many summers—perhaps as long as twenty, though no one can be sure. She's very cunning."

Koracoo says, "Who?"

Atotarho bows his head. "Have you heard the name Gannajero?"

I feel like the earth has been kicked out from under me. More legend than human, hideous stories swirl about Gannajero. She is evil incarnate. A beast in the form of an old woman.

Koracoo softly answers, "Yes. I've heard of her."

Atotarho flexes his crooked misshapen fingers. "Rumors say that she has returned to our country. Many villages are missing children. I have been . . . so afraid . . ." He rubs a hand over his face.

"That your daughter is with her?"

He seems to be trying to control his voice. "Yes. All day, every day, I pray to the gods to let my Zateri die if she is with Gannajero. I would prefer it. Anything would be b-better . . ."

Koracoo gives him a few moments to continue. When it's clear he can't, she says, "I understand."

Atotarho's mouth trembles. "No, I do not think you do. You are too young. When she was last here, you were not even a woman yet, were you?"

"I had seen only seven summers, but I recall hearing my family whisper about Gannajero, and it was with great dread."

Atotarho extends his hands to the lamp as if to warm them. His knuckles resemble knotted twigs. "When I had seen five summers, my older brother and sister were captured in a raid. My sister was killed, but my brother was sold to an old man among the Flint People. I heard many summers later that my brother was utterly mad. His nightmares used to wake the entire village. Sometimes he screamed all night long. He eventually killed the old man, slit his throat, and ran away into the forest. No one ever saw him again."

From some great distance, Sindak says, *"Towa, I swear, you're a fool for continuing to be loyal to a chief you know you cannot trust."*

Then Koracoo says, "It would help me if you told me everything you know about Gannajero. Who is she? Where is she from? I know only old stories that make her sound more like a Spirit than a human being."

Atotarho clasps his hands in his lap. "I don't know much. No one does. They say she was born among the Flint or Hills People. Her grandmother was supposedly a clan elder, a powerful woman. But during a raid when Gannajero was eight, she was stolen and sold into slavery to the Mountain People. Then sold again, and again. She was apparently a violent child. Several times she was beaten almost to death by her owners."

"And now she does the same thing to other children?" The hatred in my voice makes Atotarho and Koracoo turn. "What sort of men would help her? How does she find them?"

"I wish I knew. Twenty summers ago, we thought they were all out-casts, men who had no families or villages. Then we discovered one of her men among our own. He was my sister's son, Jonil. A man of status and reputation. He'd been sending her information about planned raids, then capturing enemy children and selling them to her."

I clench my fists. Warfare provides opportunities for greedy men that are not available in times of peace. Since many slaves are taken during attacks, it is easy to siphon off a few and sell them to men who no longer see them as human. War does that. It turns people—even children—into *things,* and gives men an opportunity to vent their rage and hatred in perverted ways that their home villages would never allow.

"Why? Why did he do it?"

Atotarho bows his head, and the shadows of his eyelashes darken his cheeks. "She rewards her servants well. When we searched Jonil's place in the longhouse, we found unbelievable riches—exotic trade goods like obsidian and buffalo wool from the far west. Conch shells from the southern ocean. An entire basket of pounded copper sheets covered with strings of pearls and magnificently etched shell gorgets."

Koracoo sits quietly for a time, thinking, before she says, "That means it will be difficult to buy the children back."

"Virtually impossible. She profits enormously from her captives. With all the stealing and raiding going on, there are too many evil men with great wealth. But . . . if my daughter is being held captive with your children, I will give you whatever I have to get all of them back."

Koracoo stares at him, judging the truthfulness of his words. Atotarho looks her straight in the eyes without blinking. Finally, Koracoo asks, "Why would you buy our children? We are your enemies."

"If you are willing to risk your lives to save my daughter, you are not my enemy."

The night has gone utterly quiet. The guards must be holding their breaths, listening. Very softly Koracoo says, "Why haven't you already mounted a search party and sent them out with this same offer? Surely you can trust your own handpicked warriors more than you can us."

Atotarho glances at the door behind him and whispers, "No. The attack on my Trading party was well organized, and they went straight for my beautiful daughter." His knobby hand clenches to a fist. "As there was many summers ago, I fear there is a traitor here. So, you see, I would rather trust an enemy who shares my interests . . . than a friend who may not."

Koracoo's gaze roams the firelit shadows for thirty heartbeats. "We will need to discuss your offer."

"I understand." As the chief rises to his feet, the circlets of skull on his cape flash. "I'll leave you the lamp; it will provide a little warmth until the oil runs out."

The effort of rising seems to have cost him all of his strength. He pants for a time before he adds, "Many of my people believe I am the human False Face prophesied in our legends. The Spirit-Man who will save the world. It has never been an easy title to bear. Especially now when I cannot even save my own daughter." Without making a sound, he starts for the door. "Let me know your decision as soon as you've made it, and I—"

"One last thing," Koracoo says.

He turns. "Yes?"

"What assurances do we have that you will keep your part of this bargain? Gannajero will not believe me if I tell her you will pay her later."

Atotarho braces his hand against the door to steady himself. "I will send a man with you who can verify—"

Gonda woke gasping as though a hammer had been swung into his rib cage. He struggled to sit up. A few paces away, Sindak turned to stare at him.

Gonda's shaking hand rose to the shell pendant he now wore around his neck . . . and he wondered what his souls were trying to tell him? There must be some connection between the dead girl's pendant and Atotarho, but he was too exhausted to understand.

He forced himself to lie down again and drew his blanket up around his throat. As his breathing began to slow, his chest tightened. Among the People of the Standing Stone, dreams resulted either from contact with the Spirit World or from the unrequited desires of the souls. To ignore a dream was to risk death. He flopped to his opposite side.

Sindak called, "Gonda? Are you all right?"

"Leave me alone," he growled. "I need to rest."

Sindak tucked his war club into his belt and walked toward Gonda. "Well, I was considering not telling you, but since you were just so polite to me . . . it's your watch."

Seventeen

Sometime in the night, they'd made camp. But Wrass didn't even remember stopping.

He squinted against the light cast by the small blaze that flickered in the middle of the clearing. Around it, several people lay rolled in blankets. He was the only child still in the canoes. He didn't see the other children. One guard stood to the south along the bank. Another stood to the north, watching the wide bend in the river.

And . . . another man stood in the river before him. Had he just appeared? Why hadn't Wrass seen him immediately?

The man was no more than three paces away, wearing a long black cape. He watched Wrass curiously. For some time, Wrass returned his stare. There was nothing threatening about him. Except that the man never blinked or looked away. *And he wasn't one of Gannajero's warriors.*

Wrass rubbed his eyes, but when he lowered his hand, the man was still there. If it hadn't been for his crooked nose, he'd be handsome. His black hair had been carefully plaited into a long braid that draped over his left shoulder.

"I've seen you before," Wrass whispered.

Several times as the canoe passed, he'd seen the man staring fixedly at him from behind trees, or calmly sleeping in the frost—but he'd thought the man a figment of his fever. No human being could out-run a canoe powered by the arms of muscular warriors. But this man must have, or he would not be here now.

"I'm still dreaming," Wrass whispered, and focused on the night sky. The brightest campfires of the dead shone like fuzzy white balls. Against that background, the bare branches above him painted delicate black brushstrokes. He wondered if his dead father was up there, sit-ting around the fire joking with his Ancestors. He'd died in the fight that destroyed Yellowtail Village. The People of the Standing Stone believed that each person possessed two souls. One soul remained with the body forever, while the other, the afterlife soul, ordinarily traveled to the bridge that led to the Land of the Dead. The bridge spanned a black abyss. On this side of the bridge, the life side, were all the animals a man had known. Those that had loved him protected him from those that had not, and gave him the time to leap onto the bridge and run for the death side. Oftentimes, a man was chased across the bridge by snarling beasts who tried to shove him into the abyss, where he would fall forever through darkness. Even if he made it across, the trial was not over, for on the death side he met all the people he'd known in his life. Those who had loved him protected him from those who had hated him. If there were more people who had hated him, the mob might drag the man back onto the bridge and cast him over the edge while his loved ones wailed.

As the man in the black cape waded closer, firelit rings bobbed across the water and collided with the shore.

Wrass squinted. "Did you come to take me to the bridge?"

The man smiled sadly. *You're not dying, Wrass.*

"I want to. Please, take me. My family is dead. I want to go to them."

No. Not yet. You have many things to do.

The man's body wavered, as though Wrass were seeing him through a wall of water. He waded to the gunwale of the canoe, where Wrass looked up at him. He was very tall. Oddly, the firelight did not flicker from his cape. It remained utterly black, like a hole cut out of the world.

Wrass whispered, "Are you the human False Face? The one who is to come?"

His people had a story about the end of the world. The story pre-dicted the appearance of a human False Face who would don a cape of white clouds and ride the winds of destruction across the land, wiping away evil so that Great Grandmother Earth could be reborn pure and clean.

The young man leaned over and tenderly smoothed Wrass' hair away from his eyes. His fingers were cool.

No. But you will know him. I promise you will.

There was a long pause, and Wrass heard a sound like the roar of putting a seashell to his ear. He studied the pale translucence of the man's skin, the smooth line of his jaw. "Are you a *hanehwa*?"

The *hanehwa* were enchanted skin-beings. Sometimes sorcerers skinned their human victims alive, then cast spells upon the skins, forcing them to serve as guards. *Hanehwa* never slept. They warned the witch by giving three shouts.

The man's brown eyes softened. *We are all husks, Wrass, flayed from the soil of fire and blood. This won't be over for any of us until the Great Face shakes the World Tree. Then, when Elder Brother Sun blackens his face with the soot of the dying world, the judgment will take place.*

"I—I . . . ," he stuttered. "I don't understand."

The man tilted his head. *Don't worry about it now. You must sleep and heal.*

He gently stroked Wrass' hair again.

Wrass heaved a sigh of relief, and his gaze wandered across the camp. The Great Face was the chief of all False Faces, and he guarded the sacred World Tree that stood at the center of the earth. Its flowers were made of pure light. The World Tree's branches pierced the Sky World where the Ancestors lived, and her roots sank deep into the underworlds, where they planted themselves upon the back of the Great Tortoise floating in the primeval ocean. Elder Brother Sun nested in the highest branches of the World Tree.

Get well, Wrass.

The man waded away through the water, and Wrass called, "Wait. Don't go. K-Keep talking to me."

The man didn't even slow down. He faded as he walked away, until he was transparent, then gone. At the place where he'd vanished, Zateri appeared, and walked toward Wrass. Her chipmunk face glowed in the firelight. She seemed to be floating, weightless, like a milkweed seed on a warm summer wind, noiseless and beautiful. A smile turned his lips. As she got closer, she started looking over her shoulder, as though she feared one of the guards would try to stop her. When she climbed into the canoe, it rocked as she walked down to sit beside Wrass. She wore a blue-painted deerhide cape. He didn't recall ever seeing it before. Had one of the warriors given it to her?

"Did you see him?" Wrass asked. "The man? Did you s-see him?"

Zateri frowned. "What man? One of the warriors?"

"No. The Forest Spirit. He was just here."

"I didn't see anyone near you, Wrass. I came because I need to talk to you. And I brought you these."

She pulled freshly cut willow twigs from her legging and slipped them into Wrass' hand.

As he nibbled on the bitter twigs, his thoughts drifted. He tried to imagine Elder Brother Sun blackening his face with the soot of the dying world . . . and wondered if it was warfare that was going to kill Great Grandmother Earth. Fighting had gone on for so long that no one in Yellowtail Village could remember a time without war.

Zateri said, "I heard Gannajero tell Kotin that Toksus is halfway home."

"Halfway? To Bog Willow Village?" Elation warmed his veins.

"I guess so."

The more Wrass thought about it, the more unlikely it seemed. "It's not possible. Even if he ran f-flat-out the entire way in the darkness, he couldn't have made it that far."

"I thought the same thing, but . . ."

Zateri wet her lips, and her front teeth stuck out. She glanced at the guards again. "Just after we made camp, she walked away into the forest and pulled the dead boy's eyes from her belt pouch. She held them up over her own eyes, as though she was seeing through them. Then she talked to them for a long time."

In a hushed voice, he said, "The eyes talk to her?"

Zateri lifted a shoulder. "I didn't hear them say anything. But I guess she did."

Zateri twisted her hands in her lap. The gesture was more forceful than any of her spoken words. They both feared that all the evil creatures in the world gathered around Gannajero. How could they fight an army of Spirit creatures?

"Wrass, I'm really scared," Zateri said. "Someone is coming for us, aren't they? Odion, Baji, and Tutelo found their families, and they organized a search party to find us . . . didn't they?"

Wrass held her desperate gaze for a time. Trying to comfort her, he said, "Baji promised she'd return for us with a war party at her back."

"Yes, but who can say what might have happened after she got away? She might have tried, and no one would listen to a twelve-summers-old girl."

Wrass smiled. "Baji is not that easy to ignore."

"Then . . . you do think someone is coming?" Her voice shook.

Wrass carefully considered what to say. If he sounded too optimistic, she wouldn't believe him. Zateri had been a slave as long as he had. She knew the way of things. On the other hand, hope had kept them alive this long. "Yes. Someone is coming. But I don't think we c-can rely on them to rescue us. Figuring out our trail isn't going to be easy. It could take them another moon to find us, and too much can h-happen." Her eyes tightened. Wrass continued, "We have to do this ourselves, Zateri. And soon."

She expelled a breath and glanced at the guards again. Both men seemed to be ignoring them, studying the forest shadows and the river. "Do you have a plan?"

He shook his head. "I've been too sick to think, but I'm starting to feel a little better, so I'll—"

"I have a plan." Zateri leaned very close to him and whispered, "They don't know it was us who poisoned their stew pot. Maybe we can do it again. I just need a few days to collect the plants."

Wrass nodded. "Do it. I'm not sure we'll have a chance. Gannajero has been watching her p-pots like a hawk. But it won't hurt to have the plants just in case we have an opportunity to use them."

"I'm pretty sure she thinks it was one of her own warriors who tried to kill her."

"To take all the children for himself?"

"Yes. She picks her men because they're slit-eyed thieves with no honor. She can't trust them."

Zateri pushed black hair behind her ears, and they sat for a while in companionable silence. The sound of the river seemed louder. Wrass let his gaze wander to the smoke that wreathed the treetops like gauzy shreds of mist. In the firelight, the treetops seemed to flicker, as though lightning lived in their hearts.

Finally, Zateri frowned. "Wrass, there's one other thing."

"What?"

"One of the new guards . . . the one named Akio?"

"What about him?"

She made an uncertain gesture with her hand. "I think he's from my village."

Blood surged through his veins, and his headache pounded. "From Atotarho Village? Are you sure?"

"Pretty sure. My father didn't allow me to spend time with warriors, but I know I've seen him."

"Do you think he's a spy? Is he here to help us? To r-rescue us?"

Zateri turned to face the camp, searching for the man amid the blanket-wrapped bodies near the fire. She subtly shook her head. "Just before we left on the Trading mission where I was captured, I heard my father whispering to our war chief, Nesi, that he feared there was a traitor in the village. I'm afraid—"

"Zateri, are you saying that you th-think Akio is the man who sold you to Gannajero?"

Zateri stared at her moccasins, as though tormented that one of her own had done something so terrible, but she replied, "He's not here to help us. I can tell by the way he looks at me."

"How does he look at you?"

"I don't know. . . ." She shrugged. "It's a kind of gleeful pride, as though he knows something I don't, something he would really like to tell me."

"Like the fact that he betrayed your father?"

One of the guards glanced at them, clearly listening, trying to hear what they were saying. He must have caught a few words. Among the trees behind him, firelight flashed and danced. The scents of cooking food wafted on the cold night wind.

Wrass leaned forward until his mouth almost touched Zateri's ear. "If he is the traitor your father suspected . . ." He hesitated, suddenly not sure he should finish that sentence.

Zateri pulled away slightly to look at him. "It's all right, Wrass. I know. If he's the traitor, he can't let me escape."

They both knew it would be to Akio's advantage to get rid of the evidence—to have her dead. The man's only stumbling block was that she was now Gannajero's property, and the punishment for killing one of the old woman's slaves was a very unpleasant death. But if there was an opportunity, he'd probably do it anyway.

"From now on, you need to stay as far away from him as you can."

"I will. I just wish I could ride in the same canoe as you, but she'll never allow it."

"No." The distant hooting of owls penetrated the trees. "We're troublemakers. Which means she's probably going to sell one or both of us at the first opportunity."

Tears blurred her brown eyes. "Wrass, if she sells you, I don't know if I can . . . do this . . . without you."

He reached out to clutch her hand. "You won't have any choice. You can't l-let the other children down."

Zateri clenched her teeth to hold back sobs. When she could, she said, "I hope that she sells me first. You're better at saving people than I am."

He shook his head. "No. You're smarter than I am. Without you and your knowledge of Spirit plants, I'd have never been able to help Odion and the others escape. *We* did that, not me."

Zateri wiped her tears with her hands, and some of the struggle seemed to go out of her face. It was replaced by resolve. "Sleep, Wrass. I'll be back to check on you later. If they let me."

Eighteen

Red and angry, Elder Brother Sun climbed above the mountains, but his gleam barely penetrated the smoky miasma that stretched for as far as Sindak could see. The haze-choked forest had a dull crimson glow.

Sindak shook his head, and Towa, who marched beside him, said, "What's wrong? You look like you ate something crawling with maggots."

Towa's long braid and oval face bore a coating of ash, as did the rest of him. He'd tried to wipe it from his forehead and cheeks so often that black streaks slashed across his skin.

At the sight of the abandoned warriors' camp, a sensation of panic filtered through Sindak. "Finding Gannajero's trail is going to be even harder than I thought. I hadn't anticipated this layer of ash."

All night long, the black blizzard had drifted over the forest, blown from the smoldering ruins of Bog Willow Village. The breeze had obviously been coming from the east, because the western sides of the spruces and pines were green, while the eastern sides bore a thick coating of gray. Worse, every time the branches swayed, ash wafted down over the trail.

A whimper sounded, very faint. Sindak cocked his head. It seemed to be coming from somewhere ahead. "Do you hear that?"

"What?"

"That whimpering. It sounds like a lost child."

Towa stopped and listened. "It's just the frozen trees creaking in the breeze."

Sindak shook his head, doubtful. "Are you sure?"

"No, but I think so."

The rest of their party continued up the trail into a copse of white cedars that seemed to pulse orange in the dusty surreal gleam.

Sindak took a moment to pull his water bag from his belt. As he drank, he studied the line of people. Koracoo and Cord led the way, followed by the children, then Wakdanek, then Gonda. He handed his water bag to Towa.

Towa took a long drink and handed it back. He squinted at the blowing ash. "You're right. The ash is going to make tracking very difficult. And our chances are dropping by the instant."

Sindak irritably jerked the bag's laces closed again and retied it to his belt. "It doesn't help that we've just clasped two snakes to our bosoms and are almost certain to be killed by them in our sleep." He tipped his chin to Cord and Wakdanek.

"Yes, I'm surprised we haven't been shot in the backs yet."

"Give it time."

Towa nodded. "I just hope they don't cut us apart and leave the chunks scattered through the forest. If they do, our families will never find our bodies, and our souls will be doomed to wander the earth forever as homeless ghosts."

"You mean because no one will requicken our souls in new bodies?"

"Not if your grandmother has her way. She—"

Sindak broke in. "You are not cheering me up."

"Sorry. I'm in a bad mood. I've spent all morning planning my funeral."

"Ah. You've been thinking of Chief Atotarho and his secret orders."

"Of course."

If they failed in their duty, Atotarho would make certain they were disgraced, perhaps even killed.

"Am I invited?" Sindak asked.

"What?"

"To your funeral?"

"I don't think you'll be around to attend. If I know your clan matron, she'll demand the right to sacrifice you first; then she'll give your heart to Puksu as a gift."

Sindak grimaced. "Impossible. Puksu ate that while we were married."

"Then maybe your brain, as an apology."

Sindak's mouth quirked. He stared at his friend. "You *are* in a bad mood."

"Well, you know I'm right. Matron Tila has never liked you."

"True. Even as a boy, the old witch used to hunt me down and force me to wash her bedding hides."

"Her bedding hides? That's odd. Why would she do that?"

"I used to urinate on them when she wasn't looking. I didn't like her either."

Towa squinted at the flame-colored ball that seemed half buried in the murky sky. "We should catch up."

Towa trotted away, and Sindak fell into line behind him. They passed through the white cedars and emerged into a grove of enormous chestnuts and white pines. As Elder Brother Sun rose higher, wan sunlight fell through the branches and warmed the frosty ground. Where it touched, steam rose. Throughout the forest thin misty streamers coiled into the cold morning air.

When Gonda heard their steps, he turned around to give them a threatening glare. "I thought perhaps you'd been captured by Dawnland refugees."

"Were you coming to look for us?" Sindak asked.

"No," Gonda answered. "I figured it was your own fault for falling behind."

Sindak smiled. "I'll remember that if you're ever captured."

"If I'm ever captured, it will be in a fight where I was outnumbered ten to one, not because I was a dimwit."

War Chief Cord propped his hands on his hips and studied them through narrowed eyes before he said, "Our fire was on the far eastern side of the camp last night, on the river. Where did you find the children?"

Koracoo aimed her war club. "There. On that deer trail that runs back through the trees to the west." She must have gotten hot on the run. She'd rolled her cape and tied it around her waist. Her knee-length war shirt clung to her body like a second skin. Sindak's gaze traced the line of her full breasts, down around the curve of her hip, and followed one long muscular leg.

Gonda asked, "Do you value those eyes, Sindak?"

He started to respond, but Koracoo ordered, "Let's move out."

They marched ahead in silence, being vigilant. Last night the laughter and singing of warriors had filled the air. This morning the sound of grieving people rode the wind.

Koracoo called, "Wakdanek? You might want to trot ahead to prepare your people for our arrival."

The big Healer trotted past her and vanished into the trees.

Koracoo gave him a short head start, then followed, leading them out to the edge of the clearing that marked the boundaries of the camp. "Let's wait here."

The party halted.

The ash-covered frosty ground was littered with crushed pots, torn baskets, and the refuse cast off by warriors glutted with victory. Several Dawnland survivors moved through the chaos, collecting old blankets, threadbare capes, seedbead bracelets, cracked wooden cups, and other things of small value. Things that had undoubtedly been replaced during the looting of Bog Willow Village. Wakdanek stood talking with an old man in the center of the camp. The elder propped himself up with a walking stick and threw hateful glances at their party.

"No arrows are flying," Sindak noted. "That's a good sign."

Wakdanek trotted back to Koracoo and said, "You're safe. For now. My relatives just want to collect their belongings and care for their relatives. They found several dead children lying in a row along the riverbank. They're preparing them for the journey to the afterlife."

Koracoo studied him uncertainly. When she turned to face the party, she looked directly at Cord. "What is your opinion, War Chief? Are we safe?"

Gonda jerked around to stare at her, obviously angry that she'd asked Cord's opinion and not his.

Cord studiously ignored Gonda and appeared to think about his answer before he responded. "We should all stay fairly close together. We don't want to tempt the grieving relatives. They've probably already declared blood oaths against their attackers."

"They have," Wakdanek said, and eyed Cord coldly.

For a long uncomfortable moment, their gazes locked.

Koracoo broke the staring contest by saying, "All right. Let's stay no more than twenty paces from each other. And search every pack you find for food. We may have a long journey ahead us. We'll need every moment to paddle. Hunting will be a luxury."

The smell of death permeated the cold air. Even through the smoky gloom, Sindak counted fifty or sixty corpses across the camp. Most had perished from arrow wounds—the shafts still protruded from the bodies—but a few had been clubbed to death. Some recently. He could tell because red blood covered their faces. They'd probably been wounded in the Bog Willow Village battle, and had their pain ended at dawn by friends who could no longer stand their cries.

Odion called, "Mother? That's where we were held." In his fist, he clutched the stiletto Sindak had given him.

Sindak followed the boy's arm to a small clearing surrounded by scrub bladdernut trees. Another dead body sprawled there. *The guard killed by Wrass?*

He took a moment to watch Odion. The boy kept licking his lips and breathing hard, as though he were straining against an overpowering desire to run away. He was walking practically on top of Gonda's heels. Baji wasn't doing much better. She had a deerbone stiletto in her fist, holding it before her. Rage twisted her pretty face, which Sindak understood perfectly. He had often smothered fear with rage. Perhaps all living creatures did. He'd watched terrified dogs go into snarling enraged frenzies when cornered. Little Tutelo seemed to be the only one who was not petrified to be back here. She appeared cautious, studying the forest carefully as they walked, but no panic shone in her eyes.

And then there was Hehaka. Sindak didn't know what to make of the boy. He kept sniffing the air like a dog searching for its pack—as though desperate to scent Gannajero or one of her men.

"Where did Baji get the stiletto?" Sindak asked.

Cord turned. The ugly scar that slashed across his square jaw had collected ash. It resembled a line of black paint. "I gave it to her."

Sindak nodded. "Good idea."

Koracoo shoved aside a clump of brush and cut through the forest, heading directly for the clearing Odion had pointed out.

Sindak brought up the rear, proceeding at a snail's pace, his gaze searching the haze as though his very life depended upon it. Which it might. Though warriors traditionally left their camps just before dawn, there were often men who remained behind to stay with dying friends or ransack the packs of the dead. There could be fifty men hiding in the trees.

By the time he reached the clearing, the others had created a semicircle around the dead body. Wooden bowls, freshwater clamshells, and a half-eaten dog leg scattered the ground. The sleeping places of the children were clear. The grass had been mashed flat, then dusted with ash. The dead warrior lay to the east, facing toward the river. His last sight must have been the hundreds of warriors camped just a few paces away.

Koracoo placed her feet carefully, so as not to disturb any tracks, and circled around to stand over the dead man's head.

Sindak could tell he'd been clubbed in the back of the head, and in the face. His nose and cheekbones had been crushed by the blow. Congealed blood filled the hollow. His half-open eyes had frozen in a surprised stare.

Sindak said, "Is that the guard Wrass killed?"

Almost simultaneously, Baji and Tutelo answered, "Yes."

"Did you see it happen?" Sindak asked.

Baji looked at him as though he were an idiot. "We were sitting right there. How could we have missed it?"

"Oh. I see."

Gonda walked over to stand beside Koracoo. A thin layer of ash coated his round face and painted a dark line across his heavy brow. Softly, he said, "This isn't good, Koracoo."

"What isn't good?"

"This entire area is a morass of crisscrossing trails. All night long, hundreds of warriors tramped around obliterating each other's tracks. Then Wind Mother whirled ash over everything." He spread his arms in a gesture of futility. "I don't know how we're ever going to find—"

"Don't give me excuses," she replied coldly. "Start looking."

Gonda clenched his jaw, nodded, and walked away.

"Mother?" Odion was shaking, but just barely. Only his shoulder-length black hair quivered. "Gannajero's camp was over there, where those dead bodies are." He pointed with the stiletto.

Koracoo turned. The bodies sprawled beside a smoldering fire pit. Next to it, a pot hung from a tripod, and a large woodpile stood beside it. "Is that the pot Wrass poisoned?"

"Yes."

"Where did he get the poison?"

Tutelo piped up and proudly said, "Zateri found it, Mother. She knows Spirit plants. As we marched, she collected thorn apple seeds, swamp cabbage root, and spoonwood leaves. She hid them in her legging."

Sindak's heart twinged. He hadn't known the girl well. Zateri was a chief's daughter, not allowed to fraternize with ordinary warriors, but he remembered her bright smile and sparkling eyes. She'd been studying to become a Healer. How strange that she'd first use her knowledge to kill . . . and thereby save her friends.

Wakdanek frowned. "Even small amounts of those plants would be enough to kill several people."

"And she collected a bag this big." Tutelo put both her fists together to show the size.

Wakdanek stood for a moment, staring at the pot, then walked toward it. While he knelt and sniffed the contents, Sindak scanned the forest. Between the trees, scrub thickets of nannyberry bushes and prickly ash saplings spiked up. To the south, he could see the hill where they'd hidden last night; it appeared and disappeared in the shifting haze.

Koracoo suddenly looked down at the war club in her hand and frowned. After a few instants, she switched it to her other hand, as though it had grown too hot to hold.

"Koracoo?" Sindak asked. "What's happening?"

War Chief Cord caught the panic in his voice and stared hard at Koracoo; then his gaze dropped to CorpseEye. Like every other warrior in the world, he probably knew the war club's magical reputation.

Koracoo didn't answer. As though CorpseEye was tugging her to the north, she turned toward the long rocky ridge covered with spruces and white walnuts that sloped down to the river. "What's down there, Odion? Where the rocky hill meets the water?"

The boy pulled his moosehide blanket tightly around his shoulders. "I don't know. We never went over there."

War Chief Cord said, "It's a canoe landing. Forty or fifty canoes were beached there last night. I—"

Wakdanek interrupted, calling, "This pot was poisoned, all right. In addition to everything Tutelo named, Zateri also added a good deal of musquash. The parsnip smell is very strong."

Koracoo slowly worked her way toward him, searching for anything in the frost or wind-blown ash that might be significant. Sindak, Cord, and Towa placed their moccasins in her tracks, as though it would make a difference in a clearing covered with ash-filled indentations.

Behind him, Sindak heard children walking, but didn't turn to look. His gaze had focused on the dead men around the campfire.

Koracoo stepped wide around a looted pack. Broken strings of shell beads filled the bottom and sprinkled the ash-sheathed frost.

She passed the bodies and went to the stew pot where Wakdanek stood.

When Sindak closed in on the first body, his eyes narrowed. Beneath the ash, the man's arms were twisted at impossible angles, suggesting he'd died in convulsions. He looked at the others. One man, a muscular giant, still had his hands clutched around his own throat. Their deaths had not been easy.

Towa slowed down and waited for Sindak to catch up, then said, "Isn't that War Chief Manidos?"

"From the Mountain People?" Sindak studied his contorted features. "Maybe. I'm not sure."

Last summer, Manidos had assaulted Atotarho Village with over five hundred men. Atotarho's War Chief, Nesi, had organized a brilliant defense and driven Manidos back; then they'd pursued his fragmented war party for two days. Sindak and Towa had been there. Nesi's warriors had killed over half of Manidos' men before they'd reached home.

"Were all of these warriors Gannajero's men?" Koracoo asked.

Baji walked around to the body of a tall skinny warrior and said, "This one was. His name was Chimon. I don't know about the others. She hired a lot of new men last night."

"Odion may know, Mother," Tutelo said. She called, "Odion? We need you."

Sindak twisted around and spied Odion standing at the edge of the clearing, alone, watching them with half-squinted eyes.

The boy shook his head.

"Odion, we need you," Tutelo repeated.

He didn't move.

Koracoo tilted her head, examining her son. She called, "Odion? Come here."

Sindak was twenty paces away, and he could see the boy start to shiver violently.

Wakdanek moved to stand beside Koracoo. The ash had stuck to the bones of his starved face, giving it an oddly shaded, almost skeletal appearance. "I'm not sure that's a good idea, War Chief."

"Why not?"

"Sometimes it does more harm than good to force a child to face—"

"Life?" she asked. "To force him to face life? He must, Wakdanek, especially when it isn't easy. The sooner the better."

"*Odion?*" Koracoo ordered. "Come over here. Now."

Gonda walked up behind Odion, said something to him, and put a hand on his shoulder, pushing him forward. The boy stiffly stepped out with Gonda at his side.

A dull thud sounded, followed by a grunt, and Sindak spun around to see Baji level a kick at Chimon's head. Stiff with death, and frozen to the ground, the head barely moved. Baji clenched her jaw and kicked it again, then stepped down to his middle and leveled a brutal kick at the dead man's privates. Her eyes took on a savage glow. She drew back and kicked him again as hard as she could.

Sindak whispered to Towa, "That little girl is quickly becoming my hero."

"Well, enjoy it. A few summers from now, I suspect you're going to be looking into her eyes across a bow. If she has the chance, she'll shoot you through the heart and do the same thing to your dead body."

"You're in *such* a bad mood today. I wish—"

"Odion?" Gonda's voice made Sindak and Towa swing around. Odion had stopped dead in the trail and was staring unblinking at the dead warriors.

"Why did you stop? Keep walking, Son," Gonda said. "Your mother needs you."

Odion took a new grip on his stiletto and obeyed, but the boy who'd been so brave yesterday looked like he was about to shatter into a thousand pieces.

Nineteen

Cord grimaced as he watched Odion approach. The boy's terror affected even him. His stomach muscles clenched tight.

When Odion got to within two paces of the dead bodies, he stared at the muscular giant who still had his hands around his throat, and a small cry of terror escaped his lips. *"No!"* he shrieked. *"No, no!"*

Odion backpedaled, slammed into Gonda, and wildly shoved past him. As he charged for the trees, he pulled the blanket from his shoulders and threw it to the ground.

"Odion?" Baji yelled, and ran after him. "Odion, he's dead! He can't hurt you again. He's dead!"

Baji caught Odion at the edge of the trees and wrapped her arms around him, holding him tightly while he sobbed against her shoulder.

Koracoo and Gonda stared at each other. After several agonizing moments, Koracoo turned toward the dropped moosehide blanket and said, "Where did Odion get that blanket?"

Gonda shook his head, and murmured, "I don't know. I just assumed—"

"I think that man gave it to him." Tutelo pointed to the muscular giant. Her pretty face had a look of concentration.

Koracoo glanced at the man, then back at Tutelo. "Why do you think that?"

"Odion didn't have that blanket when he left camp with that man last night. But he did when I saw him later."

"He left camp with this . . . this man?" Horror was slowly congealing on Koracoo's face.

As the probable truth filtered through Gonda's veins, his face flushed.

"Yes, Mother. Kotin told Odion that he had to go. And he told that man, I think his name was Manidos, that he would refund half the price if Manidos didn't like Odion."

Koracoo's fingers tightened around CorpseEye in a death grip, but before she could say anything, Gonda lifted his war club, stalked over to Manidos, and viciously began pounding the dead man's skull to bloody pulp.

Hehaka yelled, "What are you doing? You can't do that! He deserves to be buried with honor. He was a *war chief*!"

"Was he?" Gonda asked in a matter-of-fact voice. "Well, then, he does deserve more."

Gonda set his war club aside, pulled his chert ax from his belt, and hacked the man's head off.

Hehaka's mouth dropped open in shock, and Tutelo leaned against Koracoo's leg to watch her father with wide eyes.

"Wakdanek," Gonda ordered, "build up that fire."

"Why?"

"Because I asked you to."

"Very well," Wakdanek replied uneasily, and knelt. As he pulled a stick from the pile and began separating out the warmest coals from last night's fire, he kept glancing at Gonda.

Koracoo walked over to Gonda and whispered, "Be thorough."

Gonda grabbed the severed head by the hair, swung it up, and hurled it toward the fire pit. The head thudded soddenly against the ground, rolled, and came to rest staring up at the morning sky. "Oh, I plan to. His afterlife soul is doomed."

Gonda bent over the left arm and brutally began hacking it apart with the ax.

Sindak squinted at Gonda for several moments, then called, "Do you need to do this yourself, or can I help?"

"Take the legs," Gonda said.

Sindak pulled his chert knife and went to work. He sliced through the muscles, then sawed down to the hip joint. When he'd severed the right leg, he moved to the left.

Towa said, "I'll take care of the pieces."

He picked up the leg and dragged it out into the middle of the camp where a flock of crows squawked, dropped it, and returned.

Cord was an outsider. It was not his place to interfere unless asked to do so, but . . . he walked around to crouch near Gonda. "Tell me what to do."

Without even looking up, Gonda said, "The other arm."

Cord pulled his knife from his belt and knelt near the dead man's shoulder. He worked in utter silence, slicing through the meat toward the joint, neatly disconnecting the arm in fluid strokes.

Gonda was focused completely on the task at hand, and Cord heaved a sigh of relief. When Koracoo had asked Cord's opinion, he'd felt Gonda's anger like a knife in the air. It was a simple courtesy. They were both war chiefs. Koracoo wanted him to know that despite the fact that he had willingly subordinated himself to her authority on this war walk, she considered him to be an equal. Cord appreciated the gesture.

Just as Cord finished severing the last bit of sinew, he heard the whimper. It was very faint, as though coming from beneath a pile of hides, almost not there—but he swore it was more than the cries of the grieving Dawnland People. He straightened up, and his gaze drifted over the broken pots, torn blankets, and looted packs that scattered the camp.

Nothing moved, except people and the feasting birds.

From the edge of his vision, he saw Wakdanek blowing on the coals. They reddened quickly, and flames licked up around the wood. He added more branches.

Towa grabbed one arm, and the other leg, and hauled them to different areas of the camp.

Gonda rose, and Cord glanced up. The man looked like he was ready to burst at the seams, but he gave Cord a grateful nod. Cord nodded back.

Gonda grabbed the arm Cord had severed and, with a hoarse cry, swung it around in a circle, then flung it as far away as he could. The arm cartwheeled across the frozen ground.

Cord wiped his bloody knife blade on the dead man's cape and studied Gonda. He'd turned his back to the children and stood with tears running down his cheeks as he gazed out across the camp.

Koracoo softly said, "Gonda?" and walked over to him. "We need to—"

"When we find the old woman, she's mine," Gonda hissed in a shaking voice. "Do you understand? *Mine!*"

"She's yours. If possible."

With sudden violence, Gonda grabbed Koracoo and crushed her to his chest. In her ear, he hissed, "Dear gods, what are we going to do? How can our son ever find—?"

"If you want to help him," she said without a shred of emotion, "show him how a man faces something like this."

Admiration filled Cord. How could she stay so calm, so focused? The boy was a stranger to him, and still every fiber in his muscles longed to lash out at something. Being able to defer emotion in the most emotional of circumstances was the hallmark of a great war chief. A goal he had never quite managed to achieve.

Gonda's shaking embrace slackened. He released her and wiped his face on his sleeve. After he'd sucked in a breath, he said, "You're right."

Gonda stalked over to the fire and piled on more wood. When the blaze roared, he turned. Odion and Baji stood at the edge of the trees, watching wide-eyed. Gonda called, "Odion, come over here."

Odion shook his head.

Gonda shouted, "I told you to come over here. Do it *now* or I will drag you over here!"

Odion's contorted face resembled a winter-killed carcass as he marched forward with Baji at his shoulder.

When he got close enough, Gonda grabbed Odion's hand and forcibly led him to the severed head.

"Put away your stiletto, and pick that up. Throw it in the fire."

"No. F-Father . . . *please*! I don't want to touch—"

"Pick it up!"

Odion shook so badly his body seemed to be spasming as he tucked the stiletto into his belt, twined his fingers in the man's hair, and staggered forward to toss it into the flames. By the time he'd finished, he was sobbing openly, and turned to run.

Gonda grabbed him by the back of the shirt, swung him around, and forced him to stand there.

"Watch," Gonda commanded.

The hair burst into flames, and a stinking black cloud of smoke rose. Next, the skin began to peel and char. When the frozen eyes shriveled into black husks and sank into the skull, Odion leaned heavily against Gonda. The smell of burning meat rose on the air.

Through the entire thing, Koracoo stood silently by, watching her son and former husband with sober eyes.

Finally, Gonda crouched in front of Odion and gently smoothed tangled hair behind his son's ears. "His family will never find him. Together, we have made sure that no one will ever be able recognize his body. His people cannot call up his afterlife soul and perform the Requickening Ceremony to place it in another human being. No one can save him now. He will never travel to the afterlife. He will be a homeless ghost, condemned to wander the earth alone, forever. Do you understand?"

"Yes." Odion wiped his runny nose with a blood-coated hand, then looked at his fingers. Tears filled his eyes. As though to get them as far away as possible, he extended both hands to Gonda. "Father? His blood. I—"

"Come on. Let's go down to the river."

Gonda took Odion by the hand, and they marched down to the water.

Koracoo silently removed her red cape from around her waist, shook it out, and slipped it over her head again, as though cold to the bone. The cape made a great bloody smear against the sickly haze.

No one said anything until Wakdanek murmured, "That was difficult to watch. More difficult for the boy."

Koracoo blinked as though she'd just awakened from a nightmare. "Was it?"

"Well . . . yes," Wakdanek said in confusion.

"It was necessary."

"Really?" Wakdanek said as though in disbelief. "I doubt that . . ."

When she turned to look at him, his voice died in his throat. Her black eyes were hard and clear. "For the rest of my son's life he will see two faces: one living and one dead. Every time he starts to relive what happened to him, he will see that charred head. He can hold onto that image. Eventually, the dead face will blot out the living face—and he'll be all right."

Wakdanek swallowed hard. "I just . . . I don't think I could do that to my own child."

Koracoo looked out across the camp and seemed to be weighing whether or not to continue the conversation. Finally, she added, "Children need to know that evil can be killed, Wakdanek. They need to know *they* can kill it. That's what war is about. Killing evil."

Koracoo walked away and began moving through the other bodies, searching the ground for a sign. Towa followed her.

When Cord, Sindak, and Wakdanek stood alone, Wakdanek shook his head, and Cord asked, "What's the matter?"

Wakdanek gestured weakly. "I was just thinking about words. In the most terrible of moments, they are everything. They lend form to horror—define its contours and shape—make it real so that it can be borne. Though I think she's wrong about the heart of war."

"You're a Healer. What do you know of war?"

"I know that the aim of war is revelation, not the destruction of the enemy. Not killing evil."

"Revelation? Really?" Sindak's brows plunged down over his hooked nose. "That's not what my war chief tells me. Is that what you tell your warriors, Cord?"

Cord laughed softly. "No."

"I didn't think so. Please enlighten us, Wakdanek. What needs to be revealed?"

Wakdanek remained silent. Probably because he thought discussing anything sophisticated with savages would be an exercise in futility. After all, Sindak was from the Hills People and Cord was worse: a man of the Flint People. The Flint People and the Dawnland People had always been enemies.

Sindak pressed. "*What* needs to be revealed?"

As though annoyed, Wakdanek expelled a breath. "My friend, we all have an amnesia of the heart. We've forgotten that we were once the same people."

For a moment, the strange purplish smear of wood smoke shifted, and wan sunlight penetrated the haze, falling in streaks and bars across the abandoned warriors' camp. Cord took a moment to appreciate the beauty; then he said, "Well, if we were one people, it was a long, long time ago. What does that revelation get us now?"

"Get us?"

"Yes. Does it put more food in the mouths of our families? Will it bring back the rains, or make our crops more productive? Will it make our enemies stop killing us?"

When Wakdanek just stared at Cord with a sad expression, Sindak made a low disgusted sound and walked away to join Koracoo.

The Healer said no more, and Cord turned to follow Sindak.

Behind him, very quietly, he heard Wakdanek reply, "It might."

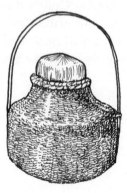

Twenty

Odion

By noon I'm shaking so badly, I can't keep my head still. I try to focus on the tawny velvet distances, but they possess a fuzzy gleam, as though the sky is a golden painting that someone has tried to erase with a rough piece of hide.

The other children who sit on the riverbank don't know what to do. Baji and Tutelo glance worriedly at me and try to pretend nothing is wrong.

I pull my knees up and hug them to my chest. Cedars and white pines surround us, casting wavering shadows and scenting the cold air with sweetness. Green water flows before me. I shift to look at the adults as they search for Gannajero's trail. For six hands of time, they've followed out one set of tracks after another, then returned again and again to start over at the old woman's campsite. Strains of conversations drift on the cold breeze. They sound irritable. They're losing hope. All across the abandoned camp, Dawnland People also wander, searching the discarded items left by the warriors, hoping to find some cherished belonging, or the trails of those who were taken captive.

Throughout the day, Wakdanek has spent most of his time with his relatives, but now he crouches on the riverbank ten paces from me. His gaze seems to be searching the brush on the opposite bank, but I frequently see him staring at me. The cap he wears—made from the shoulder skin of a moose—creates a bristly crest down the middle of his skull. The two feathers tied to the cap flit in the wind as though trying to fly away. I study the sheathed knife that rests on his breast, hung from a cord around his neck. It is large. Much larger than knives carried by the Standing Stone People.

I wipe my shaking hands on my leggings. I've already wiped them so many times my fingers are swollen. *But his blood is still there.* It soaked into my skin and has been filtering, like a paralyzing numbness, through my hands and up my arms. I can barely breathe. In another hand of time his blood will seep into my heart and stop it from beating.

"Odion?" Tutelo pats my arm. "Why don't you let me go get Mother?"

"No. I'll be all right." I hold my hands out to her. "But, Tutelo, do you see any blood?"

She grabs my hands and studies the palms carefully, then turns them over. "No, Odion. Your hands are very clean."

I scrub them on my leggings again, hard, but it doesn't help. The numbness continues spreading. If I could only forget last night, I might—

"Stop ordering me around!" Father shouts. "I know what I'm doing. I've been a tracker all my life!"

I spin to see Mother staring at Father. She glances at those close by, then whispers something to him. Whatever she said, it wasn't pleasant. Father's face contorts in anger. He gestures wildly with his hands, whispering to Mother through gritted teeth. The other warriors keep their distance, but War Chief Cord's eyes narrow, as though, if he were in charge, he would not be so nice to Father.

Mother walks away and starts searching again. Every time the wind breathes, ash swirls up and resettles, covering the tracks she's just made.

As I watch her, an inexplicable panic surges through me. I rise and hurry down to the river, where I kneel and scoop handfuls of sand to wash my arms and hands. My skin is raw and red; it hurts. But I keep washing, scouring my flesh, hoping to remove the soaked-in blood. "Just forget," I whisper. "It never happened. That part of last night wasn't real. It never happened. Never. *Never.*" I repeat it silently to myself several more times.

But when I stand up, my knees wobble. After all the beatings, and the days of marching with almost no food, I can't seem to—

"Can I help?" a soft voice says from behind me.

I turn too fast, and stagger sideways. Wakdanek is two paces away, studying me with kind eyes. "Why? What do you want?"

He kneels, and the ball-headed war club he carries tucked into his belt thumps the ground. The blunt angles of his starved face are shadowed with ash and make it look like a skeleton's. He reaches for his belt pouch. "You know I am a Healer, yes?"

I lick my lips nervously. "Yes."

"I think I can help you, if you want me to."

As though trying not to frighten me, he slowly pulls out a chipped cup and two leather bags. One has a red spiral painted on it. The other has a green lightning bolt.

"What's in the bags?" I ask.

Wakdanek sets the bags and cup aside, and smiles gently. "Among my people, touching a dead body can cause ghost sickness. Many of the dead are angry. Especially those who die violently. They know they can't travel to the Land of the Dead to be with their Ancestors, and they're lonely and lost. That's why they come around in the afternoon and at night to rattle the cooking pots. They want others to die and join them. But there are Spirit plants that drive ghosts away, and keep them away."

Wakdanek gently places his hand on the bag with the red spiral. "This is a powder from the root of the bear's foot plant." His hand moves to the green lightning bolt bag. "And this is dried water lily root. Both are powerful ghost medicines."

I wipe my nose on my sleeve. It's running, and I have tears in my eyes, though I do not know when this happened. I choke out the words, "What do I have to do?"

Wakdanek pats the shore. "Sit beside me. We'll get started."

I cautiously ease down to the shore and pull my stiletto from my belt again. It comforts me to hold it.

Wakdanek glances at the stiletto as he removes a small pot and empties some coals from the morning's fire onto the sand. "We need to purify you first," he says as he gathers up a handful of white pine needles. While he sprinkles them over the coals, he blows until the needles catch and flames leap through the tinder. "Please come closer, Odion."

I slide across the sand until I'm practically on top of the tiny blaze. As the dark smoke rises, he instructs, "Lean over the smoke and use your hands to smooth it over your face and arms. It will purify your skin."

"My skin?" I cup my hands and pull the smoke toward me so that it soaks my hair and clothing. My movements are awkward with the stiletto held between my thumb and forefinger.

"Yes, when a ghost touches you, or anything else, it's like a poison. It seeps inside you, trying to drive out your soul."

I blink. He is blurry. "I knew it. I feel the poison. It's been climbing up my arms ever since I touched—"

"We're going to stop it."

Relief surges through me. "You can do that?"

"I've known how to cure ghost sickness since I was ten summers."

"Why? Were you sick?"

"No, my mother was. A fever went through our village, killing many people. She was helping carry the dead to a place behind the houses when she took sick. Our village Healer brought ghost medicine to cure her."

He opens the two leather bags and pours small amounts of powder from each into the chipped cup. Then he dips up a little water from the river and uses a piece of driftwood to stir in the powder. He adds more water, and stirs again. "All right, drink this slowly." He hands me the cup.

I drink. It has an earthy bitter flavor. "Did she live?"

"My mother? Yes, she lived a long happy life."

The other children are watching us. Tutelo's eyes are wide, but Baji wears a suspicious expression, as though she fears the Dawnland Healer might be trying to kill me. Our people have been at war for so long, there is no trust between us. That's why the slightest, unintended insult becomes a reason for battle. Hehaka's beady eyes are fixed on my face like a hungry dog's.

I tip the cup up and swallow the last dregs. By the time I hand the cup back, I'm breathing better. The creeping numbness is fading.

Wakdanek examines my face. "Are you feeling a little better?"

"Yes. Thank you."

"You are most welcome, Odion." He begins tucking the bags back into his belt pouch. "In another hand of time, you should feel just fine. But if not, tell me, and I'll make a stronger potion."

He starts to rise, and I touch his hand. "Wait. Why did you help me? I am not of your people."

A smile warms his face. "As I told Sindak earlier, we all have an amnesia of the heart. We've forgotten that we were once the same people."

"We were?"

"Yes, our legends say it was a long time ago. But I believe we are still bound together by blood memory. You are my relative. It is my duty to help you."

As he uses the driftwood to push the coals back into his fire-starting pot, I rise to my feet. My legs are stronger. They no longer tremble with weakness.

"Is it all right if I go back to my friends now?"

"Definitely."

I tramp up the bank and slump down beside Tutelo again. My sister chews on her lower lip for a while before she asks, "What did he do?"

"He said I had ghost sickness. He gave me ghost medicine."

"Are you sure?" Baji asks. Her waist-length hair dances around her body like slender black arms. She appears to be waiting for me to keel over or fall into a frenzied fit.

"I feel better, Baji."

We all go silent when Wakdanek climbs back up the bank and passes us. Without a word, he returns to searching the ground for tracks.

"We'll see if it lasts," Baji replies skeptically. "I'm not sure about him yet."

"What do you mean?"

"I don't know, it's just . . . something. He's odd."

"He's from the Dawnland. They're all odd." I fill my lungs with a deep soothing breath.

Baji swivels around to watch the people roaming the abandoned camp. "I don't know why we have to stay on the riverbank," Baji says in frustration. "We were here last night. We might be able to help them."

Tutelo says, "Mother's afraid we'll disturb the sign. The fewer feet out there, the easier it is to track."

"Look around, Tutelo!" Baji waves a hand. "There's nothing to track. The ash makes it impossible." Her long black hair shimmers softly in the smoke-filtered sunlight. She wears an annoyed expression. "They need to start talking to us about the old woman, about how she thinks. They've hardly asked us any questions."

"They will. When they need to. Mother just . . ." I halt when the strange sound erupts again. Like a baby crying. "Do you hear that?"

I cock my head to listen. Baji and Tutelo instantly go still.

After several heartbeats, Tutelo says, "Maybe we should go see if we can find it?"

Baji turns all the way around to look up the bank toward the canoe landing fifty paces away. Hehaka doesn't move. He continues frowning down the river, as he has since just after dawn. It is as though he's waiting to see a canoe coming back for him. I don't know how to feel about this. I don't understand him. Does he want to be a slave? Does he like being hurt?

Tutelo says, "It's whimpering."

I rise to my feet. "Come on. I can't stand just sitting here. Let's go find it."

Baji points. "I think it's coming from the landing."

Tutelo scrambles to her feet. "I do, too."

Baji turns to Hehaka. "Are you coming, Hehaka? We're just going to walk to the landing."

"No," he says. "I'm waiting right here." His eyes are glued to the river.

I stand awkwardly for a time before I say, "Hehaka? She kept you as a slave for seven summers. Why do you want her to find you again?"

He looks at me with an agonized expression. His triangular, batlike face and big ears have a reddish hue. "She sucked out my soul," he whispers, and glances around. "Don't you remember? She sucked it out with that eagle-bone sucking tube and blew it into the little pot that she carries in her pack."

"I remember. So?"

Gannajero does this to punish children. She places her eagle-bone tube against their temples, sucks out their souls, and tells them that when they are far, far from home, she'll let their souls out of the pot. This is a terrible fate. It means that their afterlife souls will never be able to find their way home. They'll be chased through the forests forever by enemy ghosts.

Tears leak from the corners of Hehaka's eyes. "I have to find her. She promised that if I stayed with her, she would blow my soul back into my body before I die, then take care of me so I can find my way to the Land of the Dead to be with my ancestors."

"She's an old fool, Hehaka. She can't trap souls," Baji says and turns, expecting me to support her.

I hesitate before I say, "That's right. She's just an evil old woman."

"She's coming back for me," Hehaka says. "I swear it! I'm staying right here until I see her."

I shift my weight to my other foot, then say, "All right. We'll be back in a little while."

Tutelo leads the way, trotting down the bank with her long black braid swaying across her back. Baji and I walk side by side. Her jaw is clenched hard, and it makes her beautiful face appear misshapen.

"Why is he so concerned about the river?" Baji asks.

"I don't know."

"It doesn't make any sense, Odion. Don't you recall when we heard Gannajero's men say that she hated to travel the waterways because there were too many towns, men fishing, and other canoes? She feared someone would recognize her."

I step wide around an old lightning-riven stump. Its hollow interior is charred black, and charcoal stripes its bark. The only answer I can think of is, "Maybe Hehaka knows something we don't."

Baji stops dead in her tracks. I stop, too. Tutelo runs on ahead.

"You mean . . . you think she had a plan? And maybe Hehaka overheard her talking about it?"

"She always had a plan, Baji, and she talked openly in front of him."

"Then he may know many things that we don't."

"Probably."

When we start walking again, Baji stares at the ground with her brow furrowed, deep in thought.

The bank around the landing is strewn with refuse. I have seen this before. Warriors with packs of new plunder have to do something with their shabby old belongings, so they toss them out of the canoes just before they shove off. Threadbare packs and capes, blankets with too many stitched holes, and hide bags filled with who-knows-what litter the shore. The bank is marked with dozens of depressions where canoes rested last night.

Tutelo stops in the middle of the refuse. "Do you hear it?" she whispers.

Baji and I listen. The rushing of the river is loud. It's hard to hear anything else.

Then a soft muffled "woof" erupts.

A short distance ahead, I see a sack wiggle. "There's something alive in that sack."

We all run up the bank and encircle it. The sack flops over; then whimpering starts again.

I kneel by the sack. "It's a dog."

"Hurry, open it and let him out," Tutelo urges. "There's no telling how long he's been in there. He may be dying of thirst."

I take a few moments to gently pet the warm body inside. Barks erupt and the sack writhes as the dog frantically struggles for freedom.

"Hurry, Odion!"

"All right." I work to untie the tight laces. "But get ready. He might try to bite us."

Baji takes Tutelo's hand, preparing to drag her away if necessary. The sack is flopping around like a big dying fish. Yips and panicked barks fill the air.

"Easy, boy," I say.

As soon as I loosen the laces, a soft gray nose pokes up through the opening, then scrambling begins as the frightened puppy tries to force his way to freedom. "Wait!" I cry. "Let me get the sack off before you—"

The dog wriggles the top half of his lean body out into my lap and looks around with curious yellow eyes. I pull the rest of the hide sack off him and toss it away. He is young, maybe four or five moons old, and looks like a wolf pup.

"He's probably half dog," I say.

"Well, if he is, he doesn't look like it," Baji observes.

"He's a wolf puppy," Tutelo says. "Not a dog."

The puppy examines each of us, cautiously sniffs our scents. Finally, he wags his bushy gray tail.

Baji releases Tutelo's hand and leans down to examine the puppy. "Look at those yellow eyes, Odion. Tutelo's right. He's all wolf."

When the wind blows a lock of Baji's long black hair, the puppy lets out a surprised yip, leaps up, and clamps it in his jaws. As he tries to rip it out by the roots, he growls ferociously.

"Hey!" Baji tugs to get it away from him. "Let go!"

"Puppy, no!" I say. "Stop it."

He knows the word "no." Puppy immediately drops the hair and looks up at me with hurt eyes.

I stroke his silken gray head. "He's smart."

Baji tentatively extends a hand, lets him smell it, then pats his side. "He's also pretty. I'll bet one of the warriors stole him from Bog Willow Village last night and was carrying him home to his children."

"But why didn't he just tie a rope around his neck and lead him? It would have been easier."

Tutelo's pretty face is tight with concentration. "I'll bet the puppy was supposed to be dinner."

Roasted dog is delicious, and among our people, it is the special meal cooked for victorious warriors when they return home. There's nothing better than tender puppy.

"Maybe, but it's also possible that the puppy attacked the warrior when he killed his master, and the warrior was on his way to drown him," I suggest.

"I don't think so." Baji shakes her head. "If I were the warrior, I'd have just clubbed him to death. I wouldn't have taken the time to put him in a sack and carry him down to the river."

Tutelo edges forward and pets the puppy's silken back. "He's the color of a ghost," she says. "Maybe his name was Ghost."

"Or Oki," Baji suggests.

We both turn to stare at her.

Oki are Spirits. They inhabit powerful beings, including the seven Thunderers, rivers, certain rocks, valiant warriors, even lunatics. The most powerful oki is Brother Sky, because he controls the seasons and the waves on the sea. Oki can bring either good luck or bad. People who possess supernatural powers—shamans, witches—are believed to have a companion Spirit, an oki, whose power they can call upon to help them.

"He definitely has some special power," I say, "or we'd never have found him. He called us to him. Oki sounds like a good name."

Tutelo shakes her head vehemently. "I don't like that. What if somebody thinks he's an evil Spirit? If somebody's having a bad day, that name could cost him his life."

"Well . . . then think of something else."

Puppy licks my hand and staggers down to the river. He drinks with his eyes half-closed, as though deeply grateful for the water.

"I wonder how long he was in that sack?" Tutelo looks up at me.

"I don't know. Bog Willow Village was attacked yesterday. So maybe twenty or thirty hands of time."

"It's a wonder he has the strength to walk." Baji studies him carefully. "Odion, what's going to happen to him if we show him to the others?"

"Mother and Father will let us keep him," Tutelo says with a happy smile. "I'm sure they will."

I am not so sure. Tutelo wants the puppy. Probably, we all do. After the horrors of the last moon, the puppy is like a special gift from the Faces of the Forest.

I rise to my feet. "Before we get too excited, let's see if he'll follow us." As I start to walk down the shore, I call, "Come on, Puppy. Come."

The puppy cocks his head, listening carefully to my voice, as though trying to detect anything threatening. He takes another drink from the river, and the dim rays of sunlight that penetrate the haze catch in his fur. He seems to be outlined with white fire.

"It's all right, pup. We're not going to hurt you. Come on, boy." I pat my leg and walk away again.

The young wolf wags his tail, but he's still not sure about this.

"Puppy, come on, boy." I clap my hands.

When he hasn't moved, Tutelo says, "Maybe he wants to go back to the forest to find his pack?"

Baji scowls at the puppy. "No, he doesn't." Sharply, she says, "Puppy. Get over here! *Right now!*"

The puppy's ears prick. He trots forward to stand at her side, wagging his tail sheepishly. Baji gives me a pleased look. "He belonged to a woman."

I study the puppy. He's gazing up adoringly at Baji, waiting for her next command.

"Can you get him to follow you, Baji?"

"Come on, dog," she orders.

As we walk down the shore toward Hehaka, the wolf happily trots along at Baji's heels. Whenever he lags, she scolds him, and he catches up in a heartbeat.

Tutelo runs forward and slips her hand into mine. I clutch it tightly. Love swells my chest. Without my sister's bravery, I could not have survived the past moon. I would have given up. So many times, all I wanted was to lie down in the forest and die. As I think about it, Manidos' smile flits behind my eyes—*Lie down, boy*—and my steps falter. I release Tutelo's hand and lift my palms again. The numb stinging has returned. "No, it never happened," I repeat, barely audible, even to me.

"What's wrong, Odion?" Tutelo whispers. She stares up at me.

"Nothing. I just . . . need a moment."

. . . Stop crying or I'll cut your heart out.

I think about the taste of the ghost medicine and concentrate on seeing Manidos' mouth searing and charring, turning to black ash. With it, the sound of his voice dies. *Forget, forget, forget.*

Baji arrives with Puppy. Softly, she says, "Are you all right?"

I inhale a shuddering breath. "Yes. Let's go."

We continue down the bank. Father looks up from where he's crouched and sees us with the puppy. He frowns.

"I don't like that look," Baji says.

Father rises and walks toward us. His black brows plunge down over his nose. Across the camp, the other warriors turn to watch him. Sindak wipes his sleeve over his hooked nose and follows Father.

When Father arrives, he props his hands on his hips and glances unhappily at Puppy, who wags his tail.

"Where did you find the wolf?" Father asks.

"In a sack by the canoe landing," I say. "He was dying of thirst."

"Um-hmm."

Sindak walks up behind Father. His lean face is streaked with black, and a big splotch decorates his square jaw. He glances at Father. "What are you mad about? They caught lunch. Bring him here, Baji; I'll club him for you." He pulls his war club from his belt.

"He's not lunch!" Baji says, and stands protectively in front of Puppy. "His name is Gitchi."

I blink, wondering where that name came from.

Tutelo runs to stand beside Baji, shielding the puppy. "We found him, Father. He's ours."

Sindak turns to Father. "They gave him a name, Gonda."

The lines around Father's eyes tighten. "So I heard."

"Gitchi" seems to sense that something's wrong. He sinks onto his haunches and his tail thumps the ground, but it's an uncertain gesture, as though he's saying, *Everybody's looking at me, and the voices have gone tense. Please don't hurt me.*

"We can't take a dog with us," Sindak says. "Having the children along is bad enough."

Father's gaze touches Tutelo's, and Baji's. They give him a pleading look. He does not look at me. Instead, he turns away and slowly shakes his head. "This is Koracoo's decision, not mine."

"Can't face it, eh?"

Half-angry, Father says, "It's just not my responsibility, Sindak. Koracoo is war chief."

"Oh, well, of course." Sindak drags out the last word, as though he means exactly the opposite.

Father glowers at Sindak.

"Father," I say, "please. I'll take care of him. I won't let him get in the way."

"It's not my decision, Son. Ask your mother."

As the other warriors notice us, they begin to migrate toward the shore. Mother is the last to look up from the ground. When she sees everyone congregated on the bank, her brows lift, and she stalks toward us. Her red cape sways around her long legs.

Wakdanek frowns at Mother but doesn't say a word. He's clearly waiting to see what everyone else says before he ventures an opinion about the puppy.

War Chief Cord squints at Gitchi. His hood has fallen back, revealing his mostly shaved head and bristly roach of black hair. The snake tattoos on his cheeks seem to coil tighter. "What's the problem?"

Father waves a hand. "The children found a dog. We were just discussing—"

Towa walks up, spies the puppy, and says, "Good work! Who caught the dog? I'm starved."

"He is *not* lunch," Baji says unpleasantly.

As Towa glances around the circle in confusion, his long black braid saws up and down his left shoulder. "No?"

Sindak gives Towa a broad smile and explains, "His name is Gitchi."

The puppy wags his tail, as though he already knows his name.

Towa darkly murmurs, "Oh. They named it."

Mother walks into the circle and stands between Sindak and Towa. "I take it we've all decided to stop searching for Gannajero's trail? Why?"

"It's my fault," Father says. "I noticed the children had a dog and came over to investigate."

I step forward and look up into Mother's face. She is very tall, as tall as War Chief Cord, and her small nose and full lips are coated with ash. Her short black hair falls over her cheeks. "What is it, Odion?"

"Mother, we found Gitchi in a sack by the canoe landing. He's a good boy. Can we keep him?"

Mother expels a breath. "What did your father say?"

"He said it was your decision."

Mother glances at Father, and he reacts as though he's been impaled by a war lance. His shoulders hunch forward. "You're the war chief, Koracoo. Not me."

She stares at him for such a long time, Father starts to fidget. He folds his arms, then refolds them. I notice that Sindak is smothering a smile.

I say, "Mother, we'll take good care of him. You won't have to do anything. I promise. Baji, Tutelo, and I will feed him and make sure he stays out of trouble."

Gitchi peeks out from between Baji's and Tutelo's legs and whimpers softly. Tutelo pets his head. She whispers, "Don't be afraid, Gitchi. Everything's all right." The dog licks her hand, and Tutelo smiles.

War Chief Cord says, "Some brave soul has to make a decision. I'm glad it's not me," and walks away to start searching for a sign again.

Mother studies the dog's yellow eyes. "He's a wolf pup, do you know that? They're not like dogs, Odion. They're unpredictable. You could wake up in the middle of the night with his teeth embedded in your throat."

"I'll take that chance."

"Me, too, Mother," Tutelo says proudly.

Baji just glares at Mother, as though upset that she's considering saying no.

"And what will you do in the heat of battle, Odion? If I tell you to run, will you? Or will you try to protect your dog?"

I'm not sure I can answer this. I look into Gitchi's sparkling yellow eyes. He's probably smart enough to take care of himself when he's a little older, but now? "I'll run, Mother. I promise. And I mean it."

Tutelo jumps up and down. "Please, Mother?"

Mother's eyes narrow. "All right, but if that wolf ever growls at anyone without cause it will be Odion's responsibility to club him. Understood?"

I swallow hard and look at Gitchi. When our gazes meet, he nervously pants with his tongue hanging out. "Yes. I understand."

I smile, and the puppy trots forward, cuts a wide swath around Mother, and huddles against my legs. I reach down to pet his head. "It's all right. You're safe."

His tail wags, and he licks my hand as though he's thanking me.

Mother says, "Now that we've settled that, it's time we had a discussion about last night."

Baji says, "It's about time you asked us for our opinions."

Mother gives Baji a look that would make most people melt into the earth, but Baji just stares back.

Mother turns to call, "Hehaka, come over here, please."

Though he clearly doesn't wish to leave his place on the bank, he rises and walks to stand beside me, but he keeps longingly glancing back at the river.

Mother props CorpseEye on her shoulder, and the two black dots on the red cobble head seem to be staring right at me, as though in some strange way judging me.

"Where was the last place you saw Gannajero last night?"

I think about it. "The last place I saw her was in the middle of the camp, negotiating with the Flint Trader. She was buying children."

Baji nods. "That's the last place I saw her, too."

"Me, too," Tutelo agrees.

Hehaka just nods morosely. "She was getting ready to leave. I could tell."

"How do you know that?" Mother asks.

Hehaka nervously wets his lips. "She'd selected all the children she wanted. She was just haggling over the price. I've seen her do it a hundred times. Once she pays, she leaves."

War Chief Cord overhears and walks back with a grimace on his face. "I never saw a woman Trading with Tagohseh last night. There was a man—"

"Lupan," Hehaka says. "That was her."

Cord's expression slackens. "She dressed as a man? Are you sure?"

We all nod, and I say, "She was always afraid someone might recognize her and kill her."

Cord swings around and stares at the canoe landing. Mother follows his gaze. "What's wrong?"

"Blessed gods," he whispers. "I saw her leave. She took two canoes, loaded the children and several bags of goods, and ordered her men to shove off."

Mother seems to have stopped breathing. "What time was that?"

Cord rubs his forehead. "Just before we left. I'd say around two hands of time after nightfall."

Hehaka's batlike nose wiggles as he sniffs the air. His beady eyes have a feral sheen. "If she'd known I was with you, she'd have never left. She'd have sent men out to hunt for me and bring me back."

Mother and Father ignore him. They speak softly to each other while Cord, Sindak, and Towa nod. Wakdanek stands off to the side, as though he knows he's an outsider.

Mother says, "Cord, how many men did she have with her?"

"Not many. Five or six."

Father says, "Then we're pretty evenly matched."

Mother takes two steps toward the river. "If she canoed all night long, by now she's deep into the country of the People Who Separated."

"Or . . . ," Father says, "she could have stopped at any one of a thousand places and be headed overland in a direction we can't even guess."

Towa spreads his arms. "Think about this. Even if we can find someone to sell us canoes, which I doubt—"

"I'll get us canoes," Wakdanek says. He stands two paces away with his arms tightly folded across his chest. "There are several hidden in the forest not far from here. We keep them there just in case—"

Sindak interrupts, "We have a much better chance of finding her if we split up and walk both sides of the riverbank. If we can locate the place where she came ashore—"

"That's silly," Father says. "There will be hundreds of places where canoes have put ashore. The Dawnland People ply the Quill River constantly. How will we know which trail is hers?"

"Gonda's right," Cord says with a firm nod. "It's better to take our chances on the river, ask the people we see if a woman meeting her description passed by."

"And you actually believe they'll tell us?" Sindak looks Cord up and down like a rotten piece of venison. "Within two or three hands of time, every village along this river will know that a war party composed of Flint and Mountain warriors destroyed Bog Willow Village. They're far more likely to shoot us on sight. We should—"

"Wakdanek?" Mother turns to face the big raw-boned Dawnland Healer.

Wakdanek hesitates for a moment. "I will do my best to explain our presence before they kill us, but I make no guarantees."

Silence descends like a granite blanket. The only sound is the river rushing by.

Worry carves lines at the corners of Mother's eyes. She pulls CorpseEye from her shoulder and stares hard at the war club. CorpseEye frequently warns Mother and guides her steps. I've heard her tell magnificent stories about it when she returns from war walks. Mother's head cocks, and she swivels to face the landing.

War Chief Cord follows her gaze; then he glances back at CorpseEye. "You keep looking at your club, then at the landing. Why?"

Mother says only, "I cast my voice for the river."

"Mine, also," Cord says.

Wakdanek nods in agreement. "It's our best chance."

Father, Sindak, and Towa shake their heads almost in unison.

Father is the first to speak: "I think it's a bad idea, but I follow my war chief."

Sindak and Towa shift uneasily.

At last, Sindak says, "It's suicide."

Towa expels a breath. "Yes. So, let's go."

All eyes turn to Wakdanek. His voice is soft, as if he fears to tip some fragile balance. "Come. I'll show you where the canoes are hidden."

Twenty-one

By late afternoon, the mist vanished. A soft blanket of sunlight dappled the passing aspens and striped maples. Wrass squinted against the squares of light that struck his eyes like fists. The two girls in the canoe stared out at the forest with taut expressions, probably hoping with all their hearts that around the next bend, they'd see Dawnland warriors bursting from the forest with their bows drawn.

The dream—he knew from experience—kept despair at bay.

Auma sat next to Wrass with her hands balled in her lap.

Wrass asked, "Are you all right?"

The girl turned. Her chin-length black hair had sleeked down around her face, making her broad nose appear even wider. "I'm hungry, Wrass. When will they stop to feed us?"

Wrass eased into a sitting position. The day was cold and bracing, but he felt a little better. His headache was almost bearable. "The warriors have been paddling for ten hands of time. They'll stop to rest soon."

"And then they'll feed us?" The girl's voice choked, as though she was on the verge of crying.

Wrass reached out and squeezed her shoulder. "They may feed us, but probably not. You need to be strong. Never let your enemy see weakness. They will use it against you."

Auma glanced at the warriors paddling behind them; then her gaze drifted to the bow, where Gannajero and Kotin huddled together. They spoke in low ominous tones. As the canoe passed beneath overhanging willows, cold blue shadows darkened their faces.

She whispered, "Wrass, I thought I saw a canoe following us."

Wrass stiffened. The possibility was more painful than his headache. Hope could be a knife in the belly—and she had probably imagined it. "What kind of canoe?"

"I didn't get a very good look at it. It might have been birch bark. Do you think—?"

"How long ago did you see it?"

"Two hands of time, maybe a little longer."

Wrass considered that. It might be more of the warriors heading home from the big camp last night. "Did you see any markings on the canoe?"

Auma shook her head. "I only caught a glimpse of it as we cut around a bend. When the man saw me looking at him, he immediately dragged his oar and disappeared. I think he was trying to stay hidden."

"Man? One man?"

Auma spread her hands uncertainly. "I only saw one."

Wrass let his gaze drift to where Conkesema slept on the packs. Old leaves had swirled into the boat and stuck in her black hair. He prayed her souls were walking in serene meadows far away from here.

"Do you think it's a war party?" Auma whispered.

"One man is not a war party."

"But he could be a scout. Maybe once he knows for sure that we're here, he'll turn around and go get a war party? My parents may be with them."

Auma's gaze bored into Wrass, silently begging him to say yes, that they were moments away.

He couldn't.

As the day warmed, the scent of the river grew stronger. It had a bitter tang, a mixture of rotting leaves and frost-killed plants. Wrass leaned over the gunwale to look past the bow to the canoe ahead of them. Zateri's boat was now in the lead, with Waswan sitting in the bow. Zateri knelt in the middle next to the Flint girl. Her mouth was moving, probably speaking gently, trying to ease the girl's fears.

"Ho, Waswan!" Kotin cupped a hand to his mouth and called, "Put ashore! We need to talk!"

Waswan swiveled around and lifted a hand to indicate that he'd heard; then he gestured to the warriors paddling in the rear, and they guided the canoe to the bank. At the sight of Waswan's ugly face, hatred flushed Wrass' veins. The man was sapling-thin, with dark inhuman eyes and a knobby nose, obviously broken in one too many fights. Waswan had enjoyed it as he'd beaten Wrass half to death.

Someday I'll repay the favor.

The man jumped onto the sand, followed by Akio and Ojib, who leaped out and finished shoving the canoe up onto the shore.

Wrass braced his hands on the gunwale as their canoe grounded next to the first. Kotin and Gannajero climbed out while the new man, Dakion, got into the water to continue pushing the canoe's bow up onto the bank. When he'd finished, Dakion waded alongside Wrass and growled, "Stay in the boat. All of you."

Wrass looked into Dakion's bark-colored eyes and nodded. He had broad muscular shoulders and enormous hands. A thick scar marred his chin. Dakion glowered at the children, then stalked up the bank toward where Gannajero and Kotin stood.

"What are they talking about?" Auma asked.

"I don't know, but if there really is a canoe traveling behind us, they might have seen it."

"So . . . what does that mean? Are they going to try to ambush the man?"

Wrass shrugged. "We'll know soon enough."

Gannajero and her five warriors formed a circle ten paces from the shore near a copse of maple saplings. As the old woman listened to Kotin, she sucked her lips; her mouth resembled a shriveled berry. The greasy twists of graying hair that hung around her wrinkled face flapped in the breeze blowing up the river.

Wrass took the opportunity to crawl across the canoe and call, "Zateri? Are you all right?"

She worked her way down the length of the gunwale and sat down less than six hands away. "We're all right. How are you feeling?"

"My headache is better, thanks to you."

"Keep chewing the willow twigs, Wrass. I'll gather more if I can."

"Have you heard any of Gannajero's conversations? What's she so worried about?"

Zateri nervously licked her lips and leaned as far out of her canoe as she could. He did the same. From less than three hands away, she hissed, "I'm not sure, but when we rounded that last bend, I heard her tell Kotin that she thought she'd glimpsed—"

The Flint girl in Zateri's canoe leaped out and made a run for it, dashing away through the forest. Branches cracked in her wake.

"No! Neche, no!" Zateri jumped to her feet.

Auma got on her knees as though ready to bolt after Neche, and Wrass leaped for her and knocked her flat in the bottom of the canoe.

"Get off me, you fool!" Auma shouted. "Let me go! This is our *chance*!"

Gannajero shouted, "Kotin, find her! Make sure the other children understand."

Kotin nocked his bow and charged away into the trees. Thirty heartbeats later a shriek silenced the birdsong. As though nothing had happened, Gannajero returned to her discussion with her warriors.

Wrass released Auma and sat up. His head thundered. He leaned back and fought to slow his pounding heart by taking deep even breaths. Nausea tickled the back of his throat.

Conkesema and Auma stared at the place where Neche had disappeared. The shadows of swaying branches painted the ground.

"She escaped," Auma said. "I should have run after her. I would have if you hadn't stopped me!"

Wrass said, "If she escaped, what was that scream?"

Fifty heartbeats later, Kotin returned dragging the girl by her long black hair. An arrow stuck out of her chest, and blood soaked her dress.

Auma stood up to get a better look. "Is she . . . is she . . . ?"

"Never try to run away alone," Wrass said. "Never."

Kotin hauled the girl to the sand in front of the canoes and dropped her body; then his lips parted, revealing broken yellow teeth. He smiled at the children. "Which one of you is her friend?"

Conkesema was the only one brave enough to stand up. She was shaking. Her pretty face had gone pale.

Kotin said, "So, you were her only friend, eh? That's interesting. Well, later, I'm going to cut this piece of dead meat apart and scatter the bits for the wolves. Do you want to help me?"

Conkesema's knees failed. She slumped into the canoe with tears streaming down her face.

"Answer me!" he ordered. "Or I'll—"

"Stop it, Kotin," Zateri said. "She hasn't spoken a word since her village was attacked."

Kotin laughed at Zateri's bravado. "You're getting too bold, girl. Soon, I'm going to have to teach you a lesson."

Zateri swallowed hard and stiffened her spine to keep her head from trembling. Kotin chuckled, turned his back, and stalked over to take his place at Gannajero's side again.

Auma stared at Neche's dead body as though stunned. "I can't believe it," she whispered. "You saved my life, Wrass. I—"

"Shh!" Zateri hushed them. "Listen."

Gannajero's voice was low but clear: ". . . around to the north." She used her knotted finger to show Waswan the path she wanted him to take through the trees. Next, she turned and fixed Kotin with obsidian-dark eyes. "You circle to the east. If we play this right, they won't have a chance."

Both men trotted into the shadows.

Gannajero stood for a moment. It was as though she'd suddenly been turned to stone. She wasn't breathing. Her eyes didn't blink. As though her souls had fled, leaving a lifeless shell of flesh behind, she just stared.

The other warriors—Ojib, Akio, and Dakion—kept shifting, waiting for instructions. She stood like that so long that a dribble of saliva leaked from the corner of her mouth and ran down her wrinkled chin.

Finally, Dakion clenched his fists and walked toward her. "Listen, old woman, we need to—"

"No." It was more growl than word. Still staring at some vast nothingness, she ordered, "I want you and Ojib to hide in that thicket of brush fifty paces north along the shore. Kill anyone you see. Akio, take the children down the southern trail. Keep quiet. Don't move unless I call out to you."

The pudgy, florid-faced young warrior hurried to the canoes and hissed, "Get out. Now! Come with me." He nocked his bow, pulled it back halfway, and aimed it in their general direction.

The other children scrambled from the canoe. It took Wrass longer. The instant he stood up, the world spun in a blur of colors. He had to grab the gunwale to keep his balance.

"Hurry it up, boy!" Akio snarled.

"I—I'm . . . coming." Wrass carefully made his way down the length of the canoe, braced a hand on the gunwale, and eased over the side onto the shore. The damp sand sank beneath his moccasins.

"Move!" Akio aimed his bow at the trail that led into the trees.

Zateri marched out front, heading into the cold forest shadows. Everyone fell into line behind her. Wrass brought up the rear, walking just in front of Akio.

Behind him, he heard Akio say, "If any of the others try to run, I'll know you're responsible, boy, and I'll kill you first. Do you understand?"

Wrass spread his arms in a gesture of surrender.

Twenty-two

Odion

I sit in the rear of the canoe, holding Gitchi in my lap, petting him. His soft gray fur soothes me.

Tutelo sleeps soundly on the packs in front of me, and beyond her, Mother kneels in the bow with her paddle fluidly stroking the water. Far ahead of us, Father's canoe, carrying Hehaka and Baji, slices through the mist, appearing and disappearing with ghostly regularity. Father sits in the bow, while War Chief Cord and Towa paddle in the rear. I'm not sure, but I think both Hehaka and Baji are asleep. I can only see the top halves of their bodies propped on the packs, but their eyes look closed.

I should be sleeping, too. I'm so tired I can barely think, but my body refuses. Every time I stretch out, my hands and feet twitch like a clubbed dog's. Perhaps when all this is over the terror will leak out of my muscles and I will finally be able to rest.

I glance back at Sindak and Wakdanek, who ride behind me. Their oars pull hard at the current, driving us forward. From the moment we shoved the canoes into the water, we've been shooting down the river like needle-nosed gars. Twice today Wakdanek has asked if we could stop for a while to rest. Each time, Mother answered in a clipped voice, "No. Whatever you must do, do it over the side."

Wakdanek wears a stern expression. He is a big man with wide shoulders. His facial bones stick out, and his brown eyes seem to have sunken into their sockets. Bushy black eyebrows create a single line across his forehead.

He has been watching me.

I do not know what to make of this. Every time I look up to meet his gaze, he shifts his eyes, as though in silent apology for staring at me again.

Sindak says, "Are you all right, Odion?"

"Yes." I pet Gitchi. The dog is trying to sleep. He sighs, vaguely annoyed by my constant attention.

Sindak gives me a nod, as though we are speaking man-to-man. He's never treated me like a child, and I find this a curious relief. Splotches, mostly sooty handprints, darken his cape. He has tied his shoulder-length black hair back with a piece of leather. He must have seen eighteen or nineteen summers, but he seems older to me.

Wakdanek is staring at me again. I turn, and he instantly looks away.

"Why do you keep looking at me?"

Wakdanek's heavy brow pinches. "I'm worried about you."

"It's all right. I'm better."

Wakdanek doesn't answer for a long time. Finally, he says, "Are you? I suspect you've endured many terrible things since the attack on Yellowtail Village."

I scratch Gitchi behind the ears. I don't know what Wakdanek wants. Does he expect me to tell him what I've seen? I don't even want to remember, let alone speak of these things. I swear I will never tell anyone what I've been through. If I can, I will forget it myself.

I silently stare back at him.

The crow's-feet at the corners of his eyes deepen. His voice is kind when he says, "It might help to talk about it."

Sindak orders, "Leave him alone."

Wakdanek swivels around. "I don't think you understand, my friend. We all need to talk about—"

"No," Sindak says firmly. "We don't."

"Maybe you don't, but children are more fragile. They need—"

"The moment you tell anyone about a traumatic event they never let you forget. Every time you look into their eyes, you see it. Oh, they may just squint slightly, or perhaps their smile is just a little more sympathetic than it used to be, but you know they're thinking about it, and so you have to, too." He glares at Wakdanek. "Believe me, there are things a man needs to forget. Leave Odion alone."

Wakdanek returns to paddling. Deep swirls flow away from his oar and drift through the cool green water behind us. We enter a section of the river where giant hickories and maples lean over us. Birdsong fills the air. I see finches fluttering in the branches. Gitchi sees them too. A low growl rumbles in this throat.

"They're just birds, Gitchi. They can't hurt you."

Gitchi props his nose on my leg and wags his tail.

But my gaze clings to Sindak. What has he seen that he needs to forget? He is a warrior; perhaps that is answer enough.

I say, "I'm going to be a warrior when I grow up."

Sindak nods approvingly. "Good. We need more men to help protect our peoples."

A smile creeps over my face, and my heart feels lighter. "I have a bow at home. Father made it for me."

"Are you good with it?"

Shame makes my shoulders hunch up. "No. My friend Wrass can shoot a bird in the head at fifty paces. He's the best shot of all the boys in our village. But I'm going to get better."

"I know you will. Just practice, Odion. That's all it takes. If you spend two hands of time every day—"

"Yes, practice," Wakdanek interrupts, "but please remember that the best preparation for battle is a heart at peace."

A heart at peace. Somehow, deep inside me, I know I need to remember this. Silently, I mouth the words.

Sindak gives Wakdanek an askance look. "That's ridiculous. The best preparation for battle is an enormous quiver of really sharp arrows, and even sharper wits."

"But . . . my mother is a peacemaker," I say. "At least that's what Father calls her."

"Yes," Sindak replies with exaggerated politeness. "I've heard him. I never knew any word could carry such loathing until I heard Gonda call Koracoo a 'peacemaker.'"

Wakdanek frowns. For a long time, he just paddles. I can't decide whether he looks annoyed or disheartened.

Bravely, I say, "I want peace."

"That's wise," Sindak responds. "But to get it and keep it, you have to be willing to fight for it. You—"

"Why do you say such things?" Wakdanek asks in a plaintive voice. "Don't you know that everything in the world is related? People, animals, trees, stones, the Faces of the Forest, the Cloud People? We are all One." He ships his paddle and extends his hands to Sindak. "Every time I lay my fingers upon a branch, the tree recognizes me. If I listen, I can hear her calling my name, trying to reach across the gulf that separates us and gently touch my heart so that I will know she is my grandmother and means me no harm."

Sindak says, "That's usually when the first ax blow lands."

Wakdanek stares at him.

Sindak appears lazily amused, as though he's failed some test of intelligence and is proud of it. Wakdanek, however, has a sober worried expression.

I say, "Grandmother Jigonsaseh gave me a milkweed seed once. She told me that if I blew the seed from my palm, my breath would never stop. She said it would carry across the world to touch the cheek of a deer, and then rise into the sky to sail with the Cloud People. That's what you mean, isn't it, Wakdanek?"

The Healer smiles. "Yes. Connected. Related. That's why we must name our enemies carefully, because killing the enemy has only one outcome: We kill a part of our own soul. And by doing so, we cripple the world itself."

"The world is already a cripple. Who cares?" Sindak says.

Wakdanek leans back as though utterly confounded by Sindak. "I care. Very much."

"That's nice. However, sometimes your enemies deserve to die. I mean, don't you want revenge against the people who killed your wife and took your daughter captive?"

Pain flickers in Wakdanek's eyes. He clenches his jaw for a time. At last, he answers, "Since we are all related, Sindak, right now the entire world is resonating with my grief. Even the souls of my enemies. They've already harmed themselves far more than I ever can." His gaze flicks to War Chief Cord.

Sindak glances at Cord, too; then his brows lift. His expression says that the Healer is either lying or stupid. "Well, Wakdanek, I feel better for you. However, if the same thing ever happens to my family, I plan to hunt down my enemy, chop him to pieces, and feed him to my dogs. And since we are all related, I expect that while I watch each bite slide down their throats, the world will also resonate with my thrill of justice being done."

Mother has apparently been listening. She turns halfway around in the bow, and says, "Less talking and more paddling would be helpful."

Sindak and Wakdanek both dig their oars into the water, and the canoe flies forward like an arrow. Ahead of us, there is a wide bend lined with leafless prickly ashes. As the current sweeps us around the curve, I see a few shriveled red-brown fruits still clinging to the twigs. The boat abruptly sways and leaps as we maneuver around submerged rocks. Cold spray hits me in the face. When we are through, the river spreads out again and calms down.

Wakdanek says, "We should talk more, Sindak. Perhaps, in time, we can find something we agree upon."

"I doubt it, but I'll hear you out." Sindak drags his paddle and guides the canoe around a floating log.

Wakdanek shakes his head.

They stop talking.

Gitchi grunts and squirms as I shift to lie down on the packs. I hold him against my chest. While I gaze out at the sunlight in the treetops, Gitchi licks my chin. I feel safer with him close, as though he is already guarding me. I let my eyes fall closed.

Perhaps, if I hold the puppy tightly, my muscles will stop twitching long enough for me to get some sleep.

Twenty-three

Akio herded the children down the leaf-covered trail into the forest. Twenty paces from the canoes, he found a small clearing in the brush surrounded by towering sycamores. The massive branches cast dark crisscrossing shadows across the rocky ground.

He ordered, "Lie down, all of you. Flatten out on the ground and be quiet!" At the age of sixteen summers, he was the lowest-status warrior here. He couldn't afford to fail. If even one child escaped, the old woman would surely kill him; then he'd never make it home. And he wanted to go home, badly.

The children stretched out across the bed of frosty leaves, but the hawk-faced boy, Wrass, kept staring at Akio. How did the child have the strength to move? His face was so battered and bruised his own parents wouldn't recognize him. His left eye was swollen almost closed, and dried blood covered his skull. Part of his scalp had been torn loose. It would be a miracle if he didn't lose patches of hair. Akio had seen that happen to badly beaten men. The loose patches of scalp died, leaving strips of gray bone showing in the middle of what was left of their hair.

He glanced back toward the clearing where Gannajero stood. He was doing his job. He'd proven himself, and just as he'd been told, after two moons of being allied with Gannajero he'd already acquired enough wealth to live comfortably for the rest of his life. *I get to keep that. That's what* he *said. And everything I get before I go home. It's all mine.*

Just the thought of what he'd do with such wealth left him practically panting to please Gannajero, to keep her from suspecting . . .

Zateri, who lay beside Wrass, cupped a hand to his ear and whispered something. Wrass glanced at Akio, then subtly nodded.

Akio wet his chapped lips. Had the children seen something? He drew his bowstring back a little tighter and examined every shadow.

Wrass turned to whisper, "He could just be a lone fisherman, Akio. Why don't you leave him be?"

Akio stepped forward. "Didn't I tell you not to talk? Do you want to die, boy?"

Akio aimed his bow at Wrass' head, but his gaze jerked back to Gannajero. She was moving, tiptoeing toward the canoes like a hunting weasel. When she reached the edge of the water, she hesitated— seemed to be cataloging the contents of the canoes, looking for something. Finally, she climbed into one and started shuffling through the packs.

"What's she looking for?" he whispered a little too loudly. Every child turned to look at him.

Gannajero tore open Dakion's pack. Dakion's had a white beaver painted on the front, and he could see it even from this distance. As she searched the pack, Gannajero grunted softly. The longer Akio watched her, the more his fingers tightened on his nocked bow . . . and he wondered if she'd really seen a canoe following them, or if this was just an excuse to go through Dakion's pack.

She continued her ransacking for a few more heartbeats, then made a satisfied smacking sound with her lips, pulled something from the pack, and tucked it into her belt pouch.

"The old witch is clever, I'll say that for her."

While she glanced around, she neatly tied the pack's laces and replaced it exactly as she'd found it.

"Do you see anyone yet?" Wrass whispered.

"Stop talking!" Akio glared at him. He suspected the boy was doing that on purpose, to rattle him or distract him. "The next word out of your mouth is going to be your last. Or maybe I'll shoot one of your friend—"

His voice faded when three faint shouts echoed through the trees. Gannajero leaped to her feet and crouched like a hunting stork. At the same instant, Akio glimpsed a shadow moving stealthily amid the dense buttonbushes—less than ten paces to Gannajero's right.

He considered shouting, but what if it was Kotin returning to report? She'd told him to keep quiet, not to move until she called out to him.

The shadow stopped at the edge of the leafless shrubs. The slender trunks stood twice the man's height and hid him almost completely. He . . .

"Your brother sends his greetings, Gannajero."

As her gaze darted over the thicket, her wrinkled face hardened into frightening lines. "What do you want? Who are you?"

"Your brother says he's very sorry he missed you at the big warriors' camp last night. He asked me to deliver a message."

"He was there? At the camp?"

"He tracked a traitor to the camp. A man who left with a Trader who specialized in child slaves."

Akio's pulse pounded so loudly he could scarcely breathe. What was the old man up to?

"Your brother offers a Trade. If you give him both of them," the messenger said, *"he will give you what you desire most."*

Gannajero vented a low ugly laugh. "He's too selfish to give me what is rightly mine. It would cost him everything he holds dear. And if he was in the camp last night, he's probably the one who poisoned my stew pot." As she straightened, the tendons in her wattled neck stood out like cords stretched too tight.

Akio watched the messenger silently back away through the shrubs and move into the deep forest shadows. He tried to keep an eye on the man, but in less than five heartbeats, he was gone.

Gannajero kept her eyes focused on the brush, as though she thought he was still there, and a slow expression of pure hatred carved her face. "And if he's serious about this offer, where's the *proof?* He knows I have to see it!"

When no answer came, she clenched her fists and marched closer to the buttonbushes. "Tell him I *want* it!"

The hawk-faced boy, Wrass, jerked slightly, as though he'd been bitten by something in the old leaves. He didn't say anything for a time; then he boldly sat up, stared Akio in the face, and said, "You should tell her he's gone, before she—"

"Shut your mouth, boy!" Akio hissed. "Didn't I tell you to keep quiet or I'd—"

From the corner of his eye, Akio saw the arrow gleam in the sunlight as it flashed through the trees. He let out a shriek and threw himself forward. When it drove fire into his back, Akio staggered drunkenly.

From the trees, a faint whisper said, *The old man sends you his greetings as well, Akio. He thanks you for your service, but says you're no longer useful.*

Gannajero barked, "What's happening?" and started running toward him. "Dakion? Ojib? Get over here!"

Blood dripped from the black chert point that stuck out of Akio's chest. For several moments, he didn't understand. His legs went wobbly as pain seared his chest. The bow dropped from his numb fingers and landed silently in the frozen leaves.

Wrass cried, "This is our chance. Get up! *Run!*" He scrambled to his feet. The children shot away through the forest like a flock of frightened doves.

Akio was still on his feet when Gannajero arrived, breathing hard, her face twisted with rage. "What did he say? Tell me quickly, before you die!"

A smile quivered Akio's lips. "Boy . . . must have seen . . . distracted me."

"What did the man *say?*"

Akio toppled to the ground. With his last strength, he reached out. "Help . . . Gan—"

"Tell me what he said!"

". . . followed . . . me."

"Blessed gods. You led him right to me? You worthless fool!" she shouted.

"Gannajero!" Ojib cried. "Where are you?"

"Over here," she called back.

Feeling was draining from Akio's body, but he managed to squirm onto his side, to spit frothy blood from his mouth. It created a brilliant scarlet pool on the frozen leaves.

Gannajero knelt. Birdlike, her head cocked one way, then another. Akio's facial muscles seemed to have frozen solid. He couldn't even . . .

Ojib and Dakion sprinted headlong up the trail with their capes flying out behind them. "Gannajero, are you all right? What happened?"

"I was attacked, you fools."

Dakion's eyes narrowed; then he swung around with his bow up, scanning the forest for intruders. "Who killed Akio?"

The old woman opened her belt pouch and drew out a small pot, a hafted chert knife, and an eagle-bone sucking tube. "He's not dead yet," she said.

She leaned so close that Akio could see the bizarre yellow flecks in her black eyes as she placed the tube against his temple. She sucked so hard Akio shuddered. With the tube still against her lips, she plucked out the ceramic pot stopper and blew the tube into the pot. After she'd restoppered it, she set it aside and picked up her chert knife.

"Shouldn't we try to pull the arrow out or—or something?" Dakion said.

"No, it's too late for that."

A curious gray haze began to sparkle at the edges of Akio's vision, growing darker, spreading until it consumed the world.

Gannajero said, "Dakion, Ojib, stop wasting time! Find the children. I have other business to attend to."

Steps pounded away.

Akio barely felt the sharp bite of the chert knife as she slit his belly open and continued slicing upward toward his chest, peeling back his skin as she went.

Twenty-four

By the time the lavender sheen of dawn washed the sky, Wrass' body felt like lead. The other children were just as exhausted, but no one made a sound. They kept staggering on with their heads down, trudging through knee-deep piles of old leaves. The morning was so silent that if Wrass hadn't known better, he might have believed they were the only creatures alive in the world.

But somewhere behind them—closer than he wanted to believe—warriors placed their moccasins in the ruts he and the other children had plowed through the leaves last night. Their trail was obvious. While the men might not have seen it in the darkness, with the dawn, they'd be coming.

Wrass halted. His headache was so bad, he was crying. He clenched his fists and stiffened his muscles to hide it from the other children.

From the rear of the line, Zateri called, "Are we stopping?"

"No, I just . . . we have to do something different. We can't walk in the leaves anymore. Even a blind man could follow us."

"But there are leaves everywhere," Auma said. "Where else can we walk? We just need to keep going!"

He saw Zateri's gaze lift to the massive maple and hickory trees that surrounded them; she was thinking the same thing he was. A canopy of laced branches roofed the forest floor here. "Maybe it's time to think like Gannajero."

"And fast. They're not far behind us."

The crazy old woman had taught them a great deal. Right after their capture, she'd marched them for days without ever being on a trail. They'd scurried over bare rock, waded along creeks, and climbed through trees to hide their passage.

Wrass said, "Zateri, I'll stay on the ground and try to create a false trail to draw them away from you. Then I'll follow."

Panic lined her face. "Are you sure, Wrass? Maybe I should try to lead them away?"

The unspoken words, *because you're so weak and sick,* were clear on her face.

"No, you're too valuable. If any of the rest of us are injured, we'll need you. You're our Healer. I'll do it."

She looked like she wanted to argue; then she exhaled hard and said, "All right."

She turned and considered a pignut hickory. The trunk slanted at an angle, and the branches interlaced with those of a giant sycamore. "Where should we meet you?"

"Head due south. I'll find you."

"South?" Auma said. "But home is north."

"He knows that," Zateri replied, "and so does Gannajero. That's the direction she will expect us to run."

Wrass said, "You probably won't see me until nightfall, but no matter what, keep going."

"I will," she said, but he saw the tears glitter in her eyes as she turned to Auma and Conkesema. "Follow me."

She walked to the slanted hickory trunk, and Auma said, "What are you doing?"

"Climbing this tree." Zateri spread her arms and balanced on the slanted trunk until she reached the heavy branches; then she climbed with the grace of a squirrel into the sycamore.

Auma and Conkesema continued to stand at the base of the hickory looking up.

"I'm not going up there," Auma said. Her catlike face with its broad nose and long eyelashes shone in the sunlight. "They'll see us."

"No, they won't. They'll be looking at the ground, and besides, we won't be here for long."

"Why not?"

Zateri pointed to the branches that laced over her head, connecting to another sycamore. "We're going to travel through the trees for as long as we can. So they won't have any trail to follow. Now, hurry. We don't have much time."

Auma nervously flapped her arms. "All right, but I don't like it."

She climbed, and Conkesema followed, her long black hair swaying.

Wrass watched long enough to see them move through several trees. When he lost sight of them, he started walking back along their trail, scooping leaves to fill in the rut they'd made.

His heart was pounding, and each beat felt like a hammer swung against his skull. He'd started to reel on his feet.

He propped a hand against a basswood tree and looked up. It stood twenty times the height of a man, and its branches snaked into five or six adjacent sycamores and oaks.

For a few blessed moments, he leaned heavily against the trunk and breathed in the sweet scent of the damp bark. His nausea had returned with a vengeance. More than anything, he longed to lie down in the leaves and close his eyes.

"Keep moving. Don't think about it."

He grabbed the closest branch and pulled himself into the tree. As he worked his way across the connecting branches, heading north, he thought he heard voices, men calling to each other.

Sick with fear, he hurried, practically running across a huge oak limb.

In his desperation to get away, he hadn't realized that the sunlight was warming the branches, melting the frost. When his foot slipped, it surprised him. He gasped and lunged for the nearest branch . . . but he was so sick. His arms moved too slowly.

The fall seemed to take forever.

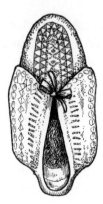

Twenty-five

When Zateri heard the scream, she swung around.

Auma, who was right behind her, hissed, "Was that Wrass? It sounded like a boy's scream."

In the distance, a man shouted. Dakion.

"They caught him!" Auma grabbed Zateri's arm in panic. "Hurry, we have to keep moving, or they'll catch us, too."

Auma tried to force Zateri to keep walking across the branch, but Zateri's heart was thundering in her chest, making it impossible to think.

"Don't push me!" Zateri hissed.

Auma stopped, but she stared at Zateri with panicked eyes. "He told us to keep going," she reminded. "He said no matter what, we shouldn't stop!"

Zateri's fingers tightened around the branch. The bark felt cold and rough. From their height in the big sycamore, she could see all the way across the forest to the river. Elder Brother Sun had coated the wide blue surface with a sparkling layer of pale gold. She thought she knew about where the camp was. Would Gannajero leave without them?

"What are we waiting for?" Auma whispered, on the point of tears. "We have to get away!"

Zateri said, "Move back to the trunk. I need to climb down."

"Climb down? But it was hard getting up here. We should keep moving over to that sassafras tree!"

Zateri tried to climb around her, but couldn't. "Move back!" she ordered through gritted teeth.

Auma and Conkesema turned around, made it to the trunk, and then one by one climbed down, using the branches like a ladder. By the time they had all jumped to the ground, Zateri felt light-headed with fear. She tried to force herself to think.

"Zateri, please," Auma pleaded. Her thin doehide dress clung to her slender body. "We have to keep running, or they'll find us just like they did Wrass!"

Zateri's gaze darted around the underbrush. Windblown leaves piled against every trunk and bush. No matter where they went, if they were on the ground, they'd leave a clear trail.

Tears welled hotly in her eyes. She rubbed them away and turned to the two other girls. "I want you to hide here until I get back. If anyone comes, cover yourselves with leaves and don't move."

"Where are you going?"

"I'm going back to the canoes to look for Wrass. I have to know what happened to him." *Or I'll go insane expecting to see him.*

"But they'll just recapture you, too!"

"Maybe," she answered thoughtfully. "I'll have to go slow, that's for sure. I can't take a chance that they'll hear me coming."

A look of horror came over Auma's face. "This is idiocy! I'm going to run north toward home."

Zateri clenched her fists at her sides. "If you wait here for me, I'll be back soon, and then I'll take you to the closest village and make sure you're safe before I go after Wrass."

Auma wrung her hands. "But Wrass told us to—"

"Do whatever you want, but I will be back here by nightfall. I promise."

Wind Mother rustled the bare branches around them, and the forest seemed to shiver in the cold. Zateri pulled her cape closed beneath her chin. "I can't just turn my back on him and run away, even if he told me to." She shook her head. "I can't do it."

To her surprise, Auma's face twisted with tears. "If he were my friend, I—I guess I'd do the same thing." She sat down in the leaves and said, "Conkesema, sit down with me. We'll wait for Zateri until nightfall. But no longer."

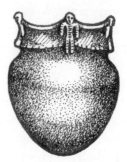

Twenty-six

Cord sat behind Sindak in the rear of the lead canoe, paddling it around a rough bend in the river. Rocks thrust up here and there but were barely visible in the choppy current. They had to be careful. Close to shore, the leafless boughs of scarlet oaks overhung the water, casting black shadows over the fallen acorns that littered the bank.

From behind, Cord heard Koracoo call, "Gonda? Put ashore."

Gonda swung around and shouted, "What? Why? We're making good time!"

Cord said, "Sindak, let's put ashore over there near the chokecherries. That looks like the best place."

While he and Sindak steered the canoe toward the brush, Gonda glowered at them. Cord and Sindak leaped out of the boat as soon as they could and helped shove it up onto the sand. Almost instantly, Koracoo's canoe slid up beside them.

She jumped ashore and said, "We're stopping for a few hundred heartbeats. That's all. Eat something, drink, and do whatever else you must; then we're leaving."

Gonda said, "We shouldn't be stopping at all. Anything people need to do, they can—"

"That was not a request."

Gonda propped his hands on his hips to watch her as she walked away from him and went to stand beside Sindak. Cord glanced at Gonda. They'd been arguing more and more, snapping at each other like warring turtles. Worse, the constant challenges to Koracoo's authority were undermining her credibility with her men. Cord had begun to notice that both Sindak and Towa were questioning her orders more often. If she didn't put a stop to this soon, she'd have a real problem on her hands.

Wakdanek, the children, and Towa disappeared into the trees to Cord's right.

Gonda strode over to Koracoo and Sindak. Each had pulled small bags of food from their belt pouches and were chewing in silence. "Koracoo, listen to me, you . . ."

Cord walked away.

The amber gleam of late afternoon coated the slender trunks of chokecherries that grew along the shore and glimmered from the river with blinding intensity.

He took the opportunity to walk upstream, where he could keep watch for canoes coming around the bend. They were well into territory belonging to the People Who Separated. The Quill River was broad and lazy, like an old woman who loved nothing better than to doze in the tree shadows. But occasional shallows ran swift and dangerous. By the time any pursuers saw their party, the enemy would have a hard time getting to shore. Still, he kept watch.

As he waded out to fill his water bag, he looked back at the group near the canoes. Wakdanek had joined the circle. One by one, the children filtered from the undergrowth and stood talking.

Cord lifted his water bag and took a long drink of the cool earthy water. He'd swallowed a stale cornmeal biscuit a short time ago. Hunger was at bay for the moment, but he had a powerful thirst. He emptied half the bag, and filled it again. As he straightened, he heard Koracoo's distinctively soft steps. It was a faint almost-not-there sound, little more than grains of sand shifting.

"May I speak with you?" she said.

"Of course." He tied his water bag to his belt and turned.

Koracoo took a deep breath and let it out slowly while she gazed across the wide glistening river, as though considering her words, but she was also avoiding his eyes—and he knew why. He felt the attraction, too. But it was not the time for either of them. Their peoples were at war.

"I have a problem," she said.

"I know."

She turned to face him, and their gazes locked. They'd been paddling hard, and sweat had matted her short black hair to her cheeks, framing her large eyes and small nose. She had CorpseEye propped on her shoulder. Even from two paces away, he could sense a presence in the war club, old and powerful. The carvings along the shaft added to the effect. The antlered wolves seemed to be chasing the winged tortoises, who were being chased by prancing buffalo. The red quartzite cobble tied to the top of the club reflected the light.

Her eyes tightened. "I didn't realize it was so obvious."

"Why don't you let me explain what I see, rather than having you tell me?"

"Go on."

Cord exhaled hard before he said, "It's clear that recently something has changed between the two of you. You want distance, but he still loves you. What appears to be anger on his part is actually, I believe, grief. He's finally realized that he's lost you, and it's tearing him apart. So . . . returning anger for anger will not solve the problem. But you must solve it. Quickly."

Their gazes held. Her eyes were as black and translucent as obsidian. It was strange for him to stand eye-to-eye with a woman. Very few were as tall as he was. And she had meltingly dark eyes.

"What is your recommendation?" she asked.

He frowned out at the water. "He's been your deputy for a long time?"

"Yes."

"Pick a new deputy. You need someone you can trust to give good orders in the worst of moments. Sindak, perhaps?"

Her eyes narrowed slightly. "Not you?"

"No. I'm an outsider. They won't listen to me."

She studied him for a long time, as though trying to read his souls.

A short distance from the shore, a flock of ducks floated, riding the swells as they chattered to each other. He watched them while he waited for her to think it over.

At last, she replied, "Gonda has been my right hand for thirteen summers. He knows my thoughts almost before I do."

"That's why this is so hard for him. He thinks you need him." Cord stared at her. Neither of them blinked. "It will be a kindness, Koracoo. He doesn't know how to step aside. Though I suspect he realizes he needs to."

The ducks suddenly took wing, squawking as they flapped away into the afternoon sky. Koracoo frowned at them for a time before she said, "He may, but this decision will still enrage him."

"Maybe. But eventually he'll understand why you did it."

Koracoo pulled CorpseEye off her shoulder and lovingly smoothed her fingers over the club as she thought. "I want you to serve as my deputy."

Cord shifted awkwardly. "I don't think that's a wise choice. Your men do not know me."

"Which means you will have to make an effort to get to know them."

"I can do that, but think hard before you—"

She walked away. As she neared the group, she called, "We're switching positions. Wakdanek, I want you with Towa in the rear of Gonda's canoe. Children, split up however you please, two in each canoe."

As the three men moved for their boat, Koracoo said, "Gonda, I need to speak with you."

She marched past him and led the way into a grove of larches. He followed her. Cord could just see them through the sunlit weave of yellow needles. Gonda had his head down, as though listening intently.

In the meantime, Odion and Baji climbed into Koracoo's canoe. The other two children got into Gonda's. Wakdanek and Towa stood at the bow, waiting.

Sindak was squinting at Koracoo and Gonda. From this angle, his hooked nose looked especially long.

Cord walked up beside him. "Sindak, go ahead and get in. As soon as Koracoo arrives, I'll shove us off. I'm already soaked to the knees."

"So am I." Sindak tucked his war club into his belt and folded his arms beneath his cape. Without looking at Cord, he said, "That sounded like an order. Did you and Koracoo have an interesting conversation?"

"We—"

A sharp "What?" erupted from the forest.

"You know it's necessary," Koracoo said. "You and I have been snarling at each other like rabid dogs."

"Why now?"

She said something no one could hear.

Branches cracked as Gonda thrashed his way through brush and shouted at Wakdanek and Towa, "Get in."

They leaped to obey, taking up positions in the rear. The boat rocked violently as Gonda shoved it off the sand and jumped into the bow. In less than five heartbeats, the man had maneuvered out into the current and was heading downriver.

Gonda hadn't even looked at Cord. But he would. By the end of the day, he'd be strutting around Cord like a stiff-legged dog. It was the way of men.

Koracoo walked out of the trees carrying CorpseEye in both hands, as though ready to bash anything that annoyed her.

Sindak's brows lifted. As Koracoo came across the sand, he said, "Gonda seemed a little upset."

She replied, "War Chief Cord is my new deputy. We're leaving." She stalked past him, climbed to the rear, and grabbed an oar.

Odion and Baji watched her with wide eyes. They knew better than to say anything. Odion clutched his puppy tighter, and Gitchi wriggled unhappily.

Sindak turned to Cord. "Do you want to ride in the rear with her . . . or am I the condemned man?"

Cord smiled. "You're the condemned man."

Sindak heaved a sigh and got in.

Just as Cord started to shove the bow away from the shore, he heard something.

A soft suffocating cry.

Koracoo heard it, too. She straightened and shipped her paddle. "What was that?"

Odion got on his knees, listened for a few instants, and pointed to the larches to the south. "There, Mother." He swung around to make sure she'd heard him.

Koracoo nodded. "Cord, go east and come up behind the larches. I'll approach from the shore. Sindak, stay and guard the children."

"But Mother," Odion said. "It sounds like a child. Can I—?"

"No."

The boy sank back to the packs with a disappointed expression.

Cord unslung his bow, pulled an arrow from his quiver, and slipped silently to the edge of the trees before he nocked it. The larches were in the process of shedding their needles, but enough remained to create a fuzzy yellow halo that extended back indefinitely into the forest. As he entered the grove, the cry came again.

Gently, so that he made no sound, Cord eased aside the branch blocking his path and stepped by. He carefully returned the branch to its former position. It made only the slightest shishing as a handful of needles pattered the duff.

He studied the dense undergrowth of dogwoods to his left. The weeping penetrated the thicket, but just barely, as though the person had his face buried in a heavy blanket to muffle his cries.

Birds hopped through the branches above him, chirping, which helped to cover the crackling of the old larch needles as Cord edged toward the thicket.

When he reached the outermost edge of the dogwoods, he saw movement and stood perfectly still, studying the shape until he made out what seemed to be four arms. Then eyes opened and stared at him.

"I'm not going to hurt you," he said in the Dawnland tongue. By now the child would have assessed his hairstyle and fitted wolfhide coat as those of a Flint warrior. He might even suspect that Cord had been involved in the attack on Bog Willow Village. Assuming the boy knew about it. They were far south of traditional Dawnland country. The news may not have reached here yet.

The boy lifted his head. He wore a ratty cape made from woven strips of weasel hide, and had a narrow face with a thin bladelike nose. Tears glued stringy black hair to his cheeks. Amid the dogwood limbs, he appeared to be perhaps eight or nine summers old. The boy's breathing sounded labored.

Cord struggled to decipher what he was seeing. When the boy shifted to sit up, his two arms became visible, but something wasn't right about the shapes. The body parts didn't seem to connect.

Cord released the tension on his bowstring and called, "Are you hungry? I have food I'll share with you."

Dark eyes blinked.

Nearby, Koracoo moved stealthily across the larch duff. If he hadn't known she was coming, he might have assumed the sound was nothing more than birds scratching through the fallen needles. She stopped. Perhaps because she'd seen the boy.

Cord slung his bow and crouched down where he could see beneath the dogwood branches. The boy was scared witless, trembling. Tears ran down his cheeks.

Cord extended a hand. "You're safe with us. Why don't you come out where we can talk?"

A shaking little-boy voice said, "I—I'm lost."

"It's all right. We'll help you. What's your name?"

The boy licked his lips nervously. "Toksus."

Koracoo slipped through the undergrowth and came to kneel beside Cord. "Toksus," she called, "I give you my oath that you are safe. I am War Chief Koracoo of Yellowtail Village. I—"

"Yellowtail?" Toksus scrambled from beneath the dogwoods. Old leaves and needles covered his hair. He stood with his fists clenched. "Wrass' village?"

In an unnaturally calm voice, Koracoo said, "Do you know Wrass?"

"He's my friend." Toksus suspiciously glanced back and forth between them. "We—we were in the same canoe."

Cord could see the vein in Koracoo's throat pounding, but she looked utterly calm when she asked, "Did you escape from Gannajero, Toksus?"

The boy's chest spasmed with tears, and his face twisted. "She let me go."

Despite the fact that Koracoo must have had a thousand questions, she said only, "Then we need to get you home. What's your village?"

"It was a-attacked. I don't know if anyone's alive."

"Bog Willow Village?"

The boy nodded.

Koracoo said, "We were just there. Many survived. In fact, we're traveling with someone you may know. He was your village Healer, Wakdanek."

Toksus took a shocked step toward them. "He's my cousin. Where is he? I want to see him."

"He just shoved off in his canoe, but I'll send people to bring him back."

Koracoo slowly moved toward him. Toksus watched her like a small frightened animal. When she was close enough, Koracoo reached out and stroked his hair. "You're going to be all right, Toksus. We'll get you home."

While Koracoo spoke with the boy, Cord tried to figure out the shapes beneath the dogwoods. Finally, he asked, "Toksus, who's the other boy?"

Toksus turned around to stare at the body half covered with leaves. "Sassacus. He—he was Partridge Clan."

Koracoo's face slackened as she connected the apparently disparate shapes. "Dear gods, it's a body."

Toksus sobbed again and wiped his eyes on his sleeve. "I don't know how he got here. I ran all night. I was so tired, I had to nap.

When I woke up a little while ago, he was lying beside me. It scared me."

"Is that why you covered him with leaves?"

He croaked, "I was afraid he'd followed me."

Cord was confused by the statement, but Koracoo stroked the boy's hair again and softly asked, "Did you see him witched?"

Toksus' mouth opened and his chest heaved, but no sound came out.

Koracoo pulled him into her arms. The boy wept, "She killed him! Stabbed him in the back. Then she—she . . ."

When he couldn't go on, Koracoo hugged him tighter and turned to Cord. "Ask Odion and Baji to come over here, then take the canoe. Catch Gonda. With the current, it'll probably be easier for Sindak to lead Wakdanek back along the shore. I want you and Gonda to remain and guard the canoes."

"Understood."

Cord sprinted away, ducked the low branches of the larches, and thrashed through the brush. When he appeared on the shore, he noticed that Sindak had gotten out of the canoe and nocked his bow. He stood guard a few paces from the children.

"Good man, Sindak."

Sindak's brows plunged down over his hooked nose. "We heard a boy's voice. Who is he?"

"He's a Dawnland child. One of the survivors of the Bog Willow battle. I'll tell you more later. Right now, we have catch Gonda."

As Cord grabbed an oar, he said, "Odion, Baji, the war chief wants you to join her."

Odion and Baji scrambled out of the canoe and ran away with Odion calling, "*Mother?* Where are you?"

Cord shoved the bow away from the sand, and said, "Come on, Sindak. We have our work cut out catching Gonda."

Twenty-seven

Wrass sat on the sandy, leaf-strewn bank with his hands tied behind his back. His balance was off. He kept falling over, then righting himself, trying to stay upright. The agony in his head was unbearable, but his ankle hurt worse.

Gannajero's four warriors had formed a tight circle three paces away. Though their voices were low, their grim expressions told him more than words. At least one of them was on the verge of bolting into the wilderness at the first opportunity.

"The boy is useless," Dakion said. He gestured with his war club, and his buckskin cape flared and buffeted in the wind. His broad muscular shoulders strained against his cape. "We should crack his skull and leave him for the wolves. We can find new children anywhere."

Ojib responded, "Even in his condition, he'll bring a few trinkets."

"But he's more trouble than he's worth! He can hardly walk now. I think he broke his ankle in the fall."

Waswan used the back of his hand to wipe his knobby nose and straightened his sapling-thin body to glare at Dakion. "The boy is *her* property. She decides what to do with him."

Wrass looked down at his foot. His ankle was badly swollen and had turned a mottled reddish purple, but he didn't think it was broken. Just badly sprained. The thick bed of leaves had cushioned his fall, and probably saved his life. He just couldn't put his weight on the ankle. One thing was certain—his hope of escape was gone. He wouldn't be able to run for days, maybe longer. The despair that filled him was like an animal eating him from the inside out.

He let his aching head fall forward. It didn't matter. Zateri and the Dawnland girls had gotten away. That made seven children Gannajero had lost in just a few days.

Dakion turned to Kotin. "Kotin, we should be far south by now. What if those girls walk into a nearby village and tell them they were held captive by Gannajero? The chief will organize a war party of hundreds to come looking for us. We need to put distance between us and—"

"Didn't you hear what Waswan said? It's *her* decision!" Kotin snarled, and jerked his head toward Gannajero.

Back in the trees, she stood bent over, working on something on the ground. She kept making small grunts, as though it was hard labor. Occasionally she lifted her knife high enough that the white chert blade glinted in the sunlight.

"What's she doing?" Dakion said. "She won't let any of us get close. Is she—?"

Ojib interrupted. "I'm more worried about that messenger who came to see her. Why won't she tell us what he said?"

"Maybe because it's none of our concern," Kotin replied. "The message was for her."

"But how did the man know where she was? He must have followed us from the big warriors' camp. If so much as a single person there recognized her"—Dakion waved an arm extravagantly—"there could be fifty canoes searching for us this instant!"

Kotin shook his head, but it was so faint Wrass doubted the other warriors noticed. Revealing broken yellow teeth, he said, "If there were, I promise you, she'd know it."

"You give her too much credit. She's just an old woman. She has no powers or the children would never have been able to escape. We'd already be far south and safely away . . ."

His voice faded when Gannajero abruptly stood up. Everyone saw her lift the dead boy's eyes. They had shriveled and turned opaque. She held one eyeball in each hand and was slowly turning around in a circle, murmuring. When she stopped turning, she let out a sharp gleeful laugh and stared off to the north.

"I don't like this," Dakion hissed. "She just does these bizarre things to scare us."

Gannajero put the eyes back in her belt pouch. Then she bent down, draped something over her left arm, and started toward them. Whatever she carried was long enough to drag on the ground. It slurred wetly over the leaves.

Dakion shook a fist at Kotin. "We have to do something now, before she—"

"Are you the hero, Dakion?" Gannajero asked in a low menacing voice as she emerged from the trees.

"What?"

She walked into the clearing, and Wrass frowned at the thing draped over her arm. Slowly, like poison working through his veins, he realized it was a human skin. Thin and coated with blood, the arms and legs swung as she walked. Revulsion wrenched a small cry of horror from his throat. He scrambled backward, trying to get as far from her as he could.

"I'll let you be the hero, Dakion," she said with mock kindness. She'd started to tiptoe forward, like a hunting cat. "You should have asked."

In less than a heartbeat, Dakion had his war club in his fist. "You're crazy, old woman!"

"Yes, I am doomed to walk this earth alone forever. *I* have nothing to lose." Her toothless mouth widened. "What about you?"

Dakion swallowed hard. "The boy is worthless. Just tell me why we can't kill him?"

Gannajero's smile froze on her wrinkled face. Without taking her gaze from him, she said, "She'll come for him."

"Who will? What are you talking about? There could be one hundred canoes on the river behind us, chasing us down, and all you can do is blather nonsense? Just let me kill the boy, so he doesn't slow us—"

"I've already told you I'll let you be the hero. Why are you still so worried about the boy?" She cocked her head in that strange birdlike manner, eyeing him first through one eye, then the other.

Dakion appeared totally confused. He took another grip on his club as though the shaft had grown slick with sweat.

The other warriors backed away. Kotin, in particular, looked terrified.

"The boy"—Gannajero gave Dakion a cruel toothless grin—"is mine. Understand?"

Dakion looked as though he might burst at the seams. He waved his war club threateningly. "What are you going to do with him? Is he a hostage? Why won't you tell us what the messenger said? What are you hiding?"

An old hatred, something grown fine and sharp over the long summers, flickered in her black eyes. "The messenger said that my brother promises me wealth and power beyond my imaginings. Would you like to share in that?"

"Your brother?" Dakion said. "Who is he? How rich is he?"

The old woman scanned the faces of her warriors. "Anyone who wishes can walk away now with no punishment." She adjusted the limp skin over her arm. "Go on. Get out of my sight. But anyone who chooses to stay will be richly rewarded."

The men glanced at each other. She'd already bestowed enough wealth upon them to make them very rich men. Wrass studied the gleam that came to each man's eyes. How could they still want more?

"So," Gannajero said. "No one wishes to leave."

They shifted; someone mumbled; all of them glanced at the skin over her arm.

"Then get out of my way," she growled.

She walked through the middle of their circle. Men stumbled backward to clear a path for her. As she knelt and began rinsing the skin in the river, graying black hair flopped around her wrinkled face.

Kotin gave the other three men an evil look. "I've been with her a long time, and she's never failed to keep her promises. In a few short moons, you could all have enough wealth to ransom a village. Keep that in mind the next time you threaten to betray her."

Wrass—beside the maple tree—saw Gannajero smile.

Dakion kicked at an old branch. "She'd better keep her promise. I expect to live long enough to enjoy my earnings."

Gannajero stood up and stretched the clean, dripping skin out from arm to arm. Without turning she called, "Who would like to help me make a frame? As soon as he's dry, I'll enchant him. Then we'll leave."

Kotin and Ojib trotted to her side. Dakion shook his head. Dust swirled and sparkled faintly in the still air around him.

With practiced ease, Gannajero collected and tied together four long sticks of driftwood, creating a rectangular frame. Ojib and Kotin then helped Gannajero stretch the feet, hands, and neck into place to keep the skin taut while it dried. The vaguely human-shaped skin continued to drip onto the old leaves.

The shape fascinated Wrass. He couldn't take his eyes from it. The old woman had skinned Akio as a man would a deer, her knife slitting up from the ankle to the groin, then peeling back the skin. The legs and arms appeared to be twice as wide as they had been when alive and sheathing muscles. Only the head was missing.

Something clinked. Wrass' gaze shot back to Gannajero as she pulled a beautiful copper bell from her belt pouch. Pounded into a thin sheet then twisted into a cone, such copper bells were traditionally used to adorn the moccasins of ceremonial dancers. A shell bead was hung in the center of the cone and made it tinkle pleasantly.

Dakion shouted, "Where did you get that? That's mine!"

He tramped over to where his pack rested in the canoe and began digging through it, searching, as though to make certain.

While he occupied himself, Gannajero carried the bell to the skinned neck and tied it on. Even the slightest breath of wind encouraged it to make music.

Dakion roared, "You took it!"

Gannajero touched the bell with gnarled fingers. It had been polished to a beautiful sheen. She took a few moments to stare at it before she glanced at the other warriors and whispered, "It's like giving a fresh fox skin to a dog just before the hunt. By the time you release the dog, he's so desperate for the taste of fox blood that he's lunging at his tether and frothing at the mouth."

Fear prickled Wrass' skin. What was she talking about?

Dakion climbed out of the canoe and stalked back with his club swinging. "Why did you tie it to the skin? Give it to me." He extended his hand.

Gannajero laughed softly. "I'm training a new dog."

"A dog? Are you calling me a dog?"

She smiled, but it didn't reach her eyes. "This *hanehwa* has one duty. No matter where you go, he'll track you down and tell me where you are."

As the implications sank in, Dakion's extended hand slowly clenched to a fist. Where only moments before he'd scoffed at her powers, now he licked his lips and his eyes darted to the others. "She's insane. I don't believe any of this."

"Yes, I can see that." Gannajero straightened, and the shells and twists of copper on her cape flashed. "Kotin, untie Hawk-Face. He can't run. Then bring the skin and come find me. I want to talk to you. Alone."

"Yes, Gannajero."

Kotin quickly walked over and slit the ropes tying Wrass' hands. "Don't try anything stupid," he growled.

Wrass struggled to give him a defiant glare. "I can't even walk. How could I?"

Kotin turned away and went to retrieve the frame with the stretched skin. As he walked back into the trees where Gannajero stared up at the sky, the old woman said, "Hang it up there where it can dry in the sunlight."

The other warriors gathered around Dakion, whispering ominously.

Wrass hadn't had any water since dawn. He gazed longingly at the river, but when he tried to put weight on his ankle it felt like fiery splinters were being driven into his flesh.

Wrass rolled to his hands and knees and started crawling for the water. The entire time, Dakion watched him hatefully.

Tears blurred his eyes. While he'd badly injured his ankle in the fall, every part of him hurt. His ribs felt as though the muscles had been pulled loose from the bones.

When he finally reached the water, he greedily scooped it into his mouth with his hand. Rivulets spilled down his chin, but he kept drinking until he could hold no more. There was no telling when he'd get to drink again.

Wrass rolled to his back and, for a few blessed moments, lay on the riverbank staring up at the gathering Cloud People. The blue-black giants were pushing eastward.

"Load up," Gannajero's gravelly voice rasped. "We're heading south."

She and Kotin tramped past Wrass without even glancing at him. It was as though he no longer existed. Gannajero climbed into the bow of the lead canoe and irritably watched her men stow their gear. "Come on. We're in a hurry!"

Ojib clambered for the rear of Gannajero's canoe and picked up a paddle, while Waswan settled into the rear of the other canoe. Dakion and Kotin remained on shore to push off.

As Kotin shoved the lead canoe into the current and leaped into the bow, Dakion glanced at Wrass and shouted, "Wait! What about the boy? Is he riding in my canoe?"

"We're leaving him," Gannajero answered, just before the river grabbed hold of her canoe and carried it downstream.

"I don't believe it!" Dakion gestured wildly to Waswan. "She'd planned all along to leave him? Why didn't she just tell me?"

Waswan chuckled, and his small inhuman eyes glinted. "She probably thought it was none of your business."

Dakion shook his head, shoved the canoe into the river, and jumped in. As they paddled out into the current, Wrass heard Dakion say, "With all the starving wolves in this country, that boy will be dead by nightfall."

Wrass shoved up on one elbow to watch them disappear around the bend.

Stunned, an odd floating sensation came over him. They'd left him. He was free. Before he realized it, tears warmed his face. He could . . . he could go home! It might take him a while, but if he splinted and wrapped his ankle, he'd make it. There were many good walking sticks in sight. A fallen maple branch about his height lay less than ten paces away.

A few instants later, when he tried to stand up, reality returned with a vengeance. His ankle went out from under him, and he landed hard on the sand. Grabbing his screaming ankle, he rocked back and forth. The swelling was worse. Only a hand of time ago, he'd been able to fit both his hands around the joint.

Fear seeped through his relief and joy.

Dakion had been right. Many large predators ran along this shore. It was a primary hunting trail for wolves, bears, and cougars.

Wrass looked back into the trees. He couldn't see it, but he knew it wouldn't take the wolves long to catch the scent of Akio's freshly skinned corpse.

He had to get as far away from here as he could.

Twenty-eight

Gonda! Wait!"

Gonda spun around at the call and pulled his oar out of the water. In the rear, Towa and Wakdanek turned to watch the approaching canoe. Sindak and Cord were stroking hard, trying to catch them. Their canoe shot forward, piercing the green water like an arrow.

Gonda realized that Koracoo and the children were missing, and he shouted, "Put ashore. Hurry. Something's wrong!"

Wakdanek and Towa backed water, turning the canoe; then they all fought the current to head to a small spit of sand on the eastern shore. Thick willows filled in the spaces between the towering trees. The spit was the only place to land. Gonda leaped out as they glided in and helped drag the boat up onto the bank. As the cold shadows of the trees enveloped him, a thousand possible explanations for Koracoo and the children's absence skittered across his souls—none of them good.

As the canoe sliced through the water toward them, Tutelo got on her knees, and called, "Father? Where's Mother? Where's Odion and Baji?"

"I'm sure they're fine," he answered. "You and Hehaka can get out. Just stay close."

"Yes, Father."

Tutelo's long braid switched across her back as she climbed over packs and oars to get out of the canoe. Hehaka followed more slowly, but both children ended up standing beside Gonda, staring up at him worriedly.

Towa and Wakdanek slogged ashore and waited beside the canoe.

Gonda yelled, "Where are Koracoo and the children? What happened?"

Cord shipped his paddle and shouted back, "We found a Dawnland boy. They stayed with him while we came after you."

"A boy?" Wakdanek called. "Who is he?"

Sindak's canoe grounded with a loud grating sound. As Cord jumped into the water and waded ashore, he answered, "The child was hiding thirty paces from our camp."

The two feathers on Wakdanek's moosehide hat wafted in the wind as he closed on Cord. "What's his name?"

"He said he was your cousin. His name is Toksus."

Wakdanek straightened. "Blessed gods! Is he all right?" He ran forward.

"He appears to be, but Koracoo wants you there immediately. Sindak will guide the rest of you back. Gonda and I will remain here to guard the canoes."

Gonda vented a low ugly laugh. "I'm not staying here. You can guard the canoes by yourself. I want to talk to the boy. How did he get this far south? What—?"

Cord turned to Sindak. "Hurry. We know we're on the right path now. The sooner we're on the water again, the sooner we'll catch Gannajero."

Sindak dipped his head in a nod and called, "Everyone, follow me."

Towa, Wakdanek, and the children gathered around Sindak.

When Gonda started to join Sindak's group, Cord caught him by the arm and forcibly pulled him back. "These aren't my orders. They're hers."

Gonda's muscles bulged as he shook off Cord's restraining hand. Murderous rage was filling him up, threatening to burst loose in a frenzy of fists or clashing war clubs. It took every bit of strength he had to calm himself enough to say through gritted teeth, "She did this on purpose, you know."

Cord just stared at him. "What?"

"Left us here together."

"Why would that be?"

"Don't be a dimwit. You've seen how she splits up her warriors."

Cord appeared to think about that for a moment; then the knife scar that cut across his jaw tilted up in admiration. "Yes. I've marveled at it. Or rather, marveled at the fact that it seems to work. I would never separate friends and create teams of enemies. I'd be afraid they'd kill each other before they arrived at some sort of reconciliation."

"This time her strategy isn't going to work."

"Why not?"

"I'm not going to get over being demoted and having an enemy warrior installed in my place—even if I do come to respect him."

Cord's mouth set into a grim line. "I'm not sure I would either."

As his anger began to drain away, Gonda had to clench his jaw to steady his nerves. He said, "Tell me what happened with the child. How did you find him?"

Cord's wary attention remained on the river, the trees. "Just before we shoved off we heard him crying. He was hiding, entangled with a corpse, beneath a thicket of dogwoods."

"A corpse?"

"Yes, there were actually two Dawnland children—one was dead."

"What killed him?"

As though to ease his tension, Cord ran a hand over the black roach of hair that lined the top of his head. Several yellow larch needles fell out. "The living boy, Toksus, said that the dead boy had been witched, and then stabbed, by Gannajero."

"Gannajero? Toksus was with Gannajero?" Panic tingled Gonda's veins. He grabbed Cord's arm. "H-How long ago?"

"Yesterday."

"So she's just ahead of us on the river?" He swung around to look downstream, as though expecting to see her canoes. Only swaying maples met his gaze. A few old leaves blew from the branches and fluttered into the rushing water.

"Apparently."

"The other children with her, what did Toksus—?"

"He said he'd talked to Wrass. That's all. But we shouldn't make too much of that. Koracoo ordered me to find you, and I left immediately."

Gonda felt light-headed. He took a few steps away from Cord and struggled to control his hope. What would Koracoo be thinking? She'd be vacillating, wondering what to do with the Dawnland child. They couldn't just leave him wandering alone in the forest. It was inhuman. The boy had been through unimaginable terrors. He needed to go home to his family . . . whatever was left of it. But they didn't have the luxury of turning around and taking the boy home. They had to . . .

"It will be a problem." Cord still had his attention focused on the trees.

"What will?" Gonda turned around.

"Another child."

It didn't surprise him that the Flint war chief was worried about the same thing he was. The danger increased tenfold with every additional child: more noise, more distractions, more chances that they'd all be killed.

Gonda gave the man an annoyed look. "So . . . what am I supposed to call you now? War Chief Cord or Deputy Cord?"

Cord calmly responded, "Our duty is to rescue the children, Gonda. She asked me. Not the reverse. And since she did, I plan to carry out my responsibilities to the best of my ability. You can call me whatever you like."

Gonda had the irrational desire to shout at him, which was sheer foolishness. Instead, he shook his fists at nothing and said, "I know this isn't your fault. I just . . . I thought Koracoo and I had resolved our differences. Obviously, I was wrong."

After a long pause, Cord asked, "What happened between you, Gonda?"

Taken aback by the boldness of the question, Gonda snapped, "What makes you think I'd tell you?"

Cord lifted a shoulder. "I'll find out anyway, but it will come from Sindak or Towa. Maybe small details from the children. Is that who you want to tell me?"

Gonda felt slightly ill. It was actually chilling to imagine Sindak relating the story of the fall of Yellowtail Village. He rubbed his forehead. "I disobeyed one of Koracoo's orders."

Cord shifted slightly. "Why?"

"*Why?* Because she was wrong. She wasn't there. I was. I had to make a decision."

"And what happened as a result?"

Gonda laughed softly, more in despair than amusement. "Do you know Yenda?"

Cord's mouth puckered. "The Mountain war chief? I've fought him many times. He's a worthless, arrogant fool. Why?"

Gonda searched the surrounding forest before he replied, "On the morning of the attack, a Trader came through bearing news that he'd heard Yenda was skulking around Yellowtail Village with a huge war party. The rumor could have been false. Koracoo, however, leaves nothing to chance. She took half our warriors out to investigate. She left me in charge of the village defense."

"Was your 'decision' the reason the village was destroyed?"

Images of the battle flooded through Gonda. He saw again the dead piling up in the plaza, heard the screams and cries of the wounded . . . felt the palisade catwalk shake as the onslaught of warriors hit it. He squeezed his eyes closed.

Finally, Cord asked, "How many warriors did Yenda have?"

"I'm not sure. My scouts reported somewhere around one thousand. But they were terrified; they could have exaggerated."

"How many did you have?"

"Three hundred."

When Gonda opened his eyes, he found Cord staring at him in sympathy. "So . . . in the last desperate moments something changed that made you disobey Koracoo's order. What was her order?"

Gonda crossed his arms over his aching heart and gazed out at the river, where an uprooted tree bobbed along in the current. As it rolled over, whole branches spun up and glittered in the sunlight. "Before she left, Koracoo ordered me to keep everyone inside the palisade. She feared that if I split my forces by sending even a handful of warriors outside, I'd never be able to hold the palisade."

"Was she right?"

"At the time, it seemed the only hope of saving a few of our people."

"So, you split your forces?"

"Yes, but I didn't make the decision hastily. I waited until the last possible moment. The palisade had been burned through in fifty places. Mountain warriors were crawling in and out like rats in a corn bin. Every longhouse was on fire."

Cord's gaze took on a faraway look, as though he was seeing it all play out on the fabric of his souls. "How many men did you send outside?"

"I led one hundred warriors out with our women and children, hoping we'd be able to protect them long enough that some could escape."

Cord didn't say anything.

Through a long exhalation, Gonda finished, "Everything fell apart. The village was overrun. Most of the warriors I'd led outside were killed, and many of the women and children were rounded up and marched away as slaves. Including my own children." The incapacitating ache he'd been suppressing swelled around his heart.

"Did some escape?"

"Yes. But not many."

Cord rubbed his chin with the back of his hand and nodded. "And when Koracoo returned, what did she do?"

"She found me in the forest, held me tightly while I wept . . . then she walked back into the village and started questioning people. She listened to the stories told by our remaining elders, talked to the people I'd left to guard the palisade, and questioned the few surviving warriors who'd gone outside with me. They all agreed I was to blame. They said I should have never split my forces. After that, Koracoo marched straight to the smoldering husk of our longhouse, gathered what remained of my belongings, and set them outside the door. We'd been joined for twelve summers, and she divorced me without ever asking me a single question."

A thousand summers from now as he slumbered in an old oak tree, that wound would still be bleeding. To make matters worse, his heartache was suffocating him. He'd do anything to be able to hold her in his arms again.

A gust of wind rattled the branches, and a whirlwind of old leaves swept out across the river. Gonda watched them settle upon the surface. Like a fleet of tiny rafts, the current swiftly carried them downstream.

Cord said, "I know it means nothing now, but I doubt that splitting your forces is what caused the destruction of Yellowtail Village. If I'd been in your situation, outnumbered three to one, with the village collapsing around me, I would probably have taken the same desperate risk you did. By the time you made the decision, the battle was already lost. It was the only thing you could have done."

For a brief instant, Gonda's pain lessened. He had the feeling Cord meant it.

"Well, you would be wise not to mention that to Koracoo. She'll demote you and name Sindak as her new deputy."

Cord smiled. "Actually, I suggested him for the position. I think he'd make a good one."

"Yes, well, you don't know him very well yet. He's young."

Cord dipped his head in deference to Gonda's experience. "If you say so."

In irritation, Gonda unslung his bow and pulled an arrow from his quiver. As he nocked it, he said, "I've had enough of making friends with you. I feel like killing something. Let's hunt."

Cord shook his head. "Koracoo ordered us to guard the canoes. However, I have no objections to allowing you to hunt, providing you stay within sight of the canoes. Agreed?"

Gonda jerked a nod. "Agreed . . . Deputy."

Twenty-nine

Koracoo stood guard two paces from where Odion, Baji, and Toksus sat talking. Now and then, one of them jerked around to look out into the larches, as though certain Gannajero and her warriors were sneaking up on them.

Koracoo understood the feeling. Toksus might well be bait for a trap. His story about how he'd gotten here was curious enough, but his insistence that he'd awakened beside the dead boy was truly bizarre.

She clutched CorpseEye and started walking in a small circle around the children, studying the ground for tracks. If Toksus wasn't making it up, someone must have placed Sassacus' body beside him. Who? Why? Had someone been trying to frighten Toksus? That seemed unlikely. Perhaps in some twisted way, Sassacus had been a gift. Company for a lost little boy? Or something more sinister. A warning not to tell anyone what had happened to him?

"Did you actually see Zateri?" Odion asked. He smoothed his shoulder-length black hair behind his ears. Sunlight falling through the branches striped his round face. "You're sure she was all right?"

Toksus pulled open the laces on a bag he carried and drew out a handful of huckleberries. As he chewed them, he said, "The last time

I saw her, she was fine. Then the canoes shoved away from shore and went off down the river, leaving me alone."

"You were smart, Toksus," Odion praised. "You knew to walk straight north along the river. You weren't really lost. In a few more days, you'd have been home."

Toksus swallowed his huckleberries and plucked another handful from the bag. "I was so scared."

"Well, you're with us now. My parents will take you home."

Toksus chewed the berries in silence, as though he wasn't sure whether or not to believe it.

Baji was eyeing Toksus severely. She said, "How did you escape?"

"I didn't escape. Gannajero let me go."

"She's never let a child go in her life. They're worth too much. Why you?"

The next handful of huckleberries stopped halfway to Toksus' mouth. He lowered it back to his lap. "After she stabbed the dead boy, she dragged him over and put him on top of me. She . . ." His eyes went vacant, as though his afterlife soul had briefly been scared from his body.

In a dire voice, Odion said, "Why did she do that?"

Toksus waved the fist of huckleberries, but it was a weak gesture, as though his strength had vanished in an instant. "She was witching us."

"Both of you? Why?"

Toksus' fingers seemed to go numb. The berries dropped from his hand, and he began rubbing his palms on his leggings, as though to rid them of an unseen taint. When his eyes started rolling around in terror, Odion slid closer to him.

"Toksus, don't worry. You're safe. We're just trying to understand. . . ."

Their voices faded as Koracoo's attention was captured by a set of tracks almost hidden beneath the dogwood boughs. She walked over and knelt near them, wary not to disturb the ground. As she used CorpseEye to lift a section of branches, her breath caught. The dense thicket had sheltered the earth from windblown needles and leaves. And the ground had been damp when he'd stepped here.

There were two tracks. Both clearly visible.

Her gaze lifted and swiftly examined the area. Was he still here? The tracks looked fresh. No rim of frost outlined the shapes, and there was no ice in the bottom of the tracks. They'd been made after the day had warmed with sunlight.

She edged closer and bent to examine them more carefully. The weather had turned cold and wet, but these were not moccasin prints. He was wearing sandals—the distinctive herringbone pattern woven only by the Hills People.

"She put his *soul* in me," Toksus wailed.

Koracoo lifted her head. Odion had gone pale.

Baji said, "Why did she want you to have the dead boy's soul?"

"I don't know. She said, 'Find him for me.' But I didn't know what she meant."

Baji cupped a hand to Odion's ear and whispered something. Odion nodded; then he swiveled around to face Toksus again. The boy looked at Odion as though afraid he was about to be left alone. He suddenly reached out and grabbed hold of Odion's sleeve.

"It wasn't my fault," Toksus explained. "I didn't do anything bad."

"She's a witch, Toksus," Odion said. "You're not to blame for what she does. Was she trying—?"

"She cut out his eyes, too."

Odion and Baji both looked at Koracoo, as though silently begging for an explanation.

She rose and retraced her tracks to where they sat in a circle. Toksus had started to cry. His chest heaved, and soft whimpers vibrated in his throat. The sight of him wrenched Koracoo's heart.

Baji said, "War Chief, have you ever heard of the ritual he described?"

"It's witch Power, Baji, evil. I know little about such things."

Baji's delicate brows lowered. She examined Koracoo as though she suspected she was lying, that she really did know but was withholding the information. Baji resented being treated like a child.

Koracoo relented and said, "She was probably trying to force Toksus to catch the dying boy's last breath. But Wakdanek is more familiar with such things. When he arrives, we'll—"

A shudder went through CorpseEye, and he warmed in her hands. As the heat increased, she shifted the club to her other hand. He was old and wise in the ways of the unseen forces that moved through the forest. *He sees something I don't.*

Her gaze swept upward from the bases of the trees to the highest limbs, then down to the brush, searching for any color or shape anomaly that would signal a hidden enemy warrior.

Very softly, so as not to startle her, Odion said, "Mother, what's wrong?" He glanced at CorpseEye.

She touched her lips with her fingers, telling the children to be quiet. They reacted like grouse chicks at the sound of a wolf's stealthy paws, their muscles bunched, ready to scatter to the heavens.

When the breeze picked up, the larches swayed and creaked, and a shower of yellow needles cascaded from the sky. Koracoo kept her eyes on the most likely places a war party might burst from cover.

After twenty or thirty heartbeats, Odion lifted his chin and his nostrils flared.

Then Koracoo caught the scent. It smelled faintly like the foul miasma that hovers around week-old carcasses in the summertime. She turned into the wind to see if she could pinpoint where it was coming from . . . and heard steps.

With ghostly silence, she rose and spread her feet, then grasped CorpseEye in both hands.

"Koracoo?" Sindak called. "Where are you?"

She relaxed. "Over here, Sindak. In the larch grove."

A short while later, Sindak and Wakdanek emerged from the trees, followed by Tutelo and Hehaka. Towa brought up the rear.

Wakdanek called, "Toksus?"

The little boy leaped to his feet. "Cousin Wakdanek!"

Wakdanek knelt, and Toksus ran into his arms, weeping. "I thought you were dead. I thought everybody was dead!"

"No, Toksus." Wakdanek stroked his back gently. "Many of us survived. Your mother is alive. I saw her just a few hands of time ago. She'll be so happy to see you."

Toksus sobbed against Wakdanek's broad shoulder. "I didn't think I'd ever see my family again."

"Well, you will. Now, tell me how you got here, little cousin? You're a long way from home."

Toksus pulled away and wiped his nose on his sleeve. As the wind gusted, tree shadows painted his face. "Just after the battle, that ugly Flint Trader bought us, then sold us—"

"Bought who? How many Bog Willow children were with you?" The desperation in his voice was painful. "Was Conkesema—?"

"There were four of us. Me, Auma, Conkesema, and the dead boy."

At the sound of his daughter's name, tears entered the big raw-boned Healer's eyes. He made an effort to swallow them and said, "Is everyone else—?"

"They're still Gannajero's slaves." As though he couldn't keep his eyes away, Toksus turned to the half-buried body beneath the dogwoods.

"Who is he, Toksus?"

The boy whimpered, "Sassacus."

Wakdanek rose and went to crouch beside the body. He examined it for a long time before he grabbed one of the feet and pulled the boy out into the amber gleam. As he brushed dirt from the child's face, his heavy brows knitted into a single line. The boy's empty eye sockets were clotted with old blood.

Koracoo said, "Do you know him?"

Wakdanek jerked a nod. "What happened—?"

Toksus rushed to answer. "Gannajero stabbed him; then she dragged him over and put him on my chest, and she—"

"Did she put your mouths together, Cousin?"

Toksus jerked a nod and twined his fist in the shirt over his chest. "Ever since, I've felt something inside me, coiling around."

Wakdanek's expression slackened. He rose to his feet and went back to embrace Toksus. "It's all right. I brought ghost medicine with me. We'll banish his soul from your body, and you'll start getting stronger right away."

"Thank you. I'm so scared." Toksus propped his chin on Wakdanek's shoulder, and a peaceful expression came over his young face.

Koracoo said, "After she forced Toksus to catch his last breath, she cut out the dead boy's eyes. Do you know why?"

"It's witchery," Wakdanek replied. "Who can say why?"

He hugged Toksus again and released him; then he tilted his head to Koracoo, gesturing that they step away.

She followed him into a small clearing where the sound of the river was louder and she could smell the mossy fragrance of the water. "Now tell me the rest."

Wakdanek crossed his arms tightly over his chest. "I've heard of the ritual. A witch transfers someone's soul to another body, but keeps his eyes. No matter where the afterlife soul travels in its new body, the eyes can still see whatever the soul sees. In this case, the soul she placed in Toksus is seeing us."

A creeping sensation worked its way up her spine to the back of her neck. "You mean she could be using the dead boy's eyes to watch us right now?"

"It's possible. But it takes a very powerful witch to do such a thing, and I doubt . . ."

A scream rent the afternoon. They both lurched through the brush in time to see Toksus topple to the ground with his jaws snapping together like a rabid dog's. He began jerking violently, locked in a seizure.

Sindak and Towa were on him instantly, holding his arms down so he couldn't hurt himself. Sindak cried, "Wakdanek!"

As the Healer ran, the children scrambled back, and Hehaka started yelling, "I didn't do anything! I swear it! He just fell down. I didn't even touch him!"

"What happened?" Wakdanek grabbed the boy's contorted face and stared into his rolling eyes. "Did he say anything?"

"No!" Odion shook his head. "He just asked Hehaka his name, and when Hehaka told him, Toksus got a strange look on his face. . . ."

The seizure stopped. As Toksus' body began to go limp, his jaw gaped and his head lolled to the side.

"Toksus?" Wakdanek fell to the ground and put his ear over the boy's chest. "No. No!"

Sindak and Towa rose and backed away as Wakdanek grabbed Toksus beneath the arms, lifted him, and shook him hard, crying, "Toksus, breathe!"

Sindak followed Towa over to where Koracoo stood. Though Towa had left his waist-length hair loose, Sindak had tied his back with a leather cord. The style made his narrow face look even more aquiline.

Sindak murmured, "That looked very much like the effects of poison."

Only Koracoo's eyes moved as she met his hard gaze. "You think it's retribution for the stew pot?"

"It may be. Where did he get that bag of huckleberries?"

"He had them when we found him."

Sindak seemed to be listening to the melody of birdsong that filled the trees. Finally, he said, "What good would it do to poison the boy unless we knew she'd done it?"

Towa frowned. "Are you saying that she let the boy go and told him to walk down the riverbank, knowing that we'd find him?"

"Not necessarily us, but whoever is after her. She must know she's being followed. This way, her pursuers would find him . . . and after hearing Toksus' story, they would be a lot more hesitant to continue pursuing—"

"*Toksus!*" Wakdanek shook the boy again. Toksus' body flopped like a soaked corn-husk doll in the Healer's muscular arms. For a protracted interval the light seeped from Toksus' eyes until he stared vacantly at the afternoon sky.

"Is he dead?" Hehaka demanded to know. His batlike face contorted.

Odion walked over to him and said, "It wasn't your fault, Hehaka. He'd been witched."

Wakdanek clutched the child to his chest and held him, but thoughts churned behind his frantic eyes. As though he was dealing with priceless statuary, the Healer placed Toksus' body on the ground and rose to his feet. His huge fists balled at his sides. He seemed to be straining against the overwhelming desire to commit murder.

"Wakdanek?" Koracoo called. "Why don't you join us? We need to talk."

It wasn't good to give men too much time to whip up their rage. It was like a dam being filled with runoff. The instant a trickle went over the edge . . . the flood washed away the world. *I have to force him to think.*

"Was it poison?" she asked.

The man wiped his eyes on his sleeve as he walked over to join their circle. The blend of shock and rage had left him shaking. "What did h-he tell you before I arrived?"

"You heard most of it," Koracoo said, speaking calmly and clearly. "He said Gannajero had stabbed the other boy, then forced your cousin to catch his last breath. After that she cut out the eyes—"

"Yes, I know all that, but there must have been more."

"Your cousin said that he walked all night to get here, and had to rest, and that when he awoke from his nap, he found the other boy lying beside him."

Wakdanek tilted his head and blinked as though trying to figure it out. "Someone carried the other boy here and placed him beside my cousin while he slept?"

"Apparently."

"But . . . who would do such a thing? And why?" Wakdanek started flexing his fists.

Koracoo glanced around at the men's faces. Sindak and Towa

seemed to sense the danger. They gripped their war clubs harder and edged back slightly. Koracoo stood her ground.

"Come with me. I want to show you something. Sindak and Towa will understand immediately. I'll explain the history to you as we march back to meet Gonda and Cord."

She guided them over to the dogwoods and used CorpseEye to lift the branches so that the three men could see the tracks.

Towa sucked in a breath and dropped to his knees. "Are they the same?"

"I think so. Take a good look. I need to know if you agree with me."

Sindak fell into a crouch beside Towa, and while they discussed the herringbone sandal tracks, Koracoo rose to face Wakdanek.

"We've seen similar tracks before," she explained.

"Where?"

"Everywhere Gannajero travels."

Wakdanek frowned at the ground. "One of her *hanehwa*?"

"Skin-beings wear sandals?" Sindak asked, confused.

"They are like ghosts. They wear whatever they had on when they died," Wakdanek said. "But I—"

"It's Shago-niyoh." Odion's voice rose from right behind Koracoo.

She turned to look at her son. Odion was standing less than one pace away, sucking on his lower lip, trying to see what Sindak and Towa were doing. His shoulder-length hair dangled over one brown eye.

"Who's Shago-niyoh?" Wakdanek gently asked.

Odion wet his lips, as though he feared no one would believe him. "He helped us escape Gannajero. He's very powerful."

Tutelo said, "He's a human False Face."

Koracoo frowned. "Why haven't you told me this before now?"

"You were busy, Mother," Odion softly replied.

Koracoo heaved a breath. She had been busy, apparently too busy to ask her own children the kind of questions that would have helped her understand what had happened to them. With as much patience as she could muster, she said, "Odion, I need to know everything that happened. Every detail."

Tutelo walked up to stand behind her brother. "Mother, Shago-niyoh used to come visit us in Gannajero's camps. He—"

"That's true," Baji said. "I think he's a Forest Spirit that takes care of children."

"Takes care of children? Is he . . . ?" She waved CorpseEye in frustration. "Is he a child?"

Odion shook his head. "I'm not sure what he is, Mother. Gannajero calls him the Child, but I've never gotten a good look at him. Sometimes . . . I think he's a—a crow. He seems to be able to fly. Other times . . . maybe a wolf . . . he runs so fast. I . . ."

Koracoo's expression must have reflected her disbelief. Odion closed his mouth and blinked self-consciously.

Towa stepped to Odion's side and put a hand on his shoulder. "I believe them, War Chief. When the children told us, we—"

"The children told *you*? When?"

Towa winced. "Right after we made camp in the plum grove. You and Gonda were standing guard. Tutelo heard us talking about the herringbone sandal prints, and she—"

"That's not right," Tutelo corrected him. "You were talking about how scared you were when you heard Father first call Odion's name. You said that the night you were chased by the warriors you'd heard the man wearing the herringbone sandals call Odion's name." She aimed a small hand at Towa. "Then I told Towa that it was Shago-niyoh. Because Shago-niyoh had been calling to Odion for days. Don't you remember me saying those things?"

The air seemed to go out of Koracoo's body. She leveled lethal glares at Sindak and Towa. "She told you all of these things and you never told me?"

Sindak's shoulders hunched. "Koracoo, it's not as though we've had time to sit around the fire and have a long conversation. We told you everything we thought was really important, like the fact that Towa thought he'd seen Atotarho in the big warriors' camp, as well as—"

Wakdanek stiffened. "Atotarho? The Hills People chief? In that camp? Did his warriors attack our village, too?" His voice kept rising until it was shrill.

To ease the tension, Koracoo said, "Wakdanek, Towa *thought* he saw Atotarho there. He wasn't sure. He saw the man from a great distance. He may have been mistaken."

Wakdanek's shoulder muscles relaxed a little, but his expression remained grim. To Tutelo, he said, "What else did you tell Sindak and Towa that night?"

Tutelo glanced at Koracoo as though no longer certain who to answer. Koracoo nodded. "Continue, Tutelo."

"Well, I told Towa that Shago-niyoh was a human False Face, and Towa pulled the shell gorget from his cape and said, 'Does he wear one of these?' That's when Hehaka woke up and said that his father used to have a gorget like that."

Wakdanek stared at Towa as though waiting to see it.

Koracoo aimed CorpseEye at Towa's chest. "Show Wakdanek the gorget."

"But, War Chief, it's not a thing for ordinary eyes! Atotarho told me never to—"

"Do it."

Grumbling, Towa reached into his shirt and pulled it out. The magnificent shell pendant covered half his chest. The hideous bent-nose False Face in the center, representing Horned Serpent, was surrounded by falling stars.

Wakdanek stared uncomfortably at the pendant. Very few people had ever seen it up close, and outsiders were never allowed to gaze upon it. Koracoo could feel the Power pulsing around the gorget. CorpseEye warmed in her hand. It was almost as though the Spirits that lived in the objects were speaking to each other in voices humans could not hear. A tingle ran up her arm.

"What does it signify?" Wakdanek whispered reverently.

Towa explained, "It chronicles the story of Horned Serpent and the destruction of the world in the Beginning Time."

Sindak stared at it in awe. The ancient pendant told the most sacred story of all: the great battle between human beings and Horned Serpent.

"Tell me the story," Wakdanek said sharply. "The whole story."

Towa's brows drew together. "I'll tell you the part that we tell outsiders."

Wakdanek nodded.

Towa said, "At the dawn of creation, Horned Serpent crawled out of Skanodario Lake and attacked the People. His poisonous breath, like a black cloud, swept over the land, killing almost everyone. In terror, the People cried out to the Great Spirit, and he sent Thunder to help them. A vicious battle ensued, and Thunder threw the greatest lightning bolt ever seen. The flash was so bright many of the People were instantly blinded. Then the concussion struck. The mountains shook, and the stars broke loose from the skies. As they came hurtling down, they hissed right over the People. Thousands slammed into Great Grandmother Earth. The ferocious blasts and scorching heat caused raging forest fires. The biggest star fell right into the lake on top of Horned Serpent. There was a massive explosion of steam and—as Horned Serpent thrashed his enormous tail in pain—gigantic waves coursed down the river valleys and surged over the hills in a series of colossal floods that drowned most of the People. Of the entire tribe, only five families remained—the five families who would become the Peoples that today live south of Skanodario Lake."

Sindak added, "That pendant is especially important because legend says that at the time of the cataclysm, two pendants were carved by the breath of Horned Serpent. This one has been handed down from clan matron to clan matron for generations, and now belongs to our chief. The other belongs to the human False Face who will don a cape of white clouds and ride the winds of destruction across the face of the world in the future."

Wakdanek turned to Hehaka. "Your father had one like that?"

Hehaka's nose wiggled. "I think he was my father. I don't remember very much from before I became Gannajero's slave, but I remember that gorget. It used to swing over me when the man bent to kiss me at night." He hugged himself as though it hurt to remember. "The last time I saw it, I was four summers."

Wakdanek's brows lowered. In a menacing voice, he said, "Are you telling me your father is Atotarho?"

Hehaka looked as though he'd been struck with a club. "You—you mean my father is a chief?"

"No," Koracoo stated. "That's just one possibility."

"But who else could it be?" Wakdanek asked sharply. "Surely you're not suggesting—"

"My father is a great Hills People chief?" Hehaka blurted. An expression of almost horrified delight came over his face. His nose wiggled as he sniffed the air, clearly smelling for the gorget.

Sindak offhandedly replied, "We don't know that, Hehaka. The war chief is right. It's just as likely that your father is the human False Face who will ride the winds of destruction."

Hehaka gasped, and Koracoo gave Sindak an annoyed look.

"It's even more likely," she said, "that there are many copies of that gorget, and your father owned one. Gonda and I found an exact copy of that gorget resting near the dead body of a girl on the border of Hills People country."

In unison, Towa and Sindak blurted, "You did?"

"What happened to it?" Wakdanek asked.

"We left it. We had no use for it."

Baji's gaze went from person to person, and she flapped her arms against her sides. "We're wasting time, War Chief. Gannajero must be just ahead of us on the river. We need to go find the other children before it's too late."

Sadness twisted Wakdanek's face and made the barely fleshed bones seem to stick out more. "I can't just leave the boys here. If wolves find them . . . I can't even bear to think about it. I have to take care of them. Please, go on ahead. I'll find a way to catch up."

Sindak walked forward. "Can I help you?"

Wakdanek gave him a suspicious look, but said, "I would appreciate that."

"Very well, but we can't wait for you." Koracoo propped Corpse-Eye on her shoulder again. "If you're not at the canoes within one finger of time, we'll go on without you."

"Yes, go." Wakdanek waved a hand. "Sindak will be there. I'll make sure of it. And if I'm not, I'll meet you somewhere on the river."

Koracoo nodded. "All right. Towa, take the lead. Children, follow him. I'll bring up the rear."

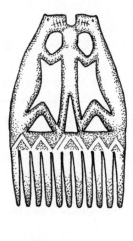

Thirty

Zateri had almost reached the camp when she heard moccasins shishing in the leaves behind her.

She turned to see Auma and Conkesema dogging her steps, threading their way between birches and maples. She shook her head and waited for them to catch up. They both had old leaves and dry grass in their hair.

"We thought you might need help," Auma explained. Her thin dress clung to her tall, slender body.

"You mean you were afraid to stay there by yourselves."

Auma had a guilty look on her face. "Well, we thought we heard warriors. It turned out to be two elk, but—"

"Just be quiet." Zateri breathed the words. "I think the camp is abandoned, but I keep hearing something just ahead."

Auma and Conkesema went silent. The faint crackling sound came again. Zateri studied the Cloud People. They had formed a bruised blanket overhead, and the temperature was dropping. Every time she exhaled, her breath frosted before her. The only thing that kept her warm was walking.

Auma whispered, "How close are we to the camp?"

Zateri pointed and continued toward the river. She could hear the rushing water. Three people made a lot more noise than one. Leaves rattled. Twigs cracked. She heartily wished they'd stayed behind. She could stand being recaptured, but she couldn't bear the thought that they might be. They had not yet seen the extent of Gannajero's cruelty. More than almost anything, she wanted to spare them that. When they got closer, she would force them—

"Look!" Auma hissed, and pointed. "In the tree. What . . . what is that?"

Only slowly did Zateri become aware of the thing floating in the maple. It appeared in the deepest shadows, then fluttered into view. It looked vaguely human, and wore a shimmering translucent material. As she squinted, it seemed to be flying, rising upon each icy gust, then falling down only to rise again.

"Blessed Spirits," Auma hissed. "It's a ghost!"

Zateri had never seen a homeless ghost before, though she knew they roamed the forest, along with other kinds of Spirit beings. Fear warmed her veins.

"Maybe. Let's get closer."

"Are you mad? I just told you it's a *ghost*! I'm not getting closer to it!" Auma said.

Zateri wound through the underbrush until she could see it swaying in the maple branches. A rectangular frame lay canted at an angle in the brush below, but she had no idea what it was.

When the Cloud People parted and sunlight streaked across the heavens, the ghost became even more fantastic. It was nearly transparent, but it crackled as it floated up and down. The kind of crackle that made the breath still in Zateri's lungs.

Then something miraculous happened. The wind shifted, and flashes of color appeared and disappeared. The ghost held a prism, a rainbow, in its heart. The ground beneath it glistened with wings of light.

"Oh, gods, no." Frantically, she began searching the forest floor, thrashing through the underbrush until she saw the body.

Carefully, Zateri picked her way around old stumps and brush to reach it. She had to clench her hands to still them.

The old woman is a monster.

"What is it?" Auma murmured as she worked through the brush to get to Zateri.

"It's a body," Zateri said. "He's been skinned."

Dark red flesh covered the bones and looked startling against the white teeth in the gaping mouth.

Conkesema trotted up behind Auma. When she saw the body, her mouth opened, but no words came out—only a single note, soft and sweet, like the beginning of a phoebe's song. The purity was stunning. It went on and on, then abruptly rose to a breathless shriek.

"No, Conkesema!" Auma leaped for her and put a hand over her mouth.

The little girl fought like a wildcat, tearing at Auma's hands, struggling to run away. Auma clamped her lips against Conkesema's ear and snarled, "Stop it. *Stop!* They'll hear us. They'll come!"

Conkesema sagged in her arms, sobbing. Auma stroked her hair. "It's all right. Just don't cry. Don't cry."

Zateri moved into the clearing and bravely walked beneath the ghost. Rainbows danced upon her upturned face. "It's the skin. A dried human skin. It must have been stretched over the frame, but the frame fell off when the wind—"

"Who is it?" Auma released Conkesema, and the girl sank to the ground and covered her face with her dress hem. Auma walked to stand beside Zateri. "Is it Wrass?"

"The corpse is too big. It's probably that guard Akio. This was his punishment for letting us escape. She turned him into one of her *hanehwa.*"

Zateri studied the ground. The leaves were thick in this small clearing, and Wind Mother had stirred them around. There were no tracks, no trails. But Gannajero's men must have walked back to the river where the canoes were stowed.

She carefully made her way down to the shore and frowned. Near one of the places where they'd shoved off, there were strange drag marks.

"What's this?" she said just above a whisper.

"Did you find something?"

"Yes, but I'm not sure what it is."

Zateri knelt. When her eyes narrowed, the reflections off the water seemed to grow brighter. "One of them must have been hurt. I see handprints beside the drag marks, but no footprints. The handprints are small."

"A boy's?"

Hope was rushing in her veins. She put her fingers over one of the handprints. It was only slightly larger than hers. "Yes," the soft cry erupted from her lips before she knew it. "I—I think it's Wrass."

Auma hurried over to look. "He escaped?"

Zateri sank down on the sand to look at the handprints more closely. Something was wrong. A frightening sensation constricted her chest, squeezing it until she couldn't breathe. "Auma, if he's dragging himself, he's hurt badly."

"Maybe that's why the old woman left him. He was dying."

The words were like a deerbone stiletto in Zateri's heart. She longed to strike the girl. But she got to her feet and let her gaze follow the drag marks up the shore. He couldn't have gone far. "I'm going to find him."

Thirty-one

Sonon leaned against the trunk of a hemlock and watched the snow fall out of the lingering blue dusk. The storm had quieted the forest and given it a luminous serenity. Even the sound of the nearby river seemed hushed.

He tipped his face up and let the cold flakes land on his skin. The boys whispered to his right. He didn't look at them, but knew they sat atop the rounded humps where Wakdanek and Sindak had buried them less than one hand of time ago.

He closed his eyes and just tried to feel.

One of the boys laughed, and it filled his tired heart with warmth. As long as Wakdanek lived, they'd be all right. The Healer would come back and make sure they got home to their families, who would in turn make sure they were properly prepared to cross the bridge to the afterlife.

He shoved away from the tree and turned toward the river. In the subdued light the water had a leaden sheen.

He wasn't needed here.

He headed south down the shore.

Nothing mattered now except his steps; they would decide everything. Steps always did. A man might plan for every detail and try to prepare himself for all the things that could go wrong, but in the end steps were all that mattered. Steps created the path. Steps brought you to the final moment when you had to stand face-to-face with all the grief you'd ever been asked to shelter in your heart. Your own, as well as that of others. It didn't matter who you were, or how you'd lived . . . the enormity was unbearable. It slammed you down. When you struggled up again, the grief either transformed into the Healer's balm or it became a murderer's inspiration.

He concentrated on placing one foot in front of the other.

Somewhere just ahead, he would take the final steps.

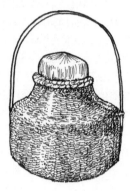

Thirty-two

Only the muffled tramping of their feet on snow-covered leaves filled the twilight.

"We'll have to stop soon," Auma said from behind her. "It's getting too dark to see the drag marks, and the snow is falling harder."

Zateri didn't answer. Panic was running hot and fierce in her body. She couldn't believe Wrass had dragged himself this far, but she knew him. The darkness and snow wouldn't stop him. He'd keep moving, trying to put distance between himself and Gannajero, until he was physically unable to continue and collapsed in a dead faint. If she didn't find him soon, she never would. The snow would fill the drag marks, and his trail would be erased from the world.

"Did you hear me?" Auma asked. "We should stop for the night."

"I'm not stopping." Zateri kept her gaze on the ground. A shallow swale marked the path where Wrass had dragged himself through the falling snow. It led around a thicket of willows and up into the trees. As she walked along beside the swale, gigantic flakes swirled around her, landing cold and silent on her hood and cape.

"*Zateri!* We have to stop!"

She swung around with her jaw locked. She was too exhausted and frightened to tolerate weakness. In anyone. "If you can't keep up, then sit down. I'll come back for you as soon as I find Wrass."

Auma clutched the collar of her doehide dress closed beneath her chin. "I wasn't trying to make you angry. We're tired and hungry. We can barely see. I—"

"Stop complaining. I can't stand it. Don't you think I'm tired and hungry, too?"

Zateri glared at her and turned back to the trail.

She followed his path around a massive sycamore trunk, then down a slope. Auma and Conkesema resolutely plodded along behind her.

Zateri's taut nerves hummed. Every noise, even the whisper of an owl's wings overhead, left her shaking. She loved the woods at home, but this forest lay as though under some dread enchantment. She could sense Forest Spirits moving around her, tracking her through the haunted darkness, peering at her between the frosted branches. Every now and then, she glimpsed something blacker than the shadows drifting through the trees. And there was more than one.

But she couldn't let fear stop her. Auma was right about one thing: the light was almost gone. Time was running out.

Ahead of her loomed the dark bulk of a toppled maple. The roots thrust up into the air like crooked arms. Straining her eyes against the falling flakes, she thought the trail led toward it.

Her moccasins squealed in the snow as she trudged ahead. In the hollow beneath the upturned roots, there was a dark splotch, a mound, like an animal curled on its . . .

"Wrass?" she cried. Down the swale she ran, slipping across the snow, her cape streaming behind her. "Wrass? *Wrass!*"

He woke with a start and shoved up on his elbows. Weakly, he answered, "Zateri?"

"Thank the gods we found you."

She launched herself at him, but the instant her arms went around him, her joy vanished. Earlier in the day, the snow must have melted on his cape as he'd dragged himself, soaking it. He was cold to the bone . . . but he wasn't shivering. She pushed away and stared at him. He was wobbling, and his eyes had a dreamy half-awake look, as though he wasn't sure she was real.

"Zateri?" he said again in a faint voice.

She spun around in panic. "He's freezing to death. Gather wood. We have to warm him up."

Auma wrung her hands. "But . . . won't Gannajero see the fire?"

"Get wood *now!*"

Auma and Conkesema scrambled through the falling snow, break-ing off the dead branches at the bases of the trees. They would be the driest wood around. In the meantime, Zateri pulled Wrass' wet cape over his head and draped it across two roots to serve as a kind of roof over his head. Then she pulled off her own cape and slipped it around him. As she tugged it down over his arms, he blinked up at her. Snowflakes coated his narrow face and perched upon his hooked nose.

"Zateri." As he said her name, tears filled his eyes. "I hurt . . . my ankle. Can't walk."

"I'll take care of it, I promise. For now, I need you to stay awake."

"But I'm so t-tired."

She grabbed him by the shoulders and stared at him. "I don't care how tired you are. Stay awake or I'll beat you with a stick. Do you hear me?"

His head wobbled, but a smile came to his lips. "You really are here. I . . . I wasn't sure. Been s-seeing things. Faces . . . in the forest."

Auma and Conkesema returned, piled wood beside Zateri, and went back for more.

As Zateri started digging a hole in the snow to create a pit for the fire, she said, "Yes, I'm really here, and I'm going to take care of you, Wrass. You're going to be all right."

But as she arranged the kindling in the pit, she kept glancing out at the dark forest.

Thirty-three

A gloating smile curled Gannajero's toothless mouth. All around her, her men crouched in the brush or stood behind tree trunks. In the falling snow, they blended perfectly with the forest shadows. She couldn't even hear them breathing.

For Kotin's ears alone, she said, "I told you Chipmunk Teeth would never leave the boy. Order our men to slowly spread out. I don't want any mistakes this time."

Thirty-four

The evening breeze was freezing cold and carried the distant howling of wolves.

"Tree." Koracoo leaned out of the bow to point.

Cord moved trancelike, dipped his oar, and steered the canoe around the snag that bobbed along in the water. The snow was falling so heavily he could barely see the spinning branches. If they struck something like this in the darkness, it would rip the bottom right off the birch-bark canoe. But he wasn't about to be the one to suggest to Koracoo that they stop for the night. For the past hand of time, she'd been terse, concentrating on the river.

Cord dipped his paddle again. Waves spun away, colliding with the whitecaps and leaves floating on the muddy surface. Somewhere upstream, the storm must have been violent. Debris, including whole trees, had washed into the Quill River.

Sindak, who sat in the stern just behind Cord, murmured, "She's going to get us killed."

"We can still see. We're all right."

"What makes you think she'll stop when we can't see?"

Sindak's snow-covered hood shielded most of his face, but Cord could see one of his eyes and his beaked nose. Uneasy, Cord asked, "Have you ever seen her canoe through a blizzard at night?"

"No, but this isn't any ordinary night, is it? She knows we're close. There's no telling what she'll—"

"If you're trying to be secretive," Koracoo said from the bow, "your voices are not nearly low enough."

She turned to stare at them over her shoulder. Some time ago, she'd shoved her hood back so she could see better, and her short hair stuck wetly to her face. "Stop complaining."

Sindak called, "I just thought I should tell you that I can no longer see my paddle."

She just dipped her oar again.

Odion glanced back and forth between them. He sat in the middle of the canoe with his puppy asleep in his lap. He'd barely let the wolf out of his hands since Toksus' death. Atop the packs in front of Odion, Tutelo slept soundly. Long black hair haloed her pretty face. She reminded Cord a little of his daughter, and that brought him both pain and joy.

"I'm trying to tell you . . . ," Sindak began, but halted when Koracoo suddenly pulled her oar out of the water and tugged CorpseEye from her belt. Her gaze darted over the shore.

"That's worrisome," Sindak noted.

Cord watched her for a time; then he whispered, "What's happening? I've seen her do this before. It's as though . . ."

"CorpseEye is speaking to her? Oh, my friend, I have seen things you would not believe."

"For example?"

"CorpseEye is old," Sindak replied, and calmly stroked the water. "He often hears or sees things that humans do not, and when he does, he tries to get Koracoo's attention."

"How?"

"She told me once that Power flows from CorpseEye into her hands. It's a warmth that can be painful."

As he said the words, Koracoo shifted CorpseEye to her other hand and scanned the trees on the eastern bank as though deeply worried.

Sindak said, "There must be something out there."

"Something good? Something bad? Is CorpseEye warning her?"

Sindak shook his head, and snow caked off his hood and piled on his shoulders. "The last time I saw this, we had completely lost the children's trail. We were desperate, biting each other's heads off. CorpseEye led us to the trail again. Good? Bad? We'll find out."

"Curious," Cord murmured.

Every warrior breathed Spirit into his weapons, and knew they were alive. For that reason, they were cared for and treated with respect. In the worst of times, the weapon's soul might save the warrior. But CorpseEye was different. He'd been around for so many generations that warriors for two moons' run in any direction knew the club's reputation. It was rumored that CorpseEye could kill even when it was not being wielded by its owner. Just looking at the ancient weapon with lust or greed in your heart was said to bring death.

Cord had known many shamans who possessed great Spirit objects. Usually it was a carved mask, or a stone fetish, maybe a tortoiseshell rattle. Once he'd seen an old woman who carried a turkey tail fan that she claimed cured illness. But very few weapons were endowed with such Spirit power. That's what made CorpseEye the subject of legends.

Koracoo shifted to face the eastern shore, and her forehead lined.

Cord called, "What's wrong, War Chief?"

She didn't answer. Instead, she lifted a hand and waved them toward the shore. "We're stopping for the night. Sindak, call back to Gonda, and make sure he hears you."

As Cord dragged his paddle, turning them toward the bank, Sindak cupped a hand to his mouth and shouted, "Gonda? We're putting ashore!"

From the torrent of snow, Gonda answered, "We see you."

When they neared the bank, the swift current jostled the canoe, sending it bucking and splashing through the waves until they got close enough that Koracoo could jump into the shallows and guide the bow onto the sand.

"Keep your eyes on the trees," Cord said. "My stomach muscles just went tight."

Sindak's eyes narrowed. He stowed his paddle in the stern and nodded. "Yes, War Chief."

Koracoo reached into the canoe to collect her weapons, and while she slipped on her quiver and slung her bow, her eyes continuously scanned the towering trees.

The underbrush was especially thick here. Willows and maple saplings crowded against each other. No clear trail could be seen through the thicket. And if the animals couldn't penetrate it, could a human? Still, Cord felt uneasy. There might be warriors hiding in that dense undergrowth, and they'd never see them until too late to get to the canoes. To make matters worse, there was nowhere to run except down the thin skirt of sand that lined the water.

"Mother?" Odion called. "Can I get out?"

She studied the forest for a long time before she answered, "Yes, but try not to wake Tutelo—and I want you to stay close to the canoe."

"Yes, Mother."

Odion picked up the heavy puppy and carefully climbed around his sister to leap ashore. Sindak grabbed his war club and followed the boy.

Cord remained in the canoe, gathering his weapons. He slung his quiver and bow over his left shoulder, checked to make sure his stilettos and knife were tied on his belt, then clutched his war club. As he started forward, Gonda's canoe came slapping across the waves, and the man called, "Sindak? Give us a hand."

Sindak trotted over and waited for the canoe to come in close enough that he could grab the bow and drag it onto the bank while Wakdanek and Towa paddled hard to keep the boat from being dragged back out into the current.

Gonda wasted no time. He seemed to sense something was amiss. He picked up every weapon he owned and strapped it on, then leaped ashore and stalked toward Koracoo. He said something to her that Cord didn't hear. She nodded and replied, "CorpseEye . . . this grove of maples."

Baji and Hehaka scrambled ashore behind Gonda and whispered to each other.

An eerie sensation of impending doom prickled Cord's spine. He stepped silently around the sleeping Tutelo, braced a hand on the gunwale, and vaulted to the sand. He walked to join Sindak and Towa.

As the three of them stood in the falling snow, Towa said, "Did CorpseEye lead us here?"

"Yes," Sindak replied. "How did you know?"

Towa pulled his hood forward to shield his face from the storm. "This is a bad place to camp. Koracoo wouldn't have chosen it."

"You think her club is brainless? Or just a bad judge of campsites?"

"I think CorpseEye could care less about our safety or comfort. He has other priorities."

"What other priorities?" Cord asked.

The two warriors had been with Koracoo and Gonda for about a moon. They knew far more about the war chief's weapon than Cord did.

Sindak's eyes lifted to the trees, searching the limbs. "I wouldn't be too eager to find out, if I were you."

Towa shivered and rubbed his arms. "It's going to be a freezing night. We should collect wood before it gets too dark to see."

Cord used his club to point to a copse of elms. At some time in the past, they'd been attacked by worms. Half the branches were dead. "Those will be the driest branches."

Sindak's breath frosted when he answered, "Towa and I will do it."

Willow stems clattered as Sindak and Towa shoved through them to get to the dead branches. For a time, Cord let them work while he scrutinized the area. The snowfall was still steady, but it had slowed down. About half as many flakes whirled from the sky.

He glimpsed movement to his left, and turned to see Odion and Gitchi walking along the sand toward him. The boy had a moonish face, with soft brown eyes and a short nose. Inside his hood, Odion's shoulder-length hair clung wetly to his jaw. The young wolf trotted happily at his side with his tongue hanging out.

As he approached, Odion said, "Mother told me I could walk down the shore so long as I keep you in sight."

Cord nodded. "Very well, but as soon as we've gathered wood we'll be walking back."

"I won't go far."

"Make sure you don't."

Odion nodded and continued down the shore with Gitchi bouncing along at his heels.

Cord took one final look at the forest and river; then he waded through the brush to help Sindak and Towa collect wood.

Thirty-five

Odion

A faint pewter gleam lingers as I walk down the shore through the falling snow. Twilight is rapidly giving way to night. Gitchi lopes at my side. The strip of sand is very narrow here, bordered on my right by the wide river and on my left by thick brush. Beyond the brush, trees rattle as Wind Mother blows the storm across the forest.

I step wide around a big rock, taller than I am, that is lodged in the middle of the sand. It narrows the path until it's just barely wide enough to edge by without stepping in the water. As I slide past, Gitchi splashes through the river, swerves around the rock, and trots ahead into the darkness.

"Gitchi, wait! Don't get too far ahead. Come here, boy."

I find him on the other side. He's standing with one wet paw lifted, staring to the south, sniffing the air. The dim gleam of evening makes him look like a ghost dog. He is a dove-colored phantom wavering in and out of the falling snow.

A low growl rumbles in his throat.

"What's wrong, boy?"

Gitchi scents the wind again and turns to me expectantly.

Wind Mother is blowing up from the south, swirling snow around and thrashing through the brush. I turn to face into the wind and my eyes widen. "That's smoke."

A campfire? A village?

Fear twists my stomach as I back away. "Come on, Gitchi. We're going back right now."

His ears prick, and he trots to me with his bushy tail wagging. I reach down and stroke his silken head. "Good boy. Thanks for warning me."

My moccasins crunch in the snow as I head for the rock. Just before I edge around it, Wind Mother's howling dies down, and the river's hushed roar seems louder. I tip my head back to look up into the falling flakes. They are half the size of my palm and silently spiral down to melt on my face. When I lick them from my lips, they have a clean earthy flavor. I turn back to the trail.

It's grown so dark that without the snow on the path, I'm not sure I'd be able to tell where the water began and the shore—

Voices.

Behind me.

Gitchi growls, and my heart thunders.

Ahead, I hear War Chief Cord speaking with Sindak and Towa, but this is something else. I'm *sure* it came from behind me, to the south.

I concentrate on listening. I don't hear anything now, but fear is burning up from my belly into my chest and filtering out to my fingertips. It is as though my soul hears the voice even if my ears don't.

Gitchi must smell or sense my panic. He goes as quiet and still as the dead, but his yellow eyes peer intently at the night, searching for the threat.

I swear there's something there, just below my ability to hear. And it's *familiar.*

I close my eyes and try to separate the human tones from the burbling of the river, the clattering of branches, and Sindak's voice. My head rotates, searching, moving toward the southeast. When I open my eyes, I am stunned. Fifty paces away, a fluttering orange gleam dances through the forest. It was probably there all along; I just couldn't see it through the snowfall.

That voice again.

The notes are sweet and high. A girl's voice.

I clench my fists and whisper, "Zateri?"

As I walk toward the voice, Gitchi whimpers, trying to tell me there is danger ahead, but I can't stop myself. The need to know is overwhelming.

The brush fades into tree trunks the size of three men standing together. Against the slate gray of night, the thick limbs trace crooked black lines. As the snow falls, the flakes pick up the orange gleam and glisten like embers floating down.

Gitchi lays his ears back, and his tail sticks straight out behind him. His gaze rivets on the flickering firelight. His steps are utterly silent. He can tell from my stealthy movements that we're hunting, and he's spotted the prey. He knows silence is of the utmost importance now.

When I stand ten paces away, flame-shadows gyrate, turning the frosted branches into liquid amber.

The girl cries, "Let me go!"

Desperation makes me sick to my stomach. I edge forward another two steps. I'm breathing hard. I suck in a breath, and her name comes out like a sob, *"Zateri?"*

I stand trembling, waiting for—

Gitchi barks suddenly and leaps at something. I spin around in time to see the puppy clamp his teeth around a man's arm and start snarling and ripping, his paws scratching the ground for purchase in the slippery snow. The man wears his black hair in a bun at the back of his head and carries a war club.

"Filthy cur," the man says as he clubs Gitchi, and the puppy falls into the snow with his legs twitching. A desperate whine escapes Gitchi's bloody jaws.

"No!" I run forward. When I fall into the snow beside him, Gitchi looks up at me pleadingly. Blood pours from his head wound. I reach to pick him up, but the man grabs my arm, drags me to my feet, and clamps a hand over my mouth. In my ear, he whispers, "How many people are with you? Nod your head for each one."

I will not. I claw at his fingers. He's pressing so hard my teeth are cutting into my lower lip. Blood wells in my mouth.

"You're a little warrior, eh? Well, don't worry, we'll beat that out of you."

The man half drags me to a deer trail that winds through the trunks toward the fire. Many people have walked this trail recently. The snow has been trampled, leaving a black slash through the white.

As he shoves me into a small clearing, a cry climbs my throat. A boy is huddled before the fire, rocking back and forth, shivering hard.

Against the man's hand, I try to scream his name, but only a garbled sound vibrates in my throat.

The man's breath is fetid as he bends down to hiss in my face, "Make a sound and my men will kill your entire party."

I nod, and as he slowly removes his hand, I wipe blood from my lips with my sleeve. My knees have gone wobbly. *"Wrass?"*

He turns, and I see the tears on his cheeks. He looks utterly broken. He's shivering so hard he can't seem to keep his eyes on me, but his shaking voice is clear. "S-sorry, Odion. So s-sorry."

The man shoves me hard, and I careen toward the fire. "Sit down, and stay quiet."

I drop to my knees beside Wrass, and he whispers, "They I-let me go. . . . Knew I'd . . . lead them . . . to the others."

"Others?" I whisper in sudden terror. "What others? I thought I heard—"

"Close your mouths," the man orders, and swings his war club to emphasize his words.

I stare at him, but Wrass' head falls forward, and he starts sobbing as though his heart is breaking.

Thirty-six

"What was that?" Cord stared southward. "Did you hear that? I thought I heard a boy's voice."

Sindak cracked off another branch, placed it in the crook of his left arm, and replied, "I heard something, but I don't know what it was."

Towa's handsome face tightened. "It sounded like a dog's bark to me. Where's Odion?"

Cord dumped his armload of wood and pulled his war club from his belt. "This could be nothing, but get back to camp. Tell War Chief Koracoo that if I'm not there with Odion in five hundred heartbeats, something is wrong."

Cord didn't wait to see if they obeyed him; he trotted down the shore.

The clouds had parted. Moonlight slanted across the snowy forest in bars and streaks. Where it touched, the ground gleamed as though coated with silver dust.

Cord slid around the boulder that blocked the path and heard a pathetic whimper. He eased his head out and peered at the trail. Almost invisible in the moonlight, the young wolf was dragging himself along Odion's footprints, whimpering and struggling, trying to get to the place in the forest where firelight flickered.

Hot blood surged through Cord's veins.

A warriors' camp? No. If a warrior had clubbed a puppy, he would have already spitted him and had him roasting over the flames. The man who clubbed Gitchi didn't have the luxury of picking him up. . . . He needed both hands, one for his weapon and one for Odion.

Cord surveyed the grove of maples and sycamores, then slowly made his way to the puppy and knelt down. As Cord petted him, Gitchi's tail weakly thumped the ground. "Were you trying to get to him, to protect him?" Cord asked softly. "You're a brave boy."

Gitchi whined.

"Don't worry. I'm coming back for you."

Cord silently rose and started for the orange halo of firelight.

Odion's footprints marked the way.

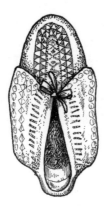

Thirty-seven

Odion

The man turns away from us to scan the forest, and I whisper, "Wrass, we're going to get out of here. I'm not alone. Just down the shore—"

"Shh!" Wrass hisses, and glances at the warrior.

As though I'm trying to help keep my friend warm, I put my arm around Wrass' shoulder and draw him close while I whisper in his ear, "Where's the rest of the war party? I don't see them."

His chin subtly tips toward the forest to my left, then indicates other places. I can't force myself to look. I'm too afraid of what I'll see. "How many?"

He shakes his head as though he doesn't know for sure. This isn't like Wrass. He is a warrior. He always knows who and what he is facing. Has the cold taken his senses? There is a woodpile beside the fire. I grasp a branch and lay it on the flames. As the fire eats through the bark, it crackles, and sparks flit toward the limbs above.

Wrass has his head bowed to hide the movements of his mouth. "The old w-woman hired more men. Don't know how many."

Thirty-eight

From where Koracoo stood guard beneath the leafless maple branches at the edge of the clearing, she could see Gonda and Wakdanek adding twigs to the fire, preparing it for the larger branches that Cord's wood-gathering party would bring. Already a weak amber gleam flickered through the trees and reflected from the river. Tutelo and Hehaka crouched before the tiny blaze with their hands extended. Both were shivering. Their soft voices seemed to echo in the snowfall and increased the deep sense of unease that tormented her.

CorpseEye was warm against her fingers, telling her there was something out there. She spread her feet and gripped the ancient club in tight fists, preparing herself for the worst.

Gonda called, "What's keeping Cord? We could use that wood now."

Wakdanek replied, "Why don't I take the children and collect some more of the driftwood along the shore? We'll add it to the pile. That should be enough to keep the blaze going until—"

"Quiet!" Koracoo stiffened at the sound of feet pounding up from the south, coming hard along the shore. "Gonda?"

He was instantly on his feet, his club in his hand. From many summers of warring together, he had learned every possible tone in her voice, and he knew this was more than just Cord returning from wood gathering.

"Where?" he softly asked.

She tipped her chin to the south.

Wakdanek rose to his feet and pulled his club from his belt. "It's probably just Cord, or Sindak and Towa."

Gonda turned to the children. "Baji, take Tutelo and Hehaka. Get in the canoe. Hide yourselves under the packs."

Baji didn't ask a single question. She scrambled to her feet and led the other children to the canoes. As they pulled packs over the top of them, Gonda said, "Wakdanek, if anything happens, I want you in that canoe and headed down the river with the children. If we're able, we'll catch you before dawn. If we haven't caught you by then, don't stop. Do you understand?"

Wakdanek swallowed hard and nodded. "I do."

As the steps pounded closer, Koracoo silently slipped behind the maple trunk and shifted CorpseEye for an easy swing at the first man's head.

Most of the storm had passed, though Cloud People still filled the heavens and cast dark shadows as they journeyed northward, apparently following the river. Snow fell lightly, obscuring Koracoo's view. She stared hard at the moonlit trail . . . and made out Sindak, coming fast. There was only one man behind him. Towa. She could tell from the way he moved.

As he ran for the clearing, she called, "Where's Cord? Where's my son?"

Sindak stumbled when she stepped out from behind the maple and onto the trail in front of him. "Odion," he said, breathing hard. "We heard a shout and a bark. Cord went to find him. It's probably nothing, but Cord said that if he wasn't back in five hundred heartbeats, you should—"

Sindak's voice faded as his eyes lifted and rapidly darted over the trees around the clearing. He said only, "War Chief."

"Koracoo?" Gonda called almost simultaneously.

She turned to see faces gleaming in the faint light cast by the fire. They stood behind trees, but she could see their drawn bows. The fletching on the arrows shimmered.

"Lay down your weapons," a man called from the shadows. "We have you surrounded. If you don't do as I say, we'll capture the children and make you watch while we gut them."

Every eye turned to Koracoo. Gonda was gritting his teeth, glaring in disgust that they'd allowed themselves to be cornered like this. Wakdanek's face had gone stony.

"Do as he says." Koracoo gently placed CorpseEye on a snow-covered pile of old leaves. As she slipped her bow and quiver from her shoulder and placed them beside CorpseEye, she whispered to Sindak, "I count eight. You?"

"Eight," he replied, "maybe nine. I think there's someone standing at the edge of the firelight to the north." She heard snow crunch as he and Towa placed their clubs within reach.

Towa added, "And two behind us, War Chief, blocking the trail."

"Our only escape route," Sindak said in a vaguely annoyed voice. "They've been watching and assessing us for a long time. Probably since we landed. Their camp must be nearby."

Koracoo glanced at CorpseEye. He had never led her into a trap before. There had to be more here than she was seeing.

A tall man with broken yellow teeth stepped out of the forest and walked into the firelight. He moved like a gangly stork wading the shallows and wore a beautiful red leather cape trimmed with seashells.

More warriors emerged from the trees, spreading out, circling them like a pack of hungry wolves. Each carried a drawn bow, and several of them were warriors from the People Who Separated. She could tell from their hats, made from the shoulder skin of a moose, which were very similar to the one Wakdanek wore. Her brows drew together as she tried to figure it out. The People Who Separated did not ally themselves with any outsiders, but the red-caped man's accent marked him as a man of the Mountain People, and she suspected by the distinctive way he moved that the skinny man to Red Cape's right was from the Landing People.

Eight men in the clearing. But Sindak was right. There was another shadow at the edge of the firelight to the north. It swayed slightly as though watching the proceedings, merely observing. And there could be many more out in the trees.

"I am Kotin," Red Cape greeted. "Messenger for the powerful—"

"Kotin!" The cry came from the canoe. Packs scattered as Hehaka leaped to his feet and scurried across the boat to get out. He charged headlong for the man, calling, "I'm here! I'm right here. I knew you'd come for me!"

As Hehaka raced by Gonda, he grabbed the boy, swung him into his arms, and held him like a shield over his chest. "You're not going anywhere."

"Let me go!" Hehaka pounded his fists into Gonda's shoulders. "They've come for me. I have to go to them!"

Kotin lunged toward Gonda, and Gonda shouted, "Come one step closer, and I'll snap his neck."

Kotin stopped dead in his tracks. "That would be very foolish. A short distance away, we're holding two Yellowtail Village children as hostages, your son and a hawk-faced boy named Wrass. Do you want to see them dead?"

A weightless sensation possessed Koracoo as the horrifying realization sank in that they had not accidentally stumbled upon a war party, but . . .

Gonda turned just barely toward her, and she saw the same stunned knowledge on his face. He called, "Koracoo, I assume you're going to negotiate with this piece of filth."

She started forward, and Sindak said, "I'll be right behind you."

"No," she replied. "I want you and Towa to stay out of the clearing for as long as they let you. Be ready to grab your weapons when the fight starts."

"The sooner the better."

The men who formed the circle at the edge of the trees shifted as Koracoo walked toward Gonda, altering their aims to follow her. Her souls were doing a mad dance, calculating strategy, trying to find some way . . .

Kotin didn't mention Cord. If they'd captured a Flint war chief, Kotin would have boasted about it.

As she made her way into the firelight, her glance searched the shadows, praying he was out there watching this, waiting for his chance.

Thirty-nine

Cord silently eased through the moonlit trees east of the campfire. He'd followed Odion's path to the place where the boy had been captured, studied the two sets of tracks, then backed away and taken the long way around. After he'd followed the river south for a few hundred heartbeats, he'd circled back to the east to approach the fire through the woods rather than the noisy brush. A dense stand of maples surrounded him. The bed of moldering leaves that covered the forest floor was damp and quiet to walk upon.

He slipped from behind the trunk where he'd been hiding and moved to the next. The earthiness of freshly fallen snow suffused the air. From his new position, he could see the low fire built in the hollow beneath the uprooted tree. It cast reflections upon the long, crooked roots. But he saw no one sitting around the flames.

Was the fire a lure, meant to draw in the enemy? He suspected that the first man to walk into the light would find an arrow through his heart.

Somewhere close by, one or two warriors would be watching the fire. Where?

Dark shapes covered the ground; most of them were bushes, or saplings, but a few might be hunching men. His gaze lingered on those shapes, searching for movement. Even the most diligent warrior moved on occasion, adjusting his cape, shifting his weapons, drinking from his water bag. Unless of course, he knew he was being watched; then he froze. But in that case, Cord would already be dead.

Down the incline near the place where Odion had been captured, a vague ripple touched the darkness, like a voluminous coal black cape whipping in the wind. When the figure moved toward Cord, floating across the snow as though weightless, Cord's fist went tight around his war club.

Black Cape moved into the trees and seemed to hover between the tree trunks as though examining the tracks that led to the fire.

Cord hesitated. He had his bow and quiver. He could have easily shot the man, but . . . he wasn't sure what he was seeing. A man, for certain, but he moved with an almost eerie grace. Barely a whisper of his cape disturbed the stillness as the figure glided behind the trees and continued at a leisurely pace up the hill to the northeast, starting and stopping often enough to convince Cord he was following a trail.

Cord remained perfectly still, watching until the man disappeared over the low hill.

Then Cord faded back across the leaf mat to the shadowy well behind a maple trunk and waited, listening. His four summers as a war chief, and ten summers as a warrior before that, had trained him well. He could smell peril; the forest stank of it. The silver brightness of the moonlight winking from the snow made the stillness all the more ominous. But he had the odd sense that this man was not the source of it. Something else was out here with them, and it breathed the darkness like a hunting bear.

Keeping to the tangle of shadows that weaved latticelike through the moonlight, he softly crept along behind the man, who seemed completely unaware of Cord's presence. His black cape swung when he looked down.

Cord eased behind a sycamore.

The man never turned. He kept walking straight north, paralleling the river.

Conscious of the weight of his body, Cord moved a few steps, then halted, careful not to snap twigs buried beneath the leaf mat. By angling his head, he could see through the dense trunks to a moonlit meadow ahead. The man appeared to be heading for it.

He followed.

Long before he reached the meadow, Cord was aware of the sound of children's soft voices. The hair at the nape of his neck stood up. As he crossed the ice-skimmed leaves, silvered by the night, he felt something. No sound accompanied it, no smell. It seemed to drift around him in the cold air. He shivered, trying to shake it off, but the sensation grew stronger, until it was almost overpowering. He didn't know how to explain it. . . . It was a . . . a hunger, a hatred that would outlive the passing of centuries, a need for vengeance that went far beyond his comprehension.

But it called to his warrior's blood like the singing of a thousand bows fired at once.

Blood started to pound in his ears. He blinked and looked around. Black Cape had vanished. Cord hadn't even seen him move. He'd thought the man was still standing, looking down at the meadow, but . . .

A child sobbed.

As though the girl was buried beneath a pile of leaves ten hands deep, the sound was muffled.

Cord set his jaw and continued on down the trail that curved through the dogwoods. Just as he veered around a clump of brush . . . Black Cape stepped from behind a tree less than five paces away.

Cord froze.

The man's ability for stillness was unnatural. Eerie. Black hair hung like silken strands around his oval, bent-nosed face. Fine as cobwebs, it shone brilliantly in the moonlight. His eyes were black as eternal night, with a wolflike luminosity. Cord couldn't take his gaze from that strangely pale face. The man's pallor contrasted so sharply with his black cape that he more resembled a corpse than a living man. And stranger still, he carried no weapons—at least none that Cord could see.

Barely above a whisper, Cord said, "Who are you?"

"One of the condemned. But no threat to you, my friend."

Cord hadn't seen his mouth move, but perhaps he'd just missed it. "You have a Hills People accent, but you're not one of them or you wouldn't be out here alone tracking them. What—?"

"If you're going to help your friends, you'll have to hurry. They're surrounded."

"Surrounded . . ." A chill sensation of terror went through Cord.

"And outnumbered almost three to one. Go. *Now.*"

Before his souls had even thought it through, he was backing away, then running across the snow, headed back for the river camp.

Forty

Odion

When we finally reach the clearing, tears are streaming down Wrass' face. I have his arm stretched across my shoulders, supporting him as we fight our way through the snow. I'm practically carrying him now. He won't say it, but I know the pain in his injured ankle is very bad. He can't put any weight on it, and I keep losing my sweaty grip on his hand and stumbling to stay on my feet, which causes him even more pain.

"Keep moving," Dakion orders. "It's not much farther."

"We'd be moving faster if you'd help me carry him."

Dakion sneers. "Complain one more time, boy, and I'll lighten your load for good." He swings his war club in case I missed his meaning and adds, "Your friend is a troublemaker. We should have killed him long ago. Don't give me an excuse."

Wrass whispers, "I'm s-sorry, Odion. I wish I—"

"Save your strength, Wrass. There's a fight coming."

He gives me a sidelong look, as though he can tell I'm secretly trying to warn him that we're going to make a break for it. Wrass' expression goes sober. He knows he can't run and must be trying to figure out what I have planned.

I'm not sure myself, except that I will not become the old woman's slave again. I'll die first.

"There," Dakion says, and points to a small clearing just over the low hill. "That's where you're going."

I take a new grip on Wrass' damp hand and haul him another five paces before I have to stop and catch my breath. Ahead, I see one guard standing over two children. A strange longing rises in me. I want to see Zateri. To know she's all right. But as we get closer, the girls' faces shine in the moonlight. She is not here. Panic surges through me. I whisper to Wrass, "Where's Zateri?"

He winces and croaks, "They took her. Gannajero said they were going to need her."

"For what?"

"The old woman . . . said Zateri had to be there."

"Where? For what?"

Wrass shakes his head. He's breathing hard, biting his lip with every step. At least he's no longer shivering. As I haul him over the hill and into the clearing, two girls leap to their feet and call, "Wrass! Wrass? Are you all right?"

The guards chuckle to each other. They find our concern for each other amusing.

When I reach the girls, I lower Wrass to the ground. He smothers the whimpers that try to escape his throat and looks at the girls. "Auma, are you all right?"

The older girl nods. "Yes, but they took Zateri."

Wrass uses both hands to adjust his ankle, stretching it straight out in front of him and heaving a deep sigh of relief. While he tries to get comfortable, the girls stare openly at me.

"Who are you?" Auma asks suspiciously. She is tall and slender, and has a broad nose and long eyelashes.

"I—"

"His name is Odion," Wrass says. "He's my friend. From my village. He—"

"Wait," the older girl says. "Isn't he one of the boys you helped to escape?"

Wrass nods. "Yes."

As though horrified, she asks, "What's he doing here? Did they hunt him down and drag him back?"

Guilt fills me. The fact that some of us escaped must have given them hope, and now, seeing me here . . .

"She didn't hunt me down," I explain, and cast a glance over my shoulder. The two guards have walked a short distance away and stand talking to each other. I keep my voice barely audible. "I came hunting for you with a war party. They are camped on the beach less than one-half hand of time away. I swear it."

"But . . . what are you doing here? Why aren't you with them?"

I square my shoulders. "Right after we made camp, I walked a short distance away and glimpsed Wrass' fire. Then I heard Zateri's voice. I had to see if they were really out there."

"But the war party will come looking for you, won't they?"

"Of course they will."

The girl wipes her eyes with her hands. "I am Auma, from the Otter Clan of the People of the Dawnland, and this is Conkesema. She—"

My eyes go wide. "Conkesema! You're the Healer's daughter. Wak-danek's daughter."

Conkesema lets out a cry, then stutters uncontrollably as she scrambles across the ground on her knees to get to me. When she twines her hands in my cape and stares hard into my eyes, she gibbers. I don't understand any of her words, but I say, "Your father is here. Right now. He came with us to find you, to find both of you."

Conkesema lunges to her feet to run to find her father, and I grab her around the waist. Against her ear, I hiss, "Not yet. They'll kill you. We have to wait!"

She whines and sobs against my hair, *"No, no, no, no—"*

Auma gasps. "She's speaking! She hasn't spoken since the attack on our village."

I pull Conkesema down and say, "Wait. For now, that's all we can do."

The little girl sinks to the snow beside me, sitting so close I can barely move. Her gaze has fastened to my face and won't let go.

I notice that Wrass is subtly surveying the guards, who stand five paces away, and I wonder what he's looking at. The shorter man, whose name I don't know, has a bow and quiver slung over his left shoulder and carries a war club in his hand. He wears his hair in a long braid. Dakion has only a war club, though his belt bristles with stilettos, knives, and a throwing axe.

Dakion says, "I don't know how she knew. . . . Witchery . . . She said there would be a boy and a dog. . . . All I did was . . ."

My heart flutters like a bird's after it's been shot with an arrow. I can't seem to catch my breath. She *knew* I would be there?

Dakion continues, "I'm relieving you. Go tell her where we're holding the two Yellowtail villagers. . . . I'll wait . . . as she ordered, until . . ."

The shorter man says something low, then trots away into the darkness. Dakion props his war club on his shoulder.

Wrass tilts his head, motioning me to come closer. I slide away from Conkesema and go to sit by him. "Wrass, how could she have known that I would be there?"

"Doesn't matter now. Listen to me." He reaches into the knee-high moccasin on his wounded leg and pulls out a wooden stiletto. It is made from hardwood, probably maple, though I can't tell in the darkness, and has been ground to a sharp point. It's about three times as long as the deerbone stiletto that Sindak gave me. Long enough to puncture a lung or heart. Wrass hands it to me and says, "I made these in case I had to fight off wolves. I have another in my other moccasin, but I don't think I can . . ." He clenches his jaw to hold back tears. "When the time is right, you're going to have to do it, Odion."

Fear constricts my throat. I close my fingers around the smooth wood. It's warm from being close to his body. "All right, Wrass."

I'm scared, but not scared enough to fail him. Wrass risked his life to help me escape, and dying is less frightening to me than letting him down. I glance around at the other children and tuck the stiletto into my moccasin.

Forty-one

Sindak gritted his teeth and glared at the people in the firelight.

Gonda had Hehaka's thin body clutched against his chest and was growling, "Stop fighting me!"

The boy let out a shrill cry and kicked his legs harder. "No, I have to go to them. They're my family!"

Gonda glanced at his war club, bow, and quiver where they lay in the snow near the small fire, as though wishing he could grab one. Gonda, as well as he and Towa, still had deerbone stilettos tucked into their leggings, but none of them dared to reach for stilettos until they had no other choice.

"Let me go!" Hehaka shrieked.

"What about your father, the chief?" Gonda yelled in the boy's ear.

Hehaka's shrieking dropped to a wail. "He doesn't even remember me. He won't know who I am."

"No man ever forgets his son. He's probably spent most of his life trying to find you."

"No one came for me. No one! I used to lie awake praying someone would come. But no—"

"Hush!" Gonda ordered, and turned to watch Koracoo lithely stride into the firelight.

Her short hair clung wetly to her face, highlighting her high cheekbones, full lips, and slitted eyes. Out in the forest, whispers started as men began discussing her. They probably all knew her reputation . . . and that of CorpseEye. Sindak looked at the club resting in the snow. He was surprised no one had come to get it yet. Did that mean Gannajero needed every man exactly where he was?

Koracoo stopped two paces from Gonda, facing Kotin, and the man's gaze traced the line of her breasts, narrow waist, and lingered on her hips. He chuckled softly, as though she were already his.

Koracoo, who had undoubtedly endured such arrogance many times, called, "You're an outcast, little better than a slave. Where is your master?"

Kotin threw out his chest. "I speak for the mighty Gannajero."

"If Gannajero is here, why am I talking to you? Is she too cowardly to face me?"

Kotin chuckled again, and his yellow teeth reflected the firelight like those of an old dog. "In a few moments, you'll all be dead. Why should she waste her time—?"

"*Because,*" Towa called, "I bring a message for her from the great chief Atotarho."

Sindak spun to stare at his friend. As Towa marched past, Sindak said, "What are you doing?"

"Carrying out my chief's orders."

"What? *Now?*"

Towa gave him an irritated look, held up his hands, and continued into the firelight. The amber gleam turned Towa's buckskin cape golden and shaded every determined line in his handsome face.

"Kotin?" a warrior called from behind Towa.

"Let him come!" Kotin said with an exasperated look.

Towa walked to stand on the other side of Gonda so that the three of them—he, Towa, and Koracoo—formed a defensive line in front of the canoes.

"What's the message?" Kotin demanded to know.

When Towa shook his head, his long black hair swayed across the back of his cape. "My orders are to tell only Gannajero. Where is she?"

Kotin turned to his right, as though looking at someone who stood deep in the forest shadows.

Sindak followed his gaze, but saw nothing. Then the brush rustled, parted, and an ugly old woman tramped out of the trees. Greasy twists of hair fell around her wrinkled face. Her lips were sucked in over toothless gums, but her eyes were like boiling cauldrons of sheer hatred.

"Gannajero! Gannajero!" Hehaka screamed, and threw himself into a fit in Gonda's arms.

Holding onto him must have been like clutching a wiry weasel with sharp claws. The boy scratched Gonda's face and throat until Gonda squeezed the air out of the boy's lungs and left him bug-eyed and gasping. "Don't fight me!"

Hehaka weakly pounded Gonda's shoulders. "I—I'll stop."

Gonda relaxed his hold enough to let the boy get a full breath of air into his lungs, whereupon Hehaka started sobbing.

The old woman didn't even glance at Hehaka as she walked over to Kotin. The shells and twists of copper on her cape shook with every move, creating small flashes in the near darkness.

"So," Gannajero said in a rough gravelly voice, "my brother sent a second messenger to follow the first. Smart. Do you carry the proof?"

Sindak wondered what she was talking about. Atotarho had already sent a messenger to her? Who? What message?

Towa cautiously walked toward her. "Is this what you're looking for?"

He grasped the leather thong around his neck and pulled the magnificent gorget over his head. When he held it out to her, the enormous carved shell swung back and forth. Kotin's jaw slackened in awe, probably calculating the extraordinary value, but Gannajero stood absolutely silent and still. Her gaze clung to the gorget, transfixed.

"Bring it here," she ordered, and extended a clawlike hand.

Towa shook his head. "Not until our negotiations are concluded. Atotarho wishes to make a Trade. He will—"

"Look around you, boy!" Gannajero said. "All I have to do is kill you and your friends and the gorget is mine!"

"Yes, but you won't have everything that goes with it. In exchange for the rights and privileges of owning this gorget, Atotarho wants both of his children back . . . and your guarantee that our party will not be harmed."

"He sold me and my brother into slavery when we'd seen eight summers, and he thinks I *owe* him something?"

The ground beneath Sindak's feet seemed to tremble. *That's* what had happened to the twins? Atotarho had sold the children into slavery? Blessed Spirits, it couldn't be true.

"He doesn't think you owe him anything. He thinks you *want* something. In exchange, he demands his children." The gorget dangling from Towa's hand lowered a little. "That is the Trade."

Gannajero vented a low disbelieving laugh. "When he sent me his four-summers-old son, his only condition was that I keep the boy alive, and keep my mouth shut. In exchange, once a summer, he sent me a messenger with big bags of pearls. Do you understand? He willingly let me have Hehaka. All these summers I've treated the boy as if he were his father. I made Hehaka go through every horror I did as a child. Now, suddenly, my brother offers me everything I've ever dreamed of? Why?"

Koracoo flexed her fists. "Do you agree to the Trade, or not?"

Gannajero shook her head, as though denying some inner admonition. "It's not enough."

Towa shifted. "What do you mean 'not enough'? He's offering you the rulership—"

"I know what he's offering, imbecile. My brother, the *great* chief Atotarho, grew rich and powerful off spoils that should have been mine!" She thumped her chest. "I'm the one who should have been living in comfort, wielding the power of the clan. But for thirty summers—"

"He only wants his children."

"You already have Hehaka." She waved a hand in the boy's direction and turned slightly away, checking the positions of her warriors.

"M-me?" Hehaka said in a tiny pained voice. He pushed back to stare at Gonda. "The chief wants me?"

"Of course he does," Gonda said.

Hehaka threw himself into a kicking frenzy. "No! I'm staying with Gannajero and Kotin. They're my family!"

As though the hidden meaning of the transaction had just dawned on Koracoo, she leveled a glare at Towa. "Hold on. What do you mean 'rulership'? What are these rights and privileges Chief Atotarho is promising?"

Towa swallowed hard. "The chief, and his clan, are offering to restore Gannajero to her rightful position as matron of the Wolf Clan. If she accepts, she will become the most powerful woman in our world."

Koracoo's eyes narrowed, and Sindak knew exactly what she must be feeling: insensible rage. After all the things the old woman had done to their children, and scores of others, her clan was going to reward her with . . .

Gonda lowered Hehaka to the ground and softly said, "Get in the canoe."

Hehaka turned to look pleadingly at Gannajero. The old woman shooed him toward the boat. "Do as he says. Get in the canoe."

"But . . . don't you want me? I want to go with you!"

"Want you? I never wanted you. You were my revenge. Get in the canoe!"

Tears filled Hehaka's eyes. He waited for a few more moments, as though certain she would change her mind. When it was obvious she wasn't going to, he ran for the canoe. Whimpering, he climbed past Baji and Tutelo, then over the packs to go sit in the rear, as far away from the commotion as he could get. Wakdanek said something to him, and Hehaka jerked a nod, but Sindak couldn't hear their exchange.

"What about Zateri?" Towa asked.

Gannajero extended her hand again. "Let me see the gorget first. I want to know it's genuine."

Towa hesitated. After several moments, he apparently convinced himself it would do her no good to possess it without the rest of the bargain being fulfilled, so he walked forward and extended the thong. Her fingers clamped around it like a bear's jaws, and she lifted the carved shell to examine it in the firelight. Her lips moved, as though speaking to it, or perhaps counting something. Her eyes widened.

"It's . . . true," she said in a stunned voice. "It's real." After five more heartbeats, her cold gaze lifted. "What's the trap?"

Towa stared at her. "There's no trap. He wants his children."

She chuckled darkly. "That hardly seems like him."

Kotin moved closer to her to stare at it and said, "What about the rest? When do you get all the riches?"

"When I return to the village, fool! Did you think my brother would send a flotilla of canoes carrying all the wealth of the Wolf Clan? Of course not. We—"

"Our business is not finished," Towa interrupted. Gannajero turned to glare at him, and he repeated, "Where is Zateri?"

Gannajero slowly, reverently, slipped the thong around her neck and adjusted the gorget. It covered her entire chest. "What are your orders once we've concluded our negotiations?"

Sindak had been wondering the same thing. It bewildered him that after all they'd been through, Towa had remained loyal to Atotarho.

Towa's expression was grim when he said, "My orders are to obey you as the new high matron of Atotarho Village and to protect you until you arrive home."

Sindak blurted, "What? You're joking! She's a monster!" Sindak felt betrayed. The Wolf Clan intended to bring this evil old woman back to live among the children of the other clans? *Horrific.* No one would stand for it.

"Those are our orders, Sindak," Towa replied through a taut exhalation.

Gannajero's jet black eyes darted from face to face. "And are your cohorts also obliged to serve me?" Her gaze fixed on Koracoo.

A humorless smile turned Koracoo's lips. "Of course," she replied, much to Towa's surprise. "Once the Trade is made, our duty is to help escort you and the children back to Atotarho Village."

"We will follow you in our own canoe, War Chief," Gannajero said suspiciously. "So we can keep track of your treachery."

Kotin said, "When do we get paid? We don't have to follow you all the way back to Atotarho Village, do we?"

As she stroked the gorget, Gannajero offhandedly replied, "Open my small pack. Pay the new men we hired yesterday. Separate the contents of the pack into six equal piles. Once we are finished here, they're free to go."

Kotin walked into the trees and grabbed her pack. As he walked back, he called, "You men. Come down."

Five warriors trotted into the firelight; then another swerved around Sindak and loped forward. As Kotin doled out strings of pearls, shell gorgets, bags of beads, and sheets of pounded copper, the men giggled and danced around like children.

Gannajero said, "Pick up your earnings and return to your positions. You are still mine until this is finished."

The warriors grabbed their earnings and ran back to their positions, smiling and yipping like demented dogs.

Gannajero turned to her own men. "The rest of you have a choice to make. You can either split my four packs, or you can pledge yourselves to the new matron of the Wolf Clan, and earn vastly more as my personal guards. If you decide to—"

Towa shouted, "*Zateri.* Where is Zateri?"

Gannajero paused, grunted, then lifted a hand and motioned to one of the men in the trees. "Waswan, bring the girl."

A very thin man with a broken nose came out of the darkness shoving a girl before him. Zateri was even smaller and more slender than Sindak recalled. She was wearing a blue-painted cape that was much too big for her. It dragged the ground. At some point in the past moon, she'd cut her hair short in mourning. It hung around her chin in irregular black locks.

Koracoo ordered, "Put her in the canoe with the other children."

Waswan's inhuman eyes went to Gannajero, and the old woman nodded. "Do as she says."

As Waswan marched Zateri to the canoe, he laughed and taunted, "I'm going to miss you, Chipmunk Teeth," and he groped her young breasts.

Koracoo's eyes flashed with rage, and Sindak's breathing went swift and shallow. Before they reached home, he was going to kill that man.

Zateri climbed into the canoe, and Tutelo and Baji leaped forward to hug her in a tearful reunion. He heard Zateri say, "Where's Odion?"

"Now," Koracoo said with a threatening tilt of her head. "Where are the other children?"

"You mean the two Yellowtail Village children?" Kotin said. "They're safe."

"Not just the Yellowtail children," Koracoo responded. "We want all the children, no matter their nation."

"We didn't promise you *all* the children," Kotin insisted. "Only your own—"

"Let them have them." Gannajero turned to one of the Dawnland men and barked, "You. Go fetch Dakion and the other brats. Bring them here."

"Yes, Gannajero."

After he'd trotted away into the darkness, Gannajero scowled at her remaining men. Kotin was seething. He looked like he longed to get his hands around her throat. Gannajero said, "Well? Which of you is willing to serve as the personal guard to the matron of the Wolf Clan of the Hills People?"

Waswan trotted up and grinned. Kotin continued standing beside her, but he made no sign of assent.

From behind Sindak, a man shouted, "I'll take what's in your packs."

Kotin growled, "You've always been worthless, Ojib! You disloyal cur!"

"Give him half the packs," Gannajero said.

"Half!" Kotin objected. His mouth hung open. "You were going to force four of us to split four packs—that's one each. Now you're giving Ojib *two*."

"Do as I say! You're going to get far more over the next few summers."

"But I was supposed to get the two Dawnland girls that you just gave away! If Ojib gets two packs, I want the other two as compensation!"

"You can't have them. When Dakion returns, he may want to be paid, and what will I—?"

Sindak flinched when he heard the hiss of an arrow behind him and, from the corner of his eye, saw Ojib fall. The arrow had taken him through the throat. He was trying to scream, but couldn't. Five heartbeats later, Cord appeared, slit the man's throat to silence him forever, and then lifted a hand to get Sindak's attention. When he knew Sindak was looking at him, he pointed to his own chest, and Sindak nodded, understanding that he was to wait for Cord's signal. Cord slipped back into the darkness.

A flush of hope filtered hotly through Sindak.

There was no one behind him now. As Kotin and Gannajero's argument grew louder, all attention fastened upon them.

Kotin shouted, "This isn't the first time you've promised me girls and then sold them out from under me. Two moons ago—"

"Stop whining! I've already told you I'll pay you for your losses when we get to—"

Sindak reached down, picked up his club, and tucked it beneath his cape. Next, he sidled forward to stand beside CorpseEye. Slowly, he lowered his hand and grasped the legendary club. As he rose again, he hid it behind his back, and it was as though Koracoo felt his hands upon the weapon. A shiver went through her. She turned to look at Sindak . . . and smiled.

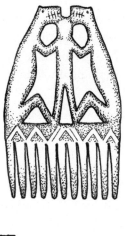

Forty-two

A few of the Dawnland men kept glancing uneasily back into the trees, as though they sensed Cord's presence, but the fire had obviously blinded them. They squinted, fidgeted with their bows, and turned back to watch Gannajero and Kotin. The old woman was shouting in his face.

Cord dropped to his knees atop a low hill with a clear view of the camp and pulled six arrows from his quiver, laying them out in a neat row at his side. By now, he trusted Sindak had collected weapons.

Cord nocked his bow and sucked in a deep steadying breath. As he sighted down the shaft, he heard steps just barely crunch the snow behind him.

I'm dead.

He clenched his jaw, waiting for the impact of the arrow.

When it didn't come, he shot a glance over his shoulder. Black Cape stood three paces away with his gaze focused on Gannajero. There was a bizarre quality to the man, a stillness so total it was as though he had been standing behind Cord for thousands of summers, waiting for this moment. He had his pale hands folded in front of him, and Cord noticed for the first time that he wore sandals, as though he was immune to the cold.

"What . . . ?"

In an unsettlingly soft voice, Black Cape said, "She was telling the truth, you know. Our brother did sell us into slavery when we'd seen eight summers." Heavy lids gave his eyes a sleepy expression that made their unnatural wolfish gleam even more sinister.

"You're her brother?"

"Her twin."

Cord saw no resemblance, except that they both had utterly mad eyes.

"Shortly after that, we were sold again, to different men in distant villages. I didn't see her for another ten summers. She had just bought her first children." Hatred inflected the tones, but subtly. "I was a warrior. I had been with the war party that attacked the village. She came to our camp to purchase some of the orphans we'd rounded up as slaves." He hesitated, as though he had all the time on earth to finish this story. "At first I—I wasn't sure it was her. Then I saw the gorget she'd made for herself. It was as though she believed she was matron of the Wolf Clan, as though nothing had ever happened to us. I couldn't stand it. I stole the gorget and freed every child. Most of them made it home. Alive or dead. I made sure. I carried them in my arms."

Cord slightly eased off his drawn bow. "I want to hear the rest, believe me I do, but right now—"

"Don't kill her. The others, yes, but not her." He spoke as though he weren't breathing; his chest did not move with air.

Somehow, it reminded Cord to exhale the lungful of air he'd unwittingly been holding. "Why not? She is the problem, my friend. Her men are just—"

"Yes," he answered in a sad voice. "She has always been the 'problem.' But there are many who have claims on her life. You are not one of them."

Cord shook his head. The obsidian eyes held his. The man did not blink, or look away. No expression lined his face, only a strange serenity far more frightening than anger.

"And if I do kill her?" Cord asked.

Black Cape moved his pale hands, reclasping them. It was a sort of weightless gesture, as quiet as the light snowfall, and Cord had the distinct impression that he was not flesh and blood. The man said, "You must help me with this one thing. It is not your right to kill her." The desperation in his voice never touched the glassy stillness of his face. He remained oddly immobile, as if centuries had taught him that, like the serpent in the leaves, survival rested in stillness.

As the voices in the camp rose to a crescendo, Cord became acutely conscious of the blood surging in his veins. It was now or never. "Very well," he said, "but I can't speak for anyone else."

Black Cape's head moved faintly, a dip of gratitude that seemed stripped to bare bones, a far-off echo of a human gesture. The man's gaze shifted to Gannajero. There was an instant of terrible silence where Cord had the feeling he was gazing upon a starving monster biding its time, motionless, waiting to strike until the prey came close enough.

Cord drew back his bow, aimed, and released. Before the arrow had even struck Kotin, he had another arrow nocked and aimed at Waswan.

He let fly, and glanced at Black Cape. The creature seemed frozen in time.

Cord nocked his bow and drew back again, but a hail of arrows began striking the trees around him. Cord flattened himself behind the hill as shouts went up and men started running for cover.

"Get down!" Cord yelled.

Black Cape just stood serenely staring at Gannajero, as though oblivious to the rain of death.

Forty-three

Sindak's muscles hardened and swelled against his leather shirt as he waited for Cord. What was taking him so long? Sindak's hand ached where he was gripping CorpseEye, hiding the club behind his back. To make things more interesting, CorpseEye had started to warm his fingers, and it terrified him. Was the club trying to tell him something? What was he supposed to do about it?

Gannajero and Kotin's argument had grown violent. The old woman was shoving Kotin with both hands while he waved his war club. He must have been weighing the momentary pleasure of beating her to bloody pulp for humiliating him in front of his warriors against the next twenty summers of untold wealth, and perhaps even status as the matron's personal guard—

An arrow flashed in the firelight, the chert point glinting as it drove into Kotin's back with enough force to send him staggering drunkenly across the ground.

One of the warriors shouted, "We're being attacked! Kill them!"

"No!" Gannajero yelled. "If you kill them, I lose everything!"

Before anyone could react, another arrow *shish-thump*ed into Waswan, and the man let out a hideous cry. Then a melee broke out. Shouts and screams rose. Men started running in all directions. Two men launched themselves at Gonda and knocked him to the ground, while several others wildly fired arrows into the darkness, trying to stop their attacker.

Sindak lunged into the clearing, shouting, "War Chief!" and when Koracoo turned, he tossed her CorpseEye.

As it spun through the air toward her, her eyes lit with a feral gleam. Koracoo snatched the weapon out of the air, pivoted on one foot, and charged into the fight spinning and leaping like some Spirit creature from the old stories. Two men sprang at her, grinning and whooping. She used a side-handed swing to crush the shoulder of the first and send him stumbling for the forest; then she spun on her toes and knocked the feet out from under the second man. Before he had time to roll, she brought her club down on his skull and moved on, running deeper into the fight.

A big warrior with missing front teeth shrieked a war cry and barreled toward Sindak, his club up. Sindak had just enough time to pull his own club from his belt and parry a blow meant to crush his skull, but the force of the assault toppled him. As he scrambled to get up, the warrior hissed, "Die, Hills dog!" and swung his club down hard, aimed for Sindak's spine.

Sindak rolled. The club whomped the ground less than a hand's breadth from his body. Gasping for breath, Sindak clawed his way to his feet, and they circled each other like buffalo bulls, growling and panting.

"Are all your men so slow?" Sindak taunted with a grin. "Or are your knees just weak from rutting with your sisters?"

"You filth!"

Their clubs collided with arm-numbing force, and the man's superior weight drove Sindak back five steps before he recovered, side-stepped, and slammed his club into the man's chest. As the man stumbled backward, gasping, Sindak took the opportunity to cave in his ribs.

Then he charged for the fracas around the fire. His gaze instinctively searched for Towa . . . but his friend had vanished. Gannajero was gone, too. Towa hadn't dragged her off to protect her, had he? Despite their chief's orders, the old woman deserved to be dead a thousand times over. And Towa knew it just as well as he did.

"Sindak?" Wakdanek cried. He was fighting a losing battle against three warriors, trying to keep them from getting to the canoes and the children. They were taking turns swinging at him, forcing him backward while they laughed. Sindak's gaze briefly flitted to the canoe, noting that he didn't see Baji or Zateri. Were they hiding beneath the packs?

Sindak swerved for Wakdanek just as an arrow *zizz*ed by his ear. *Blessed gods!* He gasped in surprise, thinking it was meant for him, but the arrow neatly sliced through the chest of one of Wakdanek's opponents. *Cord.* He was still alive! The enemy staggered, looked down at the brightly fletched shaft protruding from his lungs, and a bizarre smile lit his face before he collapsed to his knees and started howling.

With only two left, Sindak shouted, "Take the canoe. Get the children out of here!" and leaped a war club aimed at his knees. Before the man could recover, Sindak crushed his right hip and was spinning for the last man. "Go, Wakdanek!"

The big Healer leaped forward, shoved the canoe away from the shore, and ducked a whistling arrow as he madly paddled out into the current. The other canoe sat alone on the bank.

The last man roared and charged Sindak. Sindak skipped sideways. The momentum of the man's rush carried him past. Before Sindak could batter his brains out, an arrow slashed through Sindak's left shoulder and punched through the other side just above his collarbone, pinning his cape to his chest and rendering his left arm useless.

"Ha!" his opponent crowed. "You're a dead man."

Panic seized Sindak, but he managed to lift his club to block the warrior's next blow.

As the man lifted his club again, he bellowed, "Now, Hills coward, die!"

Sindak jerked when an arrow pierced the back of the man's skull. The warrior staggered, and his mouth opened as though to scream, but he just fell facefirst to the ground and started shuddering spastically.

Cradling his wounded arm, Sindak ran for cover. He got into the trees through a shower of arrows and dropped to his knees behind a head-high pile of deadfall. In the snow, he saw the small tracks of two children. They'd been running.

"Think about it later," he whispered to himself as he propped his club against a fallen log and gripped the blood-slick arrow that pierced his shoulder. He gritted his teeth to prepare himself, snapped the tip off, then reached behind him for the fletched shaft. When he jerked it out of his back, it was as though the cry was ripped from his throat by a jagged fish hook. The pain left him panting breathlessly.

From the edge of his vision, he saw several of the enemy warriors fleeing into the forest.

Fighting nausea, he forced himself to pick up his club again. He saw Gonda get stabbed in the side, but the wound didn't slow the man down. Gonda jerked the deerbone stiletto from his legging and plunged it into the throat of the man on top of him; then he rolled and scrambled to his feet just as another warrior swung his club at Gonda's head. Gonda ducked and drove himself headfirst into the man's stomach, bowling him backward, where they both collapsed to the ground. As they grunted and gasped, struggling for the club, Sindak searched the clearing. Dead men scattered the ground. CorpseEye had cut a swath through the enemy. No one was left standing.

Where is Koracoo?

Was she down? He didn't see her. Had she followed someone into the forest? Baji and Zateri?

No . . . there were no adult tracks mixed with those of the children.

Terror chittered through Sindak's souls. Koracoo wanted Gannajero dead . . . and Towa was sworn to protect her. Had she gone after Towa?

Gonda let out a hoarse cry, pulled the club from his opponent's grasp, and brought it down squarely in the middle of the man's skull. The sodden crack echoed through the trees. As though completely spent, Gonda collapsed on top of the dead man. He just lay there for several moments, breathing, before he rolled off and began probing the stab wound in his side.

Soft whimpers erupted behind Sindak, and he turned to see Gitchi staggering up the trail. Blood covered the wolf puppy's head, and one of his eyes had swollen closed. He kept stumbling, wobbling, obviously clubbed. The wolf braced his shaking legs and lifted his nose to sniff the breeze, looking eastward; then he let out a low growl.

Through the wavering firelit shadows, Sindak made out two men. One crouched on the hilltop twenty paces away. The other stood beside him, clearly visible, seemingly unaware that he made a perfect target.

Moments later, Cord rose and trotted out of the trees. He carried his nocked bow and scanned the clearing as he ran for Sindak. The other man remained standing alone in the darkness.

Cord said, "Where's Gannajero?"

"I don't know. I was occupied when she left. Who were you talking to up there?" He tipped his chin toward the man.

"A friend. I think. I'll explain when we have less pressing concerns. Wakdanek made it away?"

"Yes. But I didn't see Zateri or Baji in the canoe, and I don't know where Towa went. He may have thought it was his duty to carry out our chief's orders and protect that miserable old woman. If so—"

"Koracoo went after him?" The serpent tattooed on Cord's cheeks writhed as he grimaced.

"I think so. I have to find Towa before she does. I have to talk to him."

He gestured to Sindak's shoulder. It was streaming blood down his cape. "Are you able?"

"I'll manage."

"Then go. I'll care for Gonda's wounds."

Forty-four

Odion

Dakion hisses, "Shut your mouths! I can't hear anything," and cocks his ear to the night.

I hold my breath and listen. The other children go still. Someone is coming. We all hear feet rapidly slogging through the snow; then we hear cursing. As the man climbs the low hill just beyond the clearing, a thin layer of Cloud People cover Grandmother Moon, and her light dims. The distant chaos of screams and shouts carries on the freezing wind. We've heard it off and on for about one finger of time. The longer it takes Mother and Father to come striding over that rise, the more my stomach aches. I fight not to imagine what happens if they are both killed and Gannajero is the one who returns.

"Dakion?" a man calls from below the rise, and Dakion rushes to look down the slope.

"What? What's happening? I keep hearing the sounds of—"

"So do I!" The man appears on the crest of the hill. He is of medium height, with an oval face and a pug nose. He stands before Dakion, breathing hard. "When I left, everything was under control. I have to get back immediately. You have to bring the children. Follow my tracks and you'll have no trouble finding the camp on the river."

"Bring the children! Are you insane? What good—?"

"That's what the old woman wants. In exchange for the children, Chief

Atotarho and the Wolf Clan have offered her the leadership of Atotarho Village. Whoever chooses to serve as one of her personal guards will be rich beyond his wildest imaginings. Now, bring the children!" The man turns and runs back, slipping and sliding, disappearing over the hill.

Dakion licks his lips and grumbles something under his breath, as though deciding whether or not he will follow Gannajero's orders.

Wrass looks at me, and I shake my head. I can't believe that Chief Atotarho would . . .

Wrass whispers, "Two days ago, a man found Gannajero alone at our camp and told her that in exchange for 'both of them' her brother would fulfill her dreams. Do you think Atotarho—?"

"Is her brother? I know he is."

Dakion snarls, "Shut up, brats! Get on your feet. We're going to the river."

Auma and Conkesema rise. I try to help Wrass up, but he cries out the instant I lift him. "I can't do it, Dakion! Leave me. I'll be here when you get back."

Dakion stalks over the hill with a hateful gleam in his eyes. "I'm not coming back. No one is. You're not worth the effort."

As he strides for Wrass, Auma and Conkesema back away, and I lock my knees. The wooden stiletto in my moccasin seems to be growing larger, pressing against my leg.

Conkesema whimpers when Dakion lifts his war club over Wrass' head and says, "I've wanted to do this for a long time."

Wrass throws up his arms to block the blow and cries, "No!" just as I grab the stiletto, step into the space below Dakion's uplifted arms, and plunge the weapon repeatedly into his chest, belly, arms—anything I can reach. Someone is shrieking, but it takes me a long time to realize it's my own voice. From the corner of my eye, I see the war club swinging toward me, but it seems to take forever to impact my shoulder and drive me into the ground. I hear bone snap and topple to the snow.

For a few instants, the world goes black; when my eyes see again, Wrass is on top of Dakion, plunging his stiletto into the man's chest over and over. Every time he pulls the stiletto loose, the wooden tip slings blood, but Wrass can't stop. Dakion is still weakly flailing and trying to yell, though the only thing that bubbles from his throat is blood. Wrass does not stop until Dakion goes limp and his eyes fixedly stare at the snow-flakes drifting out of the gleaming sky. Even then, Wrass hesitates with the stiletto poised over Dakion's already mutilated heart, waiting for him to rise again. When it's clear that he's dead, Wrass sobs and crawls away, dragging his injured foot behind him. The first thing he says is, "Odion? Are you all right?"

I shake my head. The pain is stunning. I'm crying breathlessly. "I—I think he broke by shoulder. My collarbone. I—"

"Odion, listen to me. You have to go look for the other man. Did he hear us and turn around?"

Fear surges through me. I drag myself to my feet, whimpering in pain, and trot over the crest of the hill. The forest below is still and glistening. "No, he's gone. I think we're safe." I tuck the bloody stiletto into my belt and pull my left arm against my chest. Without warning, I throw up. The agony runs through my entire body. I gasp, "We should run."

Wrass is sobbing brokenly, but he nods. "I can't, Odion. But the three of you have to. You—you're the leader now. Make sure they're safe."

A strange feeling comes over me. Wrass has passed the mantle of leadership to me, but I'm terrified and hurt. "Wrass, I don't . . . think I can. I—"

"Yes, you can," he insists. "Now get away from here! When Dakion doesn't show up in the camp, they'll send more warriors. You can't be here when they arrive!"

I vomit again. When I finally turn to Auma and Conkesema, I'm choking on my own bile, but I manage to say, "Follow me. We're going to run east, away from the river."

Auma squares her young shoulders and calmly says, "All right. But first, let's take Dakion's weapons. We're going to need them."

Her sensibilities in the face of extreme danger leave me in awe. "You're right. Take them all. We'll divide them later."

The three of us trot back to his body and begin stripping it of weapons. Auma takes the ax and two deerbone stilettos, while Conkesema gingerly pulls a hafted knife from Dakion's belt. My head is spinning when I pick up the man's war club, then his bow and quiver. I carry the bow down to Wrass and lay it, along with the quiver, beside him. "The moonlight is bright. Don't let them get too close."

Wrass smiles gratefully and pulls the bow and quiver onto his lap. As he nocks an arrow, he stammers, "Not if I can help it."

The pain in my shoulder has grown so stunning I can't stop the tears that flow down my cheeks, but I call, "Auma? Conkesema? Let's go."

The girls fall into line behind me, and I start leading them out into the gloom, trudging through the light snow.

I'm praying that Mother and Father have already killed Gannajero's party and are, even now, trying to find me. But the past moon has taught me that I can't count on anyone rescuing me or my friends. We have to save ourselves. As my breathing begins to return to normal, the horrifying realization is sinking in. I killed a man. I can't feel my left hand, but the blood on my right has grown sticky. It glues my fingers to the war club. The only thing that helps keep my souls from fleeing my body is the fact that if I hadn't killed Dakion, Wrass would now be dead, killed with this very club, and I might be dead as well.

We haven't gone more than one hundred paces when I hear something. Ahead of us, on the other side of a wall of brush, *someone* is walking toward us. . . .

"Shh!" I hiss, and extend the war club to block Auma and Conkesema from taking another step.

The feet are almost silent. Warriors fleeing the fight? I take a new grip on the club. The pain in my shoulder is unbearable, but I have to concentrate and do what I must to give Auma and Conkesema a chance to run. *Stay focused. Focus!*

Two dark shapes appear and disappear through the brush. Just before they emerge, one stops and whispers something to his companion. Then both charge from the brush at dead runs, heading straight for me.

Zateri shouts, *"Odion? Odion!"*

Hot blood stings my veins. I can't help it. The mixture of hope and relief is so great, I stagger and can barely stay on my feet. My knees long to buckle. "Zateri? Baji?"

Zateri rushes to hug me, but hesitates when she sees my bloody shoulder. She stops and just stands in front of me, tears in her eyes. She is a head shorter than I am, and the arm she extends to tenderly touch my good shoulder is skinny. "We were so afraid we'd be too late. As soon as we could escape, we came looking for you."

Baji breaks in. "Where's Wrass? Is he . . . ?" Baji's eyes suddenly go huge. She is looking to my right, toward the brush.

I jerk around and see a hunched form weaving through the tangle of branches. *No . . . it can't be . . . My heart won't let me believe . . .*

Baji turns to Auma. "I don't know who you are, girl, but give me that ax you're carrying."

Baji's tone is commanding. Auma instantly hands it over.

"And I want one of those stilettos," Zateri says, and extends a hand to Auma, who pulls it from her belt and places it in Zateri's hand.

Auma sobs, "What if it's a warrior? What are we going to do? We can't fight! We have to run!" She starts to back away.

"You can run if you want to," I whisper. "But I can't. I won't. Not ever again." Though I can barely walk, I stiffen my spine and stagger toward the brush.

"I'm right behind you, Odion," Baji says.

"So am I." Zateri's steps are catlike.

Forty-five

As the Cloud People drifted through the night sky, the landscape alternated from pitch black to moon-silvered in a matter of moments. When moonlight streamed through the maples, Koracoo picked out the trail again. Dredged through ankle-deep snow, it cast a crooked black line through the white. Towa was taking the old woman away from the river and out into the dark depths of the forest where gigantic trees loomed.

Koracoo silently paralleled his course. After spending almost one moon on the trail together, she knew Towa: He had an implacable sense of honor. Following his chief's orders must be tearing him apart. But would he kill her to save Gannajero?

Ahead, a tangled stack of rotted timbers created a dark wall. The trail vanished when the clouds shifted, melting into the utter blackness. Five heartbeats later, it reappeared silvered in moonlight, veered wide around the deadfall, and snaked back into a grove of maples. A few old leaves clung to the branches and rattled in the breeze, but Koracoo heard no human sounds. No feet crunching snow. No whispers.

She circled the deadfall, keeping her eyes on the fallen timbers. The tangle made a perfect hiding place. Wind Mother whistled through the dead branches, carrying the earthy fragrance of decaying wood. One step at a time, she followed the wide curve past the deadfall and halted behind a massive sycamore trunk.

Cloud People darkened the sky again, briefly turning the world dark and cold. She shivered beneath her cape. Her shirt was sweat-soaked from the fight. Now that her body was cooling, the warmth was draining out of her muscles. When the clouds moved on, snow-flakes pirouetted from the heavens like white wisps of eagle down, softly alighting on the ground and branches around her.

Koracoo gripped CorpseEye in both hands and examined the way the trail slithered around the tree trunks, heading off to—

A carefully placed foot squealed in the snow behind her. She knew how he moved.

Without turning, she called, "Towa? Let's talk."

"Toss CorpseEye aside and spread your arms, then turn around."

Koracoo reluctantly did as he'd instructed and turned to face him. In the icy wind, his long black hair played around his broad shoulders. She said, "Do you have any idea what you're doing? This is wrong, Towa."

As he walked closer to her, his cape swayed around his long legs. "I know you want to kill her. So do I. The gods know she deserves to die for what she's done, but I can't let that happen."

"Do you trust Atotarho? Really? You actually believe the Wolf Clan is going to install her as the new clan matron?"

As Towa came nearer, she could see his grimace. He was having a very hard time with this. "If they do, it's a death sentence. It may be her birthright, but the other clans will instantly start plotting her murder."

"Then I doubt that she'll live more than a few days after you get her home."

"I doubt it, too. But it's still my duty to get her there."

"I admire your loyalty to your chief, Towa, but why would he give you such orders when he knows the other clans will never allow her to rule? You need to think this through, before you—"

"I have." Towa nervously licked his lips. "I've done little else over the past moon. My guess is that once he gets her home, he's going to turn her into some sort of prize he can parade around to elevate his status among our people. He'll boast that he captured her; then he'll send word out to all the surrounding villages so he can sacrifice her to the cheers of a huge crowd."

"Blessed Spirits." Koracoo's hard jaw went slack. Towa had always been the thinker, the one who worked a problem every step of the way until his conclusion was more than probable; it was a near certainty. "That makes perfect sense."

"The irony is that the only way he could get her to go along with it was to send her the most cherished artifact of his clan—the Horned Serpent gorget. She'd have never believed him otherwise. Never once in the entire history of our people has the gorget left the hands of our leader. Sending it to her was a stroke of genius."

A flush of revelation sent heat surging through Koracoo. "This journey had nothing to do with rescuing his children, did it?"

Towa gestured weakly. "The only thing I can say for certain is that the story convinced you to help him. You'd have never helped him if it hadn't been for Zateri, would you?"

She laughed softly. "No." It didn't matter now. She had more important things to worry about. "Did Gannajero tell you where she'd hidden Odion and the other children?"

"Somewhere in the forest, that's all I know, but they can't be far away."

Koracoo closed her extended hands to fists. "What are your plans, Towa? You going to kill me to keep me from killing her . . . even knowing she's destined to die shortly after you get her home?"

He braced his legs. In an agonized voice, he replied, "From the first instant that Chief Atotarho pulled me into his longhouse and gave me these orders, I've been sick to my stomach. I hate this, Koracoo. But please don't force me to make that choice. I can't—"

"No, you can't, good friend," Sindak called from the darkness. "I won't let you do something you'll regret for the rest of your very short life."

Towa spun to look at Sindak. Though Koracoo couldn't see him, apparently Towa could. He stared directly into the darkness near the tangled wall of deadfall and said, "What do you mean 'very short life'?"

"I mean, if you make any move to kill Koracoo, I'll have to kill you. And doing so will destroy my life, Towa. I love you like a brother."

"Sindak, what am I supposed to do? Disobey the orders of our chief? How can I ever go home and face my family—?"

"Atotarho isn't worthy of your loyalty. Don't you know that by now? All of this has been an exquisitely well-planned ruse to elevate his status. It wouldn't surprise me if Akio was an unwitting part of it, just like we were."

Towa's head cocked. "Are you saying he wasn't a traitor?"

"Of course he wasn't. Zateri was the bait to draw Gannajero in. If the chief had called Akio into his longhouse and given him special secret orders to make sure his daughter was captured, Akio would have been just as goggle-eyed with loyalty as you are tonight."

"You mean . . . that's why the chief went out on that Trading mission? It was the setup to make sure his daughter was captured?"

"Makes sense, doesn't it? You always wondered why he picked the two worst warriors in the village—you and me—to undertake the mission of rescuing his beloved daughter. The only thing that makes it worse is that he actually picked the *three* worst warriors: you, me, and Akio. He must have thought we were idiots. Of course we've proven that, haven't we? Especially you."

As Towa's aim began to quake and dip toward the ground, Koracoo said, "Towa, we need to know where Odion and the other children are. Where did you stash the old woman? We have to ask her."

Sindak called, "Stop being an idiot. Tell her, Towa."

Towa let out a shaky breath and closed his eyes. He gestured to the right with his bow. "She's over there, hidden in that copse of dogwoods."

Koracoo's eyes narrowed. The copse was only twenty paces away, close enough that the old woman could have heard every word they'd—

Koracoo grabbed CorpseEye and lunged for the dogwoods, running with the club out in front of her to help her keep her balance in the slick snow. When she veered around the dogwoods, she saw the place the old woman had stood, listening and watching. The snow had been tamped down from constantly shifting feet.

Koracoo shouted, "She's gone!"

Forty-six

As Gannajero waded through the snow, headed south to where they'd stowed their canoes on the riverbank, she burned with rage. Most, maybe all, of her men were dead. She could always hire more—that wasn't the problem. In the past twenty summers, she'd hidden stashes of wealth in ten different places—enough to pay an army if necessary. One of her stashes was less than two days north of here. In four or five days, she'd be back to Trading as vigorously as before. But she had to make it to a canoe before dawn. Her trail through the ankle-deep snow was impossible to hide. The instant War Chief Koracoo had enough light to track, she would come, hunting like a starving wolf following a hapless rabbit.

Gannajero grasped the upthrust branch of a fallen maple and studied the moonlit forest. The gleaming silver patina that covered the trees seemed dull in contrast to the brilliant snow. Ahead, a small clearing created an irregular oval on the low hillside. A deer trail threaded across the snow and through a thicket of brush, then wound through the middle of the clearing. She stepped onto the deer trail and plodded forward. If she were lucky, several deer would run this trail throughout the night, obliterating her tracks. But that would only slow Koracoo down.

As Gannajero headed for the clearing, her rage grew to a conflagration. Her brother thought he could trap her by sending her the sacred gorget! *And it had almost worked.* All of her life, she had dreamed of that gorget. Her earliest memory was of her mother slipping it over her head and saying, "Someday this will be yours." Though Gannajero wasn't allowed to play with it, she used to sit next to her mother in council and stare at it. She had counted the stars and knew every graceful curve and color variation in the carving. Deep inside her, in the dark space between her souls, the gorget's voice lived. It had called to her for thirty-two summers. Even when she was far away in distant alien empires, it begged her to come home. That's why twenty-five summers ago, she'd made an exact copy for herself. Carved it from memory with painstaking attention to detail. Though she'd known it wasn't the sacred artifact, it had comforted her. At least until her demented brother stole it from her.

Her gnarled hand rose to caress the gorget where it lay upon her chest. So many times she had tried to get home. Once, when she'd seen sixteen summers, she'd made it to the gates of her village—by then it was called Atotarho Village—only to be told by her brother's henchmen that she was an imposter. The Wolf Clan said that Atotarho's only sister was long dead. They'd dispatched a war party to drive her away.

"My brother, the great Atotarho, couldn't stand to look into my eyes."

She followed the trail through the brush, and when she emerged, movement on the far side of the clearing caught her eye. It resembled a black spider stepping across the snow on three enormous long legs. Occasionally beads or shells flashed in the moonlight. Then she realized with a start that the "legs" were actually long shadows being cast by three—

A single high-pitched cry of recognition pierced the trees. She gasped and ran. Feet thrashed the snow behind her. Wailing at the tops of their lungs, their voices blended to create one inhuman cry. She kept stumbling over roots and rocks hidden beneath the snow, falling and dragging herself to her feet, plunging on.

Her legging caught on a piece of deadfall and flung her forward. Before she could thrust out her arms to cushion the fall, she hit the ground hard, and the platter-sized gorget made a loud crack.

"No!"

When she sat up, she saw half the gorget shining in the snow. Her hand shot out to retrieve it . . . and they closed in around her.

Their pale faces seemed to have no other features than eyes. Huge black eyes. Their chests were rising and falling swiftly.

They were just children. Little more than scared mice. Gannajero rolled to her knees and shouted, "Get away from me before I witch you and rip your hearts from your bodies, you stupid brats!"

That high-pitched scream erupted again. It was earsplitting. With one hand, the boy swung a war club over his head and charged her. The Flint girl, whose name she couldn't recall, followed him swinging an ax . . . and Chipmunk Teeth leaped forward with a stiletto clutched in her fist. The other two girls stood by with stunned expressions. The pretty little girl that she'd had such high hopes for had a vague sweet smile on her face.

Forty-seven

The child's scream momentarily froze Koracoo in her tracks; then as recognition filtered through her shock, she shouted, *"Odion!"*

Her feet kicked up puffs of snow behind her as she rounded a clump of brush and dashed headlong toward the snow-bright clearing ahead, where dark patches—people—moved against the white. Corpse-Eye had gone fiery in her grip, leading her on.

"Koracoo?" Sindak called. "Wait! This could be a trap!"

She didn't even slow.

An eerie chorus of children's screams rang through the night, possessing a terrifying animalistic rage—pure emotion without reason or remorse.

She charged across the clearing toward where the children stood, calling, "Odion? Odion, answer me! Are you all right?"

When she was twenty paces away, her son turned to look at her. He blinked as though awakening from a dream and seeing her for the first time. Even in the soft moonlight, she could tell that he was drenched in blood. It covered his face and cape as though poured over his head. His left arm was hanging limply at his side, but in his right hand, he carried a war club clenched in his fist. The expression on his face wasn't that of a child, but of a victorious warrior standing over the dead body of the man who'd killed his family.

Baji stood beside him with a dripping ax, and Zateri stood two paces away with a stiletto. A short distance away were two other girls. She did not know them. One was standing. The other, younger, lay on her side curled in the snow. She had a finger tucked in her mouth, sucking it as an infant would.

In a shaking voice, Odion called, "Mother, she—she was trying to escape. We had to stop her!"

Koracoo dropped to her knees in the snow, laid CorpseEye on the ground, and—careful of his wounded shoulder—enfolded Odion in her arms. "Thank the gods you're all right."

"We couldn't let her escape, Mother," he repeated as though explaining. "She threatened to witch us. She was going to get away."

"She would have just bought more children," Baji said with unnerving calm, but as she lowered her hand, the bloody ax toppled into the snow, and tears slid down her cheeks. "We had to end it."

"Mother, I think my shoulder's broken."

Koracoo gently probed the injury with her fingers. His collarbone had been snapped, but it hadn't broken through the skin, which would protect him from the evil Spirits who fed on such wounds. "You're going to be all right, Odion, though it's going to be agony for a while. Is anyone else hurt?"

Baji and Zateri shook their heads; then they all turned and looked at the little girl curled in the snow. Her long black hair feathered across the snow. "When Odion hit the old woman in the spine and flattened her in the snow, something happened to Conkesema," the older Dawnland girl said. "She collapsed like her feet had been knocked out from under her."

"Is she your sister?"

"She's my cousin. I'm Auma."

Sindak and Towa halted a few paces away, and Towa said, "What happened?"

Sindak softly replied, "I can't tell."

Koracoo's gaze moved to the body. Had it not been for the broken gorget around her neck, the mutilated corpse would have been unrecognizable. The children must have kept striking her long after she was dead.

Odion suddenly shoved away to stare Koracoo in the eyes. "Mother, we left Wrass. He's hurt. We have to hurry. We have to go get him before the warriors find him!" He broke into a run, heading up the hill.

"Her warriors are dead, Odion," she called after him. "They can't hurt anyone now."

"All of them? Some must have escaped." He stopped long enough to hear her answer.

"A few escaped, but I think they're long gone."

Odion took a deep halting breath, then exhaled the words, "Maybe, but maybe not. They may still be out there. We have to find Wrass. I have to know he's safe." He charged up the hill again.

As Koracoo rose to her feet, Sindak walked to stand over Gannajero. For a time, he just frowned; then he bent and pulled the broken gorget over her head. "Where's the other half?"

"I don't know, but we'd better find it," Towa said. "Chief Atotarho will want it." Towa knelt on the opposite side of the body and began brushing at the snow, searching for it.

"Forget it," Koracoo said. "There's no time. Towa, I want you to get back to camp as soon as you can. Take Cord and Gonda and go find Wakdanek. Wait for us along the eastern shore. We'll meet you."

"But, Koracoo, that gorget belongs to the Wolf Clan. If I don't return it, Atotarho—"

"Once I start asking questions the last thing your chief will be worried about is the gorget. Go on. Conkesema needs her father far more urgently than you need a broken piece of shell."

Towa looked at Conkesema lying in the snow. Her sweet face looked oddly happy. "You're right." He sprinted away.

Sindak turned to Koracoo. "And what of me, War Chief?" Locks of his black hair had come loose from their tie and danced around his beaked face in the breeze. He kept glancing at Baji and Zateri, then at the old woman's body, clearly shocked by what the children had done.

Koracoo used CorpseEye to gesture to Sindak's wounded shoulder. "I need you to help me get the children back to camp. Can you carry CorpseEye?"

An expression of awe creased his face. "Yes." He extended his hand, and she placed the club in it. Sindak drew it back as though he'd just grasped hold of a deadly serpent.

When Koracoo knelt at Conkesema's side, the child didn't even blink. She just sucked her finger and stared blankly at the night sky. "I'm slipping my arms under you," Koracoo announced. As she lifted her, the girl let out a faint whimper. "Everything's all right. I'm going to take you to your father."

Koracoo turned. "All right, let's all follow Odion."

Forty-eight

The screams and shouts had stopped, but Odion still had not returned, and Wrass was shaking badly, more afraid than he'd ever been in his life.

If she killed Odion, there's nothing left, no hope. . . .

"Wrass?"

He went stone still. The faint call seemed to swirl around on Wind Mother's breath, like a distant echo bouncing through the trees.

He pulled his bowstring tighter and tried not to move.

There was something out there. An odd tang rode the wind, like the tang of carrion. His hands clenched on the nocked bow as his gaze swept the trees and brush that fringed the clearing. If his first shot missed, he'd never be able to nock a second arrow fast enough to defend himself. Which meant his first arrow had to fly true. He braced his shaking arms on his drawn-up knees.

He'd dragged himself down the hill to the edge of the trees to get away from the sounds and small jerks Dakion's body continued to make. He was almost invisible here. If he could . . .

He twisted around when something wavered in the darkness to his left.

Like great black wings flapping, the man's cape billowed around him when he walked out of the forest. He stopped five paces away, his back to the snow-blanketed clearing, and lightly clasped his hands before him. The man carried no weapons. The old copper beads that ringed the neck of his cape had turned blue-green from lack of polishing. The man's face, as white and luminescent as seashell in the gloom, flashed when he cocked his head to study Wrass.

Wrass whispered in awe, "You . . . you're real. When I saw you on the river I thought you were just a figment of my fever. Are you . . . ? You're Shago-niyoh, aren't you?"

The man stepped closer, and as he knelt in front of Wrass, shining strands of his fine hair blew across his cheeks like moonlit spiderwebs.

In an eerily quiet voice, he asked, "Do you recall what I told you that night on the river?"

Wrass licked his cracked lips. "About Elder Brother Sun blackening his face with the soot of the dying world?"

The man nodded, but it was such a subtle gesture, Wrass almost missed it.

"Yes, I remember. Why?"

"I made you a promise."

Wrass had to think about it. "You said that I would know the one who is to come. At the end of the world. The Human False Face who will don the cape of white clouds and ride the winds of destruction. . . ."

Wrass stopped when the man turned, lifted a hand, and pointed to the opposite side of the clearing, where a boy ran across the snow. He was holding his left arm, running as hard as he could, calling, *"Wrass? Wrass, are you all right?"*

A strange light-headed sensation came over Wrass. In awe, he whispered, "Are you sure?"

The man smiled, but it was a sad smile, filled with loss and longing, as though he could see the way ahead, and it was not an easy path. Softly, he said, "Help him, if you can."

The man's cape flared as he rose to his feet and walked away into the trees. In moments, he was gone, swallowed by the darkness.

Odion charged straight for the last place he'd seen Wrass, and when Wrass wasn't there, he panicked. He spun around and cried, *"Wrass!* Wrass, where are you?"

Two adults and three children followed a little way behind Odion. One of the adults seemed to be carrying something.

"I'm down here, Odion!" he shouted back. "Near the trees!"

People started running toward him, but Odion was in the lead, his legs pumping, trying hard to get to Wrass first.

Forty-nine

Odion

I lie on the packs with Gitchi curled against me. The puppy's head is healing, though he still whimpers in his sleep. I pet his fur gently and watch Wakdanek on the opposite side of the canoe. He rocks Conkesema in his arms and whispers in her ear. She hasn't spoken or taken her eyes from him since we found him waiting along the riverbank with Hehaka and Tutelo. The little girl has one hand twined in Wakdanek's shirt sleeve, as though she'll never let go.

The night is quiet and cold. Mist hovers low over the river, and I imagine that if I just reach out I can touch it. Along the banks, it creeps among the tree trunks like ghostly white arms.

Gitchi shifts and props his nose on my hand. "Everything's all right now," I murmur. "We're going home."

Ahead of us on the water, Mother and War Chief Cord paddle against the current, trying to stay close to shore. In the middle of their canoe, Zateri and Baji sit side by side with their arms around each other, talking. I don't know where Tutelo and Auma are. They must be sleeping in the bottom of Mother's canoe.

Wakdanek has told us that he will be leaving us tomorrow, taking Conkesema and Auma back to find whatever remains of their families. After that, War Chief Cord will take Baji away with him to Flint country, while Mother and the rest of us head for Atotarho Village to make sure that

Zateri and Hehaka make it home. Finally, Mother will lead the way to Bur Oak Village, where, hopefully, we will find the last survivors of Yellowtail Village. As I gaze at Zateri and Baji, my heart aches. I miss them already. Over the past moon, our souls have woven themselves together into a fine tight weave. We are part of each other. I'll be ripped apart when they go home.

My gaze shifts to Father, who paddles in the bow of our canoe while Towa steers the canoe from the rear. Sindak and Hehaka sleep on the packs just in front of me, and Wrass sits in front of them. Every time I turn, I find Wrass watching me with glistening eyes.

I shift my aching shoulder. Wakdanek bandaged it and made me a sling, but it hurts badly. Father says he doesn't know if I'll have the full use of it when it heals. Right now, I don't care. I'm alive. So are my friends.

Gitchi growls in his sleep, and his feet twitch. I whisper, "You're safe, boy. You don't have to run anymore."

And for the first time in over a moon, I think maybe I can stop running, too.

Father turns and frowns at me for several moments; then he ships his paddle and carefully climbs over the packs and around sleeping people to get to me. The lines at the corners of his eyes crinkle as he scans my face. "You are a man now, Son. A warrior," he says with pride in his voice. "There's something I want to give you."

"What is it, Father?" I sit up straighter.

Father pulls a False Face gorget from around his throat and drapes it over my head.

In awe, I say, "This looks just like the one that Towa—"

"It's not the same. It's just a copy, but it has Power. I've felt it. I want you to have it. Perhaps it will protect you in the days to come."

Father smiles again, then makes his way back to the bow and picks up his paddle.

I reach down to trace the stars with my fingers. When I look at Wrass, he's still staring at me. I nod to him.

He nods back and calls, "I didn't think you'd get that so soon."

"What do you mean?"

"Nothing." He shakes his head. "It's beautiful."

A strange sensation filters through me. It is as though I have just awakened from a long sleep and discovered that it is winter and the trees are bare and coated with snow, and I realize I am cold and very tired.

Wrass' gaze shifts to Baji and Zateri. They are talking and smiling. A sad smile creases his face, and my heart aches. Wrass must feel the same sense of loss that I do, dreading the moment when our friends go away. I don't even want to think about it.

For now, I'm safe. They're still here. We're still together.

I curl my body around Gitchi and watch the endless trees pass by.

Fifty

As they were escorted across the village by Nesi and twenty warriors with war clubs, Odion's gaze drifted over the broad plaza. Zateri walked close beside him. She kept licking her lips and staring around as though this was just another dream, and it might disappear at any instant. Ahead of him, Koracoo and Gonda walked, and behind him, Hehaka clung onto Towa's cape as though he feared he was about to be eaten alive. Sindak had insisted upon staying outside to guard Tutelo and Wrass until they returned.

The four longhouses were arranged in a rough oval around the plaza. Odion studied them. This was a huge village, perhaps the largest village anywhere on earth. On the eastern side, near the forty-hand-tall palisade wall, four smaller clan houses and another house, probably the prisoners' house, stood. The magnificent longhouses—surely the biggest ever built—were constructed of pole frames and covered with slippery elm bark. The house they walked toward stretched over eight hundred hands long and forty wide. The others were shorter, two or three hundred hands long, but still stunning. The arched roofs soared over fifty hands high.

Laughing children raced by, followed by a pack of dogs wagging their tails. Zateri craned her neck, trying to see faces, but the group of warriors was packed too tightly around them. Odion could barely glimpse eyes. People began to run across the plaza, coalescing into a large crowd. They surrounded the warriors, calling questions, trying to see who was being protected inside the circle.

"Is that Zateri?" a woman cried. *"Zateri?"*

"Aunt Dinaga! I'm here, I'm right here!"

"Thank the Spirits, you're all right! We had feared the worst."

Aunt Dinaga tried to force her way into the warriors' circle to get to Zateri, but War Chief Nesi shouted, "Stay back! The chief wishes to speak with them first. You can all talk after the chief is finished."

Aunt Dinaga faded back with a heartbroken expression on her face. Then the grumbling began. People shouted curses at Koracoo and Gonda. Someone threw a rock at Gonda. He ducked and glared.

Zateri whispered, "Odion, stay very close to me. I won't let *anyone* hurt you." She grabbed his hand and held onto it, dragging him forward.

The big war chief, Nesi, must have sensed that the mood was changing. He picked up his pace and led them forward at a run.

"Towa!" a man yelled from the right, and Odion glimpsed the man running at the edge of the warriors. He had seen perhaps thirty-five summers and had gray-speckled long hair. "Are you all right?"

Towa lifted a hand, and called, "I'm fine, Father! I'll see you soon. Tell Sindak's parents he is well, also."

"I will!"

When they approached her longhouse, tears filled Zateri's eyes.

Odion asked, "Are you all right?"

"Yes, I just never thought I'd see home again." Her gaze lifted to the two massive log pillars carved with faces and painted in rich shades of red, blue, black, and pure white that stood outside the door. "All of my life, every summer, I've watched people repaint the Faces that protect our longhouse. They are like old friends looking down upon me."

She reached out as though she longed to touch them, to speak with their Spirits, but Nesi drew back the leather curtain that held in the longhouse warmth and ordered, "Hurry. Get inside before I have a riot to put down."

As Mother and Father passed War Chief Nesi, they exchanged threatening glances, and Odion wondered if they'd met before. Perhaps in battle?

Odion ducked into the longhouse still holding Zateri's hand, and Nesi said, "Lonkol, I want half of the warriors guarding this end of the house, and other half stationed at the opposite end."

"Yes, Nesi."

Feet pounded the frozen ground as men trotted away. Odion blinked, trying to rush his eyes into adjusting to the firelit darkness. He'd been staring at brilliant sunlight reflecting from snow for forty-three days. It would likely take a while to adjust.

All he could see now were the forty fires that burned down the length of the house. They resembled a chain of amber beads. As his vision began to clear, he looked up. High over his head, blue wood smoke crept along the ceiling until it was sucked out through the smoke holes. Cornstalks, vines of squashes, and beans, as well as whole sunflowers hung from the rafters, curing in the rising smoke. The sudden warmth made him shiver.

"Grandmother?" Zateri called, her voice breaking. "Mother?"

She released Odion's hand and lunged forward to run down the length of the house, but Nesi grabbed her arm as she passed him. "Stay here. Your father is coming." Scars crisscrossed his face like thick white worms. They writhed when he glowered at her.

"But, Nesi, I live here. Why can't I go look for Mother?"

"Ask your father when he arrives."

Zateri swallowed her hope and returned to stand beside Odion. "Something's wrong," she whispered.

"It may be nothing. Don't worry yet."

His gaze drifted, searching the low shelves stuffed with pots, baskets, and personal belongings, and the sleeping benches that lined the walls above them. Bark partitions separated each family's space, providing some privacy. And far away, down at the end of the house, people were gathered. Soft voices echoed.

Koracoo, Gonda, and Towa moved closer together and spoke in whispers. Their expressions made Odion's belly knot up.

"Where's our father?" Hehaka whispered as he edged forward to stand beside Zateri. Fear tensed his triangular face, and his bat nose wriggled as he smelled the air.

Zateri balled her fists. "I don't know. Probably down there."

"What's he doing?"

For a long moment the question didn't make sense. The gathering was obviously a village council meeting. Then it occurred to Odion that Hehaka had not been raised in a longhouse or even in a village.

He'd spent his entire life moving from camp to camp with a small party of outcast warriors. He knew nothing of village life.

Zateri explained, "Each clan has its own council, but the village also has one big council of clan elders. This is the village council."

Hehaka's small black eyes narrowed. "I don't like this. I don't want to be here. Who are the people standing on the right?"

"Those are the Speakers. Different groups elect one person to communicate their decisions. There is a Speaker for the Women, a Speaker for the Warriors, each clan has a Speaker, and there are many more."

Hehaka folded his arms beneath his cape, looking worried and confused.

"Don't worry, you'll learn quickly. I'll help you. You . . . you're my brother."

An old man with a crooked body broke away from the group and hobbled toward them. Zateri took a deep breath.

"Is that your father?" Odion asked.

"Yes. I'm not sure how to feel."

She had learned things about her father that no child should know. After hearing that he'd sold his younger sister and brother when they'd seen eight summers, her eyes probably saw him differently.

"No matter what he's done, he's still your father, Zateri," Odion said.

"I know." Her gaze clung to him.

He must have seen over fifty summers. As he came closer, Odion saw that he had braided rattlesnake skins into his gray-streaked black hair, then coiled it into a bun at the base of his head and secured it with a wooden comb. The style gave his narrow face a starved look. He wore a beautiful black cape covered with circlets cut from human skulls.

Gonda said to Koracoo, "Here it comes."

Koracoo straightened and squared her shoulders, as though anticipating a fight. "Towa, are you ready?"

"Yes," he responded softly. In the firelight, Odion saw his handsome face go hard.

Chief Atotarho stopped two paces away, knelt, and opened his arms. "Zateri, I've missed you so much."

She let out a small incoherent cry and threw herself into his arms, crying, "Father, I'm so glad to be home." The last word turned into a high-pitched wail.

The chief crushed her against his chest and kissed her hair. "For-give me for everything you've gone through," he said. "I would have gone through it for you, if I could have."

"It's all right," she sobbed. "I'm home now. Where's Mother?"

He pushed her back to look into her eyes. "She'll be here soon."

At the far end of the longhouse, the council members began leaving. The curtain lifted over and over, allowing in long rectangles of sunlight. A handful of people remained. They stood like dark pillars, watching.

Chief Atotarho gently touched Zateri's cheek and rose to face Koracoo. She spread her feet.

The chief asked, "She's dead?"

"Yes."

Atotarho briefly closed his eyes, as though the news grieved him.

Koracoo said, "I assume you do not want to speak further in front of the children."

Atotarho opened his eyes. "I must. After what they've been through, they deserve to know the truth."

Koracoo gave him a suspicious look. The blue buffalo painted in the middle of her red cape seemed to walk with her uneasy movements. Finally, she nodded. "Very well."

Atotarho put a hand on Zateri's shoulder. "Someday Zateri will lead this clan, and perhaps this nation. The things she is about to hear may help her do that." He looked down at Zateri, and his eyes tightened. "But they will not be easy for you. Do you understand?"

She glanced at Koracoo's distrustful expression, then at Odion, and finally looked back at her Father. "Yes."

Atotarho had not asked a single question about Hehaka, and Odion saw Hehaka fidgeting, perhaps longing to be held as Zateri had been, or just simply to be acknowledged. The chief stared only at Koracoo.

"You must have many questions, War Chief. Ask. I will answer, if I can."

With only the barest hesitation, Koracoo said, "You used your own daughter as bait. Why?"

A swallow went down Atotarho's throat. "It had to end. I had to stop her. It was the only way I knew."

It was as though the earth beneath Odion's feet had suddenly turned to mud and was sucking him down into the dark underworlds. *It's true, then. Hallowed Ancestors, he sold Zateri. . . .*

Mother tilted her head to stare at Atotarho, and it was like Eagle spying Mouse. Her intent was deadly. "And you lied to us."

"You mean about what happened to my brother and sister. I—"

"Is it true that you sold them when they'd seen only eight summers?" Gonda demanded to know. His short black hair glistened in the firelight.

"Yes." Atotarho's voice was so low, we almost couldn't hear it. "But there's much more to the story."

"So, she didn't tell us everything?" Koracoo asked.

A brief flicker of panic touched Atotarho's expression, but it vanished quickly. Cautiously, he asked, "What did she tell you?"

Koracoo didn't move a muscle. She didn't blink. She just stared at the chief with burning eyes.

Atotarho looked away. "Well, it doesn't matter what she told you." He smoothed a hand over Zateri's hair. "It started when Jonodak—that was her name—had seen eight summers."

The circlets of skull that decorated his black cape flashed as he opened his palms to Koracoo. "She hurt her twin brother first. They'd been inseparable. No one would have ever—"

"How did she hurt him?"

Atotarho pulled his hands back. Koracoo's interruption was an insult to the chief. If she had been a Hills warrior she'd probably be dead in a less than a handful of heartbeats.

But Atotarho just replied, "One night the entire longhouse was awakened by screams. When I rushed to my younger brother's bed, I found him sitting up, covered in blood. She was crouched beside him with a sharp chert flake in her hand, smiling. She'd sliced his throat. Fortunately she'd missed the big artery. We cared for him, and eventually returned to our blankets. Just before dawn the screams started again. She had apparently carried a rock to bed with her. She must have hidden it somewhere. She'd slammed it into my brother's face."

"Was he disfigured?"

Was Koracoo thinking about Tutelo's descriptions of Shago-niyoh and his crooked nose? Odion found himself breathlessly waiting for the chief's answer.

"Yes. Our village Healers tried to set the bones, but it was impossible. She'd crushed them." Atotarho ran a hand over his face as though he still couldn't believe it had happened. "A few days later, Jonodak attacked three other children. Two died from their wounds.

One was the grandson of a clan elder." He paused as if trying to remember, then said, "His name was Skaneat. He'd seen only four summers."

No one said anything. But Odion noticed that Zateri was breathing hard.

"Why both of them?" Koracoo asked in a low menacing voice.

Atotarho seemed confused at first; then his jaw clenched. "It wasn't my decision. I was Towa's age, a warrior of some repute. I followed the orders of the council of elders. It tore my souls apart. You cannot possibly imagine what it was like . . ." His voice died as though he couldn't continue. "You know the requirements of the Law of Retribution."

Koracoo's face slackened, and she saw Towa's eyes suddenly go wide in understanding. Hehaka was gazing from one person to the next in confusion.

The chief gazed down at his daughter. "Do you understand, Zateri?"

"Yes, Father. Murder is the worst crime. Clans have a right to demand retribution."

Gonda nodded. "Murder places an absolute obligation on the relatives of the dead to avenge the murder. They may demand reparations, exotic trade goods, finely tanned beaver robes, maybe food. They may also claim the life of the murderer, or the life of another member of his clan."

Koracoo said, "Then the families of the murdered children claimed the lives of both your sister and her twin brother?"

Atotarho bowed his head. "They did. The Wolf Clan council ordered me to carry out the duty, but I was too much of a coward to do it. I tried. I took them out into the forest. I was a warrior. I should have been able to carry out the order without question."

Towa silently walked forward, and his cape swung around his long legs. "You sold them and told the village elders that you'd killed them?"

Shame filled the chief's eyes. "There is a very important lesson here, my daughter. Never, *never* disobey your clan elders. It's because of my cowardice that Jonodak became a monster."

A log broke in the fire, and sparks crackled and whirled upward toward the smoke holes.

"When did the elders discover your deceit?" Gonda asked.

"There had always been rumors. Over the long summers, many

young women showed up here claiming to be her. But the elders didn't know for certain until seven summers ago. A Trader came through saying that he'd met an insane woman who said she was the rightful matron of the Wolf Clan. Everyone laughed. Then three moons later an outcast warrior trotted in with captive children for sale. He said he'd bought them from Jonodak, who he said was now calling herself . . . well, you know that part."

"Your clan must have been unhappy," Koracoo said.

A pained smile came to the chief's face. "The dead children's clans were livid. They claimed the life of my son." He gestured weakly to Hehaka, and Hehaka's mouth fell open. "They ordered me to kill him, then to finish the job and kill Jonodak, or they threatened to claim the life of my mother, or perhaps my grandmother. I hired men. They told me they'd killed her and my son. The clans were satisfied. I didn't know until much later that Hehaka—"

"You never came for me," Hehaka cried in a plaintive voice. "I waited."

Atotarho didn't look at him. He stared straight at Koracoo with his jaw clenched.

Koracoo asked, "Why did you use Zateri?"

The chief's mouth trembled. "I knew she was the only thing that might draw Jonodak out. Zateri was Jonodak's only competition for the leadership of Atotarho Village. I thought if I could capture my sister and kill her for her crimes . . . I never thought . . . I mean it never occurred to me that she might actually capture Zateri."

Zateri stared up at her father with her eyes narrowed, clearly not sure she believed him.

Koracoo glanced at Zateri, then propped her hands on her hips. Her red cape flared out, pulling the blue buffalo tight across the middle of her chest. "We heard a different story about Hehaka."

The chief shrugged. "I'm sure you did." He turned to Towa. "I assume you brought the clan's sacred gorget back?"

Towa tugged the leather thong over his head and extended the broken gorget. "Your sister broke it. We couldn't find the other half in the snow."

Atotarho grasped the gorget and angrily pulled it from Towa's fingers. As he frowned at the broken shell, he said, "I'll dispatch someone to see if he can find the other half."

"Very well."

Atotarho hesitated before he asked, "Did you bury her?"

Koracoo vented a low laugh, and the chief's eyes immediately lifted and slitted.

She said, "No. In fact, we made certain her soul will be wandering the earth forever. We left her for the wolves to tear to pieces and scatter far and wide."

Hehaka let out a pathetic whimper, turned, and ran out of the longhouse. No one went after him.

A small shudder passed through Zateri. Odion suspected he knew why. For the rest of his life, he would fear that the old woman's ghost was waiting out in the forest. Watching him. Always about to catch him again. Zateri must be feeling something similar.

Gonda stood with his feet braced and his fists at his sides. To his right, around the fire, dishes were neatly stacked. The bowls were made from human skulls and the spoons from ground and polished human leg bones. Gonda seemed to be looking at them; then his gaze shifted to human finger-bone bracelets that encircled Atotarho's wrists, and disdain twisted his face. All the people in this village seemed to wear jewelry and eat from dishes made of human beings.

Voices echoed, and Zateri turned. At the far end of the longhouse, the elders appeared impatient. They kept looking at Atotarho and whispering behind their hands.

Koracoo said, "You treated Hehaka badly."

Atotarho's expression turned cold. As he tilted his head, the rattlesnake skins woven into his graying black hair shimmered. "I've heard he is a monster. I fear he may be another Jonodak. Besides, how long do you think he has to live? It may be my duty to kill him in the near future."

A faint cold smile turned Koracoo's lips. To Gonda, she said, "Well, that was an interesting story."

"Yes. Very entertaining. Clean. Every detail carefully worked through."

Koracoo tipped her head to the group of elders. "Is all of this for Zateri's benefit? Or the people down there?"

Atotarho made an airy gesture with his hand, and his finger-bone bracelets rattled. "I don't care if you believe me."

Koracoo said, "Really? Then what are they waiting for?"

Atotarho eyed her malevolently, and Gonda's right fist flexed.

"I have been . . . mistaken . . . in the past," the chief explained. "They rightly wish to be assured that she is truly dead this time."

"She is."

Atotarho slipped the broken gorget around his neck and adjusted it over his cape. "I am grateful to you for bringing my children home. You are under my protection until you pass beyond the boundaries of Hills Country. At that point, War Chief, you and your friends are no longer my allies. You will be my enemies again."

Koracoo's red cape swayed as she lowered her hands to her sides. "Yes. We will be."

Atotarho dipped his head in a nod and turned to Zateri. "Come, my daughter. The elders wish to hear your tale."

She clenched her fists and turned to Odion. For a few moments, they just stared at each other with their hearts breaking; then Odion walked forward, wrapped his good arm around her, and hugged her with all the strength in his body. "I will never, *never*, forget you, Zateri. If you ever need me, send word. I will be here as fast as I can."

Crying, she answered, "I love you, Odion. I always will."

A strand of her black hair had caught on his sleeve and pulled free. He twined his fingers around it, keeping it. In the future, when he was scared or desperate, he wanted to be able to touch her, to remind himself that she'd been real.

Atotarho put a hand on Zateri's shoulder and tugged them apart. "We must let our guests leave, Zateri. They have a long way to go before Elder Brother Sun sets."

"I know, Father."

As she walked away at Atotarho's side, Zateri turned several times to look back at Odion.

Koracoo continued to stare down the length of the longhouse at the assembled elders. Odion couldn't read her expression. It seemed to be a mixture of curiosity and hatred. At last, she said, "Let's go," and strode for the door curtain.

Epilogue

Odion

Night is falling, draping the forest with gray velvet shadows. Wrass keeps glancing at me from where he walks at my side, and I wonder if he feels the same dread I do. Like a sleeping monster, terror lives just behind my eyes. Breathing deep, dreaming.

I focus on the trail ahead, where Tutelo trudges with her head down, following Mother and Father. Far in the distance, Gitchi trots, scouting the way. The scent of damp trees and earth is strong.

"We're on our way home, Odion," Wrass says. "Everything is going to be all right." He reaches out to touch my shoulder.

I give him a vague smile and nod. The sound of my friend's voice, the touch of his hand, softly stir the ashes in my heart—the ashes of the days before the attack on Yellowtail Village. A sad hunger for them fills my chest.

"Our relatives will be waiting for us. They'll be so happy to see us. There will be feasting and dancing. Songs will fill the air. There will be great joy."

He sounds so happy.

Under the spell of Wrass' voice, the darkening forest fades and the moons roll away, leaving us racing across the plaza together in a long-gone summer. As his light grip on my shoulder tightens, I hear old half-forgotten laughter, see the sun glinting on the faces of the other racing boys, and watch our spears, cast almost at once, sail through the air toward the stone that careens across a plaza that is no more. There is the far-off barking of dogs in the autumn-hued trees and the smell of roasting corn. Old friends come marching back laughing as though they have not been dead these many moons, and the whisper and fragrance that is Grandmother Jigonsaseh's cape carries on the wind. Behind it all rests a sense of security and warmth, a knowledge that tomorrow will bring the same happiness today brought.

"Odion?" Wrass calls, breaking the spell. He leans forward to make me look at him. Concern lines his hawkish face. "Please talk to me."

"I'm all right, Wrass," I say. "I just miss them. Baji and Zateri."

His brows lower as though he's grieving, too. There are so many other children who are slaves, lost, and desperate to get home. I must *never* let myself forget that, but I must also start trying to look ahead. No man can survive if he is always looking backward.

Wrass playfully bumps my shoulder and leans against me for a few awkward steps. It makes me smile. Having him close is like cool water on a fevered wound. I feel safe for the first time since I lost sight of Zateri.

"I miss them, too. But we'll see them again. You know that, don't you?"

Neither of us speaks of Hehaka. He was never one of us. Never one of the trusted few for whom we would have willingly given our lives.

"I know we will," I whisper. But I'm lying, and he seems to know it.

"We *will*," he answers in a strong voice, as though the desperate wanting alone will make it come true. "I'm sure of it, Odion."

I want to believe him, but we are at war with everyone around us—and we are men now. Warriors. Deep inside me, I fear that someday I may be ordered to attack their villages. I will refuse, of course . . . and then my clan will accuse me of treason. What will I do? Has Wrass thought of these things? Is he thinking them even now? The sound of our moccasins hitting the trail is faint, barely there.

"I had a strange dream last night, Wrass," I abruptly confess. "It scared me."

He grips my shoulder and forces me to stop walking. His stare seems to pierce my heart. "What dream?"

I hesitate. "It's many summers from now. You and I are together. We're standing in a clearing surrounded by Mountain warriors."

His fists clench. "Go on."

I lift my hand and gesture futilely. "It's . . . bizarre. It's the middle of the day, bright, too bright. I can't feel my body, just the air cooling as the color suddenly leaches from the forest, leaving the land gray and shimmery. It must be summer, because hundreds of butterflies settle into the grass at my feet, and the world goes strangely quiet. You call my name and point, and my gaze moves to the west, where I see a black cloud rising from the depths of Skanodario Lake. It slithers along the horizon like Horned Serpent in the Beginning Time. Elder Brother Sun seems frightened. His blazing face begins to darken, and I know he is about to turn his back on the world and flee, leaving us all to die in the cold blackness." Shivering racks my body, as though the end of the world has already crept into my veins. I force myself to stop. "I feel so empty, Wrass, like an old husk."

In a deathly quiet voice, he says, *"We are all husks, Odion, flayed from the soil of fire and blood. This won't be over for any of us until the Great Face shakes the World Tree. Then, when Elder Brother Sun blackens his face with the soot of the dying world, the judgment will take place."*

My heart seems to stop. I feel as though I'm floating in a vast silent sea. "The judgment?" I whisper. "That's what it feels like. Where did you hear that?"

Wrass looks away, up the trail, and expels a breath before he answers, "It's something Shago-niyoh told me."

"What?" I ask breathlessly. "When?"

"On the river. I was fevered. It may have just been a dream, but I think it was real."

My gaze instinctively scans the twilight forest, searching for him, praying to see a shred of his windblown cape or hear his deep voice call my name. There is only the distant howling of wolves.

"Gods, Wrass, I pray that means he will be there with me at the end."

Wrass swallows hard. "I don't know if he'll be there. He didn't tell me." His gaze shifts to the forest, examining the shadows as though he, too, longs to glimpse the Forest Spirit. When he finally turns back to me, his expression is somber, serious. In a very soft voice, he vows, "But *I* will be there. I promise you on my life, I will be right at your side."

Our gazes lock and hold.

Without warning, tears well in my eyes and roll slowly down my cheeks. Wrass says nothing. He just walks forward and wraps his arms around me, holding me so tightly his arms shake. Only Wrass, who shares the sunny lost days of my boyhood as well as my memories of the past few moons, can understand.

All I want are the sheltering walls of a warm longhouse, a corner in which to hide and hurt, enough peace to allow me to heal.

In my ear, Wrass says again, "We're going home, Odion. Everything is going to be all right."

I let out a breath and high above me see a dove flapping through the slate-colored sky, its wings sleek in the last gleam of day. I swear, for just a moment . . . I believe him.

The
Broken Land

A PEOPLE OF THE LONGHOUSE NOVEL

Coming in January 2012

In *The Broken Land,* the dangerous sorcerer Atotarho sets in motion a cataclysmic battle that threatens to destroy the Iroquoian world. Only three people are brave enough to challenge him: a disgraced warrior known as Sky Messenger, his friend War Chief Hiyawento, and a powerful clan matron named Jigonsaseh. To stop the madman, they must find a way to bring five warring nations together.

Jigonsaseh knows the first step is to create an alliance with an even more powerful clan matron, but the only way to accomplish it is by marrying Sky Messenger to the old woman's fourteen-summers-old granddaughter, a mousy girl who has adored Sky Messenger since she was barely able to walk. In the desperate negotiations that ensue, Jigonsaseh must do two things: convince Matron Kittle that Sky Messenger is the great Peacemaker promised in legends, and keep quiet the fact that he is a man haunted by a secret that could turn all their dreams to dust. . . .

Places to Visit

There are many places in the United States and Canada that bring Iroquois culture to life. Some of our favorites are listed below. We encourage you to visit them. Each makes a great family trip.

The Iroquois Indian Museum, Howes Cave, New York
Phone: 518-296-8949   www.iroquoismuseum.org

Ganondagan State Historic Site, Victor, New York
Phone: 585-742-1690   www.ganondagan.org

Sainte-Marie among the Hurons, Midland, Ontario, Canada
Phone: 705-526-7838   www.saintemarieamongthehurons.on.ca

Selected Bibliography

Bruchac, Joseph.
 Iroquois Stories: Heroes and Heroines, Monsters and Magic. Freedom, Calif.: The Crossing Press, 1985.

Calloway, Colin G.
 The Western Abenakis of Vermont, 1600–1800. Norman: University of Oklahoma Press, 1990.

Custer, Jay F.
 Delaware Prehistoric Archaeology: An Ecological Approach. Cranberry, N.J.: Associated University Presses, 1984.

Dye, David H.
 War Paths, Peace Paths: An Archaeology of Cooperation and Conflict in Native Eastern North America. Lanham, Md.: AltaMira Press, 2009.

Ellis, Chris J., and Neal Ferris, eds.
 The Archaeology of Southern Ontario to A.D. 1650. London, Ontario, Canada: Occasional Papers of the London Chapter, OAS Number 5, 1990.

Elm, Demus, and Harvey Antone.
 The Oneida Creation Story. Lincoln: University of Nebraska, 2000.

Englebrecht, William.
 Iroquoia: The Development of a Native World. Syracuse: Syracuse University Press, 2003.

Fagan, Brian M.
 Ancient North America: The Archaeology of a Continent, 4th ed. London: Thames and Hudson Press, 2005.

Fenton, William N.
 The False Faces of the Iroquois. Norman: University of Oklahoma Press, 1987.

———.
 The Iroquois Eagle Dance: An Offshoot of the Calumet Dance. Syracuse: Syracuse University Press, 1991.

———.

 The Roll Call of the Iroquois Chiefs: A Study of a Mnemonic Cane from the Six Nations Reserve. Bulletin No. 30. Cranbrook Institute of Science, Bloomfield Hills, Mich.: 1950.

Foster, Steven and James A. Duke.

 Eastern/Central Medicinal Plants. The Peterson Guides Series. Boston: Houghton Mifflin Company, 1990.

Hart, John P., and Christina B. Reith.

 Northeast Subsistence-Settlement Change: AD 700–1300. Bulletin 496. Albany: New York State Museum, 2002.

Herrick, James W.

 Iroquois Medical Botany. Syracuse: Syracuse University Press, 1995.

Jennings, Francis.

 The Ambiguous Iroquois Empire. New York: W. W. Norton, 1984.

Jennings, Francis, ed.

 The History and Culture of Iroquois Diplomacy. Syracuse: Syracuse University Press, 1995.

Kurath, Gertrude P.

 Iroquois Music and Dance: Ceremonial Arts of Two Seneca Longhouses. Smithsonian Institution, Bureau of American Ethnology, Bulletin 187. Washington, D.C.: U.S. Government Printing Office, 1964.

Levine, Mary Ann, Kenneth E. Sassaman, and Michael S. Nassaney, eds.

 The Archaeological Northeast. Westport, Conn.: Bergin and Garvey, 1999.

Mann, Barbara A., and Jerry L. Fields.

 "A Sign in the Sky Dating the League of the Haudenosaunee." www .wampumchronicles.com/signinthesky.html.

Martin, Calvin.

 Keepers of the Game: Indian-Animal Relationships and the Fur Trade. Berkeley: University of California Press, 1978.

Mensforth, Robert P.

 "Human Trophy Taking in Eastern North America During the Archaic Period: The Relationship to Warfare and Social Complexity." In *The Taking and Displaying of Human Body Parts as Trophies by Amerindians,* edited by Richard J. Chacon and David Dye. New York: Springer, 2007.

Miroff, Laurie E., and Timothy D. Knapp.

 Iroquoian Archaeology and Analytic Scale. Knoxville: University of Tennessee Press, 2009.

Morgan, Lewis Henry.

 League of the Iroquois. New York: Corinth Books, 1962.

Mullen, Grant J., and Robert D. Hoppa.
    "Rogers Ossuary (AgHb–131): An Early Ontario Iroquois Burial
    Feature from Brantford Township." *Canadian Journal of Archaeology/
    Journal Canadien d'Archeologie* 16 (1992).
Parker, A. C. *Iroquois Uses of Maize and Other Food Plants.* Bulletin 144.
    Albany: New York State Museum, 1910.
Parker, Arthur C.
    Seneca Myths and Folk Tales. Lincoln: University of Nebraska,
    1989.
Richter, Daniel.
    *The Ordeal of the Longhouse: The People of the Iroquois League in the
    Era of European Colonization.* Chapel Hill: University of North Caro-
    lina Press, 1992.
Snow, Dean.
    The Archaeology of New England. New York: Academic Press, 1980.
———.
    The Iroquois. Oxford: Blackwell, 1996.
Spittal, W. G.
    Iroquois Women: An Anthology. Ontario, Canada: Iroqrafts, 1990.
Talbot, Francis Xavier.
    Saint Among the Hurons: The Life of Jean De Brébeuf. New York:
    Harper and Brothers, 1949.
Tooker, Elizabeth, ed.
    Iroquois Culture, History, and Prehistory. Albany: The University of the
    State of New York, 1967.
Trigger, Bruce.
    The Children of Aataentsic: A History of the Huron People to 1660. Mon-
    treal: McGill-Queen's University Press, 1987.
Trigger, Bruce, ed.
    Handbook of North American Indians, Vol. 15: Northeast. Washington,
    D.C.: Smithsonian Institution Press, 1978.
Tuck, James A.
    Onondaga Iroquois Prehistory: A Study in Settlement Archaeology. New
    York: Syracuse University Press, 1971.
Wallace, Anthony F. C.
    The Death and Rebirth of the Seneca. New York: Vintage Books,
    1972.
Walthall, John A., and Thomas E. Emerson, eds.
    *Calumet and Fleur-de-Lys: Archaeology of the Indian and French Contact
    in the Midcontinent.* Washington, D.C.: Smithsonian Institution Press,
    1992.

Weer, Paul.

  Preliminary Notes on the Iroquoian Family. Prehistory Research Series. Indianapolis: Indiana Historical Society, 1937.

Whitehead, Ruth Holmes.

  Stories from the Six Worlds: Micmac Legends. Halifax: Nimbus Publishing, 1988.

Williamson, Ronald F., and Susan Pfeiffer.

  Bones of the Ancestors: The Archaeology and Osteobiography of the Moatfield Ossuary. Gatineau, Quebec: Canadian Museum of Civilization, 2003.

About the Authors

Kathleen O'Neal Gear is a former state historian and archaeologist for Wyoming, Kansas, and Nebraska for the U.S. Department of the Interior. She has twice received the federal government's Special Achievement Award for "outstanding management" of our nation's cultural heritage.

W. Michael Gear, who holds a master's degree in archaeology, has worked as a professional archaeologist since 1978. He is currently principal investigator for Wind River Archaeological Consultants.

The Gears, whose North America's Forgotten Past Series comprises books that are international and *USA Today* and *New York Times* bestsellers, live in Thermopolis, Wyoming.